PRAISE FOR MARGARET DRABBLE

~

'Drabble is still adroit at charting the travails of personal relationships...expertly demonstrating how a child has the power to impinge upon and enrich a human life.'
Australian

'As meticulous as Jane Austen and as deadly as Evelyn Waugh.'
Los Angeles Times

'Drabble's fiction has achieved a panoramic vision of contemporary life.'
Chicago Tribune

'One of the most thought-provoking and intellectually challenging writers around.'
Financial Times

'Reading Margaret Drabble's novels has become something of a rite of passage...Sharply observed, exquisitely companionable tales.'
Washington Post

'One of the most versatile and accomplished writers of her generation.'
Joyce Carol Oates, *The New Yorker*

'Drabble writes so penetratingly about the female condition that it is impossible not to laugh, wince and admire.'
New Statesman

'A pleasure to read...utterly engrossing'
Guardian

ALSO BY MARGARET DRABBLE

FICTION

A Summer Bird-Cage
The Garrick Year
The Millstone
Jerusalem the Golden
The Waterfall
The Needle's Eye
London's Consequences (group novel)
The Realms of Gold
The Ice Age
The Middle Ground
The Radiant Way
A Natural Curiosity
The Gates of Ivory
The Witch of Exmoor
The Peppered Moth
The Seven Sisters
The Red Queen
The Sea Lady

SHORT STORIES

A Day in the Life of a Smiling Woman: The Collected Stories

NON-FICTION

Wordsworth (Literature in Perspective series)
Arnold Bennett: A Biography
For Queen and Country
A Writer's Britain
The Oxford Companion to English Literature (editor)
Angus Wilson: A Biography
The Pattern in the Carpet

THE PURE GOLD BABY

Dame Margaret Drabble was born in Sheffield in 1939 and was educated at Newnham College, Cambridge. She is the author of seventeen highly acclaimed novels including *A Summer Bird-Cage*, *The Millstone*, *The Peppered Moth*, *The Red Queen* and most recently *The Sea Lady*. She has also written biographies, screenplays and was the editor of the *Oxford Companion to English Literature*. She was appointed CBE in 1980, and made DBE in the 2000 Honours list. She is married to the biographer Michael Holroyd.

Margaret Drabble

The Pure Gold Baby

TEXT PUBLISHING MELBOURNE AUSTRALIA

textpublishing.com.au

The Text Publishing Company
Swann House
22 William Street
Melbourne Victoria 3000
Australia

First published by Canongate Books, 2013
This edition published by The Text Publishing Company, 2013
Reprinted 2013

Cover design by Imogen Stubbs
Typeset in Sabon MT by Palimpsest Book Production Ltd, Falkirk, Stirlingshire

Printed and bound in Australia by Griffin Press, an accredited ISO/NZS 1401:2004 Environmental Management System printer

National Library of Australia Cataloguing-in-Publication entry (pbk)
Author: Drabble, Margaret, 1939- author.
Title: The pure gold baby / by Margaret Drabble.
ISBN: 9781922147516 (paperback)
ISBN: 9781922148551 (ebook)
Subjects: Families—Fiction.
Parenthood—Fiction.
Dewey Number: 823.914

This book is printed on paper certified against the Forest Stewardship Council® Standards. Griffin Press holds FSC chain-of-custody certification SGS-COC-005088. FSC promotes environmentally responsible, socially beneficial and economically viable management of the world's forests.

For Hilary and Ben

What she felt for those children, as she was to realise some years later, was a proleptic tenderness. When she saw their little bare bodies, their proud brown belly buttons, the flies clustering round their runny noses, their big eyes, their strangely fused and forked toes, she felt a simple sympathy. Where others might have felt pity or sorrow or revulsion, she felt a kind of joy, an inexplicable joy. Was this a premonition, an inoculation against grief and love to come?

How could it have been? What logic of chronology could have made sense of such a sequence? And yet she was to come to wonder if it had been so. Something had called upon her from those little ones, and woken in her a tender spirit of response. It had lain dormant in her for several seasons, this spirit, and, when called upon, it had come to her aid. The maternal spirit had brooded on the still and distant waters of that great and shining lake and all its bird-frequented swamps and spongy islands and reed-fringed inlets, and it had entered into her when she was young and it had taken possession of her. Was this the beginning, was this the true moment of conception? Was this the distant early meeting place that had engendered the pure gold baby? There, with the little naked children, amongst the grasses and the waters?

She had never heard of the rare condition which afflicted some of the members of this poor, peaceable and unaspiring tribe, and the sight of it took her by surprise, although Guy Brighouse, her sponsor and colleague on this expedition, claimed that it had been well documented and that he had seen photographs of it. (But Guy was a hard man who would never admit to anything as vulnerable as surprise.) It was then popularly known as Lobster-Claw syndrome, a phrase which came to be considered incorrect. (It is now more widely known as ectrodactyly, or SHSF, but she did not then know that. She did not then know any of its names. The acronym SHSF discreetly encodes the words Split Hand Split Foot.) In some parts of the world, with some peoples, in some gene pools, the fingers fuse. In others, it is the toes. In this part of Central Africa, it is the toes that form a simple divided stub or stump. A small group of forebears had produced and passed on this deviance.

The little children seemed indifferent to their deformity. Their vestigial toes functioned well. The children were agile and busy on the water, and they were solemn on the land. They punted and paddled their little barks deftly, smartly. They stared at the anthropologists gravely, but without much curiosity. They were self-contained. They posed on the edges of their canoes with a natural elegance, holding their spear-like poles steady in the mud. They did not speak much, either in their own language or in English, of which their elders knew some words. They were not of the tribe the team had come to study; they were a side-show incidental to the longer journey, and the team did not stay with them long or pay them close attention. They were a staging post. But in the two days that the group sojourned there, Jess (so much the junior of her team, so young that she was considered almost as a lucky mascot) observed the little children as they played a game with stones. It was one of the simplest of games, a kind of noughts and crosses, an immemorial game, a stone age stone game. Red stones, black stones, white stones, moved in a square scratched out upon the sun-hardened reddish-ochre mud. She could not follow the rules, and did not try to do so. She watched them, the simple children, playing beneath the vast African sky.

Bubbles rose from the mud of the shallow inlets, bubbles of marsh gas from a lower world. A watery shifting landscape, releasing its spirits through the green weeds. There were floating islands of tufted papyrus, a sudd that was neither water nor land. On the higher banks, the mud dried to clay. From the clay, the children had moulded toy bricks and thimble-sized beakers. They had placed them in a little circle in the rushes. A small party, awaiting small spirit guests.

The next day, on the team's onward journey, she saw a shoebill. Their guides were pleased to have sighted this primeval bird, rare, one of its kind, primitive, powder-blue, much sought after by birdwatchers. The shoebill represents its lonely family. It has its own genus, its own species. Maybe it is allied to the pelican, but maybe not. Tourism was already making its slow way towards the lake, and the guides thought their troupe would be pleased by this sighting, and so it was. But Jess, although she liked the distinguished shoebill, was to remember the children with their simple stones and simplified toes. They were not on the tourist route.

They were her introduction to maternity. She went home, she continued her studies, but she did not forget them.

They were proleptic, but they were also prophetic. And she began to think, as time passed, that they reminded her of some early memory, a memory so early she could not recapture it. It had gone, buried, perhaps, beyond recall. It was a benign memory, benign as the children were benign, but it had gone.

She took home with her a treasure, a stone with a hole in the middle of it, a stone age stone that could make rain. It was a stone of the small BaTwa people of the lake. Had the children been of the BaTwa family? She did not know, but thought they might have been.

The BaTwa's territory had receded and diminished. They had taken refuge not in the bush, as most displaced African tribes have done, but amongst the reeds and in the water.

Jess was to keep the rain stone with her all her life.

~

The pure gold baby was born in St Luke's, a National Health hospital in Central London, an old institution now relocated in the suburbs. The building where the baby was born is now a moderately expensive hotel for foreign tourists. There is a mural in one of the public rooms evoking a medical past, with surgeons in white coats and busy nurses. Some guests think it in questionable taste. The smell of disinfectant has not been totally banished from the woodwork.

The quality of this small girl child was not at first evident. She looked, at first sight, like any newborn baby. She had five fingers on each hand, five toes on each foot. Her mother, Jess, was happy at the birth of her firstborn, despite the unusual circumstances, and loved her from the moment she saw her. She had not been sure she would do so, but she did. Her daughter proved to be one of the special babies. You know them, you have seen them. You have seen them in parks, in supermarkets, at airports. They are the happy ones, and you notice them because they are happy. They smile at strangers, when you look at them their response is to smile. They were born that way, you say, as you go thoughtfully on your way.

They smile in their pushchairs and in their buggies.

They smile even as they recover from heart surgery. They come round from the anaesthetic and smile. They smile when they are only a few weeks old, the size of a trussed chicken, and stitched up across their little breast bones with thread, like a small parcel. I saw one once, not so long ago, in the Children's Hospital in Great Ormond Street in London. As I was introduced to her, and was listening to a description of her case and her condition, she opened her eyes and looked at me. And when she saw me, she smiled. Her first impulse, when seeing a stranger, was to smile. She was a black-haired, red-faced, wrinkled little scrap of a bundle, like a bandaged papoose, snug in her tiny crib. She had come safely through major surgery. She smiled.

I saw one of them in a long queue for check-in at an airport a year or two ago. You couldn't miss him, or forget him. He was about eight months old, and his mother was holding him in her arms, his plump legs comfortably astride her solid hip, and he was smiling, and making free-range crowd contact, and stretching out his little waving neat-fingered hands to strangers, and responding to their clucks and waves. Other small ones in the line were grizzling and moaning and struggling and tugging and whimpering, bored and restless as they clutched their drooping toys or dragged their brightly coloured pink-and-blue Disney-ornamented plastic mini-wheelie-bags, but this one was radiant with a natural delight. His face was broad and blond and round and dimpled and shining, his hair a soft baby silken down. He entertained the long and anxious straggle of travellers. The mother looked proud and modest, as her baby was praised and admired by all. The mother was stout and plain and also round of face: an ordinary, homely young woman, the archetype of an ordinary mother, proud of her child, as such mothers are. But the baby was supernatural in his happiness.

You don't know where they come from, or why they have the gift. Who gives it? You don't know. We don't know. There is no way of telling. It is from some profound and primal source, or so we may well believe. They bring it to us.

You don't know what will happen to them in later years. Such radiance cannot last. So you say to yourself, as you watch their smiling young faces.

The pure gold baby, born in St Luke's Hospital in Bloomsbury, was a pleasant child, no trouble to anyone. She attached herself to the nipple and fed rhythmically from the breast, she slept peacefully in her cot and breathed evenly, and her mother Jess delighted in her. She took her home to her modest second-floor flat in North London, which she rented very cheaply from a couple downstairs whom she knew from her earliest student years, and for whom she used to babysit on a regular basis. Although naturally exercised by the doubts and anxieties that beset young mothers, from the beginning she felt a love for, and confidence in, this child that took her somewhat by surprise. She had not expected motherhood to come so easily. Childbirth had been moderately painful, and was helped along with a little pethidine, but attachment came easily.

Those of you who are by nature apprehensive and suspicious will read this account as a warning, and you will be right. We worried for her, we, her friends, her generation, her fellow-mothers at the playgroup in the dusty old church hall in the quadrant. (I don't think the word 'cohort' had at that time been co-opted from the dictionary for use in the sociological thesaurus.) We worried for her in the corner shop, as we bought our tins of beans and sausages, our biscuits and our boxes of eggs, our little glass jars of what we then thought of as nourishing and innocent Heinz baby food.

She was what we now call a single mother, and that was less usual then than it is now. We thought she would have a hard time, even though her baby was pure gold.

She was a single mother with an interrupted career, which she and we had assumed she would resume more actively when the child was a little older. It was the kind of career she could pursue, after a fashion, at home as well as in the field: by reading, by study, by marking papers, by editorial work on a small scholarly journal, by teaching an extramural class or two, by writing scraps of medical journalism for periodicals. (She became increasingly skilled at the last of these activities and in time was invited to write, more lucratively, for the mainstream press.) She kept in touch. She was an anthropologist by disposition and by training and by trade, and she managed to earn a modest living from these shifts and scribblings. She wrote quickly, easily, at an academic or at a popular level. She became an armchair, study-bound, library-dependent anthropologist. An urban anthropologist, though not in the modern meaning of that term.

The father of the child was never visible. We assumed Jess knew who he was and where he was, but she did not say, and nobody knew if he had been informed about the birth of this daughter. Maybe he contributed something to the child's upkeep. But maybe he did not. Jess was not a silent or reclusive woman, and she loved to talk, but she did not talk about the man who had been, maybe still was, the man in her life. Was he a fellow-student, was he married, was he a professor, was he a foreigner who had returned to his homeland? We did not know.

We had vulgarly speculated, before the child was born, that it might be dusky. Jess had dark connections and African friends, and we knew she had once studied, if only briefly, in Africa. She knew more than most of us about Africa, which, between us, did not amount to much. But the child was fair-skinned, and her soft baby hair was light of colour.

We didn't know enough about genes to know what, if anything, that meant.

~

Jess came from an industrial city in the Midlands, and had graduated from a well-regarded grammar school via a foundation course in Arabic at a new university to a degree at SOAS. SOAS! How magical those initials had been to her as a seventeen-year-old when first she heard them, and how thrilling and bewitching they were to remain to her, even into her late middle age! The School of Oriental and African Studies, situated in the heart of academic Bloomsbury. She knew nothing of Bloomsbury or of London when she arrived there, from her provincial home in white-white-white Middle England. (London in those days was full of young people from the regions who knew nothing of Bloomsbury.) SOAS was a sea of adventure, of learning, of cross-cultural currents that swept and eddied through Gordon Square and Bedford Square and Russell Square and along Great Russell Street. Jess threw herself into its waters, and swam with its tides. She loved her first year in an old-fashioned women's hostel, she enjoyed her later bed-sitter freedom, cooking on a single gas ring and reading in bed by lamplight well into the night. Her happiness was intense. Her subject enthralled her. How had she happened upon it, so luckily? Surely, she led a charmed life. SOAS was frequented by handsome and gifted strangers from all over the world, scholars, lexicographers, chieftains, heads-of-state in waiting, and she was free to wander amongst them. It was a meeting place, if not exactly a melting pot.

At the age of twenty, walking along the ancient-and-modern thoroughfare of the Tottenham Court Road, using the august but friendly British Museum as a shortcut, sitting in timeless Russell Square on the grass in the sun, attending a seminar, listening to a lecture, shopping in shabby Marchmont Street, she was profoundly happy, her imagination filled with dreams of the future, with speculations about the lands she would visit, the journeys awaiting her, the peoples she would meet.

The bomb damage of London was at last being very slowly repaired, with spirit if not always with style, and the streets of the late fifties and early sixties were full of promise and change and hope.

Some of the big men of the future were products of SOAS and the LSE and the Inner Temple. They had occupied the square mile of colonial educational advancement, and they were now in the process of rewriting history. Jomo Kenyatta, Seretse Khama, Kwame Nkrumah . . . the potent memory of their names hung thick in the air of Bloomsbury and Fleet Street, the big names of big beasts, the stars of the savannah, the giants who would bestride the post-colonial world. But there were also all the lesser people: the witty Indian students, the tall aspiring South African boys who had graduated from Rhodes or Cape Town, the Guyanese intellectuals, the Burmese mystics, the vegans from Mauritius, the twins from Jakarta, the would-be white middle-class dervish from Southport – all united in human endeavour, all part of the family of man. The variegation of the human species delighted Jess, and she was in love with all those peoples.

We lived in an innocent world.

What did we mean by 'innocence', you may ask?

~

When Jess was a schoolgirl in Broughborough, not many people she met had heard of SOAS or indeed of anthropology. It was chance that revealed them to her and set her on her course and her life's long journey.

Her father, who worked in Town and Country Planning, had acquired during his travels with the RAF in the Second World War some little booklets of beautiful hand-coloured drawings of native peoples. He had been offered them in a bazaar in

North Africa and, much pressed to purchase, had bought them for a modest sum. He felt sorry for the vendors in those hard times, for the boys with boxes of matches, for the old men who offered to shine his shoes, using their own spit for polish. These booklets, in their modest way, were the equivalent of the dirty postcards and obscene playing cards bought by other soldiers, sailors and airmen to while away the hours of boredom. Maybe he had purchased some of those too, but, if he did, he did not leave them lying around for his wife and his two daughters to discover. The *People of Many Lands* were not on display either, but neither were they hidden, and Jess came upon them in one of the little drawers in the middle of an old-fashioned fret-worked oak bureau-cum-bookcase that stood in the bay-windowed 1930s drawing room of the Speights' home in Broughborough. They were too small to stand easily on a book-shelf. They were bound, or so she was to remember, in a kind of soft fawn kid-like leather. With the tender hide of a young goat of the Atlas Mountains.

The illustrations were a wonder to her. She found them interesting partly because of the nudity on display, so rare in those days – here were bare-breasted Africans, Papuan New Guineans with feathers, scantily clad Apaches and Cherokees, tribesmen with teeth filed to sharp points, brave naked denizens of the Tierra del Fuego. There were no visible penises, though there was a discreetly oblique view of a lavishly tattooed South American in the Mato Grosso wearing what she was later to identify as a penis sheath. But there was everything else a curious female child might wish to see. There were elongated necks, and dangling ears, and nose bones, and lip discs, and bosoms that descended like leathery sacks or wineskins below the waist, and little conical breasts that pointed cheerfully upwards.

These portraits were much more touchingly human than the photographs one could see in the *National Geographic* magazine at the dentist's. Jess did not like those photographs: they seemed rude, intrusive and inauthentic. She did not like the way that the groups were lined up to grin: it reminded her of the procedure of official school photographs, always an ordeal, and menacing in its regimentation. But the artist's work in her father's booklets was delicate, attentive, admiring. The men and women and children were dignified, strange and independent. Maybe they were idealised: she did not at that time think to ask herself about this. She did not know what models were used. Were they drawn from life? Or copied from other books? She did not know. But she was captured as a child by the mystery and richness of human diversity.

Each figure had a page to itself, and the colours were pure and clear. The scarlet of these people's robes and adornments was as bright as blood, the green as fresh as a leaf in May, the turquoise new minted as from the Brazilian mine, the silver and gold as delicate and as shining as the finest filigree. The skin tones were shaded in pinks and ivories and browns and chocolate-mauves and ebony. None of the extreme body shapes repelled, for all were portrayed as beautiful. They came from an early world, these strangers, from a world of undimmed and unpolluted colour, a world as clear as the colours in a paintbox, and Jess longed to meet them, she longed to meet them all.

These figures, these people from many lands, led her on eventually to SOAS, and thence to the children by the lake with lobster claws, and thence to the birth of the pure gold baby, whom she named Anna.

Jess is ageing now, but she is still, to middle-aged young Anna, a young mother.

Jess has not travelled much since Anna's birth. She has left the field. As a student, she had pictured herself eagerly wandering the wide world. But she has been constrained by circumstance, like many women through the ages, constrained largely to an indoor terrain. Her daughter must come first, and for Jess maternity has no prospect of an ending.

~

As an anthropologist, Jess is sensitive about public perceptions of her calling. Certain academic and intellectual disciplines, certain professional occupations, seem to be fair game for dismissive mirth: sociologists, social workers, psychoanalysts – all receive a share of public mockery and opprobrium, along with, for a different class of reasons, estate agents, dentists, politicians, bankers and what we have recently come to call financial advisers. When Jess was a student and a beginner, it did not occur to her that there was anything comic about her interests, and it came as a shock to her to discover later in life that anthropology was associated in the vulgar mind with prurience and pornography and penises. She was educated in what she believed to be a noble tradition. Flippant jokes about the sexual antics of savages were as irrelevant and incomprehensible to her as the double-entendres in the pantomimes she was taken to see in Derby as a small child. She could not see anything innately funny about the Trobriand islanders, or in young people coming of age in Samoa. Interest, yes; comedy, no.

In her sixties, she was to become interested in popular conceptions of anthropology and in its use as a motif in fiction. She wrote a paper on the subject which you may have read. In fiction, she claimed that it was usually exploited by flip and smart intellectuals: Cyril Connolly, William Boyd, Hari Kunzru – writers to whom it seemed to invite parody. Margaret Mead herself was the butt of endless reductive and sexist jokes. Saul Bellow, in Jess's view, offered an honourable exception to the tradition of anthropology-mockery, and his novel *Henderson the Rain King*, which she had read at an impressionable age, had a profound influence on her. It summoned up to her the mystery of the dignity of the tribe of the lobster-claw children, although they do not, of course, feature in Bellow's novel, or, as far as she knows, in any novel. Bellow, she believes, knew even less of the physical continent of Africa than she, but he wrote about it well, and he would not have made fun of lobster feet.

Towards the end of *Lolita*, arch-parodist Vladimir Nabokov produces a classic example of anthropology-mockery, admittedly put into the mouth of a sexual pervert pleading for his life at gunpoint, but nevertheless a vulgar and sexist passage, for all that: the novel's pervert-villain-victim, bleating *drop that gun* as a refrain, tries to buy off anti-hero Humbert Humbert's vengeance with increasingly desperate offers, including access to his 'unique collection of erotica', which includes the folio de-luxe edition of *Bagration Island* by the explorer and psychoanalyst Melanie Weiss, 'with photographs of eight hundred and something male organs she examined and measured in 1932 on Bagration, in the Barda Sea, very illuminating graphs, plotted with love under pleasant skies'. Jess was horrified by a late rereading of this classic novel. She had disliked it in her twenties, when she was too young and innocent to understand it, but in her sixties she understood it and she was appalled by it.

You may assume from that that Jess was by nature prudish, but we didn't think she was.

There are penises and penis-enhancement remedies advertised all over the internet now, where you might expect to find them, and Jess has written a paper on them too, in which she wittily analyses the bizarre vocabulary of commercial erections and sperm volume: the lingo of the solid high-performance-dick-enlarged-joystick-loveknob-supersized-shlong-cockrock. Jess has made a decision to find this sales patter entertaining rather than offensive, and to admire the ingenuity with which salesmen repeatedly penetrate her battered spam filter. She has even decided, paradoxically, to detect a male respect for the female orgasm in all the sales talk. Decency is an artefact, and has failed to save our culture or centre our sexuality, so maybe, she speculates, an overflowing flood of what used to be called obscenity will. Battered and drenched by massive earth-shattering orgasms, we will all be purified.

Initially, she had been rereading *Lolita* in search of representations of unqualified and obsessive and exclusive love, which she refound there too, as she had dimly remembered them – but tarnished, perverted, tarnished. There is genius, but there is coldness. Jess's heart cannot afford to give space to coldness. She cannot afford to allow herself to cool and freeze.

Jess has given the large part of her life to exclusive and unconditional and necessary love. That is her story, which I have presumptuously taken it upon myself to attempt to tell. But her love takes a socially more acceptable form than that of Nabokov's Humbert Humbert, the tragic lover of a nymphet. Jess has had her less reputable adventures, but she has so far remained true to her maternal calling through all vicissitudes.

I have taken it upon myself to tell this story, but it is her story, not mine, and I am ashamed of my temerity.

~

The playgroup and corner-shop mothers did not notice what was wrong with Anna for a long time, not for many months. Nor did Jim and Katie downstairs, although they saw more of her, and babysat for her reciprocally when Jess wanted to go out for an evening to have supper with friends. And as regularly as they could, they would look after Anna on Jess's working Thursdays. We all saw Anna as a pretty, friendly, good-natured, smiling little thing, with a touching spirit of sharing and helpfulness. At an age when most small children become violently possessive and acquisitive she was always ready to hand over her toys or share her Dolly Mixtures. She did not seem to resent being pushed or tumbled, and she hardly ever cried. She laughed a lot, and sang along with the jingles and nursery rhymes; she knew a lot of the words of a lot of the verses. She had a special friend, a small mischievous imp boy called Ollie, with gap teeth and corkscrew ringlets, who exploited her generosity and used her as a decoy. Ollie seemed fond of her, even though he stole the best bits of her packed lunch. (He had a yearning for those triangular foil-wrapped portions of processed cheese, regularly supplied by Jess, which Anna would trustingly offer in exchange for a crust or a broken piece of biscuit.) The two downstairs children also made a pet of her, and played hide-and-seek and run-around-the-house and den-under-the-table with her.

So it came as a shock to be told that she had problems.

She was, it is fair to say, a little uncoordinated, and was often clumsy. Sometimes she dropped things or knocked things over or spilt her juice. But what child does not? Her speech, perhaps, was a little simple, with a tendency towards a repetition of phrases, sometimes meaningless, that appealed to her. She never learnt to manage the dumpy little thick-wheeled red-and-yellow tricycle that the playgroup provided: she could not get the hang of pedalling. But she could walk, and she could speak, and she could play simple games, and assemble structures of wooden bricks and basic plastic parts, and draw patterns with crayons. She particularly liked water play, and was very happy when allowed to splash and scoop and fill little cans and beakers and sprinklers from the inflatable rubber pond in the yard. She fitted in, and was accepted by her peers. At eighteen months, at two years, even at three, her cognitive and developmental problems were not obvious, for her goodwill and eagerness to participate disguised and overcame her lack of skills. She never appeared frustrated by her failures, or angry with herself or others. She was no trouble to anyone. We all liked her. Nobody noticed how different she was.

Except her mother. Jess, of course, noticed. She checked Anna's progress against the progress of the children of her friends, and saw that in comparison she was slow. For a while she kept her worries to herself, hoping that Anna was simply (whatever simply, in this context, might mean) a late developer. The Health Visitor and the nurses at the surgery and the doctor who administered vaccinations did not at first seem unduly anxious, charmed, as were we all, by the infant's good looks and beguiling demeanour. Over those first years, we entered into a conspiracy of silence. Who wants to give bad news, who wishes to insist on hearing bad news? There are many subjects of which it is better not to speak, of which it is unwise to speak. The child was healthy enough. She ate well, she slept well, she was peaceable in all her ways. Would that all children were as well loved, as well clothed, as well cared for, as well disposed as she.

~

It was on a cold day in February that Jessica Speight set off, unobserved, with her daughter Anna, for the doctor's morning surgery in Stirling New Park, the long, wide, late-Victorian residential street that curved between and linked the two main bus routes into town. She dressed her warmly, in her little red fleece-lined waterproof jacket, her black-and-white-striped bobble hat, her well-washed matted black woolly tights, her mittens on a string, her little black boots, and she strapped her into the pushchair, and set off towards her appointment with enlightenment. There had been snow, and a few thin grimy frozen traces of it lingered still in hedge bottoms and gutters, lace-edged, like frozen dirty clusters of elderflower, stained yellow by dog urine, scuffed by tyres and shoes.

On such a day, one sets forth bravely, or not at all.

Anna was content, as always, and pointed with her woollen fist at objects of interest on the route. A bicycle, a red car, an old man with a peeling plastic tartan shopping bag on wheels. She let out from time to time little cries of surprise, of approval. Jess, as she walked, thought of the child's father, and of her extreme reluctance to share her full knowledge of Anna with him. She thought of the corner ahead around which happy mother and happy child were about to disappear for ever.

She thought also of her own father, to whom she had told some of the complicated story of her affair with Anna's father, and of her unexpected pregnancy. (She had not yet disclosed to him her anxieties about Anna, fearing that to articulate them would be to confirm them.) Her father, a tolerant, affectionate and kind-hearted man, had listened with sympathy and interest to this tale, and had condoned and indeed approved her conduct. She had done the right thing. The circumstances were indeed unfortunate, but she had chosen the right path, and he would always stand by her. He respected her independence, but if in need, she could always turn to him. Her mother's response had been more anxious and equivocal, but she too had refrained from overt criticism and condemnation.

If Anna's condition was as compromised as Jess now feared, she would be able to tell her own father about it, if not Anna's father. He would understand. That was a comfort.

Jess, as she walked, found herself thinking of her father's response to this London neighbourhood in which she was now living. He had visited it only briefly, on a couple of occasions, and had admitted that he was bewildered by its resolute shabbiness, its many-layered decay, its strange population of indigenous old Londoners, incomers from the West Indies and Cyprus and Turkey, and young married couples with professional aspirations. He had gazed quizzically at the cheap Chinese take-aways, the old-fashioned Co-ops and rustic-picture-tiled Edwardian dairies, the cobbled alleys, the junk shops full of worthless Victoriana, the make-shift garages and lean-tos, the dumped cars, the small council blocks, the large old multi-occupancy houses belonging to absentee landlords. He took in the dogs and sparrows and starlings. He liked, or he said he liked, the little jerry-built cosy Edwardian terrace where Jim and Katie and Jess lived, but Jess could tell that he found the surroundings depressing. It was not for this that he had fought in North Africa, and tried to rebuild a brave new Broughborough.

Philip Speight was a disappointed man of strong opinions, who had held high hopes for post-war Labour Britain, for the new cities that would rise from the bomb sites. His visions had been frustrated, his plans sabotaged, and his name had become attached to some of what he considered the ugliest rebuilding in Europe. Corners had been cut, money both saved and wasted, councillors had grown rich, and he had been blamed for decisions not freely of his making. The Midlands had become the badlands, and were a mess, by which he felt himself condemned. His name would go down on the wrong side of progress. The ugliness of the new weighed on him, he told Jess. The failure of Modernism depressed him.

But he was a good man, a generous man. He did not allow his depression and disappointment to infect others. He contained them.

Jess had tried to reassure him that she was happy in this cheap rundown muddle of a once-more prosperous district, but now, as she walked along in her cheap smart sixties boots, wheeling and bumping her innocent charge along the uneven pavement, her courage faltered. Maybe it was all too much for her, her fate too hard to handle.

She dreaded what the doctor would tell her.

When we look back, we simplify, we forget the sloughs and

doubts and backward motions, and see only the shining curve of the story we told ourselves in order to keep ourselves alive and hopeful, that bright curve that led us on to the future. The radiant way. But Jess, that cold morning, was near despair. She did not tell us about this then, but of course it must have been so. I picture her now, walking along the patched and pock-marked London pavement, with its manhole covers and broken paving stones, its runic symbols of water and electricity and gas, its thunderbolts and fag ends and sweet wrappings and spatters of chewed and hardened gum, and I know that she faltered.

There were fag ends everywhere. Most of us smoked in those days. We knew better – we had the warnings – but we didn't believe them. We didn't think the warnings were for us. We didn't chew gum, we'd been brought up not to chew gum, but we smoked, and, almost as soon as it became available, we took the pill.

The doctor, middle-aged, grey-haired, round-shouldered, cardiganed, not the best of doctors, but kind-hearted and good-enough, listened to Jess's story, took notes, asked questions about the baby's delivery. Had it been prolonged, had forceps been used, had there been oxygen deficiency? She did some simple tests, asked Anna a few simple questions, then busied herself writing referrals to specialists and hospitals. It occurred to Jess that this doctor, who had seen Anna several times on routine occasions (vaccinations, a bout of acute ear ache, a scraped knee that might have needed a stitch), might feel remiss for not having noticed Anna's developmental problems. Jess, in her place, would have felt remiss. Certainly the solemnity and the new and marked attentiveness of the doctor's response were not reassuring. There was no suggestion, now, that Anna would be a normal child. She would be what she would be – a mill-stone, an everlasting burden, a pure gold baby, a precious cargo to carry all the slow way through life to its distant and as yet unimaginable bourne on the shores of the shining lake.

Jess wept as she walked home, for the long-term implications of this visit, although as yet imprecise and unconfirmed, were very present to her. She was ashamed of the warm tears that rose in her eyes and spilled down her cold cheeks, of the water that dripped from her reddened nose. She wiped her face with the back of her woollen glove. Why should she weep? Her snivelling was treachery. She was weeping out of self-pity, not love. Anna smiled still, as gay as ever, wheeling royally along in her battered little second-hand pushchair. There was no difference for her, to her. There would never be any difference to her. For as long as Anna lived, provided good-enough care were taken, there would probably be no difference, thought Jess, vowed Jess.

How long would she live? Who would outlive whom?

This was also a question, and one that would become more urgent with the years. But it was far too soon to ask it yet.

It would always be too soon. The moment to ask this question would never come.

Jess decided that she would be better than good-enough. She would be the best of mothers. So she resolved, as she increased her speed and made her brisk, cold way home to a lunch of boiled egg and Marmite-and-butter toast, Anna's healthy favourite.

We didn't know about cholesterol then. It hadn't been invented.

~

I don't know which of us was the first to receive Jess's confidence about Anna's condition. Probably it was Katie, but it could have been Maroussia, or it could have been me. We were all good friends, good neighbourhood friends, with children of much the same age. I wouldn't claim I had a particularly close relationship with Jess, in those early days, but it has endured for so long that maybe it has become particular with time.

We didn't know whether the child's father knew anything about Anna at all. We weren't sure who the child's father was. Some of us gossiped about this, I am sorry to say, but we didn't really know anything definite. We gossiped, but we weren't nosy. We were well intentioned. And we didn't gossip as much as you might think. There was something about Jess, some confidently brave aura, that repelled impertinent speculation.

This is how it was. This is the version that we came to believe.

Jess, it was eventually disclosed, used to spend her Thursday afternoons with Anna's father in a small cheap hotel in Bloomsbury, making love. The regularity of this date did not detract from its vigour and its intensity. Anna's father was, of course, a married man, who had no intention of leaving his professor wife. He too was a professor, he was Anna's professor, whose lectures at SOAS she had attended.

It is strange that Jess did not resent the structure of her relationship with the two professors, but it is a fact that she did not, or not very much. She accepted it, just as she had accepted the advances of her 44-year-old lover when he had propositioned her in a corridor, and led her into his study, and locked the door, and laid her upon the institutional professorial Turkey carpet.

She not only accepted them, she welcomed them. She found him very attractive. Well, perhaps that is an understatement. She thought herself 'madly in love' with him, though in later years she came to see that this phrase (which she employed only in the schoolgirl privacy of her student mind) was merely a gloss on her finding him 'very attractive'. Love excused and gave permission to adulterous sex, but really it was sexual desire and straightforward bodily lust that possessed her every Thursday afternoon in the modestly functional Marchmont Hotel. Desire was satisfied unfailingly, and that, at this stage in her life, was quite good-enough for Jess. Not many women get that much. She knew that, from the stories of her friends, from the New Wave women's magazines, and from reading the new novels of the day, which were beginning to pay close if belated attention to the female orgasm.

Jess and the Professor had no problems with orgasm.

The arrangement they came to was, for its time and place, unorthodox, but, as anthropologists, they were familiar with the immense variety of human arrangements, and not inclined to pass temporal judgement upon them. In this, they were ahead of their time, or out of their time. It doesn't matter which. Or it would not have mattered, had there not been consequences, in the form of Anna.

It could have been Katie who was first to know about Anna, it could have been Maroussia, it could have been me, or it could have been the blond egocentric sexually athletic Professor Lindahl (a specialist, as it happened, in Chinese agrarian societies). A few months after the initial diagnosis, we all knew, and had progressed beyond the stage where we made comforting remarks like 'I'm sure she'll catch up soon' or 'She seems perfectly normal to me, my Tim (or Tom, or Polly, or Stuart, or Josh, or Ollie, or Nick, or Ben, or Jane, or Chloe) can't do up his shoelaces/ write her name/ ride a bike/ count beyond twenty.' Those were the days of tolerant, progressive, permissive parenting, when it was not the fashion to impose great expectations or much discipline upon one's offspring. The prevailing philosophy was of laissez-faire, and we believed in the noble savage, the blank slate. Original Sin had been banished, and we held that, if nurtured by kindness, natural goodness would always prevail. Our chief pedagogue Dr Spock told us that babies usually knew best, and that mothers should trust them, even if they wanted to live on a diet of beetroot or burnt toast.

Motherhood was being deprofessionalised, but not deskilled. Trained nannies were out of fashion, because they were too expensive for the new generation of struggling working mothers. Trained nannies were for unemployed rich mothers, in those days. Improvisation was in favour with the middle classes: au pair girls, amateur and cheap nursery groups, reciprocal child-minding.

This was lucky for Anna and her mother.

It is not surprising that Jess and some of her closer friends began to be deeply interested in the subject of birth defects, childhood illnesses and inherited abnormalities, despite their faith in the natural goodness of infants, and despite Jess's necessary assumption that Anna's paternity had nothing to do with her condition. This was a period when important discoveries were being made about the chromosomal basis of Down's syndrome (not that Anna was thought to have Down's syndrome), and certain inherited genetic diseases were being routinely tested for at birth, not always with the mother's knowledge or consent. (It was at this time that Jess's mind began to go back again and again, involuntarily, almost dreamily, not unhappily, to those little agile club-foot children by the shining lake.) Vaccination was then, in the sixties, a major ethical issue, though autism, with which it was later to be (as we now think erroneously) connected, was not as yet a frequent or popular diagnosis.

Autism is now, in the twenty-first century, a hot topic. Down's syndrome is not. You can't make much of a career from studying Down's syndrome. It doesn't get you anywhere. It's low key and unsensational. You can maintain, you can provide care, you can campaign to alter attitudes and perceptions, you can argue about the ethics of termination. You can admire Lionel Penrose for his research on the chromosome at Colchester, for his enlightening discoveries and enlightened Quaker principles, for his respectful attention to, and affection for, his patients.

You can respect. You can abort. You cannot cure.

Most of us were amateurs, struggling on with motherhood and learning as we went, but Sylvie had studied medicine and qualified as a general practitioner before her marriage to the dashing and increasingly absent Rick Raven, so we used to listen to her as our neighbourhood expert on medical matters. She wasn't practising at this time, when her boys were small, but she would take up her career again later, and specialise in the urinary tract. We didn't know then that she was going to do that, and neither did she.

To vaccinate, or not to vaccinate? This was hotly debated by a new generation of highly educated mothers who wished to apply intelligence as well as instinct to maternity. It was a divisive topic. Sylvie Raven was in favour, but some of us were not. To maim one's healthy child while aiming to protect it seemed a tragic choice, and yet we knew such things could and did happen. It was for the good of the wider community to vaccinate (and of course we all thought we had social consciences), but how would the wider community help two-year-old Andrew Barker, brain-damaged by a jab that went wrong? He had gone into spasm, his back had arched, he had cried out, and he had never been the same small happy child again. This was a worse fate than Anna's, Jess had to believe, and the sense of guilt endured by his mother was, although unfairly, greater.

Even Sylvie Raven conceded that.

We were surprised and a little shocked when Michael and Naomi decided to have their son Benjamin circumcised, and to have the job done by an unhygienic old rabbi in the living room, not by a doctor in a hospital. This too seemed to us like a gratuitous assault on the body of an infant.

We'd never even heard of female circumcision then.

We didn't know much about genetics, but we did know that abnormalities ran in families. Ollie's little sister had an extra digit on her right hand, an oddity which didn't seem to worry her or her parents very much, though they did eventually arrange for its surgical removal at Great Ormond Street Hospital. They said that at first she missed her little extra thumb, but then she forgot about it, unless reminded. Her grandmother had had the same anomaly. *One, two, three, four, five, once I caught a fish alive . . .* most counting games work on a five-finger base. It's not a good idea to have six fingers.

None of us took thalidomide, but we knew mothers who had. It was one of the pharmaceutical discoveries of our time.

This was the last generation of British children to suffer routinely from such common complaints as measles and whooping cough. Diphtheria was on the wane, and so was scarlet fever, now so rare that when one of the children at our nursery group contracted it the doctor did not recognise it, never having seen a case. It was diagnosed, correctly, by the elderly untrained minder of the neighbourhood, Mrs Dove, who did the Monday and Wednesday shifts at the playgroup wearing an old-fashioned flowery cotton overall. It was greeted with delight by the medical students at the Royal Free Hospital as a lucky sighting, a historic anomaly. The students made a great fuss of hot and prickly little Joe, with his red skin and his impressive fever of 105 degrees: he was a throwback to another age, and his bright blood, rocking in its tray of little test tubes, was a miracle of liquefaction.

~

Anna's condition did not seem to answer with any precision to any known descriptions. Like the shoebill, she was of her own kind, allotted her own genus and species. She did not suffer from any metabolic disorder, of either rare or frequent incidence. Brain damage in the womb or at birth was not ruled out, but could not be confirmed: Jess's labour had been long, but not unduly long, and the period of gestation apparently normal. (There were, of course, no ante-natal foetal scans in those days, no anxious calls for the dubious risks and safeguards of amniocentesis.) An obvious genetic cause was sought in vain. It is not known if or at what stage Jess proffered the identity of the Professor to the assessors, but, as far as she knew, there was nothing in his family background to suggest that a clue lay in that remote nomadic Nordic hinterland.

Jess's attitude towards the Professor and his paternal obligations was extreme and bizarre. She wished to disconnect him from the story, and she appeared to succeed in doing so. It is more often men that wish to disconnect sex from procreation. Jess was a female pioneer in this field, although maybe she did not regard herself in that light.

It was easier to ignore the consideration of paternal genes then than it would be now. We did not then consider ourselves held in the genetic trap. We thought each infant was born pure and new and holy: a gold baby, a luminous lamb. We did not know that certain forms of breast cancer were programmed and almost ineluctable, and we would not have believed you if you had told us that in our lifetime young women would be subjecting themselves to preventative mastectomies. This would have seemed to us a horrifying misapplication of medical insight, but we would of course have been wrong. We had heard of Huntington's chorea ('chorea' isn't a word you can use now) and cystic fibrosis, but we thought of them as rare and deviant afflictions. Most genes, we thought, were normal. We did not believe in biological destiny. We thought we and our children were born free.

You may pity us for our ignorance, or envy us for our faith.

So Jess did not closely pursue genealogical explanations for Anna's state. Her investigations were desultory. In her own heritage she traced a distant case of cerebral palsy, a couple of suicides and, at the beginning of the twentieth century, a child with Down's syndrome (then called Mongolism, a term, like lobster claw and chorea, now obsolete). The condition of this child was easily explained by the advanced age of his mother at conception, a factor discovered by Jess on one of her covert visits to Somerset House. (The story of the Down's syndrome boy had been handed on through family lore, through the paternal line in Lincolnshire, and reinterpreted by Jess: Jack Speight had been 'a bit simple', 'a backward boy', a young man 'who couldn't do much for himself', and he had died in his thirties.) Anna's condition did show some behavioural affinity with that of many Down's syndrome children – an innate happiness of temperament, an at times overtrusting nature, a love of singing, a lack of the finer motor skills. But of chromosomal evidence for the condition there was none.

Anna as a child and as a young person was not identifiable, visually, as in any way impaired. Her learning difficulties were not obvious to the eye. This was both a blessing and a curse. No leeway was given her, no tolerance extended to her by strangers. Jess, who quickly became expert in spotting the cognitive and behavioural problems of other young people, found this at times a difficulty. Should she smooth Anna's way by excuses, or allow her to make her own way through the thicket of harsh judgements and impatient jostlings that lay before her through her life? She tried to stand back, to let Anna make her own forays, her own mistakes, but occasionally she felt compelled to intervene and explain.

Anna loved her mother with an exemplary filial devotion, seeming to be aware from the earliest age of her own unusual dependence. As our children and the other children we knew came to defy us and to tug at our apron strings and to yearn for separation, Anna remained intimate with her mother, shadowing her closely, responding to every movement of her body and mind, approving her every act. Necessity was clothed with a friendly and benign garment, brightly patterned, soft to the touch, a nursery fabric that did not age with the years.

In those first years, before the educational attainments of her peers began to demonstrate a noticeable discrepancy, Anna remained part of a ragged informal community of children which accepted her for what she was, prompted by the kind example of their parents. The parents admired Jess for several good reasons, and they liked little Anna, so smiling, so unthreatening in every way, so uncompetitive. Ollie, Nick, Harry, Chloe, Ben, Polly, Becky, Flora, Stuart, Josh, Jake, Ike, Tim and Tom tolerated Anna easily, willingly. They indulged her and let her join their games, according to her ability.

But the games grew more complex, and Anna was left behind.

Anna could not understand why she could not learn to read, as the other children did. What was this game called 'reading'? Picture books and stories she loved, particularly repetitive stories and nursery rhymes with refrains, which she could memorise word for word, and repeat back, expressively, and with a fine grasp of content, to her mentors. 'Sing a Song of Sixpence', 'Polly, Put the Kettle On', 'Curly Locks' and 'Incey Wincey Spider' were part of her considerable repertoire. But letters remained a mystery. She learnt to draw *A* for Anna, but produced it in a wobbly and uneven hand, and was slow to get to grips with *n*.

Jess noticed that although Anna could sing her way through 'One Two Buckle My Shoe', 'One, Two, Three, Four, Five, Once I Caught a Fish Alive' and other counting rhymes, she could not count well without the aid of the rhyme. She needed the mnemonic. She found numbers on their own confusing. She would never, Jess suspected, Jess knew, become wholly numerate.

Jess and I didn't talk much in those early days about Anna's condition, but of course I was well aware of it, as were we all. A kind of delicacy prevented me from asking direct questions, and I waited for whatever Jess wished to divulge. My children – but this story isn't about my children, I haven't the right to tell their stories – my children were friendly with Anna, and she spent quite a lot of time with me and my two boys. I was working part time then, and Jess and I looked after one another, covered one another. My boys had known Anna since she was born (one is two years older, one more or less exactly the same age), and for years they didn't really notice there was anything different about her. And as they began to notice, so they gradually began to adjust their interactions with her, looking out for her when there were games she couldn't manage, taking extra care crossing the road. They used to take her to the corner shop with them on Saturday mornings to spend their weekly pocket money in a binge on Refreshers and Spangles and Crunchy Bars and Smarties. They negotiated with the temperamental grey-faced heavy-smoking old man who kept the till, and made sure she got back the right change. I didn't have to tell them to do this. They knew.

Maybe we shouldn't have let such little ones go along the road and over the zebra crossing together, but we did. They all learnt their Green Cross Code, but I think they used to go to Mr Moran's even before the Green Cross Code was invented.

They weren't saints, my children, they weren't angels, they weren't always patient, and I remember one horrible afternoon when Ike lost his temper with Anna. It was teatime in our house, and she managed to break a limb off his little wooden puppet man. Ike was very attached to that little puppet man, whom he called Helsinki, and he'd sometimes let Anna play with him and twist him about, but that day she screwed his arm one notch too far in an attempt to make him wave, and it came off.

Ike was very cross, and called her a clumsy stupid silly girl, and snatched Helsinki back and said she could never ever touch Helsinki again. Anna's eyes grew large with tears, and she retreated behind the enormous mahogany veneer radiogram in the corner. I intervened and said I was sure I could fix Helsinki with a dab of Superglue and I put on a record to distract them (I think it was 'Nellie the Elephant') and opened another packet of chocolate fingers, but Anna wouldn't come out from the corner for quite a long time.

When Jess came to collect her, Anna was still quite subdued, and I felt miserably guilty. I didn't know whether to explain what had happened or not. I didn't want to betray Ike, who was such a good lad on the whole. So it wasn't all easy, all the time. There were moments. And I never did manage to fix Helsinki properly. I couldn't get the joint to articulate. He had a stiff arm for the rest of his short wooden life.

But Anna and Ike got over this incident, and forgave one another. Neither bore a grudge.

Ike's name wasn't really Ike: it was Ian, but Jake called him Ike when he was a baby, by analogy with his own name, and it stuck. He still calls himself Ike.

Jake and Ike, my babies.

Sometimes Jess and I would have a glass of wine, after these teatime child-minding sessions, and talk about grown-up matters. I would report on ethical dilemmas in the charity where I worked, or spill Whitehall secrets from my husband's ascendant career at the Home Office, and she would tell me about whatever she was reading or reviewing, and about the thesis on which she was working. I learnt a lot of second-hand anthropology from Jess. She aired her ideas on me. I liked to hear her talk about the shining lake, the children and the shoebill, and about Dr Livingstone, whose grave she said she had visited. We were both mildly obsessed by Livingstone, then a deeply unfashionable and intellectually provocative figure. She knew far more about him than I did, but I had missionaries in my family background, and old missionary books on the family bookshelves, and as a child I had browsed through my great-grandfather's school prize of *Livingstone's Travels*, with its thrilling engravings of 'The Missionary's Escape from the Lion' and 'Natives Spearing an Elephant and Her Calf'. I was always interested in reports about Livingstone. We speculated about what he had really, truly believed.

Jess and I talked a lot. We talked about everything.

When the children got tired they would watch *Blue Peter*, or whatever came on after *Blue Peter*. Ike used to suck his thumb when he watched telly. I'm sorry to say I used to like to see him suck his thumb. It was strangely comforting. And he did grow out of it.

Children's television seemed very wholesome and educational in those days, although now we're told it wasn't all it seemed.

~

Playgroup and nursery group were easy enough for Anna, surrounded by neighbourhood friends. Jess worried that when she went to primary school she would be exposed to potentially hostile strangers, even though she would still be in the company of Tim and Tom and Polly and Ollie and Ike. Jake and Stuart, two years older, had already gone ahead to defend her in the playground and taught her the ropes. And Anna's skills sufficed in the first year of Plimsoll Road Primary, with the other five-year-olds and six-year-olds, under the benevolent and knowing eye of pretty, long-legged, mini-skirted Miss Laidman. Miss Laidman, who had studied pedagogy at an avant-garde teachers' training college in Bristol, was well aware of Anna's difficulties, and became expert at including her in group activities. Anna and Jess were lucky in Miss Laidman, and the school itself had a benevolent regime. Jess was grateful for this, but knew that such luck and such participation with her tolerant peers could not last for long. The next stage must come soon.

It was considered by the professionals and indeed by Jess that Anna would, in time, be unable to cope with the demands of state primary education. A special school of some description would have to be found, where she could acquire special skills. In the right environment, she might even be able to learn to read. Miss Laidman encouraged Anna to write her letters, but she could not teach her to read.

Miss Laidman had a colleague called Fanny Foy, who taught music at Plimsoll Road and at one or two other schools in Stoke Newington and Finsbury Park. Miss Foy loved Anna, and would spend extra time with her. Miss Foy had a little sister like Anna. Fanny Foy, I discovered, moonlighted and played the violin in a theatre orchestra at night. She had a double life. She knew all the musicals. She taught Anna the tunes and a lot of the words.

~

When Anna was seven, Jess moved out of the upstairs flat above Jim and Katie, feeling perhaps that she should not become too attached to, or dependent on, them or their residence. Or perhaps she was getting irritated by the competitive marital discord occasionally displayed in the household. Jim and Katie were relieved, though they did not say so, because they needed the extra space for their own growing family: when Jess announced that she was moving, Katie had a third child on the way. They needed the space and, prospering on two incomes, they no longer needed the rent. And probably they were not happy with a witness to their domestic discord. Better to rage

in private than in earshot of a highly acute and perceptive lodger and her innocent and perhaps too guileless child. Jim's ambitions and Katie's ambitions were increasingly in conflict, and the conflict was becoming increasingly overt.

Jess moved to a shabby little three-storey terraced property a few streets away, in easy reach of her old friends and our reliable support system. Houses were cheap then, and, although it was difficult for a single woman to get a mortgage, Jess must have produced a satisfactory deposit for No. 23 Kinderley Road N5, raised from her father, or from the Professor, or from some other undisclosed source of finance. She must have found a friendly broker. She was, after all, a graduate in what was considered respectable and regular, though not very remunerative, professional employment. Maybe the Professor gave her a good reference. He could hardly, one might think, do less: although really, when considering the Professor, it is hard to know what to think that he might have done.

Sometimes I wondered if Jess made up the story of the Professor. She told it to us in instalments, over those early years, and perhaps improved and embellished it at each telling. We are all adept at rewriting the past, at reinventing it. Perhaps Anna was the result of a one-night stand, or of a liaison with a fellow-student of which Jess was ashamed, and which she had decided to disown.

The story of the Professor was, as Jess unfolded and disclosed it to us, dramatic and colourful. It had those virtues. Jess was a good storyteller. She has told me many stories, over the many years of our friendship, and some of them have certainly altered in the telling. Some of them have become so entangled with my own memories that I feel as though I have witnessed events that are part of her life, not mine. This is partly, but not wholly, to do with Anna's love of repetition. Anna would say, 'Tell us about that time when Gramps tried to jug the hare', or 'Tell us about when you went swimming in your nightie', or 'Tell us about the tree-frog', or 'Tell us about when Gramps ate the mouse', and Jess would tell.

Jess is a good listener as well as a good narrator. I have told her things I have never told to anyone, should never have told to anyone. Jess was, and is, an attractive woman, with a hypnotic intensity of attention that tends to mesmerise an interlocutor. She concentrates on others in a manner that sucks out the soul. It would be fair to say that we were all rather in awe of her. Not a great beauty in any classical style, but noticeable, memorable, one might even say seductive, although seduction was not on her agenda in Anna's primary-school days. She must have mesmerised the Professor. When she is talking to you, she transfixes you. Her short-sighted eyes are very fierce and piercing, a cornflower-blue. This explains some of her history. Had she not given birth to Anna, her life would have been different. It might have been played at fast and loose.

She wasn't a great beauty, but she had a style that turned heads, a confident way of walking and of being in her body. I don't know how a man would describe her, but men (including the Professor, or whoever the Professor represents) were attracted to Jess. If it hadn't been for Anna, we would have feared for our husbands.

In her new home in Kinderley Road, Jess gave enterprising little suppers at which she amused herself and us by cooking, usually successfully, odd little dishes, some composed from ingredients from the West Indian store round the corner. Her pigs' trotters were a triumph, and once she ventured on pigs' ears. She enjoyed confronting taboos. She and Anna were fearless eaters. You need not feel too sorry for Jess. Some sorrow is appropriate, but she was not, as I hope I have made clear, an object of pity. We regarded her with respect, affection and alarm. She was good company. We laughed a lot, over our cheap meals and cheap wine, on our excursions to the park, on our turns on the swings and the roundabouts.

There were park attendants in those days, some of them rather bossy and disagreeable, officious little despots of their small domains, and I remember an unpleasant altercation when one of them reprimanded Anna for tipping some sand from the dog-frequented sandpit on to a miserably bare adjacent flowerbed. Jess leapt to her daughter's defence with an impassioned speech which impressed and alarmed us all. She was a fierce mother, a cat, a lioness, guarding her kitten. She never allowed anyone to criticise Anna.

And not many wished to do so. Anna was a good girl.

~

If Jess longed to pursue her academic career more actively, she did not let us know. She did not complain. She appeared to have accepted, on Anna's behalf, the home front and the life of the mind. She continued to read, to study, to think, to write, to venture into the wilder wastes of intellectual speculation. One can do all those things from a little house in a back street off the Blackstock Road near Finsbury Park tube station, with reasonable access to the SOAS library and the British Library and the Royal Anthropological Institution.

Some think, indeed, that the brain grows keener in confinement. In the field, the brain wanders and cannot settle. As Guy Brighouse's was so fatally to do.

Jess managed, during this early period of Anna's infancy, to teach two days a week at an adult education college, and with Guy Brighouse's help she obtained a generous bursary to write a thesis. Guy looked after Jess well. Her thesis, you may not be surprised to hear, dealt with the assessment and treatment of mental incapacity and abnormality in the area of Central Africa that she had visited in that first youthful escapade into what was not to her the heart of darkness. (Northern Rhodesia became Zambia even as she was working on this project.) She had toyed for a while with the idea of writing about representations of the *enfant sauvage* in the literature of anthropology, a subject of great cultural richness, but too open-ended for a beginner, or so Guy Brighouse, by now her supervisor, told her. So she confined herself under his not very attentive guidance to the impact of missionaries on the practice of traditional remedies and 'witchcraft' (for this was Dr Livingstone's realm, the land where he strove and died) – and, tangentially, with the variability of the concept of IQ with reference to 'the savage mind'. (The word 'savage' was still, at that period, almost acceptable, although it sounded better in French.) She had to rely very heavily on secondary sources, but she made the best of a bad job.

She had enjoyed exploring the nineteenth- and early-twentieth-century accounts of explorers and big-game hunters and native commissioners, discovered in periodicals and learned journals and government reports. She noted their degrees of condescension and racial prejudice and their appalled condemnation of insanitary living conditions in the African colonies. (The laziness, the dirtiness, the unhealthiness! The smallpox, the jiggers, the worms, the ticks, the syphilis, the scurvy, the leprosy!) She had learnt that the people of the big lake went mad when sent to work in the copper mines, and would not eat of the flesh of the amphibious land-dwelling fish called *nkomo*, because if you ate of this mad non-fish it would drive you mad. She longed to see a *nkomo*, but doubted if she ever would.

She had noted that tolerance of mental disability and mental disturbance appeared to have diminished with the advent of Christianity: 'lunatics' had rarely been attacked in the old tribal days, as one theory held that if you killed a lunatic, you would catch his lunacy. This superstition had served a useful purpose, Jess seemed to suggest in her thesis, and it was a pity that it had been undermined by science and by the Christian religion.

She now, several decades later, disagrees with her 1960s position. She now thinks that Christianity has had, overall, globally, historically, in Africa and elsewhere, a favourable impact on our perceptions of mental disability and birth defects and congenital irregularities. It has been kinder, for example, to twins and the mothers of twins. Some African cultures slaughter twins at birth. The mothers of twins, like slaves, were attracted by Christianity. They were reluctant to slaughter their babies and glad of a reason to defy tradition.

Jesus did not have views on twins, as far as we know, but we believe we know that he favoured the simple-minded.

Jess was then in most ways a child of her secular, progressive time, and distrusted missionaries on principle. She disapproved of Livingstone as a proto-imperial trader with a gun, as she had been taught to do at SOAS. She did not share his view that commerce inevitably elevated culture. She noted with interest the cool detachment of his comment that 'the general absence of deformed persons is partly owing to their destruction in infancy', and his equally detached views on abnormality or transgression summed up in the African term *tlolo*. But she could not prevent herself from being moved by his tender accounts of the tree-frog and the fish-eagle, the forest and the mountain and the waterfall. He had seen the natural world too closely for any kind of comfort, but he had loved some of its manifestations. Livingstone, like the lobster-claw children, worked on in her memory.

She read his diaries and letters, and worried about the poor orphan Nassick boys, the young Bombay Indians who faithfully accompanied him as servants on his travels. Jess always worried about orphans. She used to try to tell me about the Nassick boys but it was a complicated story and I've never worked out quite who they were, though their unhappy name has stuck with me. They hadn't featured in the school-prize version of Livingstone's travels that I'd read.

Jess's supervisor Guy Brighouse had spent some years with a dry, grey-black-skinned, long-legged and dwindling tribe that made, according to him, the most sophisticated pots in Africa, and the most beautiful conical dwelling places man or woman had ever seen, of wattle and decorated clay. These mason–potters were dying out, according to Guy's theory, through aesthetic despair, as modernity overtook them. Plastic and corrugated iron were killing them. Their hearts and souls were dying.

Jess liked Guy, and the freedom of his fancies. He was considered a wild card at SOAS, but she liked that too.

She managed to work into her thesis a mention of the children with fused toes, but to her regret was not able to find out anything more about them. Livingstone did not seem to have met them, though he noted the dwarf, the albino and the leper, and Guy, who had seen them, did not show much interest in them. Nobody then or now seemed to have studied them. Did they and their children and their children's children play still by the shining lake upon the immortal shore?

The analogue of the children continued to haunt her. She found documentation of a cluster group of the families of similarly afflicted children in Scotland: the parents had told the eminent investigating statistician that the little ones didn't miss their fingers and toes – 'Bless'ee, sir, the kids don't mind it, they don't miss what they've never had' – and that they were remarkably adept with the vestigial digits which they did possess, with which they produced fine handwriting and needlework.

Jess had noted how deftly the lake children had punted their small canoes.

Of all the explorer narratives, Jess liked Mungo Park's best.

She was touched by this lone romantic Scottish adventurer's desire to see the best in others, even in those who were exploiting him, robbing him, exposing him mercilessly to lions and starvation. A child of his time, he wished to believe in the universal goodness of human nature. And he did meet with some goodness in Africa, as well as much cruelty.

Jess liked best the episode when he was denied hospitality and shelter by the suspicious king of a tribe near the Niger and forced to sit hungry all day beneath a tree, and to take refuge at night in its branches from wild beasts, as nobody would give him food or accommodation. But he was befriended by a woman returning from her labours in the field. Observing that he looked weary and dejected, she heard his story with 'looks of great compassion', took him to her hut, lit him a lamp, spread a mat for him and fed him with a fine fish broiled on the embers. She assured him he could sleep safely in her hut, and during the night she and her female company sat spinning cotton and singing an improvised song:

The winds roared, and the rains fell. The poor white man, faint and weary, came and sat under our tree. He has no mother to bring him milk, no wife to grind his corn. Let us pity the white man, no mother has he . . .

This song can bring tears to Jess's eyes whenever she wants.

The less friendly and more avaricious Moors were puzzled by Park's pocket compass and the way its needle always pointed to the Great Desert. Unable to provide a scientific explanation comprehensible to them, Mungo Park told them that his mother resided far beyond the sands of the Sahara, and that while she was alive the iron needle would always point towards her. If she were dead, he said, it would point to her grave.

As it happened, his mother outlived him. He came to a sad end, though not on this recorded expedition. He pursued his fate.

Jess found these stories deeply touching.

Mungo Park didn't think much of the slave-trading, intolerant and bigoted Moors, who hissed and shouted and spat at him because he was a white man and a Christian. They abused him and plundered his goods and refused to let him drink from the well. He had to drink from the cow trough. They ill-treated their slaves and their womenfolk.

He preferred the native Africans with their simple superstitions and their kind hearts.

Mungo Park was an Enlightenment man.

~

Who could have foreseen what would happen to the Blackstock Road in the next millennium? We didn't. Nobody did. The mosque and the halal butchers took over from the barrels of salt pork, and young men with beards from the West Indians and the Irish. The friendly Arsenal at Highbury, home of the Gunners, moved to the glittering Emirates Stadium, built and sponsored by money from the Middle East, and Miss Laidman married the head of a college of further education and went to live in North Kensington. The balance of power and the balance of fear shifted. But by this time many of us, like Miss Laidman, would have moved on to more up-market neighbourhoods. Some of us are still there, in the old neighbourhood, and our properties have appreciated a hundredfold, as properties in London do, but the area is still not what you would call fashionable. Those of us who are loyal to it appreciate it, indeed love it. Some streets, with their modest little mass-produced brickwork and tile decorations, have hardly changed at all. There are old lovingly pruned rose bushes growing still in small front gardens. They predate the booms and slumps of property.

Blackstock Road has not yet, as I write, become gentrified, and may never become so. It was peaceful then, when we were young. Shabby, but peaceful. There were little shops, selling small cheap household objects, bric-à-brac, groceries, vegetables, stationery. Locksmiths, hairdressers, launderettes, upholsterers, bookmakers. A lot of people taking in one another's washing. It is much the same today, although most of the shopowners now come from different ethnic groups. There are fewer of the old white North Londoners. They are dying off, moving out. It remains on the whole a peaceful neighbourhood, though there have been eruptions of violence and suspicion, and one spectacular police raid by hundreds of uniformed officers that revealed, I believe, a tiny cache of ricin.

Even a tiny cache wasn't very pleasant, some of us old survivors thought, although we made light of it, laughed about it. It's not nice to have neighbours who are trying to kill you, even if they are not trying very hard. We tried to be tolerant, but it wasn't very nice.

There was a time, not so long ago, when hatred was preached by a man with a hook for a hand from the redbrick mosque of Finsbury Park, the mosque that Prince Charles, Prince of Many Faiths, opened with such conciliatory optimism in 1994. It's quieter now. It's not a very big mosque, not one of those extravagant imposing new mosques with great golden domes, and its minaret is made of cement and pebble-dash. It is well guarded by spiked walls and CCTV. Suburban net curtains drape its windows, with their green-painted frames. It doesn't look much of a threat. As a mosque, it is a far cry from the glories of Isfahan and Samarkand and Cairo, and I'm not sure who is watching what on that CCTV.

You can't tell what will happen to a neighbourhood. Jess studies its evolution with an expert eye. Her eye is better than mine, but we discuss its progress. I've learnt new ways of looking from Jess. She continues to find ways of employing her sociological and anthropological expertise.

Finsbury Park tube station hasn't seen much improvement. At our age, most of us tend to avoid it at night. It presents a small challenge. Too many drug-dealers. They've moved up the line towards us from King's Cross.

I visited a great and famous mosque in Cairo once. I forget its name. It was unutterably grand and sacred, lofty and empty, austere and sombre. It reared up from the deep ravine of the sloping street like a cliff face. I wandered round its solitude in silence and in awe.

The Finsbury Park mosque is small, domestic, suburban. Rather English, really.

~

Jess's thesis on contrasting perceptions of witchcraft and disability in pre-imperial and post-imperial Africa was disputed, and she was rightly accused by some of having bitten off more than she could chew. She was also accused from a diametrically opposite angle by one of her assessors of having failed to include any mention of the superstitions surrounding the birth of twins in West Africa, and the heroic work of Scottish missionary Mary Slessor in rescuing some of these twin babes from being exposed at birth in the bush. (Jess had not mentioned Mary Slessor and the twins because she had never heard of them. Her knowledge, although arcane, was very patchy. But she was still very young. The assessor had himself specialised in Mary Slessor and twin studies, and if Jess had known that she might have been more diplomatic in her selection of material.)

Theses were not nearly as rigorously overseen in those days as they are now, and the maverick globe-trotting conference-attending field-work-dabbling Guy Brighouse had been somewhat nonchalant about his duties towards her. You could get away with almost anything. You didn't have to tick so many boxes.

But her efforts, although criticised, were also moderately applauded, and she became Dr Jessica Speight. Her father, plain Mr Speight of Broughborough, was proud of her. And he loved his special granddaughter, Anna, although he was shy about paying too many visits. He told me this one cold afternoon in Clissold Park, as we sat on a bench together, while the children watched the mynah birds and listened to them screech and chatter. One of them had been taught to scream 'Arsenal! Arsenal!' My children thought this was very funny. No longer children, they still support the Arsenal through thick and thin. This weekend, as I write, it's a bit thin.

Philip Speight hoped Jess's small and eccentric little family would prosper. Maybe, one day, Jess would find another man, a better man, a husband, a father for Anna.

Anna loved her grandfather. She was lucky there. She was a lucky child. She called him Gramps, and he liked that.

Anna's grandfather was much more attentive to Anna than Anna's grandmother. We speculated (but not in Jess's hearing) that this was because Anna's grandmother feared the suspicion of a hereditary taint. Women, irrationally but not surprisingly, tend to take the idea of genetic blame more seriously than men.

And, in the cause of mitochondrial disorders, they are right to do so. Although we did not know that then. And it doesn't do us much good to know it now.

Jess's sister Vee avoided Jess and Anna, possibly for the same reasons. Or maybe it was just common or garden sibling rivalry that kept them apart. Jess was, despite the difficulties, a formidable sister.

~

The story of Anna unfolded peaceably and uneventfully over those early years of nursery school and primary school and caused, as such stories do, both happiness and anxiety in almost equal measure. Anna was a fact in all our lives, and a part of our mapping of the world.

The birth of children such as Anna may become rarer year by year. And that would be a loss, though the nature of that loss is hard to describe. It is important to recognise it as loss, although we cannot describe it.

An innocence, with children such as Anna, would be gone from the world. A possibility of another way of being human would be lost, with all that it signifies. They are God's children, *les enfants du bon Dieu*, we used to say, but now we no longer believe in God. Their lives are hidden with God, as Wordsworth wrote in defence of his Idiot Boy, but God himself is now hidden. God has absconded, but he has left us his children.

Anna had no father to miss or mourn, as she had never met him. But she had a loving grandfather and many willing surrogate-father figures in our little neighbourhood community. She knew what fathers were. There were several happy to take her on their knee with a storybook, to pick her up from school, to make sure she got her fair share of the sandwiches. Even the irresponsible and frequently absconding Rick Raven was respectful to Anna, when he was around. She provoked good behaviour.

The Professor as father and, we may assume, as lover proved disposable, as his emotional and intellectual limitations became more and more obvious to Jess, and off he went, unregretted, with his professor wife, to a year's fieldwork on the borders of Manchuria. He was something of a fellow-traveller, the Professor, but Jess was beginning to think he was also a bit of a fool. She began to wonder what she had ever seen in him, apart from the size of his penis, and it sometimes crossed her mind that he had behaved rather badly in seducing her when she was still a student in her early twenties, though she tried not to allow this suspicion to linger and fester. She brushed it away. Looking after Anna had enabled her to see the Professor as an undeveloped and childish person. She was well rid of him, and, after several years of him, she was ready to move on.

The two professors went off to make a study of child rearing and infanticide in agrarian communities in a remote Chinese border community. The two professors were prepared to consider infanticide an appropriate response to many family problems, or so it seemed to Jess. They had no children. (Anna did not count.) Sweden, as Jess did not then know, as not many people in Britain then knew, practised compulsory sterilisation of those with learning difficulties until 1975, which seems a long-lasting anomaly in what is rightly held to be a tolerant, liberal egalitarian society.

Anthropologists are a strange breed. Jess didn't like it when outsiders made fun of them, but she couldn't help noticing that some of the most celebrated anthropological narratives have curious gaps in them. You read hundreds of pages of observation and analysis, and are suddenly made aware that the observer was, all the while, not embedded lonely in an alien tribe living on worms and bats and insect stew, as he appeared to be and indeed as he frequently suggested he was, but living near by in semi-comfort with his wife and a servant or two in a de-luxe tent or a mobile home, with access to the highway or the helicopter. Much work, of course, has recently been done on deconstructing anthropological narratives, and it is sometimes hard to tell which revisionist readings are true, and which malicious. But some primary and very famous accounts are, for sure, misleading.

Living amongst the Nambikwara in Brazil, Lévi-Strauss describes a meal consisting of a few fruits, two fat poisonous spiders, tiny lizards' eggs, one or two lizards, a bat, palm nuts and a handful of grasshoppers. He claimed that the group gobbled these up cheerfully, and that he happily shared the repast.

Maybe so, maybe not. When his wife developed an eye infection, she was evacuated very promptly to the nearest hospital.

However hard we stare at Lévi-Strauss's photographs of the Nambikwara, we can never read them. Are they human? Are they of the same human species as ourselves, are they of the same branch of the family of man? What did these people make of Lévi-Strauss and his low-profile but attendant wife? We stare at them as adolescents in a more sheltered age used to stare at photographs suggesting or partially disclosing nudity: hungry for knowledge, hungry for revelation. As Jess as a child stared at her father's kid-bound booklet, as Jess as a mother stares at the photographs in Lionel Penrose's classic books on Mental Defect. She gazes at the High-Grade Feeble-Minded Girl, so demure and pretty with her dark dress and wide lace collar, at the physically less appealing Laurence-Moon syndrome man with retinitis pigmentosa and six toes on his right foot. But you can never penetrate the photograph. They do not reveal more, however long you stare at them. They remain static, frozen, sealed. They do not, cannot move. They cannot speak to us.

On the new medium of television, to which we were all beginning to succumb, the images moved. They seemed to tell us more. They seemed to be three-dimensional, those animals in the savannah, those tribesmen in their shacks and huts, those patients with rare diseases, those travellers in the outback. But you can't believe anything you see on television, ever. You seem to see more than you see in an old-fashioned ethnological photograph, but you don't. We all know that now. Look for the shadow of the cameraman. Look for the footprint of the cameraman.

It wasn't quite as bad as that in those early days. Television wasn't either as smart or as stupid as it is now. It was simpler.

Katie's Jim in the sixties and seventies worked in television for Granada. He directed a current-affairs programme. He worked very hard. Those were the heroic days of Granada, when it was inventive, investigative, radical. Katie worked part time at Bush House for the BBC World Service, reviewing new poetry from the Commonwealth and chairing a poetry quiz. This was a characteristically gendered division of labour in those days.

Both their lives are very different now.

Jess's one and only African journey was to the shining lake, where Livingstone died. She remained pure gold and told no lies. She never pretended to have been where she hadn't been. She never made up anthropological stories.

That is how we like to see her, our Jess, the shining one who did not lie and did not falter.

~

So Jess moved on, liberating herself from the irresponsible, emotionally arrested, possibly mythical, possibly mythologised Professor, and when she was well settled into her life with Anna in her own new home in Kinderley Road she began to look around for somebody more her own age, as her father had hoped she would. Or that's what I thought she was doing. And I was proved to be right.

We talked about men, Jess and I, as well as about more intellectual concerns, in those early feminist days of the sixties. We laughed a lot and complained and made fun of men and marriage. But we weren't ideologically separatist, as some women at that time were. I was married, and was to remain married until widowhood, despite some scary passages, and I did not tell tales about my husband, nor would Jess have wished to hear them. But we gossiped remorselessly about our neighbours, particularly about Jim and Katie, and about Rick Raven, whose departure from our lives and Sylvie's life we had correctly predicted. I remember one evening at my house, while Anna and the boys and Ollie were making a racket up in the attic playroom with a horrible and wholly incorrect new toy called a Johnny Seven Gun, Jess and I discovered that Rick had made a pass at each of us, and maybe in the same week.

We didn't use the word 'incorrect' then, but we were well familiar with the concept.

We were drinking whisky that evening, not very much of it, not a John Updike evening, but enough to make us mildly indiscreet. I'd been given a bottle of Laphroaig for my birthday the day before – I loved a good malt in those days though I rarely risk it now – and we were sipping in a ladylike way out of two darling little matching engraved souvenir glasses, one called 'Loch Lomond' and the other 'The Road to the Isles'. I liked water with my Scotch, but Jess preferred hers neat.

Jess told me that Rick had given Jess and Anna a lift home when they'd been to tea with Sylvie and her boys, and he'd put his hand on her thigh and propositioned her. He said he'd always fancied her and could he call round later. She'd said no, certainly not, but thank you for asking.

Rick was a smooth customer, a Fleet Street man who wrote about culture and society; he fancied his own heterodox and slightly right-wing views, and we didn't think he was very bright. But he was a good-looker, and he thought he could get away with it.

He hadn't asked me if he could call round later, for obvious reasons, but he had suggested a rendezvous in town for lunch one day, and he'd squeezed my thigh in what I imagine was much the same manner. Skirts were very short then, and I can remember to this day the one I was wearing: it was grey but it had a gold thread in the weave. I suppose we were asking for it, showing all that leg and accepting lifts from other people's husbands.

Jess told me she gave him the brush-off because he wasn't her type, and anyway she didn't want to annoy the neighbourhood with unnecessary adultery. He wasn't my type either, but I did agree to have a discreet lunch with him in Soho, and a very good lunch it was too.

I didn't tell Jess about that at the time. I didn't confess to that lunch until several decades later, at Rick Raven's funeral in St Bride's.

I was sorry when the little glass called Loch Lomond broke in the dishwasher. I've still got the Road to the Isles.

Jess didn't say that she was ready for a fling, but maybe Rick Raven had sensed it, and that's why he'd grabbed her knee. It's just that he didn't fill the bill. The chap she found, without too much difficulty and after one or two more unsatisfactory overtures and experiments, wasn't a neighbourhood man at all. There was nothing incestuous or even adulterous about him. He was new blood. He was half American, and he had long black curly hair, a hairy chest, and very smooth gleaming brown shoulders. He beautifully combined the hairy and the smooth. He had a child of his own from a previous marriage, but he'd left his wife and child behind in Chicago. He was divorced, and seemed keen to marry Jess. He was exactly the same age as Jess, take a couple of months. He was an ethnologist and a photographer, quite successful, and he took life lightly. He was a populist, and he made Jess laugh. Jess found his eagerness in itself seductive. Why not? He was an American citizen and he didn't need a passport to settle in England. He didn't try to borrow money from her. He wasn't serious, but that seemed to Jess at that stage in her life to be an advantage. She was prepared to give him a try, to have a marital fling, and see how it worked out. Anna was for life, but Bob needn't be. If it didn't work out, never mind.

We didn't trust him.

We could see that Jess needed some light relief, but Bob didn't seem quite the ticket. But who were we to warn her? We were all busy making new mistakes, or learning how to live with our old ones. And he made us laugh too. There was something a little scandalous and subversive about his attitudes to the animals and the people that he photographed: something dodgy, something exhibitionistic, something self-regarding and possessive. Like the Professor, he was another bad lot, but of a less sinister, more manageable, more entertaining species. Jess, like her father, was a purist, and happy to confront disappointment that way. But Bob was a bit of a vulgarian – a bit too interested in the naked ape. (Desmond Morris's book of this title had appeared in 1967: it was a key title of the next decade, and, although we laughed at it, we were also rather taken with it. Morris was much given to jokes about the penis.) We should have known that Bob would go into television in his forties, for a time quite successfully, but I don't think we foresaw this. We hadn't really foreseen television itself, except for *The Magic Roundabout* and *Blue Peter* and *Top of the Pops* and the BBC news and the sort of high-minded current-affairs documentary programmes that Jim made.

Bob seemed to expect to be taken seriously as an ethnologist, and he was certainly very clever. And he was good-looking. I think we may have been jealous. But Jess deserved a bit of luck, or that's what we generously decided to think. Not that it would have made much difference if we hadn't.

I liked Bob. I didn't take him very seriously, but I liked him. I'm not sure if he liked me, in those days, but he didn't need to, did he?

The Professor was a wedge, a prow, a beak. Austere, determined, rock hard and unrelenting. Bob, as his name happily suggests, was a rounder chap, with animal spirits and a good deal of energy. He was a seal, a bear, a handsome beast with fur on his chest, a healthy mammal. He tumbled and laughed and talked smartly. He seemed to take stepdaughter Anna as part of the deal: Jess, North London, SOAS, a Bohemian intelligentsia, an inner ring, swinging London, long hair, impromptu street parties, a little hash. Jess didn't smoke hash – she was too responsible in her maternal role to take any small risks – but she didn't mind when other people did. She wasn't the kind of woman who said 'not in my house'.

I think Bob first came on the scene in the early seventies, but I couldn't swear to it. Anna would have been about eleven, I suppose.

Bob was friendly and at first ingratiating towards Anna, making her laugh, teaching her the words of some American summer-camp songs he'd sung as a teenager in Vermont, helping her to join in the conversation, not minding when she spilt her orange juice on his trousers. But it soon became clear that Bob felt she'd be better off at a residential boarding school for children with special needs, financed by the local authority. An offer of a place in Enfield had come up, and Jess had been worrying herself about whether or not to accept it. Anna was growing up. Anna had left our local primary school in Plimsoll Road when she could no longer cope with the lessons, even with Miss Laidman's special attention – I think she was about nine when she moved on – and she was already outgrowing the special class that she'd been attending, one attached to a larger state primary up in Highbury that gathered together most of the special-needs children of several North London boroughs. I think she was already at the Highbury school when Bob arrived in our lives.

Secondary school, Jess knew, would be a tougher proposition than primary school, and the local options for special needs weren't immediately attractive. Maybe Anna would be happy at a boarding school, where she would benefit from expert professional attention. (So, plausibly, reasoned Bob.) She could learn to be a little more independent, learn skills that would help her to survive better, in the long run, without Jess. The local authority agreed to fund her transfer to Enfield at this stage, and was committed to funding her until the age when she became the concern of the social services rather than of the education department. All in all, it seemed a sensible move to make.

Bob didn't press it, but it was clear that he was in favour of this move. We didn't quite know what to think. Most of us sent our children to the local state schools, although one or two of the more privileged and better-off amongst us had reverted to their ancestral type and opted to pay fees. My Jake went to the local comp, and Ike would soon follow him. I reasoned that Jake was such a bright lad that he'd do well wherever he went. Bright Tim Bowles had become a weekly boarder at Harrow; his father took the opposite line from me and thought he was too clever for a comprehensive. We didn't approve of that. Stuart and Josh Raven would also be sent to public school, and we wouldn't approve of that either. We were good at disapproval.

My husband and I didn't really see eye to eye about education, but he allowed me to make the decisions. He was, I sometimes thought, too busy with his work, his stressful decision-making work, to notice much of what was happening on the domestic front, and that suited me quite well. But happily that is not part of this narrative.

Anna, we all realised, was in a category of her own. Her needs were different. Her needs were special. The comfortable new phrase 'special needs' was to fit her like a nice warm woollen glove. She didn't have Down's syndrome, she wasn't a cretin or a moron or an idiot or an imbecile or even a High-Grade Feeble-Minded Girl, but she did have special needs.

Well, perhaps that's exactly what she was, in the language

of that earlier day. A High-Grade Feeble-Minded Girl. Lionel Penrose at Colchester would have recognised her, would have liked her. He liked most of his patients.

The debate about whether to educate special children in integrated classes within the mainstream system or by themselves in separate institutions is an old one, and, despite waves of reform and new education acts, it is never finally or satisfactorily resolved, because there is no final or satisfactory solution. There is no solution that fits all, as that warm-glove-word 'special' fitted Anna.

It was in 1913 that the Mental Deficiency Act was passed, which required 'defective' children to be taken out of elementary schools and placed in schools for the 'feeble-minded': a decision that was reversed by the Warnock Report of 1978, although that reversal is under constant review. No need to try to spell out this long, ongoing debate or to dramatise it here, although the *dramatis personae* are an interesting bunch of characters. The medical experts, the geneticists, the psychiatrists, the educationalists, the psychometric testers, the Mendelian mathematicians, the frauds and the faithful and the fanatics, the sociologists and the philosophers – they did their best and their worst. The story goes back a long way: to statistician Karl Pearson, who incidentally (entirely incidentally) computed the incidence and heritability of lobster claw in Scotland; to loveless tyrant Cyril Burt and his juvenile delinquents and his dubious twin studies; to gallant Lionel Penrose in the old Royal Eastern Counties Institution at Colchester, where he observed with affection the loving Down's children and what he called their 'secret source of joy'; then on to R. D. Laing, the liberator who redefined madness; and to Mary Warnock, the steel-haired, hooded-eyed, clear-sighted, no-nonsense wise old woman of the Warnock Report.

Penrose saw the secret source of joy of the pure gold babies.

There are schools now, as Jess will tell you, that specialise in many subdivisions of special needs and learning difficulties (Down's syndrome, autism, hearing difficulties) and apply many differing pedagogic theories to the education of their charges. There are schools with spiritual or religious foundations, schools with large endowments from concerned and wealthy parents, schools with cranky dietary beliefs and schools with regimes that veer towards the rigour of the boot camp. All over Britain, there are little communities and care homes, some open, some heavily gated, where the able and the fairly able look after the less able, with varying degrees of compassion and success. Some hope to cure; some are content to manage. Some of these care homes have ageing populations, as some of the needy live longer, and their carers age too. This is a worry, as our demographic curve changes. There are new needy being born every day, as we strive to keep alive premature babies that are not really viable, but Jess says we haven't even begun to worry about that yet.

There was not so much choice of special-needs schooling then, when Anna was a child, or, if there was, Jess didn't know where to look for it. Jess and Bob, during their courtship, thought they were lucky when a place for Anna was made available at Marsh Court. Anna's social worker had made inquiries and discovered it. Anna was a lucky girl. Anna would like Marsh Court.

~

Jess went to visit the school on her own, with a predisposition to find it suitable. She needed a safe stretch of time for Anna, she needed to marry Bob and have a year or two of quasi-normal life, she needed to like Marsh Court.

Marsh Court was within easy reach of North London, and it seemed to Jess to be a pleasant enough place, with caring staff and good facilities. The director and the staff were out to make a good impression. Jess was too nervous to ask them any searching questions, but she felt that the atmosphere of the classes, the smiles of some of the young people she met, were a recommendation. She did not hear any wailing from locked rooms or see any pale faces peering through barred upper windows. No mad children in the attics, no orphans strapped into their cribs.

After her interview with the director, Jess was shown round by a well-built, golden-skinned, broad-featured, crinkle-haired handsome middle-aged woman called Hazel, with a rich contralto voice and a beautiful carriage, who said she was in charge of music: was Anna musical, Hazel wanted to know? Yes, said Jess. She liked to sing. She knew a lot of songs.

We love to sing here, said Hazel, and grasped Jess's hand warmly in hers, and held her arm, hands linked, arms linked, as they walked down the corridors. Jess felt much better for this contact, and she would continue, in a long afterlife, long after she had lost touch with Hazel, to find the memory of it a comfort. Such small gestures are so much needed and not so often offered.

As she walked away from Marsh Court, on this her first of many visits, Jess looked back, calm enough to take in the school building and its immediate surroundings, which until now had appeared to her in a blur of anxiety and hope. The main house was an early-Victorian building, not unhandsome, built of reddish brick with stone facing, and surmounted with a couple of what Jess thought were Dutch gables. Despite efforts to make it cheerful and child-friendly – pots of geraniums outside its front door, bold blue-and-orange geometric-patterned curtains, fresh green paint – it had a melancholy air, pertaining less perhaps to its institutional function than to its architecture. It looked like the kind of house that might have been occupied by a lonely old woman, the last of her line, or by an embittered miser hiding from his heirs. It looked like the end of something, not the beginning.

It survived amidst a waste of random redevelopment, of housing estates and industrial parks, and was itself surrounded by little outcrops of prefabricated schoolrooms and workshops and allotments. But an older Enfield could still be traced in it, older by far than the little two-storey 1930s neat-shabby suburban homes that lined the road down which Jess now walked towards the River Lee and Enfield Lock.

Keats had been to school in Enfield. In a special school for the children of progressive tradesmen, not a special school for the educationally problematic. He and his friend, the schoolmaster's son, used to walk the ten miles into town to go to the theatre to see Sarah Siddons and Edmund Keane. How high their hopes had been, how lofty their ambitions, those earnest talented young men.

Jess walked towards Enfield Lock and the canal and the River Lee, and then began to walk, thoughtfully, reflectively, receptively, along the tow path. Anna liked the water. Anna, Jess thought, would like the water walkway. The lock was old and quiet, with a stationed narrow boat and a cluster of old buildings from another age – the dark-brick lock-keeper's cottage with white-fretted wooden gables, a row of tidy little houses, a pub called the Rifles. Jess sensed there was a historic arsenal connection here, as in Highbury, a military link, but the waterside this day was peaceful in the sun. The track was overgrown with elder and buddleia and nettles, with long greens and purples. Jess walked on and through a gate and over a wooden stile, and the water flowed strongly. She had left the placid canal bank and joined the path of the deep full river. A warning notice leaning rakishly on a rotting board told her the water was deep and dangerous. Small golden-winged birds flew in swift flurries in a light June breeze through tall willows and reeds. Dark dragonflies, blue-black, hovered and coupled over the rapidly moving surface.

~

Jess as she walks hears the high unearthly cry of the fish-eagle, calling from another world, calling from her youth and from Africa. She hears the honey-guide and the blacksmith plover and the go-away-bird and the boubou and the bird that cries *Nkoya, Nokoya, Nkoya Kupwa . . . I go, go, go to get married* . . . She hears the sad descending call of the emerald-spotted wood dove: *I lost my mother, I lost my father, and I am alone, alone, alone* . . . That, the tribesmen had told her, was the dove's lament, the lament that Livingstone had heard as he was carried dying on his litter through the swamps and the rushes.

Great submerged intensely green plants with large leaves like the leaves of cabbages stream in the current of the River Lee, with tight golden balls of flowers on long snake stems, rooted, tugging, flowing, flowering under the water. A great force of water flows powerfully in this half-tamed landscape of Essex.

Jess sees the swamps and marshes and sedges of Lake Bangweulu, the green spikes of reed and papyrus, the rain tree, the tussocks and the clumps, the rising bubbles of marsh gas, the green tunnel of the waterway and the slow progress of the low canoe. The lechwe are as numerous as the stars in the sky, their herds cover the grasslands, but the shoebill is lonely.

When one of the lechwe is taken by a lion, the rest of the herd moves onwards, uncaring, indifferent. Not one breaks off or strays behind to grieve.

Primates are different. Primates linger with their dead.

On his death march, Livingstone heard a little tree-frog 'tuning as loud as the birds and very sweet'. A luminous green-and-yellow tree-frog had perched on Jess's bedside torch, in her tent, all those years ago, safe with her under the mosquito net.

Walking on through time by the strong, fast-flowing water, Jess hears Hazel singing with Anna and the group of simple children, the pure bronzed woman singing with the pure gold child. Hazel sings:

> The river is flowing, growing and flowing,
> The river is flowing down to the sea.
> Mother Earth carry me,
> Your child I shall always be,
> Mother Earth carry me down to the sea . . .

The children join in the round, some tunefully, some at random, but all of them intent on Hazel's divine face, her sweet rich heavenly voice, as she keeps them together, against the odds.

Hazel will be a friend, a saviour, a haven, for a short while. She has the heart and the skills. To know Hazel, even briefly, is lucky. Anna is a lucky girl.

~

Anna was apprehensive about the move, but Jess prepared her as best she could, persuading her Marsh Court was a grown-up school where she would make new friends and learn new skills to show off when she came home for holidays. Anna, always an obliging child, was extremely anxious to please and appease: if her mother thought it best that she should go to Marsh Court, she would try to enjoy Marsh Court. She struggled not to show her fear, and so did her mother.

'You'll like the music lady; she's called Hazel,' said Jess from time to time, to comfort herself as well as Anna.

Anna had missed Fanny Foy when she moved from Plimsoll Primary to Highbury Barn. There hadn't been a good music teacher at Highbury. Fanny had been to tea once or twice in Kinderley Road, but it hadn't been the same.

Jess tempted Anna with stories of the canal walks and the lock and the water gardens and the pond with white and pink lilies and the turquoise damsel flies.

Jess delivered Anna to Marsh Court in early September, for the beginning of the new school year. Anna's face on parting showed a watery crumpled look of kindness and anxiety mixed, an expression far too mature for an abandoned child. Jess did not cry on the way home, but she felt like howling. She wanted to howl like a monkey or scream like an eagle.

That night Jess dreamt that Anna was drowning in the canal. She was slowly going under, her trusting face gazing upward for help, her clothes filling with water like Ophelia's, as she made little paddling movements with her arms. (In fact, Anna could swim well, a competent dog-paddle, so why she wasn't trying to swim in the dream was a mystery, though not the kind of mystery you notice when you're dreaming.) And, as Jess gazed at her helplessly, from some out-of-frame vantage point, the green-brown weed-decked Essex canal grew and broadened and spread and swelled into a shining blue lake, and Anna drifted further and further away into its distant reaches, until she disappeared from sight.

Jess woke and lay there in the night on her old second-hand bed with its sagging mattress and tried to reassure herself that this dream meant nothing, nothing at all, that its sources were too obvious to be worthy of consideration. Anna would not fall into the canal, the school would look after her, and anyway she could swim, Jess had made sure of that. Jess lay awake, and thought of the little children in Africa with their dugout canoes. How many of them, in that watery landscape, died by drowning?

Was drowning a common fate? Too late now to go back to ask. Could they swim, did they swim? Did anybody know, had anybody ever thought to ask? What were the statistics? Had anyone counted them? She hadn't seen any of them playing in the water, but that was probably because of river blindness or leeches.

A leech had attached itself to Jess's firm brown ankle on that long ago trip, and they had all laughed as group leader Guy Brighouse burnt it off with his cigarette. It had winced and puckered, poor leech. Jess had almost felt sorry for it.

Anna never had any dreams, or so she told Jess. Anna said she didn't know what dreams were. When Jess tried to describe the act and process of dreaming to Anna, Anna was uncomprehending. That layer of her consciousness seemed to be missing. Jess didn't know whether that was a good thing or a bad thing. Maybe it was a semantic problem, maybe Anna could not explain in words about her dreams, just as she could not remember the letters of her name.

Not even Jess always understood Anna.

~

Jess did not tell Bob about her bad dreams. Bob was her fair-weather lover, her lightweight boy. He was so much younger than the Professor, so very much younger. There was no point in worrying him with her anxieties.

Jess cooked Bob eccentric little meals of offal, snails and fish-tails, chicken's feet, pigs' ears, tripe and bits of webbing. This was the frustrated anthropologist in her coming out, she claimed. She enjoyed hunting around in the strong-smelling sawdust-sprinkled local shops for unexpected morsels, some of them, in those days, stored in old-fashioned wooden casks and barrels of brine that might have come over on the *Windrush*. The courteous withered old Jamaican gentleman who ran the large open-fronted corner grocery store admired her initiative and smiled toothlessly with his hard gums at her purchases. Bob gobbled up the results of her forays, and traded them for dubious memories of dubious bushmeat from his African journeys. Ants also and caterpillars he had devoured, he assured her. Lévi-Strauss had nothing on him and his adventures.

He had photographed great apes and aardvarks and small children in Senegal and the Cameroons, but he had never been to the Shining Lake of Northern Rhodesia, with its strange and special children.

Bob was jealous of the sighting of the shoebill, and interested to learn that Jess had never even thought of taking a camera with her on her African journey.

Jess said she didn't want to take photographs. Snapping birds and people wasn't scholarly; it was *National Geographic*. She was happy to be confrontational about this issue. Bob lectured her on the great photographs of the great ethnographer von Fürer-Haimendorf, and on the importance of keeping and preserving a visual documentary record of anthropological journeys, and Jess replied with a defence of the superior reliability of the written record. The camera, said Jess, always lies. And colour photography cannot choose but to lie. Words work harder than pictures; reading is harder than looking.

She had to think this, and so she thought it.

Jess drew on her store of imagery of the lake. It swelled and spread and covered the banks and promontories. The wind in the rushes made a sound like the waves of the sea. It was hard to tell the water from the land. Its name, Bangweulu, means the lake that has no shores, or so the books tell her.

Anna would never learn to read with ease. There would be times, at Marsh Court, and at later establishments with other tutors and other methods, when it looked as though she was about to make a breakthrough, but it never happened.

Jess didn't need a picture of the children's feet. She could remember them. She didn't mention the webbed and clubbed feet to Bob. They were a private emblem. She knew she would never forget them.

Oh, yes, they had a lot to talk about, Jess and Bob, as well as things they didn't talk about, and they seemed to us to get on surprisingly well. It's just that we didn't trust Bob. This was a time when it was fashionable not to trust men, and there was quite a lot about Bob, apart from his charm and his being half American, that might be construed by us as untrustworthy. We didn't think he would go on being so patient with Anna.

Anna didn't go to the wedding, and perhaps that was a mistake. She was tucked safely out of the way at Marsh Court in Enfield when it took place. It was, for us, a jolly adult affair, sealed on a sunny Saturday morning in October in Islington Town Hall. This prominent Neoclassical edifice on Upper Street was not then the fashionable and well-restored New Labour venue that it was to become: it was a hotbed of revolt, with radical slogans from Tom Paine and William Blake scrawled in bloody paint and strung in homemade banners across its pillared façade.

Or were those banners hung a little later than Jess's wedding? I forget the sequence. When you live an area for many decades, the dates blur and merge; it's hard to remember precise dates. You remember the feel of ebb and flow, but it's easy to get the dates wrong.

I do remember that Jess's wedding was of its time, low-key, informal, secular, amateur.

Weddings are very different now, in the new millennium. I went to a grand civil partnership ceremony in Islington Town Hall not so long ago at which two young men were taking their oaths of loyalty: how changed that building now looks, how carefully restored, with its imposing staircase, its marble plaques and polished wood, its leather-topped tables, its civic grandeur, its handsome dignitaries! There were songs and singers and flowers and printed programmes and confetti and photography and smart hats and a glamorous black woman registrar dressed in a canary-yellow Chanel suit with navy trim. Everybody was photographing everybody else with mobile phones, in the bizarre self-referential mode of the third millennium, but there were professional photographers in attendance too, formally recording the occasion.

There was a lot of money around, in the first decade of the third millennium, before the banks crashed.

Jess had none of that at her wedding. We were young in the tatty, ad-hoc, do-it-yourself old days.

As we grow older, our tenses and our sense of chronology blur. We can no longer remember the correct sequence of events. The river is flowing, but we don't know on which bank we stand, or which way it flows. From birth, or from death. The water and the land merge. We lose our sextant, we follow the wrong compass. The trick of proleptic memory, towards the end of life, confuses us. The trope of *déjà vu* becomes indistinguishable from shock, sensation, revelation, epiphany, surprise. It is hard to live in, or even to recall, an unforeseen moment. Anna lived, and lives, in an eternal present, in the flowing river, but we live in a confused timeframe, where all seems fore-ordained and fore-suffered, and yet all is unfinished and unknown. Foresight and hindsight are one. The lake and the land are one.

The end is predicated, and yet we do not know what it will be.

I'm not talking about time's arrow. I'm talking about something else, something that to me is stranger.

> So the two brothers and their murdered man
> Rode past fair Florence . . .

That's a famous example of prolepsis. It's from John Keats, from *Isabella; or, the Pot of Basil.* There's a bit of alliteration there too. They used to teach you that in school. Prolepsis and alliteration. Figures of speech.

Keats died so young that he had to crush all his proleptic visions and all his poesy into a narrow space. He knew he was dying so he was obliged to make haste. He had to *have been* a great poet before he had time to become one. Time seized him and shook him and he died in its jaws. Nowadays we tend to linger on with time to kill. We plan our last journeys with care. Our exits, our funerals, our memorial services. Our string quartet, our readings from Ecclesiastes, our Ship of Death.

Livingstone mischarted his last journey. He had lost his sextant, his maps were wrong, and he was carried, dying, through the swamp and the wetlands, by mosquito-tormented men with water up to their chests. Poor Nassick boys, rescued from the Indian Ocean, and now so far inland in the endless marshes, so very far from any home. Against the current they carried him, in the wrong direction, towards a lost horizon, sustained by his faith in a dying god. They would carry his sun-dried salt-preserved eviscerated and unrecognisable body home, and one of them would pose for a photograph at Southampton where the *Malva* had docked.

We can see him clearly, Jacob Wainwright, the faithful black servant. He leans on Livingstone's strapped coffin, which rests upon a cabin trunk. Wainwright leans with one elbow on the coffin, in a weary and intimate posture of possession, not a posture of servitude or subjection. He has been through much, he has earned this coffin, this kinship, this moment of repose. In another photograph, we see his fellow-servants, Susi and Chuma, posing in the Gothic ruins of Newstead Abbey with Livingstone's heavily bearded son and his black-beribboned and black-flounced daughter Agnes. Black Africans in the garden cloister of an English country house, an English country house full of zebra skins and elephant tusks and the horned and mounted heads of many beasts, the spoils of colonial sport. There they stand, Abdulah Susi and James Chuma, the orphaned Nassick boys. Their time would come, when Black History would rescue them from oblivion, and search for every priceless scrap of photographic evidence of their existence. Their stock would rise and rise.

~

I remember the wedding in Islington, and I can remember what Jess wore. I don't need photographs to remind me, and I don't have any. I was one of the witnesses and I signed the book. She wore a long terra-cotta maxi-skirt, and shiny chestnut leather boots, and a fake-leather bright brown jacket, and a black felt hat with a brim, and a red rose stuck in her hatband. Bob wore a pale suit with girlish flared trousers, no tie, and a bold flowered shirt. We celebrated in the evening with a small party in Jess's house, during which we drank a lot of cheap wine and ate some bizarre titbits which Bob and Jess had cooked up between them. Bob had by now latched on to Jess's experimental culinary style and was trying to outdo her in effrontery. There was a row of long, black-baked, spiny, snakelike fishes from the fish shop in the Blackstock Road, a big bowl of pickled eggs, some very coarse sausages, some leathery, dark-green stuffed vine leaves, and a pyramid of triangular Turkish sweetmeats. A multicultural, multi-ethnic feast.

We brought them gifts of a conventional nature – glasses, cutlery, cushions. We were still home-making, in our amateur improvised way; despising the domestic niceties of our parents' generation, yet trying nevertheless to make ourselves comfortable. Jess liked strong colours and bold prints, but most of us went for cheap Victorian and Edwardian junk, for inlay and patterns and veneers. The little neighbourhood shops were full of bargains that had not yet made their way to the smarter markets of Camden Passage. We fancied ourselves; we thought we had style. We were eclectic, at home in the rag-and-bone shop of London.

Bob was eager and intimate, wanting to be one of us, as well as to be one with Jess. We were flattered, as well as suspicious.

Jess had of course told Anna that she was marrying Bob, and Anna had seemed to understand this. Anna was, in fact, exceptionally keen on the subject of kinship and relationships, and enjoyed repeated recitals of who was married to whom, who was whose mother, or baby, or brother, or cousin, or nephew, or niece. The word 'partner' was not yet in common usage, and I can't remember how we described the couples who were not formally married. But in fact most of us were married, for better or worse. We were more conventional than we thought we were. 'Jim is married to Katie, Jim is Katie's husband, Katie is Jim's wife, Becky is their daughter, Nicky is their daughter, Ben is their son, Ben is Becky and Nicky's sister, Jane is Ben's aunt. Sylvie's sons are called Stuart and Josh. Tim's dad is called Jeremy.' Anna enjoyed these listings. And she was happy to add the name of Bob, a name which in itself appealed to her through its round simplicity. 'Bob!' she would say, proudly, making the twinned consonants bounce from her lips like balloons. 'Bob is married to Mum. Bob is Mum's husband, Bob is my Step Dad.' The phrase 'step dad' also pleased her. Its monosyllables were cheerful, like coloured bricks.

Did the word 'step' have a physical meaning for her? I have sometimes wondered. It was hard to know how she connected words and meanings. She had her own way of making connections, a way that was not ours, but none the worse for that.

We were a verbal lot. Jess and I sometimes had the semi-treacherous thought that it might have been Anna's misfortune to have been born into a social milieu and income bracket where articulate intelligence was so widely dispersed and highly prized. In some circles, in some cultures, maybe her condition would have been less conspicuous.

On the other hand, in some circles she might have met with less kindness, less tolerance and less love.

Jess has spent many years worrying about these matters and reading the academic authorities on IQ and mental ages and developmental skills. For better or worse, that is Jess's way. She is a reader. She has read Binet and Cyril Burt and Piaget. Which societies support their weaker members best? The nomadic, the agricultural, the pre-literate, the enlightened, the modern, the post-modern? The ages of stone, or the ages of steel, or the new age of cybernetics?

Anna could read the words 'Mum' and 'Dad' and 'Bob', and learnt to write them, in a wobbly wavering hand, a strangely tentative, undecided hand. She was not good at committing herself to straight lines. She enjoyed colours, and was bolder with them. Perhaps the words themselves frightened her. Perhaps the concept of words alarmed her. But it seems more likely that it was the connection between words and script, words and text, that worried her. Her vocabulary, as all those psychometric tests showed, was quite rich. But maybe they were just words she'd heard from Jess, from Katie, from Jim, from Maroussia, from me?

As an infant, Anna had liked splashing poster paint on to sheets of paper, crayoning blocks and stripes and patches, sticking gummed shapes into patterns. Approaching adolescence at Marsh Court, she continued to do art work of a sort, though with less confidence and more deference. She became afraid to make a mess, and her natural clumsiness often involved mess.

Jess rarely reprimanded her for this (not being herself a very tidy person) but more severe reprimands, despite Jess's protection, had clearly come Anna's way, and she lost the carefree pleasure of dabbling and splattering.

The regime at Marsh Court would, Jess had hoped, allow for mess. But she recognised that in an institution, however benign, a conflict must arise between creative mess, squalor and order.

Anna needed to please, and any hint of criticism caused her a visible distress. We sometimes wondered whether this characteristic was innate, or whether an over-protective Jess had implanted it. We worried about what we had done to our own children, of course, but the case of Anna seemed to give us a clear message about maternal need, maternal love. But, clear as it was, clear as it ought to have been, we could not read the message.

Over the years Jess was to visit schools and institutions that looked after children with a very wide range of abilities and disabilities. She traced the curve of the bell. She followed with a more than academic interest the changing vocabulary that classified children such as Anna. Idiots and imbeciles and delinquents featured on a historical and linguistic spectrum that stretched on to the dull, the backward, the feeble-minded, the weak-minded, the unstable, the mentally deficient, the educationally subnormal, the children with special needs. ESN, SEN. None of these words or phrases or acronyms seemed to describe the pure gold baby that had been Anna, the trusting child sent off to Marsh Court, the child–woman–daughter that Anna was to become.

The child that never grew.

Icipuba, kapupushi, ukupena, icipumputu.

These are words from the regions of the African lake where Jess saw the children, the children who coped so well in their frail barks. These words describe a range of mental deficiencies. Jess had learnt them for her thesis.

Uluntanshe. A wanderer with no aim in life.

These words describe those without the ability to clothe themselves, those who lack the sense to hold down a job, those who are violent and need restraint, those who have fits and fall into the fire. These are the distinctions that the tribes of the lake recognise.

Anna never had a fit and she had been taught the dangers of fire.

Andrew Barker had fits. As we have seen, his mother blamed herself for having had him vaccinated against polio. He didn't get polio, but he did suffer permanent brain damage. Or so his mother to this day believes. She isn't allowed to say so very often, because it's an unpopular notion to hold these days, but nevertheless this is what she believes. Maybe medical opinion will vindicate her one day. But one day will always be more than one day too late for Andrew.

~

Marsh Court observed the state-school and the local-authority calendar, and Anna was to come home for Christmas that year, the first of her years away, to find her lively new stepfather, Bob Bartlett, in residence. It had been evident from the beginning of Jess's relationship with Bob that Jess would stay in her own house. Bob would join Jess there, and Jess would pay the bills. There was never any talk of moving out to Bob's place, or into neutral ground. And Bob's place would have been unsuitable for family life: he had lived in a damp and noisy semi-basement flat on a main bus route through Camden Town, which he wisely kept on and illegally sublet to a friend. Just in case.

Jess, on the train on her way to collect Anna, gazed out of the window at the changing townscape of suburb and estate, and at the stark leafless trees, where, in the spring, ornamental cherry blossom had gaily pinked the avenues and hillsides. Now the sedge was withered by the lake, and no tree-frogs or gilded birds would sing in this season. She wondered if Anna had made any real friends at her new school, whether she would return there happily and willingly after the Christmas holidays, whether she would adjust to Bob's at times noisy presence in the house. Her concern for Anna was a constant ache. Anna was the apple of her eye and the thorn in her heart.

Jess had been to Marsh Court during the term, of course, but not too often. Those were the days when parents were not encouraged to hang around in hospital wards and at school gates. The phrases 'clean break' and 'let her settle in' were still employed, though not very consistently: change on this front was already on the way. Jess had made weekend visits, taken Anna out for a Wimpy or a bowl of spaghetti or some chop suey. (Anna loved Chinese food, but Jess was beginning to worry about the effects of monosodium glutamate. Some authorities now said it was bad for you, which was a pity, as it was so delicious.) They'd been to see a movie in the old 1920s cinema. They'd been for walks in the park and along the canal and to the lock, and had once visited the local municipal swimming pool. Anna had been eager to show that she enjoyed these outings, but just as eager to be brave at the partings. Jess on these occasions had met other mothers (and one lone father) and had become conscious that the disabilities from which Anna suffered were much less severe than those of some of her schoolmates.

Jess had struck up a friendship with Susie from Southgate. She'd always assumed Southgate was in South London, but it wasn't, it was near Enfield. Susie worked as a district nurse, and knew a lot about the system. Susie's son Vincent was a handful. He was much less amenable than Anna, given to tantrums and some astonishing outbursts of bad language. Susie said she thought he had Tourette's but the experts didn't agree with her. Jess was impressed by Vincent's vocabulary, but hoped Anna wouldn't pick up too much of it. Sitting on a bench in the spacious square vestibule of Marsh Court (it had its original black-and-white marble tiles and a handsome fireplace with a well-polished brass fender, somehow recalling a past age of austere but progressive education), Jess listened to Susie's views on the National Health Service, on Colney Hatch, on mental institutions in general, and on some of the hopeless fools and mean-spirited bastards she came across on her daily rounds.

Jess was ignorant about these matters, and Susie filled her in. Jess hadn't even known that 'Colney Hatch' was synonymous with 'barmy' in North London slang. The Friern Barnet asylum at Colney Hatch was vast, according to Susie – thousands of patients, literally miles of corridors, grounds you could get lost in, a city of the lost and the mad and the forgotten. It would take you five hours to do a round of all the wards, somebody had measured and timed it. It was being slowly, very slowly, decommissioned, said Susie.

Colney Hatch had been purpose-built in 1850, to accommodate 1,220 of the lunatic poor, and was one of the largest of the expanding public asylums that nineteenth-century alienists and psychiatrists had gradually filled to overflowing with long-term patients.

The Colney Hatch of Jess's hometown Broughborough was called Arden Gate, and it too was purpose-built, covering acres of land on the outskirts of the industrial city. It was more rural than Colney Hatch, its late-Victorian and Edwardian redbrick buildings landscaped into what had been handsome parkland belonging to a long-demolished Jacobean stately home. Its owners had fallen on hard times and disappeared from *Debrett's*. It had an ancient well-spring and cedars and a lake with water lilies and a water tower. Jessica Speight's father, Philip Speight, had designed the small new Modernist therapy clinic by the gatehouse, and he sat on the NHS board.

(In what had been Susie's Southgate, in the twenty-first century, a new branch of an extremely expensive private psychiatric institution called the Priory would open its doors to the rich. It took in those suffering from drug addiction, alcohol addiction, gambling addiction, depression, bipolar disorder, OCD and other mental afflictions, and charged them several thousand pounds a week – a far cry from Colney Hatch and Arden Gate. Psychotherapy for the Rich, not Psychiatry for the Poor. Some of the clients' fees were paid by their insurance policies. Some of them were paid by their parents or spouses. A very few of them paid for themselves. Many, including Susie and Jess, would think it all a bit of a racket.)

Susie had told Jess that even some of the really old-fashioned asylums were now being infiltrated by psychiatrists with modern views, who didn't believe in mental illness. She had expounded this theory as they walked side by side on one of their many strolls along the canal, through the changing seasons and past the eternal unchanging anglers with their bags of maggots and their old bicycles and their patient tethered dogs.

Anna had gone ahead on the towpath, looking back from time to time to check that the mothers were still following, while Vincent lagged behind.

Susie was in two minds about it. Of course some of the wrong people got locked up and certified, everybody knew that. But, then again, some people certainly couldn't cope on their own, could they? They needed somewhere safe to be.

She could have managed Vincent at home, perhaps, but her husband, Trevor, wouldn't have it. It wasn't fair on the other kids, said Trevor.

'I'm lucky that I've only Anna to worry about,' said Jess,

wondering as she said it how Bob and Anna would get on during the coming weeks, months, years.

'Yes,' said Susie, watching Anna as Anna watched the jerking progress of the moorhens. 'Yes, I can see she's the apple of your eye.'

Jess found Susie comforting. Her dry, matter-of-fact descriptions of what Jess very soon discovered to be the experimental programmes of R. D. Laing and his colleagues were calm, fair-minded, not what you might have expected from a woman of her background and her 1950s NHS training. The anomalous and erratic behaviour of her son Vincent had softened and broadened her attitudes to others. Susie had widened her categories of the almost-normal (although clearly husband Trevor hadn't) to take in Vincent and Anna, some of the long-term patients at Colney Hatch, the schizophrenics at Kingsley Hall, and the adult Down's syndrome son of one of her regular patients in Arnos Grove.

This young man, Eddie, exercised Susie's sympathies a great deal. His mother was either recovering or more probably not recovering from a major operation for bowel cancer (Susie was on a rota to visit to help with the colostomy bag) and what would happen to Eddie if the mother died? It didn't bear thinking about. It was a lot to ask of Eddie's sister, she'd got children enough of her own. The mother had expected Eddie would go first, but it looked as though he wasn't going to. You didn't know what to hope for. Life expectation for Down's isn't all that long, said Susie, but they do need their mum.

Jess could listen to this kind of conversation for hours, engrossed.

In the summer, the moorhen chicks had scooted around on the surface of the water randomly like balls of mercury, with ugly little pink and yellow necks and greedy beaks. Jess had read somewhere that the chicks had a high mortality rate, because the parents built their nests of twigs and flotsam so badly that they were always collapsing and going under. Half of the eggs would drown. She wondered what percentage of that summer's chicks had survived, and if that bird pecking stupidly at a plastic bag near Anna's feet was from one of the broods they had seen in September.

Some species produce good mothers; others, not so good. Very few species produce what women call 'good' fathers. Feminists were at this time busily espousing the bits of socio-biology that suited them, and ignoring the rest. Seahorses are good fathers, and so are some spiders.

'Yes,' said Susie, 'Kingsley Hall was Liberty Hall, that's what I heard. No rules, no discipline. The patients did what they liked; they didn't have to take their medication if they didn't want. They could stay in bed all day if they fancied. They could paint the walls with shit if they wanted. I daresay that works out well for some. There's no two alike, after all. I've a friend who works in the psychiatric ward in St Anne's. Grim, she says. Hard cases. Screaming and yelling, and trying to slash their wrists and hang themselves all day and all night. It's nice at Marsh Court. Don't you think it's nice at Marsh Court?'

Jess didn't know. She hadn't anywhere to compare it with.

They were comforting one another, that much she did know.

There are no two alike.

Ahead walked Anna, unique Anna, in her warm brown jacket and her long dark red wool skirt with orange amoeba-shaped blobs on it, with her scarlet crocheted beret on her head. She wore short black rubber boots. She still couldn't do laces. Well, she could do them, if you stood over her and reminded her of the process, step by step, loop by loop, but it seemed simpler to buy her shoes without laces, jackets without too many buttons. The propagation of Velcro had been a blessing to Jess and Anna.

It was autumn, but the sun shone on them that day.

Anna was like nobody else on earth. She was Little Stupid, the Simple Sister, the Dumb One, the Idiot Girl, the Pure Gold Baby.

She wasn't dumb, of course. She was sociable, she liked company, she liked talking. But she had loved the film *Dumbo*. Most children love that film. Most children instinctively sympathise with the Dumbo character in any narrative, if the tale is rightly told. Much depends on the teller, and on the naming of names. Dumbo's mother, Mrs Jumbo, had been certified as mad when she lost her temper with the other elephant children for mocking her son. Jess had cried when she had seen this movie, and so had Anna. Jess hates Disney (to this day), but Anna is in tune with Disney, and, in the company of Anna, Jess forgets her superior and snobbish understanding and enters the world of innocents and sobs with the rest of us. Through Anna, Jess had joined a new sorority.

Jess did not take Anna to see *Bambi*. No doubt she would find it for herself in years to come, but Jess did not think it a good idea to expose Anna to the death of Bambi's mother.

Anna was by now a pretty girl on the verge of puberty. She had lost the golden-baby smile, the round confident trusting sunny face of playgroup infancy, but, with her clear fair skin and head of fair short-cut curly springing hair, she was still a pleasure to the eye, and not only to Jess's eye. She was perhaps on the rounded side, but attractively so. If she was a little gauche and awkward in her movements, this only made her seem pleasantly shy, though at times overeager to help.

Anna loved to help. This was her nature, her innate nature.

Vincent, in contrast, was not a helpful boy. He was small and fierce and wiry and often angry. On the other hand, his reading age was much higher than Anna's, and he was basically more dexterous, despite the tics that attacked him as it seemed randomly. His prognosis, Jess suspected, was better than Anna's, whatever 'better' might mean.

Treatment of, and attitudes to, the mentally ill had deteriorated in parts of Africa after the advent of Christianity. As we have seen, Jess had attempted to deal with this in her thesis. Christianity had proposed a different, an unattainable norm. Christianity was unfashionable in the 1960s and 1970s. We thought then that it explained nothing. We didn't believe in drugs either, as psychiatrists do now. We didn't talk about serotonin and prozac and lithium. We were not of the chemical generation.

We knew people who had experimented with LSD, we knew quite a few people who smoked hash and ate hash brownies. Some of us smoked the stuff ourselves. But we didn't see our planet as a chemical material world, made up of particles from the Big Bang. We tried to look through the doors of perception. We thought there was something to see, on the other side.

~

As Jess and Susie walked along the towpath that October, and that November, and that December, and through the flow of a year to the next year and the next, the euphemism 'care in the community' hadn't yet been coined. The Community Care Act didn't come in until 1990. In the sixties and seventies, there were no beggars squatting in doorways on Oxford Street or nesting in pigeon-fouled sleeping bags under the motorways with hungry verminous dogs. The vulnerable were looked after/ swept away/ brushed aside/ immured in cold malevolent institutions/ allowed to lie in bed all day at Kingsley Hall. The Community Care Act was created as the community fragmented, possibly for ever.

Some argue that rural communities look after their frail and dependent members better than urban communities, but others argue that the countryside is stoked with hostile prejudice and intolerance. It depends on whom you ask, on which subgroup you choose to study, on which groups you use as your control. It depends on the premise on which you begin to conduct your investigation. It depends on whether you are a Wordsworthian or a Benthamite. On whether you are Mungo Park, essentially a Wordsworthian of the Enlightenment, or Dr Livingstone, an obsessed Darwinian Victorian.

Both were Scots.

Jess, collecting Anna to come home for the Christmas holidays, had brought a present for Hazel, nicely wrapped in gold paper and with a label on it saying 'Happy Christmas from Jess and Anna'. It wasn't a very daring or exciting present (of hazelnut chocolates, which they knew she liked, or said she liked), but Hazel greeted it with delight and an appearance of surprise, and gave both Jess and Anna a big hug. Hugging seemed to come so naturally to Hazel, why couldn't everybody hug like that? Such simple things are so hard for so many.

Maybe Hazel's mother had hugged her a lot when she was a baby. Or maybe she hadn't hugged her enough. Jess didn't know and didn't like to ask. She would never know Hazel well enough to ask. But she was able to respond to the hugging.

Anna had made some presents in the Marsh Court prefab workshop to take home for her mum and her new step dad and her old schoolfriends. They were in a special silver carrier bag with butterflies and ladybirds and fishes gummed all over it, haphazardly but happily, by Anna.

~

Christmas isn't a good time for a lot of people. It's worse, of course, for the single and the lonely, or so everyone always says, but it's pretty bad for those with too much family, and most of us in our thirties fell into that category. Sometimes some of us longed to be single and lonely, as we tried to satisfy the claims of parents, children, ex-husbands, siblings, aunts, uncles, cousins, lame ducks, excommunicated alcoholics, lonely depressive poets and other riff raff. None of us had houses big enough to take in a tribe, or kitchens large enough to cook for a clan, yet somehow the tribal expectations of a large gathering had descended upon us. These were frenzied festivals of foregone failure.

In view of all of that, Jess and Bob's party could be counted a success.

The Christmas tree was chastely decorated with dangling orange clementines and white candles, and the room with oiled paper wooden parasols, gummed paper chains made by Anna, gorilla masks made by Bob. The riot, the mayhem, the broken lavatory bowl, the singing! It was an all-age-group, day-after-Boxing-Day party, eating up everybody's leftovers – we brought our plastic boxes of giblets and cold turkey and cold Christmas pudding and brandy butter with us at midday, and stayed on for hours. Jess and Bob and Anna had been up to Broughborough for a couple of days, to authenticate Bob as legitimate husband (the Speight parents hadn't been to the wedding) and, according to Bob, had spent most of their time sitting round a giant jigsaw portraying 'The Wreck of the *Medusa*', avoiding eye contact. (We think he made that up.) Jess's unmarried sister, Vee, had been there too, rather impatient with the whole thing, thought Bob. But Anna liked Auntie Vee, who had given her a beautiful tambourine with golden bells and scarlet ribbons, which she had purchased in Egypt, where she was working for the British Council – an imaginative, noisy and perhaps provocative present, which enlivened the party.

(Vee spent most of her working life abroad, in flight from Jess, Anna and her parents.)

Anna was happy. She loved parties. We were all happy. We were letting our hair down, congratulating ourselves on having once more got through the main event of Christmas Day, on having jumped the highest fence of the season. Children were marauding, running round the house and out into the street in little gangs, and we were lying back on Jess's African cushions, smoking, chatting, drinking, comparing notes on the dying year. We were wearing long skirts, high leather boots, flared trousers, necklaces. (Some of the men wore necklaces too.) Jess looked good: her nut-brown hair was very long in those days, tied back with a yellow chiffon scarf, and her freckled arms were garlanded in many-coloured cheap Indian bangles. Sexual happiness glowed from her skin and flaunted itself in the deep cleavage of her blouse. Bob kept glancing at her proudly, a look of satisfaction and possession. We talked of the schools our children went to, the films we'd seen, the books we'd been reading, the affairs our friends were having with one another. We didn't talk about property prices.

Maroussia talked about the Secret Garden. She was involved in a community project in Camden, restoring a lost garden which had lain untended for many decades in a triangle between three residential roads. Her own garden backed on to it, and she and some neighbours had devoted time to discovering the lease and the deeds, and had embarked on clearing it. They had had a big bonfire of hacked elder and sycamore and bramble on Guy Fawkes' Night, and some of us had attended, with our traditional offerings of sausages and baked potatoes and parkin. (Anna, away at Marsh Court, had missed this fun, but listened eagerly to the reports. She was always a good audience.)

Maroussia didn't mind getting her hands dirty, she didn't mind nagging the council for the public good. And she didn't get herself televised while she was doing it, although she had a public face and could have tried to use it. That's not how things worked, not in those days.

Steve the poet, Steve our own depressed poet, had thrown

himself into the slashing and burning, finding company and an escape from his heavy habitual grief. He wasn't very handy with an axe or a spade, but he made himself useful. He had written a poem about the reclaiming of the Secret Garden which was published in the *London Magazine*, and which he now read to us at our post-Christmas party. It was a good poem. He was a good, though not a prolific, poet, a well-published poet. And yet he exuded a terrible white sweat of failure. His large white face and his slack lips and his damp black hair and his home-knitted old blue jersey and his nervous stammer all spoke of invincible pursuant despair, of the furies that followed him. I didn't think he looked at all well that Christmas. He was overweight, I saw that he couldn't stop eating – he munched his way through half a dozen mince pies. I wondered if one day soon a neighbour or a rent collector would find him dead in his bed.

Steve read his poem, and we listened respectfully, because we felt we ought to. And it was a good poem, it was our poem.

Then we listened to Jim, because we had to.

Jim was working on a Granada documentary about colonial Africa and the newly independent states. The Gold Coast had long been remade and renamed as Ghana, and Nigeria had celebrated independence as Nigeria, but more recently Northern Rhodesia had become Zambia, Nyasaland had become Malawi, and Bechuanaland had become Botswana. Southern Rhodesia was the sticking point in the decolonisation of Africa. Jim tended to overwhelm us with tedious self-important inside information (in this instance from his Foreign Office contacts and a South African Afrikaans campaigner for civil rights), which made us all feel ignorant fools. And was meant so to do. We could see that Jim's wife, Katie, was getting restive as Jim told us how Rhodesian premier Ian Smith had spoken to him personally on the phone only a week before, but Jess was intrigued by this story.

I think this may have been the moment when she first

mentioned, at a seeming tangent, the secret children, the lobster-claw children, the Cleppie Bells of Zambia and Bangweulu. I don't know how many of us picked it up, I'm not sure if anyone else was really listening, we were all a bit knocked out by lunch and leftovers and Jim's discourse, but I listened and retained the reference. It's the kind of thing I do tend to remember. (I didn't know what the phrase 'Cleppie Bells' meant, at this stage, but I remembered it: it had a tragic ring to it.) She didn't say much about them, just that most of us adjust to what we have or have not, we regress, we revert, we accommodate ourselves to our missing limbs, to our little stumps and stunted digits, to our deafnesses, our blindnesses, our incapacities. They had been very simple people, she said, the people of the lake. Pygmy hunter-gatherers and fisher folk. They wouldn't like the new industrial prosperity of the copper mines.

This could have been a politically reactionary aside, in support of colonial oppression, but I didn't think it was.

I don't know why I remembered it so well, but I did, and do.

Katie was visibly and audibly about to get more than restive, and Jess broke off from her thoughts about normality and deviance to call the children back from the street and the backyard for the indoor fireworks display. Do you remember those indoor fireworks? They are illegal now. Health and Safety forbids them, though they seemed harmless enough, indeed touching in their humble harmlessness. The fireworks came in harshly tinted badly printed cheap oriental oblong cardboard packs, of acid reds and greens and yellows, and they displayed a mild variety of small activities: there was a little pyramid cone called Mount Fuji that smoked and puffed, a terrible grey worm of obscene ash called the Great Serpent that grew and grew, some little poppers, some paper flowers that expanded in a glass of water, a ball of hyperactive powder that whizzed and fizzed and then self-destructed, and a handful of stumpy sparklers.

The children were innocent enough to watch quietly in the darkened room as the adults lit the touch-papers, their faces illuminated by the candles on the mantelpiece and the small glow of the Japanese illuminations. Some of us watched the light playing on the grave sweet attentive children's faces instead of watching the small display. They composed a painting, a Joseph Wright, a de la Tour. Our children were so good, our hopes for them so high. Goodness seemed to be their birthright. How could any of them go astray?

The gap-toothed boy, the pure gold baby, the freckled fox girl, the dusky little despot, the white-faced flower, the luminous lamb, the lion charmer. Naughty Ollie, mild-mannered Anna, silent Stuart, black-braided Polly, lisping Sam, choir-boy Joshua, beetle-browed Ben, birth-marked Harry, quick and clever Chloe, angular Andrew. They were all beautiful, all good, all in bud. Even Andrew, subject as he was to spasms and to fits of incoherent rage, was beautiful, and full of undisclosed personal promise.

Most beautiful of all, at that age, was Joshua. A light shone from him, a light shone upon him. Each of us favoured our own, but we all recognised that Joshua Raven, Sylvie's younger boy, had an angelic perfection of feature. There are such children. Anna was the pure gold baby, the child without a shadow, but Joshua was the luminous lamb. He looked as pretty as a Christmas card, with his light auburn hair curling down to his shoulders, his perfect porcelain skin, his turquoise eyes. He was drawn in pencil and aquatint, a Renaissance boy. His delicate skin seemed translucent.

After the fireworks, we sang. Anna and Bob taught us 'The River is Flowing, Flowing and Growing' and we sang it as a round. Then we sang some carols, and some of the songs of the Beatles. But as the evening wore on, Jim grew more aggressive, and Katie more angry, and they began to shout at one another, and just before midnight Katie ran out into the street, screaming 'That's enough, I'm leaving, I'm leaving, I'm off to the airport!' and her children ran after her crying and the neighbours started to peer through their curtains and Jim fell into the ill-placed Christmas tree. Steve kept trying to intervene, in his bumbling, good-hearted, counter-productive way, and Jim got very cross with him and called him a parasitic shit and a great lump of useless lard and a eunuch.

Jess intervened at this point, as she didn't like to see Steven being abused, and said we'd all better go home and leave her to clear up.

That wasn't the end of Jim and Katie's marriage, but it was the beginning of the end.

Anna didn't like it when people quarrelled. She seemed to take discord upon herself, to try to absorb it into herself. When Bob and Jess in the inevitable course of things started to cross each other, she was distressed. Bob was an intruder into her relationship with her mother, but she didn't want him driven away. She would never have tried to make difficulties between her mother and her stepfather. She was an appeaser.

~

That first vacation from Marsh Court went well, warmed by the friction and activity of Christmas stress, but never bursting into angry flames, or at least not in Jess's household. Anna did not seem reluctant to return to school, to Jess's relief, but of course Anna always tried to be obliging, and was stoically adept at hiding distress. One of her characteristics was an ability to suffer minor physical pain without making a fuss: little injuries such as bruises and scratches which made our children yell for attention she would endure with the minimum of noise or complaint. 'It's nothing, it doesn't hurt at all,' she would assure us, smiling eagerly, as she dabbed at the blood on her knee with her hanky. And I don't think that was anything to do with her pain threshold, as some observers might have thought. It was to do with her good manners.

(Jess once read out to me a phrase from an early anthropological textbook on the Negro, which had clearly lodged unpleasantly in her memory, as it then did in mine: *The nervous system of the Negro is not very sensitive, and the appreciation of pain is dull.* She had also discovered research that indicated that sensitivity to pain showed a positive correlation to intelligence. Of this, she had remarked, 'It depends what you mean by pain.' Measurement of pain is a dangerous business.)

Anna didn't really know how to be bad. We were all, in our ways, bad – motivated by ambition, or rivalry, or envy, or lust, or spite, or sloth, and observing the seeds of these passions even in our beloved born-innocent children. But Anna didn't know these emotions. The only one of the traditional seven deadly sins with which she had the slightest acquaintance was gluttony, for she did enjoy her food, and was fond of talking about what she might be going to have for her supper, but she would never grab at table. She did sometimes launch into her plateful without waiting for others to be served, but if Jess caught her eye she would put her knife and fork down, guiltily.

Let you that is without sin among you cast the first stone, Jesus said. Anna wouldn't have thrown a stone at anyone or anything, not even at a gate-post. She lacked aggression.

It's hard to survive without aggression. Her old schoolfriend Ollie concealed his attacks and predations by a winning charm and a wide smile, but her new schoolfriend Vincent was openly strung with aggression. His little wiry body and his language and his gestures were charged with attacking energy. He was fierce and insistent. He was a handful. His jaw worked with fury, his eyes shot bolts. He was full of knots. He threw stones, and other things, at people and at birds. When walking by the canal, he would stone the moorhens. Susie reprimanded him, but not very forcefully, as he wasn't a very good shot, and he never managed to hit a moorhen.

Susie was a wiry person too, her face sharp and angular, her body scrawny, her legs and sinews toughened by her bicycle round, her opinions made fierce by the frequent sight of pain and distress, her hair frizzled by a violent perm and dyed an aggressive and defiant red. She too was full of knots.

Whereas Anna was a smooth, mild, benevolent person, with mild and rounded features.

Unlike her mother, Jess, Anna was not highly strung.

~

Jess registered the hints that Susie had let drop about the new views of the anti-psychiatrists and the regime at Kingsley Hall. They didn't really apply to Anna, or to her inexplicably becalmed condition, but they were interesting to Jess. She read a book or two, attended a talk or two, about the knotted regions of the mind. She did not think that Anna would ever be awakened into a more adult state of stress and conflict. Undreaming, not knowing what dreams were, Anna lived in a dream, in an innocent charmed world without progress, without a goal, without an aim. If you measure your pain or hope or despair on a scale of ten, ten being anguish, Anna's measurement was near to zero.

Sometimes Jess dreamt of going back to the shining lake. Sometimes she dreamt of the field trips she might have taken, had she not been burdened with the sole care of an ever dependent child. Maternity had become by chance her destiny.

Had Livingstone truly believed in the afterlife, believed in it as securely as he claimed? Believed in it as he believed in the existence of the maggots that burrowed into his limbs and popped their heads in and out of his flesh at him in those weary latter days? As he believed in the army of red ants that swarmed over him and devoured his foot like smallpox, and in the dark-grey swarming cannibal caterpillars that wormed their way through the waters of the lake? Did he know the afterlife of heaven as he knew the call of the tree-frog, the cry of the fish-eagle?

He said the natives of some tribes did not like to talk to him about death, or even to consider it, and he thought this a clear sign of their lost and miserable pagan state, in which only wooden charms and idols could comfort them.

He noted that birds of his domestic flock did not seem to recognise death either, for when the cock died the hens continued to try to feed him.

Two very fine young men, of a 'superior' tribe, with well-developed 'organs of intelligence', once asked him *whether people died with us, and where they went to after death. Have you no charm against death?* they wanted to know. He seems to have thought this a highly intelligent question, presumably because, as a missionary, albeit a very unpersuasive and unsuccessful missionary, he thought he had an answer to it. But of course we don't agree with his answer, so need not regard the question as an intelligent question. Although it was a natural question to put to a visitor so clearly confident that he had all the answers.

Adolescent Anna occasionally asked Jess, 'What is death?' or 'What is sex?' These metaphysical questions were difficult for Jess. She did not know how, or on what level, to attempt to reply to them.

The Africans whom Livingstone encountered were not converted, but they enjoyed watching magic lantern shows of Bible stories. Moses in the bulrushes reminded them of the shores of Bangweulu, and they liked the baby in the manger with the ox and the ass. But they did not care at all for the crucifix. They expressed the view that crucifixion was cruel, and that not even the cruel Moors went in for it. Livingstone was not sure that they fully understood that crucifixion was not being recommended by the Gospels. Teaching the heathen was not an easy task. Nor was discovering the source of the Nile. But he persevered.

~

Anna went mildly and obediently back to school in January, and Bob and Jess resumed their domestic life together, in a rhythm that was to last for a year or so. Jess says she thinks it was only a year, and she should know, but I think she and Bob cohabited for at least two years. At my age my sense of time is notional, whole decades blur and elide, let alone the years and the months, but I think I'm right about this bit of Jess's chronology.

To outsiders, Jess's arrangements for Anna and Bob seemed to be working adequately, but it was also clear that this marriage was not destined or even very seriously intended to last. Marriages were splintering all around them, and Bob and Jess had no common bond, no mutual concern, apart from sex, ethnography and anthropology. Children were the problem for most of us when we ran on the rocks. Children sometimes kept us together, sometimes forced us apart. But it was clear that Jess and Anna formed a unit that would survive and eventually exclude Bob. It was only a matter of time. We watched, we waited, I would like to think without too much malice or *Schadenfreude*, although of course none of us are malice-free.

Jess had the upper hand in the relationship. She had the house, she had the confidence, she had a network of her friends around her. It was the time of the women. She had her niche at SOAS, whereas Bob was somewhat stranded and *dépaysé*, and in that first year or two remained on his best behaviour. But there was something of the cuckoo-in-the-nest about Bob. He'd displaced Anna, and now he opened his mouth and expected to be fed. Chitterlings, locusts, honey, little cakes. He did prepare a meal, occasionally, but Jess did most of the cooking.

Also, he stuck around more than perhaps might have been expected. He was supposed to be an adventurer, but he seemed more than happy to hang out in North London. He took shots of swinging seventies London which he sold to magazines in the States. Hampstead Heath, the King's Road, the Post Office Tower, the Commonwealth Institute, the London Zoo, the Brunswick Centre in Bloomsbury, even the then deeply unfashionable ponds and lawns and aviaries of Clissold Park. Miniskirts, maxi-skirts. He was digging himself in, appropriating our city. He did 'city-scapes': people behaving in an urban environment, crowd responses to new buildings, patterns of occupation. He wanted to photograph Maroussia and the children in the Secret Garden, but she wouldn't let him. She was an actress and she didn't want publicity.

Jess was relieved when eventually he said he was going off to film fishing communities for a month in British Colombia with an old pal of his from the University of Chicago. That was more like the sort of work she thought he ought to be doing. ('Ought' was a not uncommon word in her vocabulary.) She didn't know she was relieved, but she was. She encouraged him to time his absence so that she could have Anna to herself during what I think was the second long Marsh Court summer holiday. The first summer had been a bit of a strain. She looked forward to a time with Anna during which she didn't have to worry about entertaining Bob. They'd be fine on their own, she and Anna. They were a self-contained little duo. Jess was getting tired of trying to please two incompatible sets of interests, two incompatible temperaments. She didn't know it, but she was.

Bob flew off with Jerry to Vancouver on a French Caravelle and Jess and Anna did their own things, as they'd done in the happy old days before Bob had popped up. They went out for cheap high street meals, they went to the park and to the cinema, they joined in and helped with the street parties which were a feature of that time.

Jess didn't have to worry about Bob, but a rival worry almost immediately presented itself, in the form of Steve. Our latent and long-standing apprehensions about our neighbourhood poet proved well founded. As soon as Bob took himself off to Canada, Steve saw his opportunity and attempted to move in with Jess. Jess didn't let him, but that summer she allowed him to hang around and cadge meals off her and read his poems to her. Steve was good with Anna, as Bob had been, and Jess found it hard to close the door on him. Anna had prised the door of Jess's heart open, and Steve got his foot in quickly when Bob left. The greedy presence of his misery, like a third party in the room, afflicted her, and she could not resist trying to feed it and soothe it and make it grow strong enough to go away.

For such a strong and independent woman, she was curiously vulnerable to the claims of others. She must have known that looking after Steve was an unrewarding and probably hopeless task, but she listened to him for hour after hour, as he told her of his damaged childhood and his ambiguous sexuality and his troubled spiritual journey. Steve, like many birth-damaged people, was at once extremely interesting and hypnotically dull, and some of the most cynical literary editors and hardened publishers of the day succumbed from time to time to his Ancient Mariner grasp. A volume of his poems called *The Dance of the Grieving Child*, after a painting by Paul Klee, was published by a distinguished publishing house with the Klee image on the jacket, a breach of copyright that brought the poems some notoriety if not many sales. Steve was somebody, he had made himself into somebody, and that long summer he presented that person to Jess and Anna, in hope of its salvation.

Anna didn't mind Steve. She didn't mind anybody who even appeared to be friendly. But Jess grew impatient. Too many improvised meals of scrambled eggs on toast (preferably with bacon), too many take-aways of chicken korma and chicken Madras from the Taj Mahal along the high street, too much mango chutney, too many packets of chocolate digestive biscuits. Steve devoured. He was insatiable. He devoured curry, he devoured Jess. Anna listened to his tales of wicked stepmothers and Eastern sages and his dramatic renderings of Wordsworth's ballads (*The Idiot Boy*, *The White Doe of Rylstone*, *The Affliction of Margaret*) until late into the evening, her eyelids drooping slightly with sleepiness. She loved the simple rhymes and rhythms of *The Idiot Boy*, and seemed to understand this tale of motherly pride and devotion, but it did go on a bit, and Anna could not help but yawn. Steve was not good at knowing when to stop.

Jess would make an excuse of Anna, one night too abruptly. 'You must go home now, Steve, I need to put Anna to bed.'

'I can go to bed by myself,' said Anna plaintively, to which Jess snapped 'Well, go on, then, *go*' – words meant for Steve but directed at Anna, who took herself off promptly and went upstairs in some embarrassment.

Jess was so ashamed of this tiny volcanic outburst, this little home firework, that she resolved to be sterner with Steve next time. And, disastrously, was. No, she said to Steve on her doorstep, no, you can't come in, not even for a moment, I'm writing a long review for the *New Anthropological Journal*. No, you really can't.

She said this more harshly and abruptly than she had intended, because saying it was so difficult, and she saw his long large face freeze and then flinch in response, as he bumbled an apology. As soon as he had gone, she regretted her tone if not her words, although she did settle down at once at her typewriter to bash out 2,000 ill-paid words on kinship, totemism and bark painting in a small tribe inhabiting the north coast of Australia, a topic about which she knew hardly anything, although as ever she was glad to learn. She soon lost herself in her unfamiliar subject, and forgot Steve. Anna was watching an episode of a very basic science-fiction series on television, as absorbed in its incomprehensible plot as Jess was in the domestic taboos and artistic impulses of a primitive people she would never encounter, in a land she would never visit.

One was allowed to use the word 'primitive' then.

At that time, it was still believed by some that Down's syndrome children encapsulated an early phase of the evolution of the human race, and that in their very features lingered a racial imprint of an earlier age, a long-ago migration from the East. As the developing human embryo lives through evolutionary time from primitive cell to tadpole to gilled fish to mammal, so the Down's child bears witness to a moment of past time, when the mind and the brain were simpler. This hypothesis was long ago dismissed as ludicrous in scientific terms, but clung on in the popular imagination because it had a certain poetry. It may be pleasant to believe that the world was once peopled by men and women without guile.

The skills required by survival are not always attractive.

Steve did not appear at first or third or fiftieth encounter to be a survivor, but he had learnt to manipulate others, and Jess, up to a point, had allowed herself to be manipulated. And Anna liked him.

His suicide attempt, which followed closely on his doorstep rejection by Jess, was easily interpreted as another manipulative move, but it could as easily have ended in his death, in which case it would perforce have had to have been interpreted quite differently.

It was a coincidence that Jess and Anna discovered him, but not a very extreme coincidence.

It was a Saturday, a beautiful golden late-August urban day, and Jess had arranged to meet Maroussia and Katie and one or two more of us in the Secret Garden for a lunchtime picnic. Some of the children were getting too old and sullen to want to come to a family event, but there was still a critical mass of little ones, large enough to turn a picnic into a party. It was by chance that Jess got there first. She had her own key, and she arrived on the bus with her plastic box of egg and cress sandwiches, her bottle of wine, her bottle of juice, and she let herself in. She left Anna sitting in the sun with the basket under the shade of a little red-hipped hawthorn tree which had survived the clearance, and went over to the Wendy House to get out some deckchairs and some of the plastic beakers and bits of rush matting that were stored there. We'd assembled the Wendy House ourselves from lot of awkward, obstinate and confusing wooden parts that had arrived in a large cardboard box (what we'd now call, apprehensively, a flat-pack), and we were very proud of it: our combined manual skills were not great, but the little shed was a small and suitable monument to our cooperative effort. One of us (a lawyer) had wondered if we'd had the legal right to erect a structure on this bit of waste land, to which we had responded: who cares?

Steve was sitting slumped in a striped deck-chair, just inside the hut, of which the door was ajar. He looked, said Jess later, rather like a younger John Betjeman, stranded in a beach hut on a desolate seaside promenade. (Steve did not admire the work of Betjeman.) Steve's eyes were closed, the pouches under them grey and more than ever drooping. His jaw was slack, and he was breathing noisily through his mouth. Steve never looked healthy or well, but that noon he looked peculiarly unwell. Indeed, he looked as though he were dying.

Jess, reading the scenario guiltily and self-referentially, her heart instantly pierced with remorse and self-blame, invoked his name.

'Steve,' she said urgently, 'Steve.'

Steve did not react, so she approached him more closely and nervously patted, then increasingly fiercely, shook his arm. He did not much stir, although he made a gurgling, moaning sound from his throat that could have been either a good or a very bad sign. Jess looked around for tablets or a note, and found evidence of the former on the Wendy House floor, by his dangling arm: an empty tube of Veganin, as clear a message as one might wish to receive. Jess did not dare to feel his pulse, and anyway she had no idea what constituted a normal pulse rate. She knew she must get help, and she ran back to Anna, who was sitting quietly under the tree with the picnic basket, looking like a child in a nursery rhyme.

Polly, put the kettle on
Polly, put the kettle on
We'll all have tea.

'Anna, it's Steve, he's poorly, we need an ambulance,' said Jess. 'You just wait here, don't move, don't do anything, just wait, and I'll go and get Maroussia to phone.'

Maroussia lived on one of the three streets that backed on to the Bermuda Triangle of the Secret Garden, and her house had a little gate through which she could come and go. (Maroussia sometimes went into the garden at dead of night, and just stood there, on her own, breathing in the London air, as her two children slept safely in their bunk beds.) The gate would be locked, but Maroussia would be expecting them, and Jess could shout for her, or try to climb over: it would be quicker than going down the little countrified elder-sprouting urban lane and round the sides of the triangle to her front door.

'Maroussia!' yelled Jess. 'Maroussia, help!'

And Maroussia, busy making her mustard-and-ham sandwiches, came running down her garden path, and let Jess into her tiny kitchen to dial 999, while Anna continued to sit dutifully under her hawthorn tree, and Steve continued to loll heavily like a great doll in his deck-chair.

The ambulance arrived in half an hour, by which time more of the picnic group had assembled and absorbed Anna into its care, releasing Jess to accompany Steve to hospital. She took it as her responsibility, and nobody disputed her dolorous claim. Anna wanted to go with her mother, but we insisted to Jess that she could safely be left with us.

The ambulance crew had its instructions, and it promptly transported Steve and Jess to one of those grim nineteenth-century North London hospitals that cater for a large intake of patients from the Victorian gaols of the region. In its maternity ward, as Jess happened to know, pregnant women prisoners from Holloway gave birth, sometimes in shackles. Jess felt herself met with a wave of hostility and disapproval by the staff, but also, to her relief, with some sense of urgency. The overdose procedure was well rehearsed, and the nurses went into action with a stomach pump. Steve was moving around by this stage, and Jess could see him through the window of the door of the ward. It was a pitiable, a horrible sight. The obscene rubber tubing was thrust down his gullet with a degree of brutality that seemed, and probably was, vindictive. Luckily they did not know that Steve was a poet, thought Jess, or they might have been even harsher with him.

It fell to Jess to attempt to give Steve's details: she knew his name and his address, but not his age. (Was he thirty? Thirty-five? Forty? He he had always seemed ageless as well as sexless, an amorphous, absorbent being, a negative capability.) She knew he was single but she did not know the name of his GP or his next of kin. Should she give the name of his stepmother, a woman who was not without a certain public reputation, but whose care for Steve, if he told the truth about her, could not be considered admirable? What about his champion at the small distinguished publishing house, or the literary editor for whom he wrote occasional reviews? None of these characters seemed appropriate, so Jess settled for giving her own contact numbers and describing herself as a 'personal friend'.

She had landed herself with Steve, for better or worse. No, she did not know if he had ever attempted suicide before, or whether he was on any medication. No, she did not know how many pills he had taken. No, she did not know anything about his general health. Reluctantly, she admitted that he was a 'freelance writer'.

She was protective about his status as poet. She was sure that these starched young women disapproved of poetry, as they clearly disapproved of suicide, and would take it out on him when and if he came round.

When pressed, they admitted that he probably would come round. He did not seem to have consumed an excessive amount of Veganin, and they did not think the pills had been in his system for very long. He would almost certainly recover. He might have done permanent damage to his liver (they announced this as though they rather hoped he had, and as though he would be last on the list for a transplant), but he would live through the episode. He was already beginning to respond to their unkindly attentions.

Jess, at this point, was beginning to worry about Anna and the effect that this drama might have had on her, and decided she should try to get back to the garden party. She said she needed to return to her daughter, hoping that a mention of her maternal role might soften these hard hearts. It had no such effect, but it was agreed that Dr Speight could be released. ('No, I'm not a medical doctor': Jess had at once been made to regret trying to pull rank with her doctorate). Jess said as humbly as she could that she would ring later, and perhaps call round in the morning.

What bus could she catch back towards Camden, she asked them? But if they knew, they were not going to tell her. Their care, they made it plain, ended at the ward door, where the unwelcome and unwanted Steve breathed noisily, high and heavy on a narrow railed bed, a giant cot.

She went out on to the hot street and looked around for a bus stop or a taxi. This was not taxi land. A slight wave of nausea and panic attacked her as she set off down the hill, from which she was rescued by the sight of a red London bus labelled with a promising southward destination: she ran after it, jumped on at the lights, and was on her way to rejoin us, overcome with relief at her escape from overt institutional resentment. She wasn't very pleased with Steve herself, but she didn't see why she should be blamed for, or implicated in, his act. It wasn't her fault. Was it?

~

Jess rejoined us in Maroussia's house, and told us the story. Anna listened, though what she took in we could not tell. Not even Jess could tell. The other children, bored with the gloomy adult drama, had gone upstairs to the bunk bedroom to play a very low-tech but gripping football game which involved moving little plastic men about on a green cloth. One or two of them who lived within easy walking distance had sloped off home, to join fathers watching real football on television, but Anna sat with us, listening.

The fathers supported Arsenal or Tottenham Hotspur, and enjoyed comparing their merits and their style. None of the mothers, in those days, followed the game.

Jess considered (as did we all) that Steve's choice of a Wendy House as his potential deathbed was highly significant. Poor Steve, he had found in us (and in Jess in particular) a surrogate family, and had wished to become our child, as Anna was and would ever remain our child. He was a Peter Pan, a motherless lost boy. But clumsy, never airborne, except in words. His mother was dead, his father had disowned him.

Steve had always exuded grief. He must, we thought, have been born sad and mewling and scowling. Anna was pure gold and eager to be happy, if occasionally over-anxious, but Steve was heavy cold wax, with no natural happiness accessible to him.

So that's what we do, we find a small dark cosy familiar corner of plot, and we curl up in it and die. Or try to die. We regress, we rock ourselves backwards and forwards, we climb back into the cot, the playpen, the Wendy House. We become as little children, and we try to crawl back to a safe place, to a familiar place that needs no exploring. We lose our adventurous spirit, we turn away in fear from the untracked forests and the shining waters, and we seek the comfort of a small known space, where we cling to our sucked blanket, to our worn woolly old knitted rabbit or piglet or bear. A comfort zone, we now call it.

This may happen to us when we are very old. You have seen

them, in the care homes, in their recliners, with their thin baby hair. *We go back there*. Steve had attempted to short-circuit the long and dreary circular journey, but he had failed.

We unlatch and open the little gate, and we try to go back. But the place does not always admit us, it will not let us in.

Steve had felt safe in our company, he had felt safe with Jess, he had been happy clearing the brambles and lighting the bonfire and attempting, ineffectually, to help with the construction effort. (We were all ineffectual, and that too was companionable.) We had given him somewhere to be. The sadness of our failing of him subdued us, for a while, that evening, but we were young and strong and healthy and resilient, and by the time we parted we had regained the rhythm of our selves and our selfishness, and were planning the busy week and the weeks and months and years ahead. We forgot about Steve, because thinking about him drained our energy, and we needed our energy for our own lives.

~

Maroussia did not go into the Secret Garden that night to look at the large low full moon and the stars. She stayed indoors. She looked at the ceiling, and the walls, and then she went into the bathroom and looked at herself for a long time in the mirror.

~

Jess did not forget Steve, although she tried to, because she found herself unwillingly placing herself *in loco parentis*, a default position to which she was beginning to recognise she might always tend to revert. As Steve reverted to infancy, she reverted to maternity. This is what Anna's birth and the responsibility of Anna had done to her. Her holiday from her husband

Bob Bartlett (Jess never took the name Bartlett and often forgot it was legally hers) transformed itself into a watch over Steve. She resented this, but it happened just the same.

I'm afraid some of us were not very supportive. We couldn't take the strain. We regarded Jess as our mental-health expert, as Sylvie was our medical expert, and we left it to her. She'd been through so much already, she could go on getting on with it.

Steve was kept in hospital for a couple of days, and then discharged back to his dusty hole of a £6-a-week book-filled bed-sitter over a pawnshop in garbage-strewn Chalk Farm. No psychiatric after-care seemed to have been proposed. He was on his own again, written off with visible contempt. The prison hospital had a psychiatric wing, but Jess's instinct (rightly) told her that this would not have provided a therapeutic environment, even if he had been admitted to it. When Steve turned up next time on her doorstep (and by now Jess could feel the approaching return of a Caravelle with Bob on it, although she did not have a precise date for his arrival), Jess was anxious to set up something, anything, that would divert Steve from his visits to her and his dependence on her.

Steve, eating his bacon and eggs and fried bread with as hearty an appetite as ever, was a little sheepish about the trouble he had caused, but he remained deeply depressed. His gullet had recovered from the assault on it, but neither his mind nor his spirits had recovered. Jess was convinced he would have another go. She hoped it wouldn't be in her house, or in front of Anna.

She asked Steve about his doctor, she mentioned his stepmother, but made little progress on either front. She didn't know where to turn. Steve needed somewhere with company, a refuge to contain and surround him, not a lonely third-floor bed-sit with a dangerous gas ring up steep uncarpeted wooden stairs. Could you kill yourself with a gas ring? Probably not.

Sylvia Plath had put her head in the oven, not so very long ago, and not very far from the pawnshop where Steve lived, but a gas ring wasn't as powerful as an oven, and anyway, weren't most of us on natural gas by now? You can't kill yourself with natural gas, or that's what we believed. But there was the high window over the hard street, and there was the unprotected gas fire. Jess had visions of Steve drinking a bottle of Teacher's whisky and clambering on to his window ledge and letting himself fall drunkenly on to the pavement, of Steve setting his ill-hung curtains ablaze and dying of smoke inhalation. She hoped such images did not occupy the screen of his imagination too.

But she knew they did.

After a week of hesitation and another exhausting visit from Steve, Jess rang the editor at his publishing house, hoping his literary patronage could be extended to pastoral care. It seemed that it could not. Noah invited Jess (and perforce Anna) to have coffee and a Danish pastry with him in the café in the British Museum, a neutral and inexpensive venue, and he listened to Jess's story with interest. He volunteered some colourful information about Steve's stepmother (a titled society beauty with a penchant for ageing homosexual actors and theatrical impresarios, whom she would escort to dubious nightspots and country houses), and he expressed concern for Steve, but said: 'Frankly, I can't cope with him, he's a nightmare, he's a vampire, no, not a vampire, he's a leech, keep away, he'll suck your blood.'

Had the stepmother seduced Steve? Probably, thought Noah. She seduced anything that moved.

'Not that Steve,' said Noah, 'moves very much.'

At this point I think they both laughed.

'You should just see her,' said Noah. 'The lips, the old-fashioned hair-style, the slinky hips. The Nightmare Life-in-Death is she.'

Was the phrase 'fag hag' current in those pre-gay-lib days? I think not.

'Maybe,' said Noah, as though the thought had just struck him, 'she's a transvestite.'

Noah, also a poet, had a style more animated than Steve's: angular, skinny, sharp, caustic. Manic, not depressive.

Anna ate two Danish pastries, Noah ate one, Jess ate none. Jess hated Danish pastries.

Jess batted on: did Noah know any kind and obliging analysts or therapists or psychiatrists who could advise Steve? There must be somebody who could help?

'You don't want his blood on your hands, do you?' said Jess provocatively, who thought she was getting on rather well with Noah by this stage, and sensed that before their elevenses were over he would make a pass at her.

'I know a woman at the Tavistock,' said Noah doubtfully, 'but I wouldn't recommend her to my worst enemy. And she's a Kleinian.'

'I don't think Steve needs a Kleinian,' said Jess. 'What he needs is company. Ordinary physical daily company. I can't provide it, I've got work to do, I've got Anna to look after. And my very new husband's just about to get back from British Columbia.'

'Pity, that,' said Noah.

Jess smiled at Noah, her intense and intimate and dazzling smile.

'Bob won't want to find Steve in residence, or even in attendance,' continued Jess, after a significant pause.

'Psychiatry's out of fashion,' volunteered Noah, trying now to be helpful. 'It's all anti-psychiatry at the moment. We're publishing a brilliant new book on the killer family and the throttling umbilical cord.'

'Steve hasn't got a family or an umbilical cord,' repeated Jess. 'He's all alone. That's his problem.'

Noah, at last, appeared to be trying to think.

'He needs a commune,' said Noah. 'There are some. But what kind of commune would want Steve as a member?'

'He's quite interesting,' said Jess. 'He's a good poet. That's something, isn't it?'

'A therapeutic community,' said Noah. 'We need a therapeutic community, and preferably on the National Health Service. I'll look into it.'

'Please do that,' said Jess firmly.

'I'll get back to you,' said Noah. 'I'll give you a ring. When does your very new husband get back?'

'Any day now,' said Jess.

Noah smiled.

'I'll ring you,' he said. He wasn't going to be put off by the existence of Anna, to whom he had been courteous, and he seemed to welcome the challenge of a very new husband.

'Please do,' said Jess. 'And now I'd better go, I promised Anna we'd go to look at the Egyptian mummies.'

'And you said we could go to SOAS,' said Anna, who remembered all promises. Anna had a very literal memory.

'And SOAS,' said Jess. 'I said we'd call in there on the way home.'

Anna liked the word 'SOAS', a friendly whispering bee-like word which she would sometimes murmur to herself as a reassurance. It was her mother's mysterious cradle and school and workplace, peopled by important adult names, names prefaced by titles and initials, names which her mother always mentioned with respect. Anna liked to go there, and some of the important people would greet her as well as her mother by name and in a friendly manner.

She also liked the idea of seeing the British Museum mummies, though when she visited them in their glass coffins, she was very disappointed. They were not as she had imagined them, at all. They were inert, and not at all maternal, and they were very dead.

Anna had not really taken to Noah, despite the Danish pastries. He had eyed her mother in a manner that she had found disquieting. She had not found Steve a worry. He hadn't, in her view, from her position, been a threat. There was room in Anna's life for plenty of people like Steve.

~

Jess, over the next few days, was to remember her Marsh Court friend Susie's descriptions of the new forms of asylum, of the new communities of the mad where the sick were reborn or, as a phrase of the day had it, rebirthed. (Susie hadn't used this phrase, but Jess had come across it in the articles and books she had been reading.) Even Friern Barnet at Colney Hatch, that bastion of the old schools of treatment (lobotomy, ECT, insulin, routine, regimentation, damp mattresses, prolonged neglect), now housed under its umbrella, according to Susie, an experimental rehabilitation unit where less punitive measures were being attempted. Maybe Steve could find a refuge there? She didn't have Susie's phone number, and anyway would have felt it intrusive to ring her, but when Noah telephoned (as she knew he would) she asked him to investigate. She declined an invitation to an open-air concert in Regent's Park, but she delegated to Noah the task of finding out about the new unit. It was his turn to do something, she instructed.

You will recall the movement towards redefining mental illness, towards creating safe houses for those in need of care but not necessarily of medication. Schizophrenia, rather than clinical depression, was the malady of that decade, but a label, after all, was only a label. Madness had become interesting to some very clever and articulate and innovative professionals and laymen, and big money was invested in it. The rich go off the rails quite frequently, and they can afford to pay well to be rehabilitated. Most of these ventures failed, some spectacularly, for they were, even for the rich, too expensive, they demanded too much from staff, too much from inmates, and were at high risk of scandal and exploitation, and of exposure by a hostile and mocking press. But, for a while, some of them flourished, providing a refuge for misfits and a home for the homeless. A few badly damaged people at this period experienced a happiness, a sense of belonging, that they were never to find again. Time has such patches, such pockets, and some unfortunates are fortunate enough to be reborn into one of them.

Anna's condition was not very interesting, except to Jess. It lacked drama and progress and the possibility of a surprising or successful outcome. Anna had her devoted mother Jess to care for her, and a local-authority-subsidised place at Marsh Court, and one set of well-off middle-class grandparents. What more could a girl want? She was a fortunate child. She did not need a fashionable mind doctor to peer into the still and slow-flowing rivers of her thought processes, seeking their headwaters. She was happy as she was.

Whereas Steve was in need, and might respond to a cure, and, in a suitable haven, recover. Steve's condition was not without interest, and his stepmother featured in gossip columns. He was not nearly as interesting as Sylvia Plath, a writer of genius whose tragic fate had been instantly recognised by Jess and many women of our generation as emblematic, but he had a minor talent, and a claim to human attention. There was material in Steve.

Minor talents or failing talents ask much of those who associate with them. They are parasitic. They suck, they cling, they sour, they devour, and they can kill their hosts. Disappointment is a deadly companion. We didn't yet know how many of us would end up in its grip, because we were all still striving, and some of us thought we were thriving. Steve was our scapegoat, our loser, our sacrifice to ambition. We all thought we were more viable than Steve, although he had published some good poems in little magazines.

In Halliday Hall, Steve ceased for a while to be disappointed.

Halliday Hall in Essex was a new 1960s therapeutic unit housed in a refurbished wing of an old purpose-built mid-nineteenth-century institution which occupied the site of an eighteenth-century manor and farmhouse called Troutwell. There were still vestiges of the old farm buildings standing, though the manor house had long gone. (From potato farm to funny farm, that had been one of the old jokes.) Troutwell was more rural and further away from Central London than Enfield and Marsh Court, but it lay on the same eastward trajectory. Pioneering work into the causes of mental defect had been done there in the old asylum in the early twentieth century, in the days when politicians and statisticians and eugenicists had publicly worried that the swelling numbers of the mentally subnormal would overwhelm the normal population, and sought (though not through infanticide or Swedish programmes of compulsory sterilisation) to counter this falsely perceived tendency.

By the second half of the twentieth century, inherited abnormality and excessive fertility were no longer the villains. Other culprits were sought.

In Halliday Hall, Steve was happy. The transformation was remarkable. Jess, visiting him there for the first time (guiltily, for he had already, thanks to Noah's intervention, been an inmate for three weeks), found him cheerful, outgoing, responsive, surrounded by new friends and filled with new hope. There was even a little colour in his large pale cheeks, as though he had been leading an outdoor life, as though he had been sitting more in the sun.

Spacious grounds surrounded Halliday Hall, grounds handsomely planted with cedars and willows, grounds dating back to the days of Troutwell Hall and Troutwell Farm, around which had grown a vast old-fashioned complex of Victorian buildings. Within them nestled this new unit, like a cuckoo or a dove.

On her way in, Jess had walked for more than half an hour along a mile or two of Victorian and Edwardian corridors, over the brown-and-yellow-and-turquoise-patterned tessellated ceramic tiles that paved the floors of late-nineteenth-century London and its surrounding towns and villages. She had made her way through heavy fire doors, past open doors and locked doors, past communal sitting rooms thick with cigarette smoke occupied by inert figures staring at flickering television screens, past wheelchairs pushed by fellow-inmates, past men in overalls carrying screwdrivers and planks of wood, past women pushing trolleys and carrying trays, past broken-paned conservatories where straggling plants fought for survival, and she had eventually arrived at Halliday, where Steve was holding his court.

Halliday Hall was the sanctum, the shrine, where the crème de la crème, the star patients, assembled.

Steve had a little room of his own, looking out through a French window on to a ground-floor brick-paved courtyard, sprouting pleasant little tufts of chickweed and groundsel. There he entertained Jess to tea and biscuits, and introduced her to his companions. There she met Simon and Patrick and Ursula and Raoul and Zain. They sat around in a circle, talking eagerly of poetry and politics, and of their guru, Dr Nicholls. As Steve said, it was for all the world like being back at university, like sitting in a college quadrangle. This was not a group of zombies, it was a seminar, a refresher course, a group of young people with a future. Steven and his friends were all in their thirties and forties, so they had regressed a decade or two, but not as far back as the cot or the Wendy House.

Steve poured the tea from a big brown teapot. If the teapot was an accessory of Dr Nicholls's therapy, as seemed probable, Jess saluted him.

Jess did not think Steve had become manic. She had never seen him manic, and did not consider that this pleasant engagement with others and the outside world could be diagnosed as mania. He passed the wholesome Marie biscuits round in an attentive manner that he had never shown in Jess's house. Dr Nicholls, whoever he was, had worked a miracle.

Raoul was a Lebanese, she learnt, a Marxist refugee, a medical student and a political activist who had left his homeland pursued, or so he believed, by death threats. An intellectual. He was a small, slightly built, pleasant-looking, bird-featured young man of diffidence and charm. Ursula was a grey-haired, Roman-nosed, Roman Catholic, young-middle-aged primary-schoolteacher from Croydon, and Simon was, or had been, a monk from a closed order in West Sussex. Patrick was an axe man, a tree man, whose job it had been to pollard the municipal planes and limes of Barnet and Harrow. Zain was a Sudanese, who had been referred to Halliday Hall from Bush House, where he had been working for the BBC World Service.

Jess, basking relieved in the remission of guilt and the success of Steve's new placement, liked them all, but she found it hard to take her eyes off Zain. He was a stunner. Intellectual energy and a dangerous sexual radiance poured from him. The other participants at this mad hatter's tea party seemed pale in comparison, although none was unattractive.

Zain disclosed a little of his history, with encouragement from Jess: born in a Sudanese village, he had been hand-picked by an itinerant schools inspector as a promising lad worthy of higher education, and had travelled through the network of high school and scholarships and prizes to a degree at the London School of Economics and a job with the African World Service and a disastrous marriage to a white virgin of the Anglican Church, a marriage which had ended in violent affray, criminal charges, psychiatric treatment and Halliday Hall.

That was his brief summary of his dazzling meteoric career. He had clearly told it many times, to many listeners, but it had not lost its force. Here he sat, still burning.

'They are holding my job for me,' said Zain. 'They have treated me very well. Like a prince.'

Zain's English was impeccable. He had adopted the very accents and intonations of the LSE and the BBC.

'Too rapid a journey from too far away,' hazarded Jess sympathetically, bending upon Zain the full intensity of her short-sighted, cornflower-blue gaze.

Zain nodded, and sat back forcefully on the fragile seat of his small grey plastic-framed hospital chair, making it tremble.

'Yes,' he agreed. 'The migration to the north has destroyed many. But I am set now on a survival course, I shall survive.'

Steve looked on benignly like a successful pander.

'Jess is an anthropologist,' Steve contributed.

'Ah,' said Zain, leaning forward to offer Jess a cigarette from his soft pack. 'And what field of anthropology has been your chosen domain? Do you know the Sudan? It has attracted many students from England. It has a long history with the English. It retains much of the primitive to study. Your colleagues appreciate the primitive. My own village would be worthy of your attention. It has not yet been documented, except by me. Our palm trees, our mission church, our preacher, our oasis.'

Jess accepted the cigarette, although she rarely smoked. Zain leant further forward to light it for her, cupping and enfolding her white hand and the little flame of his Swan Vestas match together inside his black and larger hand.

'I have become a North London anthropologist,' said Jess

modestly, after her first inexpert draw on the unfiltered Camel. She had never smoked an unfiltered cigarette. She picked a surprisingly adhesive shred of tobacco from her reluctant lip, and continued. 'I have become an anthropologist of the interior world. I do not travel far. Although I did go to Africa, once. I went to Central Africa. I have seen Lake Bangweulu and I have seen the Zambezi. I saw the lake and the swamps. I saw where Livingstone died. I saw where his heart was buried.'

'So you have seen my continent,' said Zain.

'Yes, I have. But it was a long way west of the Sudan.'

'This is the continent of Dr Nicholls,' said Zain. 'We are in his protectorate.'

Jess liked his florid English speech.

'Dr Nicholls,' contributed Ursula, who was also smoking a Camel, rather more competently and more provocatively than Jess, 'is our chieftain.'

Ursula may once have worn her long grey hair tethered and pinned into a neat schoolmistress's coil, but here she had released it. She still wore a knot of it on top of her head, skewered with a plastic mother-of-pearl dagger, but thick strands escaped from bondage and fell dramatically, purposefully, suggestively down to brush her bare brown shoulders. She was wearing a strapless pink-and-white sundress and, like Steve, had been sitting in the sun, perhaps too much in the sun. She had a fine neck, a long and haughty neck, and the escaping locks enhanced its swanlike curve. Her nape was proud and bare. She wore a silver cross on a silver chain around her throat.

Ursula tapped the ash from her cigarette into an ashtray extended to her in a large cupped hand by Zain, and smiled a complicit private smile at him. Jess could see that she too found Zain irresistible, and had not resisted him. Jess wondered whether Dr Nicholls encouraged that kind of thing, whether he was one of the new men who saw all sexual activity as therapeutic. She would be interested to meet Dr Nicholls. Halliday Hall was clearly a place without conventional frontiers. Maybe even Steve would find a loving partner here.

(Susie, over a gristled Wimpy, ketchup and soft limp chips in Enfield Church Street, had told Jess about a young woman who had been deliberately impregnated by one of the so-called doctors at Kingsley Hall. Responsible state-registered Susie from suburban Southgate had not approved of this, but had admitted that it was said not to have done much harm to the young woman in question, and the baby was really very sweet. 'A lovely little boy,' said Susie, with surprising warmth.)

'Zain's wife,' proffered Ursula provocatively, 'is from Durham. She is the daughter of a man of the cloth.'

Ursula stared boldly at Jess and helped herself to a biscuit.

She had called upon Zain to offer his apologia. He offered it, on cue.

'It was an unwise marriage,' said Zain. 'But she insisted.'

Jess felt she should have found this remark offensive, but failed to do so. She was too far in.

Bob should never have left Jess, not even for a month, if he had wanted to keep her. Bob appeared like a tiny figurine in her memory, very small and boyish and far away. Zain loomed large and present and overpowering. He was the enterprise, the journey, the adventure. And she wouldn't even have to catch an aeroplane or cross the ocean to find him. He had come her way.

'Another cup of tea?' urged Steve. 'I'll go and put the kettle on, make another pot.'

'I must be going,' said Jess, snapping out of her brief trance. 'I've left Anna with Sarah and Ollie, and Ollie starts to tease her if they're together for too long. I have to pick her up.'

'Come again,' said Steve. 'It's jolly here, isn't it?'

'Yes, very jolly,' said Jess. 'I'm so pleased, I'm so pleased for all of you.'

She spoke primly, like a visiting social worker or a nun. Distancing herself, detaching herself.

She gave Steve a hug on parting, and shook hands all round with the other inmates. Zain's hand grasped hers in a fierce electric grip.

'Come again,' he said. 'Come again, before they kick us all out and send us back to where we came from.'

'They won't do that, will they?' she asked, her eyes wide as he stared into them. His eyes were white and bloodshot. He was, or had been, a drinking man.

'Not yet,' said Steve. 'Not yet.'

'No,' echoed the quiet, diffident Raoul, as he stood courteously by the courtyard door to usher her on her way. 'No, I think we will have another few months, before we are evicted. They will let the experiment run for a few months more, I think. They are keeping notes on us, you know.'

And he smiled, to show that he was not suffering from paranoia, as she might reasonably have expected.

Jess retraced her way through the corridors, past the second- and third-class patients, some of them interned here for decades without trial or diagnosis, many of them to be released in a few years into care-in-the-community, into lonely bed-sits with gas rings and high windows and death at desolate weekends.

Sitting on the train to Liverpool Street, travelling westwards through the still visible bomb damage of East London, through the railway cuttings and the ragwort and the bindweed and the buddleia, she feared she would be late for Anna. Ollie's mother Sarah would be getting impatient and anxious, Ollie would be growing bored and annoying. Anna loved Ollie, Ollie tolerated Anna.

Ollie could very easily make Anna cry. His worst trick was to recite a nursery rhyme that he knew would upset her. He'd found this out by accident, but, having discovered the game, he wouldn't let it go. He would chant it at her:

Polly, put the kettle on,
Polly, put the kettle on
Polly, put the kettle on
We'll all have tea.

Sukie, take it off again,
Sukie, take it off again,
Sukie, take it off again,
They've all gone away.

This would always distress Anna, in the old days to the point of tears.

'They don't want to have tea with Polly and Sukie,' she would sob, when she was very little. 'Why don't they want to stay for tea?'

In vain had Jess tried to rewrite the lyric. 'They go away because they've already *had* tea,' Jess would explain. 'They just don't want a second cup. They've *had* tea, they've had a lovely time.'

Anna did not accept this interpretation, and Ollie and Jess knew she never would. Her reaction to the ditty had become Pavlovian. Even a phrase of the nursery rhyme could upset her.

We all suspected that Ollie was going to be the one who would go to the bad. One of them was sure to, statistically, and he seemed the most likely candidate. How wrong we were, how wrong.

~

The encounter with Zain, preceded as it had been by an overt if easily deflected overture from Noah, guaranteed an uncomfortable homecoming for young Bob Bartlett. Bob's new wife Jess had moved on in his absence, and she was not very welcoming when he reappeared, with only a few hours' warning, carrying gifts of soapstone seals and feather head-dresses and miniature carved totem poles and turquoise necklaces. She had become accustomed to having her house and her daughter to herself again, and she and Anna would find it hard to make space for the Step Dad. He found Jess unresponsive, although she did consent to wear the turquoise jewellery.

She did not really want to know him any more. She had cooled off in his absence.

She had cooled off towards him, but something was burning away in her, something he sensed but could not reach.

She did not even pretend to want him back. He was puzzled by this, and offended, and after a couple of weeks he illegally evicted his illegal tenant from his Camden flat and moved back into it by himself. 'We'll try living apart for a bit,' he said; 'maybe I'll move back when Anna's gone back to Marsh Court.'

This wasn't a very tactful remark, implying as it did that Anna was the obstacle to intercourse. He couldn't of course have known that the obstacle was Zain, because at this point he didn't know of Zain's existence. Nor did any of us. Zain was the dark card.

Most women used to feel a polite or submissive need to placate and satisfy their husband's sexual demands, at least when there was no good reason not to do so. The accusation of being a castrating woman still had some force, and maybe for all I know still has, but this element in Jess's emotional make-up seems to have been missing. If she didn't want to, she didn't want to, and that was that. She felt no obligation. Perhaps her obligations towards Anna swallowed up any other sense of duty: one woman can manage only so much personal commitment, and for Jess, this was embodied in her daughter. She didn't think she owed much to Bob. She began, unfairly, to consider that her sexual relations with him had been almost as unsatisfactory as her relations with the Professor. The Professor had provided unfailing orgasms, and these had needed no aid from Viagra or any of those other products which had not yet become commercially available. (They probably had not even been invented. Oysters and monkey glands were all our predecessors knew of aphrodisiacs.) But the Professor had not been much fun. Bob had been fun, while he lasted, but he did not last as long, and there was something trivial, something superficial, about the level of his desire. It did not go deep enough. Or so Jess now considered.

So she heaved Bob out of the brightly cushioned nest.

Anna was sorry that Bob moved away, as she did not like the sense of uncertainty and discord that this rift represented, and she had enjoyed the sing-songs with Bob. She liked life to be safe, and people to be constant and kind to one another. The abrupt and (to her) unexpected phasing out of Bob made her very reluctant to go off to Marsh Court, a reaction Jess had not anticipated, although it was easy enough for us to speculate that Anna might feel her own return from school at the end of next term, like Bob's from his short photographic foray to Canada, would be unwelcome. Going away was risky if you couldn't be sure you'd be allowed back.

What was her mother doing? Was she shutting herself, alone, into her little fortress in Kinderley Road? Was she repelling all outsiders? Was Anna to become an outsider, as well as Bob?

Anna began to cry on the train from Liverpool Street to Enfield. She tried not to, but she couldn't help it. Jess felt like a heel, watching her helpless stupid darling daughter sniffle, watching her eyes redden and her nose run. She kept offering her tissues, but Anna let the fluids drip. This made her look less than attractive. '*Do* wipe your nose,' said Jess irritably, as the shabby vandalised little train made its way through Seven Sisters and Hackney Downs.

Anna sniffed, and obeyed, and dropped the tissue on the floor, and then had to bend down to pick it up again.

'You'll be seeing Hazel soon,' said Jess bracingly; then, with less conviction, 'and Vincent.'

'I don't really like Vincent,' said Anna; adding boldly, 'he's a very rude boy.'

'Yes, I suppose he is a bit rude,' said Jess. 'But he doesn't mean to be, he really doesn't.'

'Yes, he does,' said Anna.

She very rarely contradicted her mother. Jess was taken aback.

Now she'd heaved Bob out, Jess began to think as the train travelled haltingly northwards, maybe there was no need for Anna to go to Marsh Court after all. She could come back to North London and be found a schoolplace nearer home, a day schoolplace. There must be something that would serve, something better than the one they hadn't liked at Highbury. Karen the social worker had mentioned a new Special Needs Unit at Woodberry Down; maybe she could try that. Anna hadn't learnt anything much at Marsh Court anyway, except the words of a few stupid songs.

Optional scenarios flitted through Jess's imagination on the journey home. (The leave-taking had been painful, with Anna silent, confused, lost and distraught as Jess helped her to unpack her suitcase. Jess was annoyed with herself for having forgotten to pack Anna's favourite blue sweatshirt, monogrammed in red with *A* for Anna, and that hadn't helped.) None of Jess's plans featured Bob in any starring role. It was as though the Bob-need in her had died. It had been satisfied, and then it had died. She didn't think Bob would mind very much. She hoped he wouldn't mind very much.

She had expected this to happen sometime, but she hadn't expected it to happen quite so soon. She was puzzled by her body's messages.

She had thought herself 'madly in love' with the Professor, and she had thought herself engaged in a cool mature friendly equally balanced sexual partnership with Bob Bartlett. Both conceptions had been mistaken. She had been sexually obsessed by the dominating Professor, and with Bob she had always had the upper hand.

What next?

Zain, of course, was next. Would this be 'love' or 'illness', and would she be able get it over with before Anna came home for the Christmas holidays?

She never wanted to see that sad abandoned look on Anna's face again. She never wanted to find herself speaking harshly to her daughter again. Anna was the apple of her eye. Even when her eyes were red and her nose running, she was the apple of her mother's eye.

~

We think Jess did have an affair with Zain, in fact we know she did, but at the time she didn't much want us to know. She wasn't wholly proud of it. She couldn't keep it a secret, in our community, but she didn't want us to appropriate him and domesticate him. She talked to me about most things, but she was silent about Zain.

Zain was psychotic, we know that now. His story was extreme, and his arrival in Jess's life predictable.

I don't mean *his* arrival, literally. I mean the arrival of someone like him, someone from the Dark Continent, someone from the Book of the People of Many Lands. He was Africa, albeit North Africa, and he was North Africa driven mad by the journey from the village to the air waves, from the rote-recited Sunday School Bible lessons and the palm tree to Kant and Keynes and Malinowski.

I was talking to Jess recently about her father's little book about the People of Many Lands. She had described it to me on several occasions as she and I discussed our differing vocations, as we used to do, and the other day I asked her if she'd ever been to see that famous exhibition called the *Family of Man*. She said she thought she had, though clearly she didn't remember it as vividly as I did. I saw it sometime in the 1950s on the South Bank (the quaint and whimsical Hugh Casson/Rowland Emett Festival of Britain South Bank, not today's more austere Denys Lasdun-dominated South Bank), probably when I was in the Sixth Form at Orpington. I went by myself, on one of those outings to town which I took in the school holidays to escape from my mother, who was going through a passing phase of menopausal bad temper. It was an exhibition of photographs, a famous exhibition. I still have the catalogue, and I have just been leafing through it.

Like Jess's father's book, the exhibition featured and documented the many peoples of the world. It was first shown at the Museum of Modern Art in New York, though I didn't know that when I went as a girl. I was disappointed but not surprised to read recently an account of its alleged limitations – it has been deconstructed as racist and sexist, and images that had seemed beautiful and universal to me (as the pictures in Jess's father's book had appeared to Jess) were condemned as condescending and exploitative. I can see now what is meant by these strictures, but I didn't think of them then.

Looking through its crumpled pages all these decades later, I recognise that I must have been moved and stirred by some of the more erotic photographs. They are in black and white. There are couples kissing, embracing, dancing. A boy and a girl in the grass, by an abandoned bicycle. A couple on a park bench. I was of the age to respond to dreams of kisses and I longed to feel a man's arms around me. I can feel the memory of that longing now. There is nothing pornographic in these portraits – how could there have been, at that period in time? – but to me as a teenager they were full of suggestions of passion and sexuality. I was particularly moved by the face of a woman crushed in ecstasy beneath a man's naked body. Well, we assume he is naked, but because this was the 1950s, all we can see is his naked shoulder, and her face contorted, as it were, in orgasm.

There is also (I have just been looking at it again, and am still in shock) the most astonishing photograph of a newborn baby boy, one foot held in the air by the gloved hand of a masked doctor. The still-attached umbilical cord glistens like a moist rope, and the baby's genitals are held aloft, prominent, symmetrical, dark, enormous. The legs are puny and skinny like a rabbit's legs, but the testes are large and contain, already, the germs and genes of the future. The treasury of Nature's germens. The body of the mother is out of shot beneath a sheet, so I cannot tell whether this is a natural or an unnatural childbirth. The tenderness of the portrait suggests that it must be natural.

The internet informs me that this is an image of the photographer's father delivering the photographer's son. It also informs me that the photographer, like me, is still alive. This is amazing information. I shall write him a fan letter.

My firstborn was a boy. Unlike Jess, I have more than one child. I have not been called upon to invest all my love in a one and only child.

~

Jess thinks that Steve must have given Zain her address. Having himself been deterred from turning up on Jess's doorstep, Steve handed on the address of that doorstep to Zain, and, one day, there he was. Jess now saw that, having rejected Bob and hospitalised Steve and escorted Anna back to Enfield, she had deliberately made a void for the dark stranger to enter.

As it turned out, Zain knew quite a lot of people at SOAS, including Guy Brighouse, Jess's one-time tutor and supervisor. Everybody, in all parts of the world, knew Guy. (It was said that if you came upon two men at an oasis in the desert, two men on an island in the Pacific, one of them would turn out to be Guy Brighouse.) Zain also knew Noah Trellisick, Steve's editor, who had produced an erudite little series of World Service poetry programmes at Bush House. And he knew Jim's wife, Katie, but made it clear that he didn't wish to meet her out of hours, which suited Jess fine. The intellectual community was smaller in those days, or seemed smaller. And it needed a man like Zain, to represent its commitment to what we did not yet call multiculturalism. In those distant days, we still spoke quaintly of the 'colour bar', of 'crossing the colour bar'. Zain was living proof that the Sudanese IQ was in no way inferior to the Caucasian IQ. Most people still secretly believed that blacks were mentally inferior to whites, but it was becoming more difficult to say so openly.

Those were the days of Hans Eysenck and fierce debates about racial intelligence and heritability. We needed Zain, even though we had driven him mad and egged him on to stab his wife.

We were casuists, fierce casuists in the cause of the equality of man. We ignored arguments from genes and nature and race. We were blind to so much. We ignored all those things that we did not want to know. We longed to alter destiny. Each child was born free, and born with all the possibility of the future stored up within it, packed within it. All we had to do was to release the future.

I suspect that Jess did not tell Zain much about Anna, whose IQ and good nature were immeasurable, and would not feature meaningfully on any chart or graph. Anna was absent, at Marsh Court.

Bob kept out of the way. He was said to have taken up with a pretty young zoologist in Cambridge.

We supposed that Zain and Jess would enjoy an intense affair, and that it would not last long. Jess let Zain into her bed but not into her home. We saw his arrivals and departures, we met him on the street corner, we smiled and said hello. But we did not get asked to supper.

Steve was still at Halliday Hall. He had managed to prolong his psychic convalescence for months. He would never be so happy again.

~

It was the illness at Marsh Court that ejected Zain.

That December, a severe attack of gastric flu had hit the school, and the director had decided it would have to close down early, as the sick bay was full and the bedrooms and classrooms had been turned into hospital wards, where fever-struck children were shitting and spewing into chamber pots. The director rang Jess and explained the situation. Anna was so far well, but should be removed from this epidemic as soon as possible.

He was trying to empty the school of all but the sick.

How very old-fashioned, how Victorian, all that sounds now. Like something out of *Jane Eyre*. But that's how it was.

I volunteered to drive Jess to collect Anna. God knows why, there must have been some reason, but I can't now remember what it was. Jess didn't drive, had never learnt to drive. Maybe I was at a loose end. Maybe I was curious and hoped Jess would tell me more about Zain. My children were by then beginning to be self-sufficient, well able to fend for themselves: they could cook themselves meals and run around on public transport and gang up to play football and mooch around in one another's bedrooms smoking secret cigarettes and talking about sex. (Cassie's Janie and Cilla's Chloe set the bedclothes on fire one night, on what we didn't yet call a sleepover, but they managed to put it out very promptly and efficiently.) Anna could do none of these things. My heart ached for Anna and Jess, and yet pity seemed then and seems now an inappropriate emotion.

Maybe it was guilt, the guilt of the healthy, the guilt of the normal, the guilt of the free. And yet I do not think I was guilty. I tried to be a good friend.

I do not wish to privilege my friendship with Jess. She had many friends. I was only one of many. I claim no special knowledge, no special relationship.

I must sometimes have annoyed her, I know that. My children must have annoyed her. Jake and Ike were good with Anna when she was little, I've already made that claim for them, and they continued to be good with her as they became teenagers. I tried not to rejoice too evidently in their successes, their accomplishments. I tried not to make tactless remarks or comparisons. But I must have done. I know I must have done.

~

A proleptic flash. I think this happened about ten years ago, perhaps fifteen years ago, long after that visit to plague-stricken Marsh Court, but it comes back to me vividly now, and in that context, in the context of remembering the sick schoolchildren. I was sitting on the top of the No. 7 bus, on the front seat at the right, travelling along Oxford Street. We had just passed Selfridges, that's when I saw him.

He was sitting on the opposite pavement, on a bench, holding a large placard, with homemade letters that were easy to read from the top deck where I sat. They said MUM IS DEAD.

He had a cap by him, for offerings.

The words rent my heart.

MUM IS DEAD.

We are familiar with the concept that God is dead. We accepted it long, long ago. The message that MUM IS DEAD is more powerful.

The bus stopped long enough for me to observe something of the man's age and features. Stoppages on Oxford Street are what one expects, and I was given time. He was middle aged, balding, in his forties, with large ears and a receding stubble-covered chin, and he was dressed in well-worn clothes that showed touching attempts at neatness.

Wordsworth, in London for the first time, saw on the street a blind beggar who appeared to him to be an emblematic figure. This beggar held *a written paper, to explain/ His story, whence he came, and who he was.* And so this man on Oxford Street appeared to me to be a portent, although his message was much briefer than the blind beggar's.

MUM IS DEAD.

I want to describe the man without the mother as a 'boy', but he was not a boy. He was a man. I have to keep reminding myself not to think of him as a boy.

The bench on which he sat was a grey concrete oval slab, without a back, standing on squat pedestal legs. Those benches are not designed for comfort. They are punitive, they are sacrificial.

~

On the way to Marsh Court that winter to collect Anna, as I negotiated the ill-planned nightmare traffic lanes of the North

Circular and then the A10, once such a pleasant rural highway, we did not talk about Zain. I didn't like to ask. There were things Jess and I talked about, and things we didn't talk about. We talked about Sylvie, who had just embarked on her intensive study of the bladder. We admired her for committing herself to long and specialised study in early middle age. We wondered why she had chosen the bladder, instead of all the more glamorous body parts she might have favoured. Now that we have all reached the age where our bladders grow weak and treacherous, we can see that she chose wisely and for the common good.

Last month, lunching with a colleague in a Thai restaurant in Oxford, I was obliged to retire to the ladies' room to remove my knickers to rinse them and dry them with the hand dryer. I had been caught short by a sudden burning spasm of cystitis and half a pint of Tiger beer. Bladders are important, but we took them for granted then, when we were young.

I was glad nobody caught me at it in the ladies', but the smell of hot breathy urine and cheap soap must have lingered after me. I stuffed the pants into a small resealable plastic bag that I happened to have in my handbag, a tribute to modern air travel, and returned to finish my lunch knickerless.

Air terrorism has had some small beneficial side effects, and the habit of carrying resealable plastic bags on one's person is one of them.

I told Jess this story the other day. She laughed.

No, we didn't foresee such humiliations in those early days, when we and our children were young and our bladders were strong.

We talked in the car about Sylvie and her son Stuart, who was going through a difficult patch, a delinquent adolescent patch, bunking off school, catching the bus to town, playing the Soho arcades. Perhaps he resented his mother's prolonged absences at UCH. That's the kind of thing we parents worried about then. Sylvie had the two boys, Stuart and Josh. Pretty boy Josh was still a good lad, though less perfect of feature than he had been as an infant, but Stuart had always been a handful – secretive, a little morose.

As we drove along we also spoke, Jess and I, it comes back to me now, about town planning and Modernism, comments provoked by the 1890s and 1930s suburban ribbon developments through which we were driving, and by the narrowness of the A10 and its inability to cope with the buses and cars that clogged and clutched and braked their way along it. There were some truly grim façades and stretches of shop frontage then, and they are no better now. I don't think the M25 existed then, or maybe we were avoiding it. Jess mentioned Keats and his long walks, and the yellow globe flowers in the River Lee, and the peaceful lock of old Enfield. I asked after Jess's father, whom I liked and who had always been courteous and gallant to me whenever we met. He was well, Jess said, in good health, but still downcast by Brutalism.

Broughborough had just approved a Brutal new shopping centre, windowless, fortress-like, with car parks above and below, with arrow slits in its concrete walls from which to defend the shoppers against the enemy.

Those were early days for shopping centres, the early days of the Arndale vernacular, a Northern style which was to prove a popular target for the IRA in the seventies and for Al Qaeda in the next millennium. Those arrow slits provoked attack; they incited the enemy. Nobody loved the Arndales except their begetters, Sam Chippendale and Arnold Hagenbach. Philip Speight knew Sam Chippendale well, in the years of his ascendance, Jess told me. A bustling, dapper, confident chap, a property dealer, a first-class salesman who played the Yorkshire stereotype. He lived in style in a handsome old-fashioned house in the country near Harrogate and ran a silver Jag driven by a lady chauffeur. He didn't live in a Brutalist home.

It all went wrong for him too. The property slump of the seventies got him. Now the Arndale Centres are being rebranded and their infamous names are being written out of planning history. The rebuilt IRA-damaged Manchester Arndale still defiantly keeps its title, but others are lowering their profiles.

'Sweetness and light, that's what Pa dreamt of,' said Jess, watching the grubby ugly high-street façades as they passed us by. Sweetness and light. Modernism, not Brutalism. It had all gone wrong.

Anna, excited and animated, was overjoyed to see her mother, and full of stories of the sickness that had seized the school. She was delighted that term had come to an end early, and when she had finished telling us about the vomiting in the classrooms and the blocked toilets and the camp-beds in the corridors, she interrogated us about all her friends at home: Ollie and Polly, Chloe and Jane, Stuart and Josh and Becky and Nicky and Ben. I gave her the latest on Jake's piano lessons and on Ike's latest bicycling accident, about which she was very sympathetic. She asked, of course, after Bob, and was told he had gone back to live in Camden Town. This silenced her for a mile or two, but she seemed to absorb the information, and did not refer to it again. She was a sensitive child, a sensitive young woman, and her manners were always good. She had a natural tact.

As we approached home territory, she inquired after Steve. This subject was easier to address. Steve was much, much better. He was in a very nice place, not too far from Marsh Court, where he had a lot of new friends. What were they called? They were called Simon, Patrick, Ursula and Raoul. And Dr Nicholls. Jess hadn't met Dr Nicholls, but she'd heard a lot about him. He was a very nice man, said Jess.

'Raoul,' repeated Anna. She liked the name. She made it sound like a friendly howl, a jackal laugh. Raoul. Raoul. It stayed in her memory, as odd words and phrases did, and she repeated it, occasionally, over the years. 'Where is Raoul?' she would ask. But over the years Jess did not know, did not expect she would ever know, although she sometimes thought of him.

Jess had never caught his surname, and maybe she never heard it.

Zain, of course, was not mentioned by Jess on this homeward journey. Zain's days in Jess's calendar, it was easy to tell, were numbered.

~

Jess was to look back on the Zain episode as a necessary passage, an encounter of its time and of her time. It had been intense and emblematic, at once physical and spiritual, she told herself, to still a slight sense of shame at her own too eager surrender. He had told her stories, as Othello had told Desdemona, and she had listened, for the time bewitched. He had appeased a longing in her, a longing for the faraway world she had been forbidden, just as the dean's daughter had appeased through him a more fleshly and subversive longing.

Zain had indeed been married to a dean's daughter, Jess established. That was no fairy-story. He had married her, and stabbed her, and although, unlike Othello, he had not killed his wife, he continued staunchly to maintain that it was largely her fault. She was a dean's daughter, but (and) she was a heavy drinker who could not hold her liquor. Their brief marriage had been an alcoholic haze. They had been married by Special Licence, and both, as they swore their solemn vows, had been pissed out of their minds.

The BBC drank a lot in those days. Corporately and individually, it drank. It drank before the programme, it drank after the programme, and then it repaired to the pub. It is far more sober now. Other sections of society drink far more these days, but the BBC drinks much less.

According to Zain, he and the dean's daughter had met at a garden party in a cathedral close. Imagine, Zain had said to Jess (and no doubt to many others), imagine, the slim cool young lady in the big wide-brimmed straw hat, the tasteless wet cucumber sandwiches, the sugary little iced cakes, the cathedral spire, the vestments, the distant music playing. A charming English scene, and the big black intruder. It was some kind of ecumenical fête, I'd been invited with my director, said Zain, they wanted a bit of colonial colour. I was the right colour, and I was cultured, I was a totem, I would do, I would dress the set, I would be allowed to walk on the green and pose for the photographs. She made straight for me, she hung on me, she flirted and played with me, she played the bad girl, she was wicked with me.

She had a half-bottle of gin in her handbag and behind the marquee she laced my juice, complained Zain. And then she married me, and then she provoked me, and then I attacked her with a kitchen knife, and here I am.

Jess believed most of this story. Something along those lines had surely happened.

Zain had particularly loathed the cucumber sandwiches. He had not realised, he said, that in England they were a cultural marker, a sanctified repast, a literary reference. They were disgusting. They were limp and wet. They were like slime in the mouth.

Jess had listened to this diatribe with professional fascination. It had not occurred to her, even though she was an anthropologist, that anyone could take so strongly against a harmless cucumber sandwich. Zain liked the spiced and the fiery, the burnt and the grilled, the red and the black and the orange. She found it easy to understand his dislike, to savour the sandwiches with his Sudanese palate, and she says she has never felt quite the same about them since.

She learnt a lot from Zain, but, when Anna came home early from school, she dismissed him. He disappeared, without protest, as Bob before him had disappeared.

He went home to the Sudan, but later we learnt he was back in Europe. Civil war and drought and famine drove him back. He was a very gifted man. He wrote an important book on Sub-Saharan economics which has come to be cited as a classic. Halliday Hall and Dr Nicholls rescued Zain, although Zain did not manage to rescue the Sudan. The Sudan was too much for him, and he lives in exile. He's not well. We expect to see his name in the obituary columns shortly. We think he's living in Paris.

He was lucky to be ill at the right time, in the right place. Jess still thinks at times of the large brown teapot and the Marie biscuits. Those had been kindly days.

She sometimes wonders what happened to Raoul, to Simon, to Patrick, to Ursula. Zain had thought highly of Raoul. He had predicted a future for him. A clever man, Zain had said. 'A clever man, washed up in the therapeutic wastes of Essex. Watch out for him,' said Zain.

She sometimes wonders, as she continues perforce to consider the problems of mental-health care, whether or not Dr Nicholls had been an inspired healer, or whether, more probably, he had arbitrarily and somewhat improperly selected interesting cases for his particular attention. He and his little group had certainly profited from a golden moment in NHS theory and practice. She has seen Dr Nicholls's name, occasionally, in the medical press. She thinks that he moved into private practice, not long after Halliday Hall was closed down on grounds of cost. Occasionally, sitting on a bus or watching telly with Anna, she thinks she will google him, out of curiosity, but she always forgets.

~

Jess was to enter, after Zain, into a long and stable period of celibacy, a lake with still waters. Some of us were not so lucky: divorce and desertion riddled our comfortable little encampments, adulteries laid siege to us, and disputes over property split us and scattered us. Jess had retired from the field. The strange trinity of the Professor, Bob and Zain had provided variety and conquest enough for her youth and middle years, and she and Anna settled into a calmer domestic rhythm.

After a few years Anna graduated from Marsh Court and came home to Jess. Her social worker Karen, looking ahead to the as yet unimaginable days of Jess's old age, suggested a placement at a residential sheltered home near Taunton in Somerset ('very nice' she insisted), but Jess declined. She visited, and saw that it was indeed very nice, as far as niceness goes, but she declined. She could manage perfectly well as she was, she and Anna could manage together, she'd organised her bookish working life to accommodate Anna. Anna was safe to leave alone in the house for brief stretches of time (though never for the night) and, despite the divorces and desertions, there was still a neighbourhood network of friends to help out in need, and the Day Centre, and other voluntary support groups. I was still around, and so was Katie. Sylvie had moved up-market to an elegant Georgian house in Canonbury, and Ollie's mother, Sarah, had moved too, not as smartly as Sylvie, but not very far, and still on the bus route. It seemed that Jess and Anna would continue together, companionably becalmed, through the next decades. It did not do to look too far ahead.

I saw somewhat less of Jess and Anna during these years. My boys were grown and had more or less left home, one for university and what was to be an academic career, the other for Bolivia. The after-school mothers' gatherings in one another's houses had come to a natural end. I had been promoted and the organisation which employed me was expanding rapidly, I thought too rapidly. I was now working longer hours, and so was my husband, who was wearing himself out in the service of the state. (Northern Ireland nearly killed him, and I mean that literally.) I still went round to Jess's for supper by myself occasionally, and we would arrange to meet for a walk in the park. And once or twice – I am sorry it was not more often, but I plead that I was busy – I would step in to keep Anna company when Jess had an unavoidable engagement. Anna and I went to the theatre once to see Maroussia in *Twelfth Night*, and once, God knows why, we went on a coach ride to Windsor.

Anna was easy company, always appreciative, and always very keen to say thank you for everything. But she was a worry. I worried about losing her when she was in my charge, as I grew older I began to worry more about road accidents, and I worried about strangers being rude to her. It wasn't good when she stepped on that woman's handbag on the Windsor coach. I can see that woman's ugly angry broad red pig face, her thick neck, her angry grey curls to this day. And I suspect Anna can too.

But Jess and Anna, during these years, had many happy times. Our children were changing almost beyond recognition, as they emerged from adolescence and embarked on gap years, degree courses, ambitions, careers and disappointments, as they discovered whether they were gay or straight and had tragic love affairs and, eventually, some of them, babies. It was not like that for Jess and Anna, for whom the concept of progress was in perpetual abeyance. But there were many things that they liked to do together. They liked walking, and they explored the London parks and galleries. Anna was surprisingly tolerant of, indeed keen on, exhibitions, and they visited the traditional and the avant-garde. Anna had a good eye, and could sometimes make sense of paintings that baffled us and Jess. 'Look,' she'd say, 'it's a boat'– and when you looked, you could see that it was.

They enjoyed some of the same movies. When Anna was little, they used to go to shows in the extraordinary and fantastic world of the Finsbury Park Astoria, then a twinkling oriental fairyland of fun, with a fountain full of goldfish, and balconies and cupolas and shining stars, suggesting a vast hinterland of wonder behind its stucco façades. It was a real treat and we all missed it when it closed down. (The Finsbury Park Astoria belongs to some kind of extreme religious sect these days, it's far more way out than the Finsbury Park mosque.) I can't remember which cinemas took over as the children grew up – did we have to go down to Upper Street and the Angel? I can't remember.

Anna loved Hollywood musicals, *Star Wars*, Shakespeare and Jane Austen adaptations. One of her favourite movies was a bizarre and innocent fantasia featuring a Hollywood bathing belle performing aquatic wonders under water in a great blue shining lake full of lilies and fish and mermaids and swaying greenery. She saw this one Sunday afternoon on television at Marsh Court and described it to Jess, who tracked it down on video and bought a copy. Anna played it again and again. (They weren't supposed to watch daytime TV at Marsh Court, but of course they did.) Anna admired her heroine's muscular but well-curved physique, her turquoise bathing suit with its stylish sparkling silver trim, her old-fashioned flower-petalled bathing cap, and the way, on shore, she released and shook out her long blonde hair.

Jess enjoyed this video too. It was much pleasanter than James

Bond. When DVDs became available, she bought Anna a DVD of the underwater Venus. Anna never tired of it, and Jess enjoyed glimpses of it for the pleasure it gave her daughter. And they found other swimming movies, with Esther Williams, Glynis Johns, Annette Kellerman. Mermaid movies, Neptune's daughters, synchronised swimming – all these delighted them.

But best of all Anna liked, herself, to swim. She was happy to swim in chlorinated water, in ionised water, in sea water, in fresh water, in brooks, in waves, in rivers and in standing ponds. She loved the water. She was not an elegant swimmer, though she had by now graduated from dog-paddle to what Dr Livingstone called frog-fashion, but she was strong, and bolder in the water than on land. She had been awarded swimming badges by the club at the sports centre where she used to swim. Jess had sewn them on to her bathing suit, and Anna was always pleased when people asked her what they were for: for swimming ten lengths, for diving for a brick, for jumping off the springboard, for good attendance.

In the summer, Anna and Jess would take a day trip to the seaside, to Brighton or Hastings or Seaford, and occasionally a group of us would go on an outing. Nearer home, Jess and Anna liked the Hampstead Ladies' Bathing Pond, and would catch the Northern Line to Belsize Park and walk over the Heath with their swimming things and a picnic and a book to read. Jess was to remember one sunny day in late July, when for a while the world stood still and all was well. Anna was lying sunning herself on one of the creaking dank wooden landing stages (these were the days before we were told to fear the sun), and Jess was reading Proust.

English people reading Proust often manifest a degree of self-consciousness, and Jess was no exception. She felt a sense of solid and almost visible virtue as she lay in her stalwart royal-blue bathing suit on her yellow towel on the grass, making her way through the *Jeunes Filles en fleurs*, which she was reading in the Scott Moncrieff translation. It was a good summer read, a seaside holiday bathing pool read, and it took her back to her childhood holidays with her parents and Vee in North Wales. North Wales was not very like Proust's Balbec, but she had been a *jeune fille en fleur* at the time, and had courted and caught the eye of many a fellow-bather and promenader. She had even made an assignation behind the ice-cream hut, and exchanged a ridiculous kiss with a boy from Liverpool.

Jess was reading Proust with an incentive. She was reading him not competitively but companionably, in concert with an old schoolfriend from Broughborough with whom she had kept in touch. They met rarely, for her friend Vivien lived in Edinburgh, where she was the assistant curator of a gallery, but they had preserved their intimacy through Vivien's occasional London visits and through sending one another postcards and letters. They had enjoyed their English and French classes at school together, and this was a way of perpetuating their pleasure into adult life, maybe old age. (The reading group had not yet become a nationwide phenomenon.) Jess and Vivien had already read their way through *Ulysses*, encouraging one another onwards by exchanging comments and moments of bewilderment and enlightenment, and now they were doing Proust. Would they reach the end? They were not sure. It wouldn't matter if they didn't; nobody was watching them, nobody was marking them, there were no exams to sit, no teachers to impress.

Jess had made notes to herself on sentences she had particularly appreciated, thinking perhaps to share them with Viv, and now looked back at a passage that had curiously captivated her. The Marquis de Norpois, the sententious and elderly diplomat who persists in giving bad literary advice to Proust's young narrator, is recommending as a model the career of a young friend of his who has quit the diplomatic service for the life of a man of letters. The titles of this novice littérateur's works had filled Jess with inexplicable delight. He had written, claimed the marquis, a book dealing with the Sense of the Infinite on the Western Shore of Victoria Nyanza, and a monograph on the Repeating Rifle in the Bulgarian Army – the latter 'not so important as the other, but very brightly, in places perhaps almost too pointedly written', commented M. de Norpois, 'and these have put him quite in a class by himself'.

Jess knew that these subjects were ludicrous, and intended to be so, but nevertheless she liked this ageing novice littérateur with his random mind, for she too has a random mind, and the thought of the sense of the infinite on the shore of Lake Nyanza entrances her. Proust might make fun, but she can see it, the borderless lake extending to infinity, as she had seen Bangweulu and its swamps and marshes and ant hills and its low horizons, the land of the blue shoebill and the shy dark sitatunga.

She sees also as she pauses from her reading the River Lee and the lilies and the flurries of little red and golden birds, she sees the canal and the moorhens, she sees the Hampstead Ladies' Bathing Pond and Anna and the fringe of sallows and elders and the dark brown water lapping, as she now hears the slow strokes of an elderly stout swimmer, the ripple of the water, the faint hum of hover flies, the murmurs of conversations. The pond and the little lake stretch timelessly towards infinity, the river flows for ever and imperceptibly. Out of time, all is well for the ageing mother and the ageless daughter.

~

There were, of course, many awkward moments for Jess and Anna during these years, small patches of crisis and anxiety in their conjoined lives, and the minor difficulties that arose foreshadowed more to come. Let us take one incident as an example, which Jess did not report until well after it was over. This was a worrying episode when Jess came down with a chest infection and had to take to her bed. I think Anna must have been in her late teens or early twenties – not long after the days of Marsh Court. A big girl, a grown woman. Jess was hardly ever ill, enjoying good health and a strong constitution, but that February she found she was running a temperature. Her breathing wheezed and her chest rattled and she felt very hot. She put herself to bed, with jugs of water and aspirin, and tried to keep Anna at a distance, for she did not want to communicate whatever it was that she had caught. It did not occur to her to get in touch with her doctor, even though in those days home visits were still a possibility, because she had little faith in the doctor, and anyway she reasoned that whatever she was suffering from would pass of its own accord. She did not hold with antibiotics.

She was right: the infection did pass – but not before it had caused distress to Anna.

Anna hated to see her mother lying in bed, so uncharacteristically inert and helpless, and she did her best to tend to her. She followed Jess's instruction about food, bringing to the bedside the tins of baked beans and pineapple rings that Jess kept in store as emergency provisions, and running back downstairs for the tin opener and 'one of those stripy blue-and-white bowls, you know where they are, they're in the cupboard by the fridge'. Jess didn't want to eat, she had lost her appetite, but she opened the tins (Anna couldn't really manage that bit), and she watched Anna eating. So far, so good, and not unlike a treat or a picnic, but when Anna set off down the stairs with the bowl and the tins and the spoon and the tin opener she slipped and fell headlong quite heavily and gashed her inner forearm on one of the open lids which Jess had folded down, but not quite carefully enough.

Anna was never very sure-footed, and had a tendency to fall, to trip and to walk into objects.

Jess, from her bed, heard the crash, and heard Anna's suppressed yelp of pain, and called anxiously, but the muffled tone of Anna's answering shout 'I'm all right, Mum, I'm all right' was not reassuring. Jess heaved herself out of bed and to the landing, where she saw Anna trying to upright herself, while simultaneously trying to pick up the tins and the bowl and the cutlery and to dab at the stair carpet with her skirt.

Jess saw the red blood from the shallow gash.

The open edges of the gash needed stitches, really, but Jess was not up to organising stitches. She could not face the doctor, the hospital, the ambulance, the out-patients' department, the confrontations with abusive or judgemental others. They sat together, mother and daughter, on the step, each assuring the other that no serious harm was done. Then Jess went up to the bathroom, and sat Anna down on the white-painted wooden bathroom stool with its old cork top. She found the TCP, washed the wound, pulled it together as best she could, bandaged it and tied up the bandage with Elastoplast strips. After a while the vivid scarlet blood stopped seeping through the white cocoon. The wound would leave a scar, but it would heal. Vanity might have dictated stitches, but survival did not.

It didn't hurt very much, Anna assured her mother. Jess told her she was a very brave and helpful girl. Jess reassured herself that at least her bathroom cabinet had been adequately supplied. How much worse things could have been. How very much worse.

When I learnt, much later, about this episode, I told Jess she should have called me and I'd have gone to help. But of course she didn't. She liked to be independent.

~

When you are young, you do not think you will grow old. I remember my father saying that to me one morning, over breakfast, when I'd gone back home to Kent for a long weekend to help out with my mother, who'd just had a hip operation. They were wondering whether to sell the family home, to buy a bungalow. We call it downsizing now, but we didn't then. We hadn't yet coined that familiarising, patronising, dismissive, yet helpful term for decline and retrenchment, for the beginning of the flat, slow and then descending and accelerating march to death and the little, little room of the grave.

'Nellie,' he said, 'you don't know what it is to be old. I've only one piece of advice for you, Nellie. Don't grow old.' He was smiling gently, compassionately, as he spoke.

I laughed, and ate my half-grapefruit. 'I'll try not to,' I assured him. I was young, vigorous, immortal. I knew I and my children and my children's children would never grow old, and we would never die.

I knew I would never die, but I also knew that I would, in the event, when forced, grow old gracefully. I would not complain, as my mother complained. I would not even joke about old age, as my father joked.

And then, after that, I would die.

I am not allowed to eat grapefruit now. It disagrees with my medication.

It's strange how old age creeps up, a process that is watched, with varying degrees of denial, by everyone in every generation throughout history. None escape, unless saved by sudden death. Some of us have aged well, some badly. I never see Jim now, since the separation and the divorce, but Katie looks good, her complexion unlined, a tribute to her genes or to HRT or to decades of Boots moisturiser, who can say. She still lives round the corner, having won the battle over the marital home, and will have done very well out of that deal. Maroussia looks 'wonderful', unnaturally wonderful, and has probably had a facelift, as women in her profession are increasingly obliged to do. She has homes elsewhere, on at least three continents, but she still has the old house in Camden, and keeps in touch with us. Chloe's father, Tim, has Parkinson's and does not go out much, and Chloe's mother accordingly looks lined, grey, hunched and worn out, as one would expect. Andrew's parents have moved out of the neighbourhood and beyond our knowledge: I think they went to live in Dorset. Steve has put on weight and looks like a Michelin man. Bob, who has somewhat surprisingly come back into our lives, looks as boyish and buoyant as ever. He is a sweet-natured man, and his hair is still thick and curly.

And Anna still looks girlish. Womanly, but girlish.

I think nuns used to look like that, in the old days. Clear skin, soft curves, uncorseted bodies. Anna never wears a bra. Her body is soft and yielding. I think she has no sexual interests, no libido, or very little libido, which is fortunate. Jess mentioned at one point that Anna's menstruation came late, and lightly. This again seemed fortunate. She would have been vulnerable, with her trusting nature, had she needed to go out with the boys. She talks sometimes of 'boy friends', but I don't think the phrase has a sexual meaning for her.

Some of us, on rejuvenating HRT, bled like stuck pigs. *And on our skirts and knickers gouts of blood.* As Lady Macbeth might have observed. It was one of the side effects.

Sylvie Raven's appearance does not at first glance betray the ordeals she has suffered. It is a tribute to the success she has achieved, the official eminence she has acquired. If you did not know her history (but alas many people do, or at one time did, as the press at the time did not respect her privacy), you would not know from her well-tailored, well-coiffed, confident demeanour that her life had been marked by family disgrace. Baroness Raven of Riversdale looks impregnable. Her hair is a well-cut, dyed, golden helmet, with not a strand straying. She has left the operating theatre and the hospital board for the theatre of the House of Lords, where her token female medical presence is as necessary and as useful as Zain's was at the dean's tea party in the cathedral close.

Public life suits Sylvie. Private life let her down, but public life has given her a patina, a posture and a confidently loud voice. She can be heard from the other end of the street, across a crowded room, in any public arena.

She is eminent, but simultaneously obscure. There are many such people in public life. You can read their obituaries in the press any day of the week, and wonder why you have never heard of them before. They are the honoured of the nation who have lived diligently and served their country well. They take their place in the obituary columns along with the celebrities, who usually die younger. You have never heard of most of those either. I still know Sylvie because we were neighbours in the old days, and still are, and because my children knew her children. I've followed her career with admiration.

My son Ike stuck by her son and his schoolmate Joshua, and went to visit him in his open prison near Grantham. He took him a few books and a lemon cake from the shop at Highbury Barn. I was proud of him for that.

Yes, Sylvie has weathered well. She has faced them out.

~

As for me, I look in the mirror, and I remember my aunt saying staunchly, aged ninety, 'I don't like to look in the mirror any more, so I don't.'

I think sometimes, indeed quite often, of that Sixth Form

school trip to Paris from Orpington. We went to Folkestone and caught the ferry to Calais. Most of us had never been abroad before. We were sixteen, seventeen. It was very exciting, and we were full of hope for our future. The ferry ploughed its noisy way across the Channel, accompanied by seagulls, and we rejoiced in the salt wind, and some of us were sick.

In Paris, we went to some talks at the Sorbonne, and to a performance at the Comédie-Française, and visited Notre-Dame, and bought postcards and posters at the stalls along the embankment. And we went to the Rodin Museum near the Invalides. I remember the postcards of Monet and Manet and Renoir and Van Gogh and Picasso, but I remember best of all the Rodin.

The sculptures of Rodin were already familiar to us in post-card format. He was in those days popular with schoolgirls but also acceptable to schoolteachers, because his works were sensuous yet chaste. Most of us hated Renoir. His women were so fat and so pink. They threatened us. But Rodin offered us a body image to which we could more happily if fruitlessly aspire. The doubly colourless medium of marble and of print had introduced us to his elegantly severed hands, to the eternally arrested lovers of *Le Baiser*, to the voluptuously curved spine of his mourning *Danaïd*. The women crouched and curled within the bronze and the marble, and their embryo forms as they emerged from the matrix, were pleasing to us. No skin, no pores, no misplaced hairs. We knew quite a few of those images, and we thought we admired them. We had no training in art history and very little knowledge of what we were looking at, but we walked, we paused, we admired.

It was there, in the Musée Rodin, that I came across the bronze of the old woman. This was not a smooth picture-postcard image. I was unprepared for the shock of the woman's naked body. That old woman of Rodin lacks all dignity. Her image wounds, insults, reduces. I stood, transfixed, appalled and undefended.

How did I know then what she meant? Why did I not calmly turn away, in my healthy seventeen-year-old arrogance? What was she to me? What kinship with me did she claim? Why did I fear her withered arms? Why did I even *notice* her? I have as yet no answers to these questions.

She is called by several names, although when I was seventeen I took in only that she was an old woman. Now I know that she is *La Belle Heaulmière*, or *The Helmet-Maker's Once Beautiful Wife*. She is also *Winter*. She is also *The Old Courtesan*. Literary prototypes from the works of Villon and Dante have been proposed for her, of which the Villon seems to me much the most plausible, though what I think is neither here nor there. She is old, and scraggy, and ugly. She is a *memento mori*. She is worse than a *memento mori*, for in comparison with this condition, death were welcome. She is, I suppose, witchlike, but she lacks the malevolence and the energy of the three weird sisters from *Macbeth*, the play we were then studying back in Orpington for our A-Level English examinations. She is drooped, sagged, imploded. She is passive. She is a passive recipient of the battery, the assault of time, and of the contempt of men. Her breasts are dry and dangle, her ribs stand out, her skin hangs in folds from her withering frame, her back is bowed in submission.

One of Rodin's titles for her was *Vanitas*. I suppose we were all full of *vanitas* when we were seventeen. Vanity is natural, it is normal, it is not to be punished by sculptors.

Who sat for this piece of scrag? What unfortunate creature achieved this dubious form of immortality? It's fashionable to inquire about artists' models these days, it's an aspect of modern feminist scholarship. I'm sure someone will have written about her.

Quand je pense, lasse! au bon temps,
Quelle fus, quelle devenue,
Quand me regarde toute nue,
Et je me voy si très changée,
Pauvre, sèche, maigre, menue,
Je suis presque toute enragée . . .

Standing in front of that sculpture, aged seventeen, I travelled, fast-forward, towards the end of my life, and to a condition which I have not yet reached, for there is still flesh on my ribs. My skin, although unaided by Botox, does not hang. It is still firm, at least in places. It is not as unnaturally firm as Maroussia's, but it is firm.

What shall I be, in another decade? If I am spared for, or condemned to, another decade?

Nellie, don't grow old. That's what my father was to say.

She hit me in the stomach, *La Belle Heaulmière*, the helmet-maker's wife. The helmet-maker's once beautiful wife.

I would go to look at her once more before I died.

~

Marsh Court, Troutwell, Halliday Hall, Colney Hatch, Kingsley Hall, the old Priory at Roehampton, the new Priory at Southgate, the vast ruins of Lionel Penrose's Severalls asylum at Colchester, Graylingwell at Chichester – Jess got to know about them all, and some she visited, pursuing her own agenda, her own obsessions, her own long journey.

Friern Barnet at Colney Hatch in North London has been translated and renovated, and its imposing palatial Italianate Gothic façade now fronts 'luxury' flats and a health club with a gym and a deep blue steaming tropical basement swimming pool. In the gym muscular and threatening and probably unemployed and unemployable men work out grimly hour after hour, but the general atmosphere of the club is playful and cosmetic. The cupola and the gatehouse are still for sale, for a few millions. The whole of the hilltop estate has been renamed Princess Park Manor, and its driveways are now known as Regal Drive, Balmoral Avenue, Hampton Close, Duchess Close, Baron Close, Viscount Close, Kensington Close, Earl Close and Highgrove, as shameless an attempt at rebranding as Jess has ever encountered. She rather fancied the Gatehouse. She has often thought it would be pleasant to live in a gatehouse, on a border between two domains, on a threshold.

The new Manor is a gated community, possibly even more heavily gated and patrolled and spied upon than it was in its asylum days. The extensive grounds where the trusted inmates tended their horses and cows, their pigs and sheep, their fowl and ferrets and their mangold-wurzels, are now a planted urban landscape, little patronised, it seemed to Jess, by the busy flat-dwellers.

Up near Broughborough the asylum of Arden Gate still stands, and still shelters a few inmates who have been there for decades. It would be unkind to move them now, and the authorities have turned a blind eye and left them alone. A small staff of ageing carers tends them. They will all die soon, the carers and the cared-for alike. Philip Speight had a hand in their protection. He was on the hospital board at the time when decisions were made. It was hard to decide what to do with so many acres. The water tower and one or two of the Queen Anne-style buildings (another style curiously popular with architects for the lunatic poor) were listed, and some of the ancient trees from the days of the old parkland, oaks and cedars and sweet chestnuts and a mulberry, had protection orders on them.

Philip Speight was particularly tender towards the inept and the vulnerable, because he loved his daughter and his granddaughter. They had educated him.

The asylum that had housed Halliday Hall, out in Essex beyond Marsh Court, has succumbed to time. It has been invaded by squatters and subjected to arson. Some of its buildings are listed and therefore cannot be demolished, but it cannot be developed either. It stands, a vast monument to institutional paralysis, to the inertia of mind and matter to which a campaigning and reforming minister of health called Enoch Powell had referred way back in 1962. It is a brownfield site awaiting a revelation, a new world order. All the optimism that built it has drained away. Someone has written in huge red dripping bleeding letters upon an inner corridor wall MY WOUNDS CRY 4 THE GRAVE. This is a fine biblical message of despair. Unplumbed sinks and baths and lavatories stand around, as though construction or renovation had been arbitrarily halted one day as funds ran out. Weeds push up through the broken tiles; brambles and roses nod in through the windows. It is Sleeping Beauty's domain.

Jess, disobeying warnings about 'Private Land' and CCTV, climbs over the perimeter fence, helping Anna over it after her, and they eat their tuna sandwiches and cherries in the long grass, in an ancient unpruned orchard of knotted apple trees and plum trees. The jagged initials and names of long-ago inmates are scarred into the trunks of the beech and oak trees. TOM, PK, JB, BOB. The grey bark has risen to enfold them, the sap has risen within them and swelled their lips, but still they speak.

The oaks and the mulberry long predate the asylum. The trees live for centuries.

There is a newish lavatory bowl, still swathed in its dirty builder's-yard Lazarus bandages. It stands alone, like a throne, in a derelict courtyard. Could this have been the very courtyard where Jess visited Steven and first met Zain? This expensive ceramic object had never reached its destination. It reminds Jess of something she has seen, long ago, and it comes to her that in Africa, all those many years ago when she was young, the anthropologists had been shown just such a bowl, standing surreal and abandoned on a concrete platform on a little brownish grassy African slope by a giant anthill. It had never been, would never be, installed. There was no need for it, no call for it. It was a symbol. It was a wonder of the villages, it was a wonder that it had travelled so far. It was famous far and wide through the unplumbed swamps of Bangweulu. Graham Hayter had photographed Guy Brighouse sitting on it. The only lavatory in Bangweulu.

She had forgotten it, and now it comes back to her.

The anthropologists had crapped in earth latrines and behind thorn bushes, worrying about snakes.

They were told, all those years ago, of a colonial administrator in Northern Rhodesia who'd had a lavatory installed inside an immense baobab tree, but they never got to see it.

Jess reads the Gospels, contemplates the miracles of Jesus and the acts of the apostles. Jesus cured the halt and the lame and the bleeding. He cured the diseased womb. He cured the epileptic, a lunatick who fell often into the fire and often into the water. He made the blind to see and the deaf to hear.

She cannot find much in the Gospels about the simple-minded. Are they the same category as the poor in heart?

Icipuba, kapupushi, ukupena, icipumputu.

Jess wrote a paper on Lionel Penrose's work on Down's syndrome at the Colchester asylum. Penrose's law, which stated that the population of prisons and psychiatric hospitals is inversely related, is not of particular interest to her, nor is she strongly attracted to his mathematical fantasies – the impossible triangle, the endless staircase. No, she is more concerned with his attitudes to his patients – Quakerly, respectful, mildly optimistic. She wonders if there was some redistributive element for him in his field of research. From an extravagantly gifted family, with clear marks of an inherited mathematical genius, he chose to spend years with simpletons (a term he personally preferred to the word 'feeble-minded'), worrying at causation and heredity. Penrose, like the Annual Reports of the Asylum for Idiots which he quotes so eloquently, wished to 'disimprison the soul of the Idiot'.

Disimprison is a good word, a surprising word to find in an official report. *Soul* is a good word also.

Jess studies these documents, and has been studying them over the decades. She persists.

Wordsworth, in his celebrated letter to his cocky young admirer John Wilson in defence of his ballad *The Idiot Boy*, accused Wilson of disliking and misinterpreting the poem because of the use of the word 'idiot'. *If there had been any such word in our language, to which we had attached passion, as lack-wit, half-wit, witless, etc., I should certainly have employed it in preference; but there is no such word.*

This is what Wordsworth wrote, in self-defence. Jess thinks about this a good deal.

There is no such word.

One of her old friends at SOAS, with whom she keeps in touch, had left academe and ethnography and anthropology and moved very profitably into advertising, into what we now call the creative industries. Many of the brightest and best in those days made this move, and he was one of them. He is good at brand names, at rebranding and re-creating concepts. Maybe she should ask him about the word 'idiot'. 'Special needs' and 'learning difficulties' are good phrases, useful phrases, dignified phrases, but Jess thinks there must be something still better to be plucked from the circumambient twenty-first-century air.

Something that would suit Anna even better. Anna, the pure gold baby.

Les enfants du bon Dieu.

~

Jess was right about Vincent's prognosis: it was, in the long run, better than Anna's. Years of intensive and expensive pharmaceutical research eventually produced medication that redressed whatever chemical imbalance or neurological disturbance had plagued him since birth, and he ceased to rage and swear and jerk and fret. He never became a model citizen, but he became independent, better-tempered, reasonably amenable. He got a job in a Turkish restaurant, married the boss's daughter, got stuck into dubious wheelings and dealings on Green Lanes about which his mother Susie did not inquire too closely, had two children and went regularly to the Arsenal, where he could shout as loud as he wished. It was a good outcome. He had made good progress.

Anna, as we have seen, made no progress at all. She was becalmed. There was no story to her life, no plot. The concept of progress did not apply to Anna. Events happened, but they did not impinge upon her. Unexpected crises occurred within her circle, like the melodramatic arrest and conviction of Joshua Raven, but they did not affect Anna, although they touched her. She listened to the Josh scandal with sympathy, with interest and concern, as she listened to the affairs of television stars and celebrities, as she followed the story lines of soap operas, but she did not see herself as a protagonist in the narrative of her own life.

She was unhappy when she saw Josh's photo in the press, after the conviction.

Anna loved soap operas. She loved the small daily dramas, the ebb and flow of minimal fates, the lovable characters, the bad but well-intentioned villains, the lame ducks, the matriarchs, the emotional separations and reunions, the petty crimes. She became worried when the plot took an unexpectedly violent turn, but fortunately for her peace of mind so did most of the programme producers and the scriptwriters, and daily life on screen reverted readily to the norm. Things went on and on in soap opera, as they did in Anna's life. People lived on, ageing only slowly, many of them ageing more slowly (as in Proust's soap opera) than in real life, until external and arbitrary pressures such as a star actor's desertion dictated sudden death. Anna knows all about the stars and their troubles and some of the reasons why they suddenly disappear. She is, in her way, a sophisticated viewer. She absorbs the information from the fan magazines.

Jess, watching Anna watching the screen, would think back to the shining lake, and remember the days when she had had other, less domestic horizons. Occasionally, she wondered if she would ever go back to Africa. She still from time to time dreamt of the lake and the lobster-claw children punting their little wooden barks. These dreams were, she decided, Jungian dreams of the collective unconscious, the dreams which had given birth to Anna. From that great lake all life forms had arisen, there they had all been engendered. All life came out of Africa, from the Sense of the Infinite on the Western Shore of Victoria Nyanza.

Jess did not like to see Africa on television. She disliked wildlife programmes, and not only because some of them were made by Bob Bartlett. She had forgiven herself for her bad treatment of him, and allowed him over her doorstep from time to time for a meal and a chat. But she didn't like his programmes, because they tended, although obliquely, to anthropomorphise. She didn't even like David Attenborough's programmes. She didn't like watching antelope running free on the savannah, or crocodiles lugging wounded buffalo into the Zambezi, or leopards hanging in trees like strange and lazy fruit, posing smugly for the camera. Still less did she like programmes about the Masai or starving children in the Sudan.

Programmes about deformity weren't as popular then as they have since become, but programmes about famine were ubiquitous.

I worked in those early days for a charity, once small but now of international repute, which placed teachers and student teachers in schools in what we still called the Third World. Missionary work has been taken over by NGOs, most of them secular. There are missionaries in my ancestry a long way back, as I've mentioned, lower-middle-class upwardly aspiring Methodists, but I don't think that affected my motivation, though I think Jess thinks it did. In the early years I worked part time and for very little pay, because this fitted my childcare arrangements better than the full-time post for which I was qualified. I still work for the same charity, but it is more professional now. I became one of their full-time highly paid legal advisers, and worked long hours for twenty years or so, before going back to part-time consultancy and semi-retirement when my husband first became ill. I am not sure its work is as useful as once I thought it was, and I dislike the new management style. Success has not been good for the cause. It has attracted some unpleasant characters of late. I think of retiring altogether, but I don't. I will be obliged to retire soon, but not just yet. They would like me to retire, they can't really afford me, even though they've successfully juggled my pay scale to their own advantage. I don't know whether I want to leave or not.

Unlike Jess, I have never been to Africa. Not even once. I have not been to most of the countries to which I have sent hopeful or hopeless volunteers. Some of these countries were poor and relatively safe, but others have been ravaged by famine and civil war. A few of my volunteers have come to bad ends and died on the job. I have felt small twinges of guilt. Maybe they had a death wish. Jack from Leuchars, Serena from Carstairs, Bobbie from Southport. Sometimes I think we should leave other countries to perish. My optimism has perished. When I hear rock stars and pop stars allegedly raising funds for Africa, I want to scream and tear my hair and weep. I have no personal memory of a shining lake or a powder-blue shoebill. I never visited the village where Livingstone died, or saw the old men reading the large black Bible by the fire at night. I have never heard the mourning cry of the emerald dove, although Jess has imitated it for me on several occasions. It is one of her party pieces.

She does it very well.

~

This is a story that Jess told me not so long ago. In its way, it's about Livingstone.

Jess's stories have become my stories and some of mine have become hers.

Once, when they were still small, Jess told me, she had taken Anna and Ollie on a summer-holiday trip on the river. They set off from the Festival Pier on the South Bank and sailed westwards to Westminster Pier and Westminster Abbey, where Jess had a secret intention of visiting Livingstone's tomb. She had never seen it, although she had seen the mpundo tree where his heart was buried. The children were too young to object to the cultural aspect of this outing, or even to know that it was part of the plan. They had enjoyed the boat trip, and had been indulged with ice-creams with Cadbury's chocolate flakes stuck jauntily into their soft mounds, a messy treat which had left them a little smeared and sticky. Jess, at the imposing entrance to the Abbey, had dabbed at them both with the damp flannel she kept for such occasions in a wash bag in her handbag, and then she shepherded them in. There was no entrance fee in those days: you could just walk in. The children were at first slightly subdued by the height and solemnity of the building, but soon regained their spirits and curiosity and began to wander, even to scamper, as Jess gazed at the soaring statuary.

She had been expecting Livingstone's monument to be vast and gesticulatory, like the Albert Memorial, with palm trees and crocodiles, with adoring natives in crouching postures. And there were plenty of memorials on a grand scale, most of them devoted to naval and military commanders, some famous, some forgotten. Charles James Fox reclining in a stout classical death pose was accompanied by a handsome kneeling African, representing (as she much later deduced) Fox's commitment to the abolition of slavery, but Livingstone she could not find.

She had to ask a verger, who told her that Livingstone lay under a plain black slab on the floor of the nave.

She retraced her steps, and there he was. No mourning doves, no weepers, no palm trees, just a plain epitaph, recording in plain script that his body had been brought by faithful hands over land and sea, and concluding that we should pray 'to heal this open sore of the world', by which he had meant slavery.

He had not wanted to be buried in an English grave. He said that English graves lacked elbow room. He had become accustomed to the vast spaces of Africa. He had wished to be buried in a little forest grave, in a clearing, in a simple garden plot marked by blue stones. But he had ended up here, after a year's jolting and journeying, having left his heart and innards behind him under a tree.

She remembered his last march, his broken sextant, his tree-frog. *I lost my mother, I lost my father, and I am alone, alone, alone.* She thought of the nine Nassick Boys, slaves plucked from an orphanage in Bombay to lead Livingstone through Africa. As we have seen, one of them (although she does not yet know this) had accompanied his corpse to England. He had been a pall bearer at the state funeral, and had thrown a palm branch into the open grave, this grave where she now stands.

Mum is dead.

Livingstone had unfortunately recorded that the 'slave spirit' in the Nassick boys went deepest in 'those who have the darkest skins'. That remark has not been good for his posthumous reputation. He has been retrospectively cast as a racist, which Jess considers may or may not be fair.

There was not much in Livingstone's austere slab to detain Jess, and after reading the inscription she looked up to locate Anna and Ollie, but they were not in sight. She could hardly shout or whistle for them in this sombre setting, and although she was sure they could have come to no harm here she set off briskly to search for them. It was a good building in which to play hide-and-seek. Chapels, cloisters, alcoves, crypts, and the great dark marble royal bedchambers of the dead offered many a Gothic hiding place for two small children. She could not see them anywhere, and began to wonder if she should approach a verger to ask for an announcement. Would there be a loud-speaker system available, as on a railway station? And if she asked for help, would she be publicly convicting herself of maternal neglect?

After some minutes of perambulation, up worn stone steps and over chequered slabs and uneven paving and along a dark transept, she heard promising sounds echoing from a side chapel. It was Ollie's high-pitched childish voice, carrying clearly through the sepulchral gloom. 'Go on, I dare you,' he was saying, 'I *dare* you' – or these were the words that Jess was to think that she remembered, when she told the story to me. Anna was clearly refusing to do whatever she was being dared to do, and Jess hastened towards them, to find Ollie trying to persuade Anna to climb over a low chain to enter the precinct of a Baroque monument portraying a life-sized skeleton emerging from what seemed to be a gardener's hut. Death was poised to aim his deadly bolt upwards at the lovely bared bosom of a young woman swooning in her husband's protective arms.

Jess was cross with Ollie and with herself. She snatched Anna away from the morbid monument and grabbed Ollie with her other hand and propelled them both not very gently away from the skeleton and the woman and the surrounding displays of ostentatious alabaster grief and self-congratulatory self-perpetuation.

The skeleton was horrifyingly realistic. Its lower jaw was missing, though whether this was by the sculptor's design or by accident or through iconoclastic Cromwellian vandalism was not clear. Jess didn't like it at all, but clearly both children had been strongly attracted to it. Ollie protested, as he was led away, that they had wanted to see what the skeleton had in his little shed. The door was half open, and they'd wanted to see inside. 'There wouldn't have been *anything* inside, you little stupids,' said Jess, as she marched them down the wide nave and over Livingstone's pickled remains towards the summer sunshine of Westminster Square.

'There might have been bones, or anything,' said Ollie defiantly.

'There might have been bones,' echoed Anna, a docile pupil.

'It wasn't *real*,' said Jess; 'it was only a *statue*, it didn't have a real indoors.'

'It *looked* real,' said Anna.

'Egyptian mummies have real people inside them,' said Ollie.

'Come along now,' said Jess, as she set off towards the bus stop, dragging one infant in either hand. The good girl, the bad boy.

'Pyramids have mummies inside them, and mummies have real people inside them,' insisted Ollie obstinately, on top of the No. 24 bus.

'Don't keep kicking the seat in front like that, you'll annoy the lady,' said Jess.

'Real dead people,' insisted Ollie.

Jess found the remains of a packet of dry old Rowntree's fruit gums in the bottom of her bag. Ollie chose black, Anna orange. They sucked, exhausted, silenced, as the bus made its way past Nelson and the lions and round Trafalgar Square.

Yes, we all thought Ollie was a handful. It was brave of Jess to undertake him. But he was a bright boy, and Anna liked him. He was Anna's friend. Jess needed Anna to have a friend, even a bad friend. And Jess owed Ollie's mother a favour or two.

~

The groves of statuary, the petrified trees, the stony branching despairing and gesticulating dead.

The helmet-maker's once beautiful wife.

Roubiliac's famously macabre figure of Death in Westminster Abbey, the one that so captivated the naughty and precocious Ollie, portrays Death threatening Lady Elizabeth Nightingale with a thunderbolt. She died of a miscarriage. The mother died, but the child survived.

Queen Philippa, the mother of the Black Prince, also lies in Westminster Abbey, and her effigy does not flatter her. Was she a Moor, an African, the black mother of a black prince? Today's fashion says yes; history says no. Whatever her complexion, she spoke up for the burghers of Calais.

The burghers of Calais, centuries later, notoriously attracted the attention of Rodin.

Queen Philippa died of the dropsy in 1369, and her effigy in the abbey does not flatter her. Rodin did not flatter the burghers either, and his realism caused offence. We don't know if the helmet-maker's wife was offended by her representation.

The lonely and the distressed and the ageing haunt the dead, and they become connoisseurs of epitaphs and funerary monuments. The dead speak to them, lure them, beseech their company.

Uluntanshe. A wanderer with no aim in life.

Christ cured an epileptic, but old age he cannot cure. He offered immortal life as a placebo, but few of us trust his promise these days. I went to a funeral a month or two ago and was surprised to find the service full of references to the resurrection and the life everlasting and to reunion beyond the grave. I had thought the gaunt proud old woman in the coffin under the lilies couldn't possibly have believed in any of that stuff. But maybe that was what she wanted. It seemed very archaic to me.

~

Jessica Speight, Sylvie Raven and I went to a fund-raising fête in Sussex together. We are old friends and old campaigners, and sometimes we join forces, we keep one another company in our latter days. Sylvie was due to speak on this occasion, and we to listen. Sylvie had been co-opted as a useful and willing baroness, though not a particularly relevant one, as the event had nothing to do with the bladder. We went as supporters, and I had offered to drive. I had a new car and was childishly and vainly eager to take it for a spin, hoping that this activity would take my mind off my low spirits. As, at first, it did.

It was July, and the event was to be held in the grounds of a small country house, or perhaps I mean a large house in the country, converted into a residential home for children and young adults in need of special care. The fête had been organised to raise awareness and funds for medical research into acute behavioural problems, loosely grouped together under the controversial label of autism, although we were shortly to discover that the home also catered for a select group of young people with conditions not related to autism – dystonias, mobility malfunctions, self-harm. The word 'autism' has become a shortcut to describe other states, and not always a helpful one. That's what Jess tells me. Jess is well up in all of this.

Jess and I were not expected to make large donations, but we were good at being aware. Indeed, we were both experts in awareness. (My awareness is much influenced by, and dependent upon, Jess's.) And of course we paid for our rather expensive tickets, which included tea, cakes and a glass of wine. Jess might write about her visit. And there would be one or two people there that we might know, and to whom we could try to make ourselves pleasant.

Workers for campaigns and NGOs get to know one another. They inhabit the same world, breathe the same air. Some professionals move from one campaign to another with apparent nonchalance – from torture victims to threatened species, from organic farming in Scotland to women with fistulas in the Horn of Africa, from rescuing battery hens in Wiltshire to the removal of land mines in Cambodia, from anti-smoking to tree protection. The objectives differ, at times grotesquely, but the techniques of fund-raising and consciousness-raising are much the same. The missionary motive dies hard.

Anna didn't go with us, which turned out to be a mercy. Jess had thought she might find the visit disturbing, so Anna went instead on a coach trip to Brighton with the staff and some of the clients of the Thelwell Day Centre, a support group which she had been attending for some years on the recommendation of the social worker's successor. Anna loved an outing, and the Brighton trip offered a tour of the Pavilion, a walk along the pier and a pizza. (It didn't offer a swim: Health and Safety forbade the sea.) Anna was a trusted member of the day centre, always welcomed by the staff, who could rely on her to help to shepherd some of the more obstructive or disoriented of the flock. Her day, we heard, was going well. At lunchtime she reported to us on her mobile that she was having a Pizza Margarita and a Diet Coke and was looking forward to a butterscotch ice-cream. She had the better part.

The mobile was a godsend to Jess and Anna. It saved Jess a lot of worry. Anna had a few saved numbers that she could ring by pressing two simple buttons: Mum, Bob, Katie, Gramps, me, a few others. Gramps is dead now, and much missed, but he lived long enough to own a mobile phone, he lived to join the age of the mobile.

Anna liked butterscotch. There used to be a dessert called Butterscotch Instant Whip to which we mothers often had resort in our frantic earlier days. It was much less artificial of flavour than the unpleasant synthetic pink varieties, though its texture was equally suspect. What can they have used to make the milk coagulate like that? It can't have been good for the body or the brain. But it was a godsend.

The gods also sent us a canned dessert called Ambrosia Creamed Rice Pudding. But none of us liked that.

~

I mourn those days when the children were young. I miss them. Sometimes I look at the little drawer in my desk where I used to keep the Family Allowance book and my eyes fill with tears. A Freedom Pass is a comfort, but the Family Allowance book was more than a comfort. The woman in the Post Office on the corner used to stamp it, and hand over the cash, and I felt rich.

~

On the drive down to Sussex, Sylvie told us what she knew of the organisation, and of her contact with it through a fellow-peer with a problematic son. The peer wished to protect his troublesome and troubled son's privacy, for the sake of the whole family, and didn't want to exploit a personal tragedy, but he had allowed himself to become well known as a donor to mental health causes and as a patron of the home we were about to visit. He occasionally made enlightened speeches on mental-health issues in the House. Jess knew his name, and I let it be assumed that I too had heard of him, though I'm not sure if I had.

Sylvie was fond of fat bald baggy old Bob Germen, and thought he did his best. She wanted to oblige. He had promised her that Wibletts, despite its silly name, was a good cause. His son, now in his thirties, had spent a year at Wibletts. The son suffered from late-diagnosed PKU, or phenylketonuria, a recessive metabolic disorder associated, according to Sylvie, with seizures, mental retardation and rapid-twitching-finger movements. It was hitherto, Sylvie thought, unknown in the peerage, though many peers she knows are loony. But Bob was only a life peer, so, as she said, that didn't mean anything. Nobody knew what trick nature's germens had played on poor old Bob and his boy.

He wouldn't be there at the fête himself, said Sylvie, he couldn't face it. She was his envoy.

PKU is not wholly unconnected with the bladder, said Sylvie, the bladder queen. It's caused by an acid that dyes the urine a spectacular dark blue-green. It's amazing that nobody identified the condition until the 1930s. You don't see it often, but you can't miss it when you do.

Jess was very interested in the story of Bob Germen's son, and Bob Germen's ambivalent paternal behaviour. (I don't think the mother was ever mentioned.) Jess knew many stories of parents who had distanced themselves from or disowned their problematic children in less enlightened days, and as we made our way past Guildford on the A3 she recited some of them to us. Jane Austen's brother George, she now told us, had never learnt to read or write, and had been cared for quietly in a neighbouring village, not in the family home. There were few mentions of him in later family records, although his father had once, she thought, expressed the view that it was a comfort that he could not become a bad or wicked child.

George had lived until his seventies, presumably neither bad nor wicked.

The reverence for those whose lives were hidden with God had not, Jess thought, touched the Austen family in the way that it had touched Wordsworth. The fashionable and benign late-eighteenth-century affection for idiocy had escaped them. Jane Austen had little time for idiocy. She set a high value on rational intelligence, which George had clearly lacked.

Jane Austen's fellow-novelist Pearl Buck, on the other hand, had gone to very great lengths and much expense to support her brain-damaged daughter, whom she memorably described as 'the child who never grew'. Jess hadn't read any of Buck's many one-time bestselling Nobel-Prize-winning novels, and neither had we, but Jess had read Buck's brief account of her daughter Carol, who, like Bob Germen's boy, had suffered from phenylketonuria, although she had been born a decade or so before this label existed, and for years nobody knew what was the matter with her. According to her mother, Carol had been, said Jess, a charming blonde baby and (like Anna) a happy and pretty child, but as she grew older she was afflicted with physical restlessness and meaningless outbursts of dancing and clapping. Her mental capacities failed to develop, despite her mother's love and care and persistent efforts to educate her, and she was never to learn to read or write. The extreme conditions in China in the 1920s might have been thought to explain some of the child's maladjustment, but apparently had no connection with it. Buck travelled widely for years in search of a cure, and at last in the United States a truth-telling 'expert' had warned Buck that she should give up hope. She should find her a place where the child could be safe and happy, and leave her there. She should not waste time and grief on her. Carol was uneducable and beyond help.

Buck was not wholly able to follow this practical advice. She was a mother, and a missionary's child, and she could not forget her one and only daughter. She did her best.

As she grew richer and more and more famous, she adopted other daughters in an effort to heal the maternal wound, and founded homes and institutions (not unlike Wibletts) to care for children marginalised by poverty or hereditary abnormality. Some of them are still functioning, in the twenty-first century, commemorating Carol Buck. So Jess told us.

There is a story, and usually a sad story, behind every private care home, every institution, every act of charity. Wibletts had originally belonged to a wealthy and worldly vicar, the Reverend Edgar Holden, an old-school, Jane-Austen-style, younger-son-of-landed-gentry vicar. His son Felix, less worldly, more evangelical, had gone to Africa as a missionary to save the lepers, where he had died, as did so many, of malaria. He had saved some lepers, but he had died of malaria. The house had been gifted for the care of unfortunate young people by a later generation. A sequence of Holden deaths in the male line (as in a Jane Austen plot) had ensured that Wibletts itself, and a missionary settlement in Northern Rhodesia, had remained very well endowed.

You can read all this in the brochure. Jess will add it to her list. Jess has become an encyclopaedia, a compendium of case histories, and she was now on her way to a hothouse of such histories, a concentration of parental anxiety, a communion of distressed mothers.

Arthur Miller, Jess now reminded us, has been blamed of late for ignoring the existence of his Down's syndrome son. He placed his baby boy in a home and tried to forget about him. He didn't do as well by his son as bumbling embarrassed old Bob Germen. Despite his reputation for high ethical thinking, despite his attraction to the dramatic possibilities of the ethical conundrum, despite his having written a play called *All My Sons*, Arthur Miller hadn't been a good father to all his sons. He'd ducked the issue, he'd edited it out of the script. In his autobiography, Jess claims, he never even mentions his unwanted boy.

Japanese novelist Kenzaburō Ōe made his reputation and won the Nobel Prize by writing painfully, brutally, repetitively, obsessively about his grossly abnormal son, his son whose brain oozed horribly out of a hole in his head.

Nobel-Prize-winning Doris Lessing (who does not like Ōe's work) was locked for more than sixty years into a mother–son embrace of peculiar intensity, married to a son whose strangeness, whose incapacities, whose gifts, like those of Anna Speight, remained undiagnosed, indefinable. He too is one of his kind. He is much cleverer than Anna Speight, but not as simple and not as golden.

Jess broods on these examples, and wonders whether she had been wise to undertake this journey to Wibletts, which will remind her of so many unanswerable questions. She does not anticipate that the visit will lead to any new departure. She is too old for new departures. It will be, she thinks, just one more round of the familiar track, a few incremental details, a few new observations to add to the map she has been forming over the years. A new creek, a new inlet, a new promontory.

Maybe she will write a paper on the Nobel Prize for Literature and the representation (or lack of representation) of brain damage in works of literature by Nobel laureates. Saul Bellow's portrait of Augie March's simple-minded brother Georgie March is masterly and charged with loving sympathy. Georgie March loved his mother. On the first page of this epic and picaresque novel Bellow records the idiot brother's love in a little rhyme that Jessica knows by heart. It goes:

> Georgie Mahchy, Augie, Simey
> Winnie Mahchy, evwy, evwy love Mama.

For a long time now in times of stress Jess has repeated to herself this little rhyme, this little mantra, as a comfort.

(Winnie March was an overfed poodle and, according to Augie March, did not love Mama, although all her boys, all her sons, the good and not-so-good Jewish boys, certainly did.)

People who knew Saul Bellow tell Jessica that he wasn't exactly a role model for parenthood. Not an attentive father to his four children, all of them born to different mothers. But Jess isn't going to blame him for that. She might, if she were one of those mothers, but she isn't.

Jess knows how lucky she is in Anna. Anna lives safely at home with her mother. Anna has not been exiled to a care home, or treated as a leper. She does not have seizures or assault strangers. Unlike Carol Buck, she does not even dance in the street. Anna has been on many pleasant excursions, both with her mother, and on organised outings with the Thelwell Day Centre and other support groups. Anna has been to France, and Italy, and Holland, and, once, as far as Turkey. But she has never been to any country where she might catch malaria or be exposed to danger. She has been well protected.

The word 'over-protected' sneaks into Jess's mind, unbidden. Maybe it is, after all, through selfishness that she has kept Anna at home. Through selfishness, through pride.

As we drive onwards, Jess's anxiety inexplicably mounts, and my spirits sink. I keep thinking of that man in Oxford Street, with his handwritten placard announcing MUM IS DEAD. I do not think I have ever communicated this vision to Jess, but I know that she can read my mind.

Pearl Buck had worried that her daughter Carol would outlive her. She had longed, guiltily, rationally, for her daughter's death. *I would have welcomed death for my child and would still welcome it, for then she would be finally safe.*

So she wrote, in cold blood, during Carol's lifetime, knowing that her child would never be able to read these words.

Jane Austen's brother George had lived a life without incident, without complications, without any plot, for seventy years in a village called Monk Sherborne near Basingstoke. He was boarded out with a village family, who also looked after his maternal uncle Thomas Leigh. Thomas Leigh, like George, was mentally impaired. It was the Leigh gene that was defective, not the Austen gene. The Leighs were to blame. Unlike Johnny Foy, Wordsworth's idiot boy, George had no moonlit adventures, or none that we know of, none that were thought worthy to relate. Unlike Johnny, unlike Augie March's brother Georgie, George Austen was not, it would seem, loved by his mother.

Maybe the village woman had loved him, as Betty Foy had loved her boy Johnny.

Obsessive Jess has been to look for George Austen's grave in Monk Sherborne, to see if it would speak to her, as he could not. Would it cry out in grief? She had caught the bus from Basingstoke on a sunny day in April years ago. She took Anna with her but did not tell her what she was looking for. It was just a day out in the country. She could not find the grave because it was unmarked. He did not call to her from his resting place. She had known it was unmarked, so there had been no point in trying to find it. But it had made a pleasant outing.

Jess thinks of the churchyard. All Saints Church is simple, rustic, humble, the wooden beams of its porch are ancient and rough hewn, its brickwork and masonry are crumbling and patchy. Few of its tombstones have names that can be deciphered. The names are lost in time, obliterated by the unimaginable touch of time. The stones are white and grey and ochre and pale green, encrusted with sun-bleached lichen. They lean and slope. There are gaudy plastic flowers on one or two of the more recent graves. The grass is studded with daisies and dandelions and buttercups, and there are a few clumps of cowslips which the mower has left to stand.

Jess and Anna had enjoyed their day out, and the bus ride.

Jess thinks of the church, and is pleased that Anna is happy on her day out in Brighton.

Jane Austen was buried in Winchester Cathedral.

Sylvie sits quietly, girding herself for the public.

The children of the lake await Jessica Speight at Wibletts. They are the voice of another calling. Anna has been Jess's vocation for forty years.

The children appear to us on that journey through Sussex, our own children, not the poor stranger children of Jess's catalogue, or the children of the lake, but our own North London children, whose stories are not yet finished, whose stories no proleptic twist of plot can pre-empt. The spirit trembles before the leap of prophecy, of guesswork, of staring into futurity.

> So the two brothers and their murdered man
> Rode past fair Florence . . .

The children appear before us, the children of Stirling Hall Nursery and Plimsoll Primary and Highbury Barn. Ollie, Nick, Harry, Chloe, Ben, Polly, Becky, Flora, Stuart, Josh, Tim, Tom . . .

We had all thought that Sally's Ollie was the bad boy, for whom we feared the worst, but Ollie, after years of teasing Anna and committing other minor misdemeanours, had made good. He now owns a company selling organic vegetables, and a chain of up-market market gardens. He pioneers new eco-friendly planet-preserving glossy shining crops whose leaves deflect and reflect the violent sun. He is a success story of our time.

Big brother Stuart was Sylvie's drop-out boy as a teenager, but he dropped in again, and he's now a highly paid if moody and dark-tempered barrister. He wears old-fashioned clothes but sports a pigtail. It's a strong message, a strong look.

It was pretty Josh Raven who had hit the headlines, for all the wrong reasons.

I am afraid to say that we blamed Sylvie and Rick Raven for taking Joshua out of the state schools, to which we were all so loyal, and sending him to a private school, where he was bound to get into the wrong set. How smug we were and how self-righteous. What ideological prigs we were. Yes, he got into the wrong set – drugs, theft, fraud, remand, court, conviction, jail. The choir-boy turned crook, the toxic luminous lamb, the public-school swindler. It was quite a story. We blamed the school, we blamed Sylvie and Rick for sending him there. We had to blame somebody. It was hard to blame Josh, whom we had known when he was so very little, when he was in a state of grace, before he went to the bad. We had known him as a baby in a pushchair, as an angel in a nativity play, as a child gazing rapt at modest indoor fireworks at Christmas. There had been no harm in him then, no sign of Original Sin.

Young Harry Grigson, Harry with the strawberry birthmark on his face, had also been blameless. But at the age of twenty he had climbed into the lion's den at London Zoo in Regent's Park, confident that he could lie down with the lion like a lamb.

There was no harm in that faith, only delusion. The lion mauled him and he nearly died. He now spends his days in an institution, in one of those many institutions. It is not as pleasant as Halliday Hall was in the old days. The doctors say he is schizophrenic, but what is in a word? He is heavily medicated. We don't know if he still hears voices. We haven't seen him in years.

~

Our little children, what becomes of them? They set off so innocently on their long journey. It is hard to bear, it is hard to grow old and see the children age and suffer. It is hard to see them grow bald, and estranged, and some of them lonely.

~

I was feeling low again by the time we arrived at Wibletts. The temporary relief of driving and talking and listening to Jess's stories was wearing off, and I was returning to the default position of despondency into which I sank so easily that summer. As I parked the car in the cordoned grassy car park, surrounded by fields of standardised toy-farm Friesian cows, a sense of despairing futility almost overwhelmed me. It came upon me like nausea as I looked around at the Peugeots and the Hondas and the BMWs and the four-wheel-drives. What were we all doing here? We were eking out our latter days. That's what we do in our afterlife: we stand there begging for alms, begging for money from the rich, although some of us who do this are rich enough ourselves, but we have nothing better to do than beg, we are thrown back on good works, we are obliged to resign ourselves to good works. No longer very active, we choose to beg so that others younger than us may continue for a while to be active.

Retirement, as I have said, threatened me. I've reached retirement age, even by today's shifting standards, and I've had my Bus Pass for years now. It's been hinted that I should depart soon, for the public good. My salary, although trimmed, was too high for the charity, they wanted and needed to employ somebody younger and cheaper and easier to sack. I didn't need the money, and they knew that. I had a pension, and a mortgage-free house, and what seemed to me a generous proportion of my late husband's civil service pension. My children were grown and able-bodied and independent. I didn't need the work, except as occupational therapy.

We become, in our latter days, unnecessary. I wasn't any longer enjoying my work, as I had done in my thirties and forties, when I thought it was useful, when I thought it was leading to a better world order. I hadn't yet concluded, as some do, that it was a form of neo-colonialism, but its impact on the client populations had been negligible. And maybe, yes, I agree, maybe even malign. Not even the wise can see all ends.

Jess and I agree that we have come to hate fund-raising professionals and fund-raising techniques. They are disgraceful and distasteful. The cold-calling, the faked handwriting on appeal letters, the celebrity endorsements, the celebrity auctions, the television bonanzas, the vanity of pop stars, the ridiculous little free gifts designed to induce guilt and misery. The biros, the free Christmas cards, the stick-on personalised address labels, the small unwanted devalued devaluing coins.

Once Jess was sent an unsolicited gift umbrella intended to symbolise the need for shelter of some forgotten and afflicted overseas minority. It had no doubt been assembled, very cheaply, by another forgotten and afflicted overseas minority. Jess didn't know what to do with it, so she used it, as an umbrella, to keep off the London rain. It lasted for ever. She forgot which organisation had mailed it to her, but continued to shelter under it on rainy days as she walked along Upper Street or the Blackstock Road or Southampton Row. She had it with her, in her bag, on this summer day, which threatened a thunder storm.

So what were we doing, on this charitable excursion? Supporting Sylvie, who was supporting some good cause sponsored by old Bob Germen, whom neither of us knew? What was this spree, this outing, this pilgrimage? What lodestone drew Jess on this journey? What guilt, what hope, what compensation, what restless seeking for a forgotten image?

~

The tour of the residential facility and the outreach departments of Wibletts was stressful for many of its participants. The well-wishers and parents and fund-raisers were shepherded around in little droves, gazing at stables with small ponies, at herbaceous borders, at small forestry plantations, at hutches with guinea pigs, at a shallow pond with ducks and moorhens, at a de-luxe indoor swimming pool, at classrooms and study areas and dining halls and ping-pong tables and an IT centre and a woodwork studio. Everything was well provided, and well and expensively maintained, but then it would be well maintained for an Open Day, wouldn't it? This was Psychotherapy for the Rich, not Psychiatry for the Poor, as notoriously practised at Colney Hatch and Friern Barnet (see here, if you are interested, the work of the mother-and-son team of analysts, Hunter and Macalpine). Everyone spoke a little too cheerfully, a little too heartily. Jess was reminded of her first nervous visit to Marsh Court, when she had been on the lookout for signs of abuse or distress, but had been too anxious to look very carefully. She remembered Hazel, the caramel-skinned and golden-eyed Hazel, Hazel who could teach the deaf and the tuneless to sing, to lift up their voices in song.

She could not identify the Hazel of Wibletts. Maybe there was one. She hoped there was one.

She thought again of Pearl Buck, and of the story of the child who never grew. It was much in her mind. She had read it very recently, in a tattered battered little 1952 edition which had arrived from the outlying shelving of Boston Spa to her desk at Humanities Two in the British Library on the Euston Road, humbly apologising for its condition, assuring readers that it would shortly be on its way to the binders. It had brought tears to Jess's eyes, with its strange mixture of obligatory optimism and honest despair. Buck had inspected many institutions while looking for a safe home for her daughter Carol, and however often she had recited the tale of her tours and sanitised or exaggerated her impressions, however much licence or fiction she had employed, her tale of these inspections still rang true. Jess recognised them all. The headmistress-type who instructed her charges on pain of punishment to walk properly with heads high and backs straight, and who taught them how to hold a hand of cards and look as though they knew how to play a game of bridge. The young man who saved a sanatorium from filth and squalor and brutality, who rescued babes, children and adults from a regime where food was thrown on the floor as for dogs, and bodies hosed down like cattle. Elderly Uncle Ed, the kindly principal with his pockets full of little sweets, who believed in the combination of a good discipline and a social spirit.

Good care homes, warned Buck, perish when their founders retire or die. You need, as a parent, to keep a watchful eye, all the time. You need to be vigilant, and make your presence felt.

Care homes and research into mental impairment require private funding, said Buck. The state will fund research into armaments and warfare, but it has no interest in the handicapped. It is up to you. You are on your own. You have to raise your own funds.

Buck was a good earner. She's not much admired now, but she was a good earner. She still is a good earner.

That was how it was in America in the 1950s, and how it is now in Britain in the third millennium. Some mental-health issues are hot and attract research money, but most of them aren't and don't. (There is big money, smart money, in autism research.) And care is expensive. Staffing, we were told, was more than one on one in Wibletts, at the luxury end of the caring market.

But Wibletts was a home to some hard cases, distressing to witness, and there was evidence that summer afternoon of its daily difficulties. Not everything had been tidied up or brushed under the carpet. Some examples were on display, intentionally or unintentionally.

Nothing could disguise the pain of the shock-haired bespectacled boy who could not cross the threshold of the canteen, of the pale girl with brown braids and braced teeth who through terror could not release the handle of the classroom door.

They both had threshold problems, we were told.

The girl's fingers stuck to the well-polished brass handle and could not be prised away. Her face was contorted with anguish. The boy could not move his feet. He tried to put his foot across the line of the doorway, but he could not do it. He lifted it, advanced it and then withdrew it.

No physical barriers blocked them, no strait jackets constrained them. Both these children were able bodied, but they were paralysed by some inner prohibition, some flaming invisible sword that debarred them from movement and transfixed them in stubborn postures of refusal. Patiently the staff coaxed and manoeuvred, calmed and cajoled them, but the terror held its grip, and eventually the visiting group and our guides had to unlock another set of doors and retreat, leaving the frozen children in possession of the small spaces which they had occupied and from which they dared not move. Perhaps the visitors had disturbed them. But perhaps this behaviour was normal to them, a daily performance.

Jess could not tell. She had never seen these particular behavioural manifestations before, although she was well read in behavioural problems. She wanted to question the guides further, about lintels and limens and spatial prohibitions, but she did not wish to make herself conspicuous. She followed, silently, as the group left the purpose-built classrooms and converted dining areas and was ushered up the pink-carpeted staircase of the main house towards the Map Room, advertised in the brochure as the building's architectural showpiece, where the Holden family archives were still kept. This, we assumed, was out of bounds to the inmates, or patients, or clients, or customers, or paying guests, or sufferers, or whatever else the residents were correctly or incorrectly called. But we, the privileged, were to be allowed a viewing.

Portraits in dark oils hung on the lower walls of the stairwell, and on a plinth at the stairwell's turning stood a noble, bald-headed, eighteenth-century bust of black marble, suggesting a blend of Roman and Christian philanthropy. One of the oils portrayed a dark sombrely clad silver-haired churchman in clerical robes with white bands, but there were also, as we ascended, lighter portraits of sand-coloured explorers and big-game hunters in khaki shorts with lions and wildebeest.

Jess paused at the threshold of the Map Room, in the aperture of the high doorway, her mind troubled.

The threshold was curiously marked by a slightly buckled punched-brass ribbon strip, dividing the crushed and well-trodden dusty pink carpet of the stairs and the landing from the golden polished wooden blocks of the Map Room's parquet and its vast and richly patterned oriental carpet. The room within, at least on first sight, gleamed with luxury and polish, with scholarly calm and tranquillity. Two of the walls were lined with leather-bound books in ornate shelved cages, imprisoned by diamonds of gilded ironwork grilles. The lower open shelves contained lavishly illustrated ethnographical studies of the People of Many Lands and aged copies of the *National Geographic*. The third wall was covered with elaborately illustrated maps and sepia photographs. Manuscript letters were displayed in glass cases, and in one of the three large window bays stood an antique globe as high as a man. There were small tables with intricate hardstone inlay, and one larger table with a plain deep oxblood-red lacquered surface on which lay a half-assembled jigsaw of the map of Africa, an original late-eighteenth-century hand-tinted Spilsbury dissected map, showing the delicate pale turquoise of the sea and the faded pink tectonic plate of the continent of Africa, showing the rivers and lakes and states and kingdoms of Africa at the time of Mungo Park.

The softly spoken and deferential guide reverently ushered the visitors into the room, and Jess stepped forward, over the brass metal strip, into Africa.

This was the Africa where Felix Holden had died, explained the guide. The bookshelves housed a fine collection of atlases and of travel books, many of them first editions, recounting the explorations of Mungo Park and Dr Livingstone and Speke and Stanley and other pioneers. There was a large section devoted to the journeys of missionaries, with accounts of their missions and settlements. There were volumes of sermons deemed suitable for infant congregations in open-air gatherings or in corrugated-iron missionary churches. There was a section on tropical diseases and medical research in the nineteenth century, which had been the subject (we were told) of an interesting book by Dr Jaynes from the Wellcome Institute. Scholars were permitted access for study, and the work of missionaries, after a century of neglect, was now receiving renewed academic attention. The family was very proud of having kept the collection together. Many private libraries are dispersed and sold when their owners die, but this had been preserved, catalogued, cherished. The Holden legacy was more or less intact.

'We like to think that Felix Holden's good work continues, though in a different form,' said our well-spoken guide. 'We lend items for exhibitions,' she said, 'but we keep the core of the collection here. We like to feel it is at the heart of our work.'

The guide wears a long off-white cotton skirt, and a neat blue short-sleeved shirt, and serviceable leather sandals. She is a nun, a nurse, a carer. Jess does not really take to her.

Some of us were wondering about the insurance costs. Insurance in a home for the physically unreliable cannot come cheap.

Jess is glad Anna is not with her. There are too many things to knock over in this room.

We were directed towards one of the most valuable items in the Map Room, which lay enshrined in a glass-topped cabinet, protected by green baize. The guide folded the soft covering back for us, so we could gaze at a letter written in a firm, sloping, looped hand. It was from William Wordsworth to the young Reverend Felix Holden. Felix Holden had corresponded with William Wordsworth in the 1820s about the Scriptures and the Heathen and the Simple-Minded and his sense of vocation as a missionary. He had felt a calling to help the simple people of the world, directly inspired, he claimed, by Wordsworth's poetry. He was interested in the concept of the simple savage. He wished to know Wordsworth's view of the correct translation of the words 'feeble-minded' and 'faint-hearted' in the epistles of Saint Paul. Were these conditions one and the same? Jess, who has sometimes wondered this herself, is oddly touched and shaken by his words. He had also asked Wordsworth for practical advice. Should he give up the comforts of Oxford and travel to Africa? He felt sure that in the great continent of Africa some revelation, some vision, awaited him. The knowledge of the crime of slavery had profoundly affected him, the anti-slavery campaign had moved him deeply. The African people had been cruelly torn away from their villages and their shining rivers and their huge savannahs and their palm trees, and they had been shipped in shackles into torment. He felt called upon to right the wrongs done to an innocent race, to heal the woes inflicted upon them.

He looked to the poet as to a source of moral comfort and enlightenment.

There lies the poet's reply, or one of his replies, for some of the correspondence appears to be missing. It is from Wordsworth, verifiably in his own hand, although the signature has been thriftily cut away by some Holden vandal.

The poet advises caution. He speaks of the noble impulses of youth, which should be tempered by reason and good sense. The young man should consider his own flock, his own sheep. There is much work to be done among the poor and the simple here at home, in England. The poet mentions a young friend of his who had been for a while carried away by a romantic longing to travel and see the world, an impulse which should not, the poet suggests, be mistaken for a true sense of vocation. (The young friend, as Jessica suspects, was almost certainly John Wilson, he who had written to Wordsworth about *The Idiot Boy*, and who became not a missionary or an explorer but an opinionated literary critic, writing as Christopher North.)

Wordsworth's letter was sensible, kindly, paternal. But Felix Holden had not heeded the warning. He had followed his noble impulse, and some years later, under the auspices of the London Missionary Society, he had set off for Africa, where he had died. We do not know if Wordsworth knew either of his departure or of his death. But the name of Holden did not perish: it was remembered still, we were assured, through the communities he had helped to found.

Most missionaries went forth from oppressed lives, from lives without prospects, to better themselves as well as to improve those worse off than themselves – they were mill workers, Presbyterians, Congregationalists, the children of drunkards. Unlike Mary Slessor and David Livingstone, Felix Holden had left a life of comfort. He had relinquished more, for he had had more to relinquish.

Jess, turning away from the ghostly missive and the well-informed guide, and wandering over to the wall of photographs, remembered the impulses of her own youth. They had not taken a Christian colouring. Anthropology had not been her vocation. We do not speak so much of a sense of vocation now, although some in the caring professions, such as our guide that day, may be assumed to feel it. Anthropology, for Jess, had been a curiosity, an exploration, a way of seeing. She had not dignified her pursuit of it with any altruistic or sublime motives. The Family of Man, Jess whispered to herself aloud.

She does not give up.

And now, to her surprise, and yet she is not surprised, she finds herself standing in front of a large late-nineteenth-century photograph of an expanse of shining lake, which is captioned in twentieth-century script as 'Lake Bangweulu'. Yes, there it is, the lake itself, or at least a stretch of it, with its fringe of reeds and little islands. And next to the landscape of the lake there is a photograph of a group of little children, sitting in a row on a muddy shore and solemnly facing the camera, displaying their misshapen feet. It is a later photograph, probably from the 1920s or 1930s, though Jess is not sure why she knows this, as the children are not wearing clothes of any particular period and the photograph is undated. Perhaps her sense of a date comes from her time with Bob, from whom she has unwittingly absorbed much useful information about ethnographic photography.

The children are captioned 'Leper Children from the Holden Settlement'.

But the caption is wrong. They are not leper children. Jess recognises their condition. They are the lobster-claw children. They are the ancestors of the children that she saw, all those years ago. She had always known that she would find them again, that they would find her again, and there they are, and there she is.

They are not lepers. The label is wrong.

They are the Cleppie Bells of Africa.

Nobody else in our group spares them a glance. We are not interested in ancient deformities. But Jessica Speight sees them.

The group is ushered out again, politely, and led towards the walled garden.

~

And there was Sylvie Raven, the public woman, in her dark pink slightly car-crushed linen suit and her wide-brimmed public hat, at a garden fête in July in Sussex, in the courtyard of what had been a rich man's mansion but was now an institution that houses and cares for the deeply disadvantaged, for those born to trouble and sorrow and pain. The eddies and currents and struggles of the hot day moved slowly round us in the summer air, currents of unspoken grief, inadmissible rancour, unacknowledged despair, hopeless parental love. You could feel them: they lay over the newly mown lawn and the pebbled paths like a low invisible mist, they clung to the tall red and purple plants of the herbaceous borders, to the deep bronze foliage of the crimson dahlias. Belladonna, delphinium, mandragora, poppy. It was headache weather, close and airless. We were all standing in a soup of grief, a psychic deposit of grief. That building housed too much of sorrow, and those gathered together in the courtyard were oppressed. The Map Room had been calm, spacious, historic, settled in the past, but here, outdoors, we were exposed once more to the unfinished present.

Jess was oppressed and confused and alert, as she stood to attention in her cornflower-blue ethnic frock and her Moroccan sandals, waiting for Sylvie's address. She was the wise matron, with oil in her lamp. She had been waiting a long time. She was musing on the message from those lobster-claw children, so long for her a symbol, but of what she had never clearly known. This day seemed full of portent. It had been largely chance that had brought her here, but she felt herself to be on the edge of another threshold.

Lepers and lobster claws and the pure gold baby that was Anna: the mysteries of diagnosis turned in Jess's mind, as she watched her old friend Sylvie gearing herself up to speak. We would rather blame genes than defective child-rearing, we would rather blame genes than the vengeance of the lord. We pass the buck. Pearl Buck's daughter was diagnosed too late, far too late. Sylvie Raven could have put her right in half an hour.

The cluster of children with lobster-claw hands in Scotland, the Cleppie Bells, was held by folklore to have descended from a common ancestor. Their deformity was said to have been a vengeance on Constable Bell, a heartless officer who had presided at the drowning of the Wigtown Martyrs in the Solway Firth in 1685. Or so the unpleasant story went. 'The bairn is clepped' was a cry that mothers giving birth in that part of Scotland dreaded to hear. But the children had no difficulty in finding normal husbands and wives, suffered no reduced fertility, and were considered of average or even above-average intelligence. The gene had been handed on. Statistician and eugenicist

Karl Pearson had done a good deal of work on the pattern of this cluster. He called it, possessively, 'my family'.

Ollie's little sister had been born with an extra digit. Not too few digits, but too many. The aberration had descended through the maternal line, as had Jane Austen's brother's. Families knew how to hand on blame before they knew that genes existed.

Jess, standing there feeling slightly overwhelmed by the summer heat, cast her mind back over all these blame games. Blaming parents for their children's misbehaviour, blaming schools and teachers, blaming genes and illnesses, blaming doctors and politicians, blaming the ideologies of others, blaming fate, blaming God. See where the scarlet silken poppies flame in the borders, behind the purple-blue delphiniums. Blame the tall poppies. Blame the lawns, blame the courtyard, blame private philanthropy, blame private greed and public malice. Blame the sixties, blame the seventies, blame the eighties. Blame the Beatles, blame Mrs Thatcher. Blame the institutions, then blame the closing of the institutions. Blame R. D. Laing, blame Mary Warnock. Blame Modernism, blame Brutalism, blame Tesco, blame Prince Charles. The banner of blame flies high.

The blameless Anna sits by the sea on a bench eating a butterscotch ice-cream. It drips on to her blue cotton dress and seeps in dark yellow spots on to her uncorseted bosom. The blameless children with their fused toes play by the great lake, and do not blame their maker. The Scottish children with fused fingers do not blame old Constable Bell.

The blameless George Austen, too stupid to sin, lies safely at rest in the churchyard at Monk Sherborne.

Jess blinks in the harsh afternoon light, seeing the pale girl's thin blue-white hand gripping the doorknob, seeing the red tag on her skinny wrist, seeing the knotted boy who cannot cross thresholds, seeing Harry in the lion's den and Josh in Lewes

Prison, seeing the children's faces clustered round the indoor fireworks a hundred years ago. Clouds are gathering in the west, dark, sulphurous, with a bruised yellow tinge. Surely it will rain, but the sun still glares, hotly, without brightness, dully. She flicks to the thought of street-wise Vincent, surviving so much better than anyone had thought he might, and wonders if Susie or the greedy capitalist pharmaceutical company is to be praised for his survival. Praise or blame, wherefore and by whom should they be allocated?

Jess has worked so hard to protect and fortify Anna, but at times her courage fails her. Anna cannot be protected at all times. Anna is friendly and cheerful, but at times she stumbles into insults, rejections. She stumbles down the stairs. She stumbles as she boards the bus. She brushes against a stranger on the pavement and is reprimanded for her clumsiness. 'Look where you're going,' she hears shouted at her. And she hears worse words than those. The angry words hurt her.

Pearl Buck had wished her daughter dead.

Somebody in the small crowd is staring intently at Jess, with curiosity and recognition. Jess is aware of attention, and feels she has half caught an inquiring eye, but cannot work her way back to the moment of fleeting contact. A parent, a social worker, a patron, a donor, a fellow-journalist? Her mind is full of a sudden wave of worry about Anna. Is there somebody here who knows Anna? There are faces here from familiar terrain, welfare terrain. Is it one of them?

Sylvie begins to speak. Sylvie speaks well, succinctly, generously, mentioning the absent but benign patron Bob Germen with affectionate respect. Sylvie is used to this kind of thing. On this occasion, nobody throws stones at Sylvie. Nobody shouts at her that her son is in jail, that she has mothered a public-school-educated delinquent. The group listens, politely. Sylvie introduces the recently appointed new executive manager (he is California-trained from a twinned institution; he has an American accent) and hands over to him.

The stones, it now appears, have been saved for the new chief executive, Jerry Panks. When smooth pink-baby-faced manager Jerry (it is all first names now) begins to praise the regime of his staff and to outline the year's developmental programme, there is a disturbance. Somebody in the small and docile well-groomed crowd suddenly shouts, 'That's a fucking pack of fucking lies!'

Jess hasn't been listening to the smooth manager's smooth words very carefully; she has been thinking about Anna and simultaneously about Sylvie and poor Josh, and she cannot tell whether this sudden, aggressive and sweeping objection relates to a change of policy, or to hopes for future progress, or to Jerry's account of the past year's success, or perhaps to all of these. Jerry Panks has mentioned new research into causation, for which funds are urgently needed. Causation is always a dangerous topic, connected as it so closely is with blame. Maybe he has used the word 'cure', which to some in these circles is taboo. Whatever he said, this woman didn't like it, and she has been rude enough to shout her protest, in a high-pitched but musical upper-class tone.

Maybe the heat is overwhelming her, maybe she had been drinking, maybe she is an intruder or a terrorist. It is not acceptable to shout out like that, at this kind of private gathering. At a political rally, perhaps, but not at a fund-raising garden party in private grounds.

Chief executive Jerry attempts to carry on with his address, but the woman with long blonde hair continues to protest. 'You don't understand anything about it!' she confidently yells, her voice gathering volume. 'You don't know what the fuck you're talking about!'

It is as though all the pain and guilt and sorrow and effort of the day have come together in one woman (unlike the clouds overhead, which have not yet fully massed and broken), as though all the currents in that well-manicured and expensively gardened place have accumulated in that cry. All the disparate stories have become one story and found one voice. Sympathy and embarrassment mingle as kind bystanders and staff members so accustomed *oh so well accustomed* to uncomfortable and unpredictable outbursts attempt to calm and defuse, to restore the peace of a Sussex summer afternoon.

Twenty minutes later a kind of calm has been restored, and the air seems a little lighter for the outbreak, although it is still close, hot and heavy. Jess and the tall woman with long blonde hair and one or two more of us gather in a corner of the marquee, where we are being placated and are placating one another with cups of tea and glasses of pressed elderflower.

It is a strange little knot of people, tightly bonded by instant and spontaneously overflowing emotion. Managerial Jerry has been moved discreetly out of sight, and public representative Sylvie Raven has vanished with him, but sitting in the little ad hoc group of comforters is a slightly built, sharp-featured, hawk-nosed, dark-complexioned, dapper, grey-bearded man who has been watching Jess for some time. He has recognised Jessica Speight as the long-ago visitor to the tea parties in Halliday Hall. She has not yet recognised him, although she has become aware of his scrutiny, but he has recognised her, and that is why he has joined the group. Jessica Speight has not changed much. He would have known her anywhere, from those long-ago meetings, in that charmed courtyard with Zain and Ursula and Patrick and Steve and the brown teapot. Time has failed to disguise Jessica Speight.

Moreover, of late he has tracked her name on the internet, as now we all so easily may. He has read her articles and papers, he has followed her patched-up improvised wide-ranging diversified career.

The mad woman tells her story to her new circle of friends. She is a slender handsome woman, a confidently handsome woman, overwrought, highly strung, unapologetic. She is called Victoria.

Jess finds Victoria fascinating. She must, Jess thinks, be in her fifties, but she is well preserved, and her low-cut black linen dress reveals firm well-tanned breasts, worthy of display. A loop of large false pearls dips from her elegant throat towards the shadowy, alluring gulf between them. Her fingers glitter with a variety of rings, her large hazel eyes are long-lashed, her oval face is long and thin, her cheek bones are high and her cheeks are concave, her lips glisten pink-brushed and animate. She is emphatic, mannered, expensive. A long-legged thoroughbred, a handful, not the victim that Jess had at that first instant of disruption supposed her to be.

No, she is a trouble-maker, and she is accustomed to making herself heard. And out from her swooping nicotine-cadenced throat her story pours, like a recitative, like an aria: her son, the most wonderful boy, the most darling boy in the world, so brilliant, so gifted, so beautiful, the pride of her life, but *impossible*, impossible to manage at home, so here he is, at Wibletts, where she had been promised *round-the-clock care*, *one-on-one attention*, remedial activity, IT training, he is a genius on the computer, horse-riding, swimming, everything that money could buy and more, but it was all going to the dogs, that prat couldn't run a pet's beauty parlour, centre of excellence, what a joke, the fucking staff were fucking demoralised, the fucking hedges needed clipping, the sash cord in the bedroom was broken, her boy was out of control, he wouldn't speak to his own mother, wouldn't recognise his own mother, what can they have done to him to turn him away from his *own mother*? Out it pours, sense and nonsense intermingling in a torrent, in an outpouring of free association, an outpouring decorated with intermittent obscenities, which against all probability have an almost exhilarating effect.

It wouldn't have been exhilarating if she hadn't been so beautiful. But she was. She wouldn't have tried it on if she hadn't been so beautiful. But she was. We use our talents as we may.

So what had gone wrong, has anything *particular* gone wrong, why is she so animated, so angry? Is it with long-term fate itself that she quarrels, or has some recent incident outraged her? Has the executive's accent tipped her over, or his pale blue sporting suit, or his smooth managerial language? Why does she insist that her son is so 'brilliant'? She repeats the word remorselessly. 'My *brilliant* boy!' she cries. Is it the rage of disappointment, of love, of frustration, of despair? Jess is mesmerised, baffled. She recognises a highly tuned note of refusal, an exceptional cry. It is a spirited cry: it fills the grassy space beneath the canvas, embarrassing some of its auditors, but not the little group around the table.

I lost my mother, I lost my father, and I am alone, alone, alone. So repetitively, so musically, cries the emerald dove. And so this mother–woman wails her fluent unstoppable garrulous articulate long-nurtured song of protest.

The mad mothers of the mad children. Why should they not cry out? Why should they politely accept their tragedies? Why should they subdue themselves?

Jess joined a therapy group once, for the parents of children in care, for the parents of children with special needs. She joined it out of need and humility, and to please Anna's social worker Karen, to keep on the right side of ever optimistic Karen, but she had not stayed with it for long. It had bored her to tears and broken her heart.

(Anna sits quietly on a bench overlooking the Brighton shingle, with Rod and Isaac and Molly and coach driver Mr Greetham. Mr Greetham has tied knots in the corners of his big blue-spotted handkerchief and put it on his head, Brighton-style, to prevent sunstroke, because he has forgotten to bring his hat. They all find this very funny. Anna sits and smiles. Anna does not need to cry out.)

Twice her dear boy absconded, loudly claims the histrionically indignant blonde woman, twice they let him get out, once he was found wandering in the village trying to buy cigarettes with a plastic bag full of euros, God knows where he got the euros, then he got on to the verge of the dual carriageway, he was all scratched, must have climbed over the wire, over the perimeter fence, fucking Wibletts was supposed to be a fucking place of safety, that's what we pay so much for, that's *all* some of us pay for, it's a miracle the poor darling wasn't knocked down, anything could have happened to him, they should have watched him, they should have minded him, he was barefoot on the dual carriageway, they had let him wander out without his shoes, they had confiscated his mobile, they had lost his favourite green shirt in the laundry, a pig-faced fat girl called Marina had seduced him, he'd got an infection, a *venereal* infection, they had made him share a study room with *morons*, *they* are the morons, they are cretins, they are profiteers, they should be exposed in the press, it's a scandal, and they're trying to get additional NHS funding, it's a disgrace!

Jess is a good audience – she listens in open admiration to this tirade – and we take our cue from Jess and we listen with her. Jess is not necessarily sympathetic – she is reserving her judgement (and she can be judgemental) – but at this moment she is gripped by this extreme case, by this authentic specimen of maternal passion, so smart, so overt, so tanned and brazenly shining, so magnificently and so violently partisan.

Victoria pauses for breath as she reaches the subject of the NHS, preparing perhaps for a new section of her diatribe, but Jess interrupts with a question.

'Where is he now?' asks Jess.

Victoria stops in her tracks, looks wildly around her, outrageously giggles, and covers her mouth with her hand to stifle her laughter.

'Where is he now?' Victoria echoes.

'Where is your son now?' repeats Jess firmly. 'Is he here?'

'He's locked up somewhere in this loony bin,' says Victoria, gathering herself. 'They've locked him up with a game of chess. He likes chess. I think he's in the Games Room. Shall we go and look for him? Come on, come with me, let's go and find him, you'll see what I mean.'

She lays her quivering bony ringed hand on her new friend Jess's bare warm freckled arm, she grasps Jess's upper arm fiercely, painfully, intimately. Jess acquiesces and allows herself to be led away.

Raoul watches them go, the woman in bright blue and the woman in dull black, he watches them as they make their way over the lawn and vanish through a stone arch towards the spread of homemade huts and activity rooms that extend through what was once a field or a paddock towards the main driveway. The sky is by now very dark, but it is not yet raining.

Raoul is biding his time to reintroduce himself. He wants to ask Jess about Steve Carter the poet, he wants to tell her about Zain and Ursula and Dr Nicholls. Zain's story has come to an end, but the stories of Ursula and of Dr Nicholls continue. As does his own. He is living it now, here, and he is waiting for Jess to re-enter the unfolding of its plot. He wants to tell Jessica about his career and his son, to ask her about her career and her daughter.

The Games Room, a low one-storey bungalow edifice, is identified by a green sign above its door. The door is locked, but there is a fortified glass panel in it, criss-crossed discreetly with wire, through which the two women peer. Inside, Jess can dimly see a ping-pong table, a pool table and a card table, at which a young man is seated. He is staring intently at a chess-board covered with chess pieces, but she cannot tell whether he is planning a move or whether he is in a vacant trance. He has long brown curving hair which falls to his shoulders, and, like his mother, he is handsome. Melancholy, Gothic, lost, imprisoned. A prince in a Renaissance tragedy, a prince hidden in a closet.

Victoria raps on the glass panel, but he does not even look up.

She yells at him, in her commanding, carrying, confident voice. 'Marcus!' she shouts. 'Marcus!'

Her son stares at his chess set.

Victoria rattles the doorknob. She bangs on the door. She shouts again. The young man, very slowly, in slow motion, moves a piece. Jess cannot see what the piece is, or whether the move is meaningful or random. She doesn't know much about chess anyway. She cannot tell whether or not he is aware of his mother at the door, and, if so, whether his indifference is natural or provocative.

There is suddenly something terrible to Jess about this stasis, this barrier, this slow motion, this locked door, this new threshold, this incarceration. Inside her body, there is a collapse. She was to describe the sensation to us later, on the way home. She said it was as though all the strength and power and blood in her head and her shoulders and her upper body drained downwards, first towards where she believes she keeps her heart, and again down further into her bowels. Her strength, the strength that has kept her together for so many hard years, imploded and deserted her, it sank out of her and leaked away into liquid nothingness. Her cell walls collapsed and ceased to hold their place. As she stood there, leaning on the wooden door for support, the mobile phone in her handbag rang, and she knew it was Anna, or someone from Anna's group, needing her, needing her, but she could not reach it, she was about to lose consciousness. She could no longer support herself. Her knees sank to the ground. She had time to wonder if she was having a stroke, or a panic attack, or a fit, or a revelation. Then she passed out.

~

I think Jess fainted. I think it's as simple as that. The weather was freakish that day, and the barometric pressure had been plunging rapidly (or do I mean rising rapidly?), and it made a lot of people feel quite faint. Also, one had to take into account the stress of the occasion and the poor young people and the craziness of Victoria's outburst and the sight of that wretched young man at his chess set, sitting like a funerary monument. Or it could have been some form of migraine, but Jess swore she'd never in her life suffered from migraine, she hadn't had time for headaches and migraines. Anyway, it was a warning, and when she had returned to her proper upright self she was eventually to heed it. But she continued to believe that she had been felled by the sudden invasion of suffering, by the spirits trapped in the building, alive and dead. The unhappy Holdens, the true lepers, the false lepers, the threshold children.

Her mind and body had opened and let them in.

Well, that's one of her explanations.

I think it was an epiphany of anxiety about Anna's future.

What happened was that Jess slumped forward and fainted on to the newly mown grass, in a modest kneeling position.

Victoria, who is not as barmy as she looks and sounds, took the situation in hand. She pulled Jess up into a more upright position (she began to come round almost at once, Vicky told us) and simultaneously got on her mobile and summoned help.

Jess, as she surfaced, heard Victoria saying 'Come on, send a medic, you must have got a few to spare round here, we need a doctor here right now' – and as she peremptorily shouted this command Jess's own phone began to ring again. Again, Jess didn't get to it in time (it would later reveal itself as a voice message from Anna about the Wild River Ride on Brighton Pier, a message to which Jess listened on the way home), but the sound of the needy ring tone brought her round, and by the time the medic (an eager untrained minder aged about sixteen) arrived on the scene, Jess was sitting on the front step of the Games Room and apologising for being a nuisance.

'The heat,' said Victoria, 'the heat, it's just the heat,' which is what any sensible person would have said. The minder fetched a glass of water from the marquee, and Jess obediently sipped, and dabbed her forehead with a few drops, and it began at last to rain. Heavy spots of rain began at last to fall.

Throughout this little drama Vicky's son sat in the gloom and stared at his plastic chess men without raising his eyes to look at the would-be intruders. He did not acknowledge his mother's presence. Maybe he did not hear her, maybe he did not know she was there.

We have since discovered that Marcus can play chess, and he can play, as his mother rightly claims, 'brilliantly', but he can also sit for many hours as though locked into himself, staring at the board, without making a move of any sort. That's part of his condition. Not many people are up to playing with him. They haven't the patience.

Jess and I have never been able to play chess. I learnt the moves once, my father taught me long ago, but I couldn't be bothered to learn to play properly. I didn't have the brain or the will for that kind of activity. It's a man's game, an autistic game.

Don't say I said that.

Vicky at this point in the drama gave up on her son Marcus

and his game of chess and escorted Jess back to the marquee, where I was still sitting, having been joined by now by Sylvie, who, her duty done, was eager to get home and was looking for her lift. Sylvie had been burdened with an inconvenient bouquet which was leaking on to her pink suit from its large water-filled cellophane stem-pouch. Raindrops pocked and spattered on the canvas of the marquee and dank-smelling water leaked on to Sylvie. Raoul was also still there, and had in Jess's absence introduced himself to me by name as an old acquaintance of Jess from years ago. I didn't disbelieve him, and indeed I thought I had heard Anna invoke the name of Raoul. He seemed the kind of person Jess might well know, from SOAS, from her life as a scholar and medical journalist, from her life as a mother of a child with special needs. I didn't at once guess that they had met through Steve the Poet at Halliday Hall, although I did of course remember Jess's stories of Halliday Hall.

As Jess and Victoria rejoined us, we saw that their roles had been reversed: Victoria was now supporting Jess, who sat down and started to fan herself demonstratively with the glossy Wibletts fund-raising brochure.

'I had a bit of a turn,' she said. 'Sorry, I had a bit of a turn.'

It's the heat, we all agreed. It's very close today, we all said wisely, a chorus of wise old women.

I expected Raoul to make himself scarce at this point, but he wasn't going to back out, despite the strong indications that Jess was not feeling her best and was maybe not up to a potentially challenging reunion. But he held his ground. He was determined to effect an introduction. Having found her, he wasn't going to lose her again. And, when he diffidently but inexorably named himself, and asked her if by any chance she remembered him, she instantly rallied.

'Raoul! Good God!' she cried. 'Of course I remember you! Good God! What on earth are you doing here?'

She had wondered about his fate, she told him. She had wondered about the afterlife of all the Halliday comrades, encountered at a time of such vivid and clear intensity. So Raoul had survived, and here he was! She would never have recognised him after all these years, but she could see the shy young man in this respectably dressed elderly man with his neat little grey beard, with his slightly hooded brown eyes, his urbane and confiding smile, his sharp nose, his courteous insistence, his assumption of an old intimacy.

What had been wrong with him, all those decades ago? She had never known what his passport to Halliday had been. Had he been bi-polar, schizoid, psychotic, paranoid or a simple victim of exile?

'What *are* you doing *here*?' cried Jess.

Raoul, it appears, is now a distinguished neurologist. If he is disappointed that Jess does not know this already, he conceals his regret. Sylvie Raven, unlike Jess, recognises his name as soon as she hears it. Neurology and urology have some close connections. The neurogenic bladder was one of Sylvie's specialities. And he, of course, knows Sylvie's name, because she is a public person, and he has just heard her speaking in public in her public manner.

He tells us that he graduated from Halliday to UCL, where he took up the medical studies forcibly abandoned in the Lebanon, and moved on to graduate research at the National Hospital for Neurology in Queen Square in Bloomsbury. So near to SOAS, a stone's throw from SOAS. He says he thought he saw Jess once, crossing the wide green civil lawns of Russell Square, but that he had been too shy to speak. He wanted to speak, but he had not dared to call out to her.

He had lived and worked in the States for a while, but now was back in England, the country which had first taken him in.

Jess is delighted to see him, as he to see her. They are full of questions for one another. He looks so well, so complete, such a whole person, such a credit to the Halliday regime. And Jess appears to have completely recovered from her *petit mal.*

(I think it was Vicky who produced this sophisticated verbal diagnosis for Jess's turn. *Petit mal.* A phrase in French, which dignifies so many neurological disorders. Words, words. Ugly illnesses, pretty illnesses, ugly words, pretty words.)

I am keeping an eye on my watch, and also on the weather, which seems to be about to fulfil its threat of a heavy downpour. I have to be back for supper with friends in Belsize Park, I need to get moving, and I can see Sylvie is keen to make a move too, her duties for the day being over. But Jess and Raoul are in the full flow of reminiscence, and it seems a pity to separate friends so recently reunited. So, impulsively, I offer Raoul a lift back to London, which he accepts. I think Jess is pleased, but, if she isn't, there's nothing I can do about it. We exchange mobile numbers and email addresses with Victoria, our comrade in disaster, our new best friend for life whom I (wrongly) suspect we will never see again. She embraces all of us effusively (including a benign and mildly blinking Raoul) and sets off once more towards the main house, to pursue her endless battle on behalf of her beautiful brilliant disconnected boy.

Sylvia dumps the flowers and her big hat in the boot and clambers into the front seat of my car. Her best summer suit has been ruined, it is streaked with greenish damp and sap, it is stained and spattered with orange-brown pollen, but she is too tired to care. She unbuttons her jacket, revealing a surprising stout turquoise brassière, reclines her seat forcefully backwards on to Raoul's knees (luckily he is small and compact), shuts her eyes and leans back. She is asleep before we reach the turning to Midhurst, asleep and snoring slightly. She has done her fund-raising best. It hadn't been easy, but she'd done her best.

The chestnut trees of Sussex are huge and in heavy leaf; they arch over the tunnel of the sunken road.

Jess and Raoul, in the back seat, catch up on thirty or forty years of news. They address an occasional remark to me, but I cannot hear them very clearly (it will all be relayed to me later) and I have to concentrate on the road, as now, at last, the driving rain starts to fall in slanting sheets. We have got away just in time: the deluge will turn the grassy car park into a muddy swamp, it will batter the herbaceous borders, it will bend and crush the erect sap-structured stems of the tall poppies. The rain is majestic, torrential, and even as we drive it begins to pour down the gullies by the roadside, carrying sticks and leaves – it is falling too heavily on the dry hard summer earth to be absorbed, I wonder if there will be floods in London, as there were a few years ago, when people drowned in underground car parks and public lavatories. My new car's windscreen wipers go into frantic mode: they are self-regulating, they recognise the emergency of the storm, they respond with vigour. The air conditioning hums and sings. I am in control. Sylvie, Jess and Raoul are my passengers, my puppets, I can take them wherever I wish.

~

So this is the story that Raoul tells Jess, as I drive through the rain and Baroness Raven slumbers in her fascinating uplifting turquoise pearl-enhanced lace-edged well-boned vulgar vanity bra.

The first item of news is that Zain is dead. Jess had known this fact, but she had not known the circumstances of his death. He had died in Paris, two months ago, and she is now told that he had died alone. There was a long trail of wives and lovers, but the trail had gone cold, and he had died alone, in a large apartment in the rue de Vaugirard in the 15th arrondissement, near the Luxembourg, surrounded by books, papers, heaps of dead technology, African carpets, badly carved wooden palm trees and chunks of Roman statuary from the old Roman Empire of North Africa. In a junk shop, a magnificent and baroque junk shop, amidst the spoils of empires. Raoul had seen him on a few occasions, over the years. They had met at a conference in Cairo, at a reception in Beirut, at a seminar in Strasbourg. Raoul had visited the Vaugirard apartment, once, a decade ago, and had been made welcome. Zain had offered Raoul red wine, but had been on the wagon himself. He'd stopped drinking years before. He'd retired from the bottle.

Jess does not ask if Zain had remembered her. She knows that he did. He would have kept a tally, and she, Jessica Speight, urban anthropologist and haunter of asylums, would have been inscribed on it. Had she not kept her own tally, as women may do, as well as men? The Professor, Bob, Zain, and one or two minor episodes that had left less of a mark on her. She recalls them all. Sitting there, in the back seat of my Honda, with the rain beating violently on the windscreen as we join the motorway, she remembers Zain with interest, with admiration, with a recollection of intense physical pleasure and no regrets at all. She had done well with Zain.

She knows that Raoul knows that Zain remembered her as well as she remembers Zain, but he will be far too polite to allude to this knowledge. Raoul struck her then and strikes her now as a modest and fastidious man, who would keep his erotic secrets to himself.

Dr Nicholls, in contrast to Zain, is still alive, but he has been crossed off the medical register by the GMC. Jess has missed this bit of gossip, or has forgotten that she ever knew it. (This kind of forgetfulness recurs increasingly, as we grow older; surprises cease to surprise us, or surprise us twice or thrice over, as our memory confuses and entangles events and disclosures, as déjà vu merges with memory loss. I think I may have made this point before.)

Jess presses Raoul for details. Although she had never met Dr Nicholls, she had been curious about him. What sins had he committed, she wants to know? Jess does not have a very high regard for the ethics of the self-protecting GMC, and is willing in principle to take the side of Dr Nicholls.

It had been a matter of betrayal of patient confidentiality, says Raoul, a sin of publication. An eminent and clearly ungrateful client, a newspaper article, a fictionalised case history with not enough details changed, a law suit. Things hadn't gone well for Dr Nicholls after Halliday closed, says Raoul; he had gone private and public at the same time, he had started writing pseudonymous and highly paid articles on mental health for a tabloid and had been shopped by a colleague. He was hated as well as loved. He had carried too far his disapproval of medication, his faith in the restorative powers of a benign environment and laissez-faire, his belief in the psyche's powers of spontaneous recovery. One of his patients had assaulted him and he had hit back. That had been a mistake.

Also, said Raoul, who seems to enjoy telling this story, he had become unexpectedly, grossly fat. He had swollen up like a toad. Or like a Buddha. He had morphed into a middle-aged Buddha guru, a fat toad, with plump and swollen cheeks, wreathed in rounded layers of flesh.

Jess finds this fascinating. The only photographs she had seen of Dr Nicholls had shown him as handsome, lean, big, energetic, athletic, a tennis-playing figure of a man. Self-regarding, perhaps, but self-regarding in a manner that should surely have prohibited such weight gain.

Was it steroids, she suggested? As with Gore Vidal?

Raoul thinks not.

It was very odd, says Raoul; Dr Nicholls began to look quite Middle Eastern. Or oriental. As though he'd changed ethnicity and gender as well as body shape. Very odd.

Rather like Peter Hall, I thought, but did not interrupt them to say so. They were probably not aware that I was eavesdropping. I couldn't hear everything they said, but I could hear most of it. And if I had mentioned Peter Hall, that would have been name-dropping as well as eavesdropping.

Steve also put on weight, Jess tells Raoul. Does Raoul remember Steve Carter? Of course he does, says Raoul. So she still sees Steve? They agree that they would have expected Steve to put on weight: he was by nature indolent, he never took any exercise, he ate for comfort, he needed to eat. To be fat was his destiny. A heavy baby that could never suck in enough, a heavy man who could never eat enough biscuits. A fat old man baby. An unappeasable, devouring baby.

Raoul says he has often wondered about Steve, whose name seems to have faded from the literary record, his early promise unfulfilled. When he'd met him, he'd been a somebody, he'd been a published poet, the only poet Raoul had ever known. But he seems to have slipped away into obscurity, suggests Raoul. You can find his name through the web – you can find almost anyone's name through the web – and there are some early poems there, someone had posted them, some of the best of his early poems, poems he used to read to the circle in Halliday, but nothing recent, nothing from his later years. There is no surrounding integument of critical discourse, there are no links feeding his poems out into a living network. His work is islanded in the recent past. It has not yet hooked up with the expanding interconnecting digital world. Minor Edwardian poets with their entourage of minor commentators and minor biographers and minor research scholars are better connected than he. He is in a limbo, in the land of the unreborn.

Raoul suggests this (well, he suggested some of this, Jess and I looked up the Edwardian poets on the net later), and Jess is inclined to agree with his analysis.

Does Steve still write, Raoul asks?

Jess thinks not. His muse has abandoned him. Steve is all right, she insists, defensively, he's okay, really, but even as she speaks she knows that he isn't 'okay, really', he has suffered too much, his spirit has been too deeply damaged too early. By 'all right' and 'okay, really' she means he is still alive, he gets from day to day, he calls on her occasionally (but not too often, doubting his welcome), he gets up in the morning and passes the day and goes to bed at night and has not as far as she knows repeated his Wendy House suicide attempt in the Secret Garden. He has resigned himself to a life of unproductive daily anguish. Sometimes he thinks the gift will return, for there is no reason why he could not write a good poem even about being unable to write a poem (Coleridge did, others have done), he still has his fingers and his words and his pen and his paper, they are poor possessions but he has not physically lost them, his early poems were begotten of despair upon impossibility, so maybe the late poems will come, released by a final spasm of impossibility? At sixty-five, at seventy, at seventy-five?

He hopes, maybe.

Steve's mantra, which he once repeated to Jess, goes:

The day is agony
The night brings no reprieve.

She's tried hard to forget it, but she can't.

It is hard for Steve: he was born to guiltless misery, and for a while it seemed he had outwitted it. Anna was born happy, a pure gold baby, but Steve was born into a white misery. In his crib he was deprived and wanting. The thought of Steve's life sentence darkens Jess's pleasure in her reunion with Raoul (the successful and competent survivor Raoul), and luckily at this lowering moment she is interrupted by a call from Anna, who wants to tell her that she is on the coach on her way home and it is raining very hard.

'It's raining here too!' says Jess.

This pleases them both. It is reassuring to them to know they are in the same weather system. Their intimacy is terrible.

Anna wants to know where Jess is, and who is in the car, and when will she be home. Jess tells Anna that she is with Sylvie and Eleanor, yes, Eleanor is driving, Eleanor's new car is very smart and silver, and guess what, Jess has met her old friend Raoul, and Eleanor is very kindly giving him a lift back to town.

Anna is pleased with this news, because her mother cannot have enough friends. She rejoices in her mother's friends; the more she has, the happier Anna is. She is never jealous of her mother's friends, although she had been a little jealous, long ago, of Bob.

She has no idea who Raoul is, but she remembers his name. 'Give my love to Raoul,' says Anna, as is her generous way.

'My daughter Anna,' says Jess, as she disconnects. And yes, she is well. Raoul has never met her, Anna had never been taken to Halliday, but he asks after her, politely. Jess briefly describes the coach trip with the Thelwell Day Centre to Brighton, an explanation that explains all. She can see Raoul quickly decoding the story of Anna. He is very quick.

And you, Raoul, she risks, did you have children?

She has declared herself and so can he.

Raoul, who becomes tense as I try to get into the right lane to leave the A3 for the M25, says that he has a son. One son. An ex-wife, and one son.

He relaxes as I make it safely from the slip road into the mainstream. The windscreen is misting slightly; the new car is perhaps, for all its up-to-the-minute technology, not perfectly adjusted to this wet English summer weather, and I have to lean forward from time to time to wipe the screen with my naked knuckles. Sylvia is still asleep; I do not want to rouse her but I wish she would wake up. The poor new car is not accustomed to so many passengers, to so much breathing and condensation. Neither am I. Driving conditions are not good, and the traffic is heavy, and I can't get the air conditioning to adjust as it should.

Raoul says he has one son, who works in Geneva on particle physics and black holes and dark matter. This son is, it would appear, a multilingual stateless scholar of the universe. I cannot understand his work, says Raoul; it is too hard for me, it is all a mystery to me.

He is proud of his son, of course. His voice is full of a pride which he cannot dissimulate, cannot conceal, even though he wishes to defer to Jess, the rediscovered and long-admired Jessica. So transparent we are, so helpless, so vulnerable, as we lay bare our pride and our affections. His son is called Rachid. His ex-wife is a French–Algerian anthropologist, now connected with McGill University. She specialises in nomadic peoples, and is currently on a field trip in Mongolia.

Jess, hearing this, thinks fleetingly but intensely of Anna's father, who has so completely vanished from the field of her knowing. Maybe he, like Zain, is dead. He had been twenty years older than she, so he is probably, though not necessarily, dead. He is frozen in time for her, for ever at the age at which she had known him, in the old days of sex and SOAS. It now strikes her that he must almost certainly be dead. She hears nothing of him, no echo from him reaches the network. His very name is dead. He cannot have published much, or she would have come across his references to his work. She has not looked for him on the internet, where we all have an afterlife, but maybe, as of course he must be dead, maybe, perhaps she could look.

Yes, she knows he must be dead, or, if not dead, moribund in Sweden. He cannot be in England, or she would have known. His tenure at SOAS had been limited; he had no right of return. Maybe he died long ago in the Chinese foothills. Maybe he was an anthropological martyr, murdered by tribesmen or eaten by ants.

It would be safe to look for him now. Her shame (and she has felt at times intolerable and inexplicable shame) has died with him.

The thought of seeing the Professor's name again fills her with horror. She has been trying not to know this. For decades she has been, as we now say, in profound denial.

Maybe Raoul's ex-wife knew him.

Jess banishes the thought of the Swedish professor and returns to the present.

'Particle physics,' repeats Jess to Raoul, admiringly and meaninglessly, playing for time to reorganise her thoughts, her flashbacks, the heaped and impacting flickering particles of recollection that no prose can ever reproduce, however fancy. The neurones are far too quick for us, proleptic, pre-emptive.

'Particle physics!' says Jess. 'That's amazing.'

There is no future in talking to Raoul about particle physics and his clever son.

She decides to risk betraying stupidity and ignorance by asking Raoul to tell her more about what kind of neurologist he is, and why he had found himself at the Open Day at Wibletts.

We are impressed by his Delphic answer, delivered just as Sylvie rouses herself from her exhausted slumber.

'I specialise,' said Raoul, as we entered the uninspired repetitive landscape of the South Circular, 'in phantom pain.'

~

Phantom pain.

'I feel anguish, and it is not of the body, so it must be of the spirit.' So says a character in one of Strindberg's tragedies. I forget which.

Neurology does not accept the disembodied notion of the disembodied spirit. Raoul has been working on this problem all his life. Well, for all his life since he left the Lebanon and Marxism, suffering from what he would have accepted as 'anguish'.

I don't know what the Swedish word for 'anguish' was, or who translated it as 'anguish'. Maybe it was me.

Steve had used the word 'agony' in his mantra.

I don't know if there is any difference between these two concepts, whether one is more embodied than the other.

~

Raoul and Jessica met for lunch in an old-fashioned little Italian restaurant in an alleyway just off Queen Square, which they had each visited severally over the years, but where their attendances had never until now coincided. An unpretentious little place, it is now more committed to the pizza than it used to be, but otherwise it is little changed. It is still a family business, although the waiters grow old and will soon die, and the patron will sell to a fast-food chain and return to his native village near Bardi in Emilia-Romagna.

The restaurant is quite near SOAS, and even nearer to the National Hospital for Neurology and Neurosurgery, where Raoul had worked. It is quite near the Great Ormond Street Hospital for Sick Children, where I saw the stitched and smiling baby that I mentioned.

Raoul and Jessica were well within their comfort zone there, with ageing waiters and familiar food. They found themselves surprisingly comfortable with one another.

In the restaurant just off Queen Square, Raoul and Jessica talked about the Lebanon and the Sudan and Mongolia. (We don't use those definite articles now.) They ate fusilli and farfalle and drank a bottle of San Pellegrino. They spoke of Steve Carter, who had retreated to the comfort of the Wendy House, but had found no comfort there, or thereafter. They spoke of Zain and his long heroic journey north from the oasis. They spoke of Dr Nicholls and R. D. Laing. They spoke of phantom pain in missing limbs, and of the neurology of the traumatised bladder. They spoke of Sylvie and her son Joshua. They had a lot to talk about.

Perhaps they spoke of me, their obliging facilitator, but if they did, Jess did not report it.

~

Jessica and Raoul met for their second lunch in a Lebanese restaurant near Victoria, where they ate a variety of challenging raw vegetables, some rice and some beans and some splayed grilled quails, and drank a glass of red wine. They talked about exile. They talked about Africa and the lake. Raoul asked Jessica why she had never been back to Africa, if it had meant so much to her, and her ready answer (Anna, Anna, money, Anna) died on her lips. She stared at Raoul as he tidily nibbled at a bone. He smiled, to indicate that there was no threat, no malice in his question.

Why had she never been back to Africa? She could have cajoled a friendly editor, in the days when there was easy money in print journalism. Someone would have commissioned her to write about lepers or lobster claw or ostrich foot, had she set her heart on it. She had been good at cajoling, when she was young. But she had never even tried. She could have gone while Anna was safe at Marsh Court. She could have sent Anna home for a couple of weeks to her Broughborough grandparents, while they were still alive and willing. But she had never even tried.

She had stayed within her comfort zone, with Anna.

That useful if vulgar and irritating little phrase, that journalistic, cheap-popular-psychology phrase 'comfort zone', hadn't existed in those early days, when she had sought whatever it is that we now mean by it.

No, reflected Jess on her underground journey home to Finsbury Park tube station, she hadn't travelled far. She had made an excuse of Anna. She had withdrawn to the life of the mind, to the idle life of the busy mind. The magpie mind. This was the accusation which, prompted by Raoul, she now drew up against herself.

She had made Anna dependent. She had been wrong to make her so dependent. She had permitted too great a closeness, in too small a space. She had made Anna safe and herself indispensable. This had been short-sighted. Few had dared to warn her, but some had tried. Maybe she should have listened to Karen, her social worker.

Karen tried to warn her, but I didn't. *Par délicatesse.* I was a coward on this front.

Par délicatesse j'ai perdu ma vie.

~

Before her next lunch engagement with Raoul, Jess found herself thinking about those large horizons. She thought about the thousands and thousands of air miles that so many of her friends and acquaintances had travelled over the last few decades. In her twenties she had been the adventurer, but now even the stay-at-homes had overtaken her. Travel had become commonplace. The upper air was thickly crowded with economic migrants and refugees, criss-crossing one another unhappily in mid-air; with pleasure-seekers and holiday-makers; with executives needlessly visiting foreign branches of their companies; with trustees of boards, with politicians and NGO employees on freebies; with bankers and engineers and salesmen; with grandmothers and bridegrooms; with party-goers and pilgrims; with jihadists and journalists and novelists and poets on their way to festivals or conferences or global summits. Global displacement, for reasons both trivial and profound, had accelerated and intensified, and not even major catastrophes – airplane-engine failures, terrorism, volcanoes, earthquakes, nuclear disasters – seemed likely to halt it. Only a few neurotics and ecology fanatics stayed at home.

All the impenetrable places of the earth have been documented and filmed and probed and contaminated. You can see them on television any night of the week in all their *National Geographic* banality. Jess has been told that in the United States whole television channels are devoted to travel and ethnography. Round and round they go on a loop, the simple peoples of the earth.

Jess hates the *National Geographic* shop on Regent Street. It is as false as false can be. It is a virtual world of almost indescribable ugliness.

People don't need to travel to see other peoples. They can watch them on the loop from their beds. But people go just the same. To Africa, to Thailand, to Brazil, to Antarctica.

My Ike, always a wanderer, works for a backpacker's guidebook, and has been to more uncomfortable places than most. In theory Jess ought to disprove of this, and so perhaps should I, but Ike is a charmer and an enthusiast and we love him, despite his massive carbon footprint.

Jess's sister Vee has conspicuously avoided England. She returns once or twice a year, for funerals. She attended the funeral of their father, then that of their mother. Jess doesn't like to ask her where she will live when, in a few years, she is obliged to retire. She and her sister are not close. Vee has no children, has never married, is secretive about her personal life.

A few eccentric, green-minded, middle-class intellectuals are now turning against foreign travel. Having been everywhere they could possibly have wanted to go, having tired of queues at airports and security procedures, they now make a virtue of refusing to fly. The fox and the grapes, thinks Jess, a little sourly.

Bob still flits about a lot. He doesn't tire. He doesn't mind aeroplanes, he doesn't give a damn about global warming, in fact he says he thinks its dangers are much exaggerated. He's still based in England, but he takes off for China, for Australia, for the Solomon Islands, for Alaska, whenever a commission comes up. He can still get work. He's still restless. He hasn't finished yet. She doesn't think she envies him, because she thinks his work is shallow. But maybe she does envy him. She envies his freedom, his temperament, his weightlessness. She now thinks she was lucky to have had a happy couple of years with her surprising husband Bob.

They still haven't divorced, and when he is in London he lives happily alone in a large flat in Herne Hill, south of the river, a long way from Camden, in an area that Jess found surprisingly genteel and leafy when she first visited him. She's been over there a couple of times with Anna. It is very different from the urban North London in which she is so deeply embedded. It has large trees, green space, wide roads, tall wide houses, deep gardens.

Statistically, a high proportion of marriages that produce children with learning difficulties or disabilities founder, for obvious reasons. Jess hasn't had to worry about that. Bob hadn't really been part of that plot.

As she sets off via the British Library to her third rendezvous with Raoul, thinking of horizons broad and narrow, she remembers the powerful and well-attended funeral that she and Anna had been to earlier in the week. It was the funeral of her plumber, whom she had known for nearly forty years. He had been the plumber of all the local families and he looked after much of our neighbourhood, as his father had before him. We knew him well, and he knew us. Jimmy Parker was of the old English white artisan class, and he had prospered way beyond his father's expectations, as the gentrification of Canonbury and Highbury enriched his growing parish, as new bathrooms and showers were installed and penthouses and basements were added on and refurbished. He was reliable, and, although his prices went up and up as he acquired more vans and more employees and a new logo and extended his business to building and electrics, he was loyal to us, as we to him. He gave us reasonable rates. It was Jimmy who came round to Jess's that Christmas to fix the broken lavatory bowl, it was Jimmy who rebuilt Maroussia's top floor and created her smart new bathroom, it was Jimmy who fixed Sylvie's new house in Canonbury Square, it was Jimmy who stepped in when a boiler cranked itself to death, it was Jimmy who knew which tree roots were throttling the drains or making their way into basements. He knew our infrastructure and our secrets underground.

Jess remembers very clearly the day, six months or so earlier, when she discovered that he was dying. She'd called him round to look at the shower attachment, which had finally resisted her attempts to stick it together with silver duct tape, a plumbing matter of no great moment, and she had been prepared to greet him with her usual neighbourly cheeriness and small talk. But when she saw him on her threshold, she knew at once. 'How are you, Jimmy?' she asked brightly, trying to conceal her shock at his appearance, for she knew the answer. He shook his head as he stepped indoors and wiped his shoes on the orange-brown whiskered doormat. He didn't say anything. He had shrunk, his round and cheerful face had folded and sunken inwards, his pink complexion had yellowed, his whole body manifested mortality. He shook his head, and Jess, impulsively, put one arm around him, then quickly withdrew it for fear of offence or presumption. But he smiled wryly; he did not mind.

He was smaller than she was. He looked smaller than ever.

Together they went up to the bathroom and looked at the old shower head, and Jimmy confirmed that it wasn't worth spending time messing about with it, he'd get her a new one.

'It's done you a good few years,' he said.

'Yes,' said Jess.

At the bottom of the stairs, in the narrow London hallway, he said, 'They say the chemo might work, but they don't sound very cheery about it.'

Jess asked which hospital, and he told her.

'I hope they're looking after you properly,' she said.

'The wife and the boys have been very good,' was his reply.

Then he said, with his hand on the latch, 'I've not travelled far in my life, Jessica. I've not got far. All my life I've spent in these parts, as my dad did before me.'

He said these words seriously, as though he had been premeditating them.

'You're very well known here,' said Jess. 'You know us all. We all depend on you here. You've looked after us all for a long time.'

'No,' he repeated, 'I've not been far away from where I began.'

He opened the door, and Jess once again patted him nervously on the shoulder, and then he brightened a little and said, standing there on the threshold, 'I was born at home in Riversdale Road, you know, just off Clissold Park. No. 70. It's still a nice road, Riversdale.'

'Yes,' said Jess, 'it is.'

The thought of his birthplace comforted them both.

He came to fix the shower head, with his own hands, on what was clearly his last visit. Jess learnt that he was taken back into hospital, and expected bad news, but she met him once more, in the newsagent's on the corner, looking as though he were at death's door, which he was. He was chatting to the proprietor, but broke off when he saw Jess.

'They've let me out,' he said, with a certain bravado.

She knew that was not good, and didn't pretend to think it was. She bought her newspaper and a box of eggs, and said goodbye, leaving him to his last neighbourhood round.

The funeral was held in the Victorian church on the quadrant where Ollie and Josh used to be boy scouts, and Jess and Anna went, out of respect. So did Katie and Sylvie. There was a good turn-out. We didn't think Jimmy had been a religious man, but he'd known the vicar for many years, and the vicar had known him, which came to the same thing. The few words spoken were appropriate. We were told that Jimmy had been loyal and faithful to the last, a reliable friend in times of trouble, a pillar of his community like his father before him, a rock of strength. We were told a funny story about the night the church was flooded by a burst main in the bitter winter of 1963, and how Jimmy came to the rescue in his pyjamas and macintosh and woolly hat. 'God moves in a mysterious way, his wonders to perform, and so did Jimmy,' said the vicar. And then we sang the hymn.

We also sang 'The Day Thou Gavest Lord is Ended' and 'He Who Would Valiant Be' (Anna singing bravely and in tune), and the vicar read the familiar passage of the death of Mr Valiant-for-Truth from *Pilgrim's Progress*. 'So he passed over, and all the trumpets sounded for him on the other side.' And one of the boys, now in his forties, who had learnt to play the trumpet at the primary school round the corner, valiantly drew a breathy gasping phrase or two from his old boyhood instrument to send his father on his way. Not quite the 'Last Post', but it brought tears to the eyes just the same.

Jess, when she got home that afternoon, had taken down her old Everyman copy of *Pilgrim's Progress* to look up Mr Valiant-for-Truth and Mr Feeble-Mind, but found herself distracted by Mr Despondency and his daughter Much-Afraid. She had never noticed these minor characters before. They had been rescued, it seemed, by Greatheart from Doubting Castle and the clutches of Giant Despair. Mr Despondency, on the verge of crossing the river of death, apologised to his fellow-pilgrims on behalf of both of them for their having been 'troublesome in every company', with their desponds and fears, and as they went to the brink of the river his last words were 'Farewell Night, Welcome Day'. His daughter, on the other hand, 'went through the river singing, but none could understand what she said'.

What had happened to Mrs Despondency? Jess could not discover. Maybe she had been fallen by the wayside and been choked in the Slough of Despond.

She went through the river singing, but none could understand what she said.

Was Much-Afraid singing of the further bourne, the undiscovered country, the shore that Steve the Poet had tried but failed to reach? That bourne from which no traveller returns?

It is hard to know what Anna fears. She is too polite to reveal much. But fears she must have. She has been a little quiet of late, as though there was something on her mind. Maybe Jimmy's funeral had upset her, but it had been right for them both to go.

Jimmy had lived in his patch of London, generation to generation, and now his sons and daughters-in-law and grandchildren holidayed in Spain. Raoul was an exile, a man of the world.

His son worked at Cern in Switzerland, his ex-wife the anthropologist was, or had recently been, in Mongolia.

~

Jess and Raoul met for their third lunch in the Novotel on the Euston Road, next to the British Library, where Jess had been consulting books on the history of women's sanitary protection, the changing names under which it had been known, its VAT status, and its provision in NHS hospitals and other selected public institutions. The lunch venue was her choice, the meeting his suggestion.

She likes the spacious women's toilets in the BL. The sanitary-disposal system is labelled 'Ultimate Hygiene Solutions', which sounds more technological than it appears to be. It's just a plastic bin.

Jess was beginning to speculate about the nature of Raoul's interest in her. It is true that they had a great deal to talk about, as they covered the years since Halliday Hall – the politics of the Middle East, the rise of Islam, the wane of Marxism, the London bombings, neurology, urology, phantom pain – but did he have any more personal motive in seeking these encounters? Was there something he needed to tell her? Was there something he wanted from her?

She considered herself long past the age of courtship and romance, and assumed that his courtly manners were habitual.

Perhaps he was *sorry* for her? Perhaps her frailty and uncharacteristic fainting fit on that hot Wibletts afternoon had given him the wrong impression, had given him the idea that she needed protection, had suggested to him an entrée into her life, had given him a hold over her? Surely not. She did not think she presented a pitiable spectacle, and, even if she did, she did not see why that would have appealed to him.

Unless, of course, he was very lonely. He was still a stranger in this land. That was a possibility.

He was a man who would always be a stranger.

As she saluted him at the table by the glass window overlooking the harsh pavement and the brutal wide and unattractive street, she caught sight of herself reflected in the pane and thought she looked fine. A handsome woman, for her age. An independent woman. She was still confident in her physical presence. She was wearing a jaunty red beret and, for the benefit of Raoul, had applied a gloss of scarlet lipstick.

As she pulled out her chair and seated herself, smiling, and arranged her bag on the floor by her side, and shook out her napkin independently over her knee, the image of Noah Trelissick, poet and editor, swooped unbidden into the picture gallery of her memory, to be followed almost instantly by a more faded shot of the Professor on the carpet in his SOAS study. A momentary spasm of archaic sexual vanity and the unusual application of lipstick had summoned these shades.

She shakes them away. She has hardly thought of Noah in years, and his random and pointless intrusion is not welcome now.

The Professor is another matter. Maybe he reappears with a purpose. She does not think of him often either, but she is very slowly beginning to admit to herself that this is because she dare not think of him.

She is, after all, getting old. She is beginning to have a sense of an ending.

She returns to the present, intensifies her womanly but unseductive gaze at Raoul, picks up the menu, warns him off the buffet, asks him about the exhibition over the road at the Wellcome Institute. It is about surgery during the American Civil War (it must be some anniversary of something?), and he has had a hand in it. It connects with the discovery of the phenomenon of phantom pain, he says. She says she will visit it but knows she won't. (The subject does not wholly appeal. She is interested in surgery, but not in war.) She listens politely and orders slow-cooked belly of pork. Belly of pork is the fashionable dish of the autumn, and it reminds Jess of happy days shopping in the Blackstock Road for pigs' feet and pigs' tails. Raoul draws the line at belly of pork, although he insists that he will be happy, indeed delighted and curious, to watch her eat it. He chooses lamb cutlets.

Jess confesses that she seems irresistibly drawn to ordering taboo meals when invited out to lunch or dinner in restaurants, meals that are chosen as though on purpose to offend her hosts, or, on other occasions, her guests. Pork, hare, shellfish, nettle soup, gulls' eggs. Raoul articulates his preference for meat on the bone (which she had not yet quite consciously registered, but now recognises); he prefers it, he says, because you can see *where it has come from*. He is very suspicious of reconstituted meat. They discuss, briefly, forbidden foods, and Zain's strong views on the cucumber sandwich. Her mind still full of menstruation and the Ultimate Hygiene Solutions of the British Library, Jess almost introduces the subject of menstrual taboos, but decides she should not. Raoul is a fastidious man, even though his ex-wife is an anthropologist, and she does not want to put him off his cutlets.

She has not invited Raoul to her home. She has not asked him over the threshold. She has kept him out in the public conversational domain, in the detached domain of topics. She is wary of letting people get too close. He has not been introduced to Anna, although he knows about her, and always asks after her.

Raoul lives in an apartment block in St John's Wood. He hasn't exactly told her this, but he has intimated it. Men are not required to reveal or betray their domestic details or habits, and she imagines him impersonally tended by cleaners and guarded by a concierge, in a bachelor way of life embraced with relief after the defection of his nomadic French wife. She knows he likes to walk through Regent's Park, to glimpse the long necks of the tall giraffes in the Giraffe House and the birds in Lord Snowden's aviary. He is a man at home in the landscape of his adopted city.

But maybe he is lonely. She cannot tell.

She had not seen giraffe in Africa, but she had seen wildebeest and lechwe and marsh-dwelling sitatunga and plump-bellied zebra and fish-eagle and the rare shoebill. The rounded bellies of the zebra were as tight as drums. There had been a balding zebra-skin rug on the floor by the bed in the little hotel where they had stayed on their first night in Lusaka, before setting off towards the swamps. She had not liked it at all, and is surprised she can remember it. It was far too realistic. It was all too easy to see where it had come from, what it had once been. She did not like its legs.

As he neatly aligns his knife and fork over the curved picked neck bones of the cutlets, Raoul comes up with his proposition. She had sensed he had one, but she had had no idea of what it would be.

Does she remember Ursula, he asks. He expects the answer yes, because he has mentioned her before, but not in this newly meaningful way. He has bided his time with his update on Ursula.

'Yes, of course,' replies Jess cautiously.

He wants her to go with him to see Ursula Strawson.

She still takes some responsibility for Steve Carter, and Raoul has kept in touch, albeit anxiously and reluctantly, with Ursula. Or she, it now appears, has kept in touch with him.

'I got to know her well in Halliday,' he says. 'It was a place where we all got to know one another well. And she wrote to me. She wrote many letters.' He pauses, smiles sadly. 'Many hundreds of letters. Hundreds of letters and thousands and thousands of words.'

'Oh dear,' says Jess inadequately.

She toys with the remains of her bread roll.

'I thought she was in love with Zain,' Jess proffers tentatively.

'She was. But she transferred.'

'Oh dear,' says Jess again.

'At first she transferred to me, and then she gave up on me and transferred back to God.'

Over a double espresso, Raoul tells Jess the story of Ursula.

Ursula, he relates, had seen God when young. God had visited her in a shining light, from somewhere above the pelmet of her bedroom curtains (she was very precise about his location), and she had been converted. God had appeared to her in her bedroom in Redhill, and the glory of the Lord had shone about her, and she had risen from her bed a believer. She was sure she had not been asleep. It had been a waking vision. And, thus awakened, she had joined the Roman Catholic Church.

It was a Roman Catholic god, the God of the saints and the martyrs, who had appeared to her. She wished to be a martyr, to embrace the plague-ridden and the lepers, of whom there were few in Redhill. Her lower-middle-class, non-practising, disbelieving Church of England family had been appalled by this rebellious move. (Jess fills in some of this background detail for herself, from clues in Raoul's speech, for, although he is very quick, some of the very English social detail was meaningless or puzzling to him, although he reported it as faithfully as he could.) Ursula had flounced off, left her mother and father as Christ had commanded, changed her first name from Liz to Ursula (she had been christened Elizabeth, as were so many, in the wake of the birth of the princess) and had after much persistence been admitted to undertake a novitiate in a Cistercian convent in Hampshire. But this novitiate had gone badly, setting the pattern for a series of future evictions and rejections, and she had been politely but firmly discouraged from pursuing her dramatic sense of religious vocation.

She had been persuaded by the nuns that she was needed for service in the community, had resumed the teacher training that God had interrupted, and then had worked quietly for some years at a Catholic primary school in Croydon, until a series of spectacular psychotic breakdowns had precipitated her into ECT at an NHS psychiatrist hospital. She had been miraculously rescued from the hospital by the intervention of her concerned and conscientious GP, who happened to have heard of Dr Nicholls's outfit at Halliday.

'It's surprising,' says Raoul, 'the number of people who have taken up Ursula's cause.'

'Including you,' says Jess.

'Yes,' admits Raoul. 'She is very manipulative.'

'But,' he says, 'also she has suffered very greatly. Her episodes were very serious. They were horrifying.'

He is not making fun of Ursula's story.

Some years ago, Raoul continues, long after Ursula had been expelled from Halliday by Dr Nicholls, long after the general dispersal of NHS patients into the community, she had taken sanctuary in another nunnery, this time in a lay community attached to an abbey in Somerset, but had been evicted for bad behaviour. The nuns had not been able to put up with her any longer. Their patience ran out. She had taken to practising self-denial and austerity, and had visions of martyrdom that were very irritating to her less ambitious co-believers, whose aim was to keep going as best they could in an age of dwindling faith and finance. She was given to violent bouts of abuse and recrimination. She had been given notice and had been moved out to sheltered accommodation in Taunton, but something had gone wrong with her local-authority funding there, and she'd been turned out of that too. So she had made her way back eastwards to Essex, where she had once been happy, and claims that she is now living in a squat at Troutwell Farm, near the old site of abandoned Halliday, with a collection of tramps and vandals.

As Raoul recites this story, Jess sees why he needs to enlist her interest. This is the kind of subject about which she knows more than most people. She is a good listener. She is usually a good listener, but this story is tailor-made for her. She is transfixed. She does not suspect that Raoul had planted himself at Wibletts, hijacked a lift back to London through a rainstorm in her friend Eleanor's car and met with her thrice for lunch simply in order to offload responsibility for Ursula, but she can see Ursula may have figured in his otherwise somewhat surprising interest in Jess.

She confesses to Raoul that she too had been drawn back to visit Halliday and Troutwell, that a summer or two ago she and her daughter Anna had trespassed over its barbed-wire boundaries and picnicked in the grounds. It had a powerful pull, that place, a scenic and a spiritual pull, as, in its more majestic Italianate urban way, did Colney Hatch, high on its North London ridge. But she and Anna had seen no sign of any residents at Troutwell, legal or illegal. No puffs of illicit smoke, no washing hung out dry, no Kentucky Fried Chicken cartons. They'd seen graffiti, and a lot of CCTV notices, but no people.

'Well, she's there now,' says Raoul. 'Or she says she is.'

Has he been to see her? No, he hasn't braved the journey; he wouldn't know how get there. He hasn't been near the place for decades. He had been in a bad way when he was first referred from UCH, and he was never quite sure exactly where he was throughout all of his stay. He says this apologetically. It had been an island for him, a refuge, an anchorage. He'd been a lost man from the Middle East.

'I know it's in Essex,' he says, 'but I don't know Essex.'

'How do you know she's really there?' asks Jess in a challenging tone. 'I think it's a very unlikely story.'

'I did see her when once she was in Taunton,' says Raoul, but he knows that's not an answer. 'She was living in a maisonette in an estate behind the station. It was quite pleasant in its way. Pleasant little houses with front gardens. But she had to leave. Or so she told me.'

'It could be a fantasy,' says Jess, her mind flashing back to Steve slumped in a deckchair in the dubious safety of the Wendy House. 'It could all be a fantasy.'

'It isn't,' says Raoul, and she is inclined to believe him.

'She must be getting on by now,' says Jess, still playing for time.

'She's very robust, physically,' says Raoul. 'She looked strong when I saw her in Somerset. She was' – he pauses, looking for a word – 'imposing?'

(His English is subtle. French and Arabic were his first languages, but his use of English is precise and delicate. His accent is now mid-Atlantic, but a refined mid-Atlantic.)

'Does she say she wants to see you?' asks Jess.

He nods his neat head primly.

'Always, always,' he says.

'The postmarks,' he says, 'would fit with Halliday and Troutwell. Essex postmarks, an Essex postcode.'

Jess wonders if Ursula remembers her. She doubts it. Ursula had visibly enjoyed being the only woman in a group of men, the queen of the little refuge. She had not welcomed Jessica's visits. If she remembers Jess at all, it would probably be with resentment. Jess had stolen Zain.

Ursula's grey hair had been abundant, her complexion fair but her colour high, the naked nape of her neck proud. Ursula reassembles herself in Jess's memory; she comes into focus.

'Do you ever reply to her letters?' asks Jess.

'Not very often,' he says. 'She gives a PO box number. And she uses second-class stamps.'

He offers this as though it were convincing circumstantial evidence of his tale.

Ursula, it appears, had written to Raoul at great length about her religious or pseudo-religious revelations, about the demonic and angelic voices she has heard, some of them urging her to acts of violence. He did not read these letters scrupulously, and indeed much of their content was impenetrable, as she used cyphers and symbols for parts of her message, but he had got the gist of it. She was using him as a confessor, as once she had used the priest, and, after the priest, Dr Nicholl. She spoke, or she wrote, but it was not necessary to listen or to read.

'She is,' says Raoul, 'in her own way, impressive. Not to say fascinating. Bi-polar, schizophrenic, hard to tell.'

'And,' he repeats, 'I have to say, manipulative.'

Jess agrees that she will go with Raoul to Troutwell, to see if they can find Saint Ursula.

'That would be very good of you,' says Raoul.

Jess suggests that if he is serious about this enterprise, as it seems he is, it might perhaps be wise to contact the local social services in advance to see if Ursula is known to the authorities.

She can see from his holding expression that he does not wholly approve of this practical proposal. Might it not be compromising, might it not cause trouble, might it not suggest a degree of commitment and responsibility which he – they – would then be obliged to honour? She recognises that this may be what he thinks, although he does not articulate it. It hovers between them, over an unwise second double espresso.

Jess thinks she has enough to worry about, with Anna.

But maybe he hasn't got enough to worry about.

Maybe she ought to take on Ursula too.

She says she'll think about it, she's got to go now, she looks at her watch, she's got to get back to her desk in Humanities Two. (She hasn't really got to get back to her desk – the Reading Rooms are very full, so she's dutifully cleared her desk and left her laptop in a locker – but he won't know that.)

It is his turn to pay the bill, and she thanks him. She will get in touch, she promises. She might make one or two non-committal and, as it were, semi-anonymous inquiries.

He is right to think she has contacts in the social services in Essex. She could ring her young friend Lauren, who will tell her the name of somebody in the community mental health team, who may know of Ursula's case. Somebody must.

Jess saw Lauren quite recently, and appropriately, at Birkbeck at a seminar on the Death of the Asylum. Lively Lauren had updated her about Essex County matters, including one notorious and much misreported child-abuse case which had lingered in the headlines, and she had also described a rare sighting of Anna's beloved Hazel, who had been seen teaching group singing on a holistic holiday course on an island in the Atlantic. Hazel had left Marsh Court for the sun, and the Essex canals for the ocean. Lauren, another member of the band of the warm and golden-hearted, is an Essex girl, and she sticks it out in Essex.

One of the speakers at the Birkbeck seminar had given a vivid account of Friern Barnet in the old days. She had done her earliest psychiatric work there. She had slides of the curious egg-box motif that had decorated the ceilings: dirty cream when she had first observed it, and later what she called a surprising shade of pink. She also commented on the curious properties of the lava floors of some of the old wards, which were cold to the feet and had seemed specially designed to soak in and retain urine. When replaced by wooden flooring, bedwetting had diminished appreciably.

Friern Barnet had left a deep impression on the speaker.

Friern Barnet had been a vast institution. Arden Gate had

been vast, and so had Severalls, and so had Troutwell. They had once housed multitudes, those old palaces.

Ursula is sheltering fiercely in a little space, a little, little space, her last refuge. So thinks Jess, with pity.

On the way to King's Cross tube station, as Jess walks past the perpetual building site and *Big Issue* vendors of the façade of the St Pancras Hotel, she checks her mobile phone. On this stretch of beleaguered waif-tormented pavement she always checks her phone. There is a voice message from Anna at the day centre, describing her lunch (hamburger and chips, but, although Anna likes hamburgers more than she should, she sounds faintly disappointed, almost rather anxious?), and two texts, one from Victoria and one from Bob. Victoria's text reads SPARE TICKET 4 WIG HALL FDY, CAN U CUM? For some reason Victoria thinks Jess likes concerts, which are as little to her taste as the American Civil War. Victoria thinks she is doing Jess a favour by inviting her, and Jess cannot disabuse her. And Jess does not like Victoria's abbreviation of 'come'. It is louche. Victoria's diction and spelling are louche. She reminds Jess very strongly of Virginia Woolf. Maybe she has consciously modelled herself on Woolf.

Bob's proposition is more attractive. She pauses to read it in the windy mouth of the tube station on the Euston Road. Bob writes: BOTSWANA KILBURN TUES 22? CAFÉ LAUNCH, GREAT AFRO FOOD, BRING ANNA?

Bob knows her appetites. This might be shaming, was once, but is no longer. Great Afro food sounds good.

Yes, she and Anna will probably go to the Kilburn party. Bob and Anna enjoy a party. Bob is thoughtful about suggesting occasional outings that can include Anna.

Maybe at this point Jess was already asking herself if she could ask me to drive her and Raoul to Troutwell, if it should come to that. As I had driven her and Sylvie to Wibletts. I was a useful friend, an old friend with a new car, and she'd already softened me up for future requests by her entertaining descriptions of Raoul's gallant lunches and menu preferences. (I was particularly gripped by his views of the superiority of meat-on-the-bone, and have found myself becoming phobic in sympathy about anything skinned, boned or filleted.) She gossiped freely about Raoul, in a way that she had never gossiped about Zain or even about Bob. That's how I knew she hadn't been to bed with him, as, I suppose, even at her age, even at our age, she might have done.

Standing on the Piccadilly Line platform, Jess gazes at the advertisements on the hoarding opposite, with their disparate sales pitches: an ancient brand of whisky matured in charred oak barrels, a sober black-and-white poster in a serious font announcing a course on Meditation and Spirituality, a dating agency for the colourful and nubile, and cut-price air fares to Africa offered by a safari company. It says it costs under £300 to fly to Cape Town or Namibia or Kenya and back again. Once you could live in London on £300 for months, but now it doesn't seem a lot of money. Would Anna like to go on safari? Would an insurance company cover Anna and Jess to go on a safari?

Kenya is represented by a zebra. X is for Xylophone, Z is for Zebra. Anna knows that. Anna knows her alphabet by heart, and can recite it as correctly as Jess, but its higher uses still remain largely mysterious to her.

A little dark black-brown dusty velvet mouse is scuttling busily between the tracks over the nuggets of spent coke and clinker in the gulf below her. It is spotted by a lank young man with a scruffy red beard and a blue rucksack, and other passengers including Jess spot him spotting it, and a row of newly arrived foreigners, indigenous commuters, multi-ethnic students and bag-burdened shoppers lines up to gaze down with interest at the lively indifferent little creature going about its own business. They all seem well disposed towards it, and most of them are smiling. Perhaps that is because it is safe down there, safe in its own subterranean dominion. It will not climb up on to the platform and attack skirts and trousers. It has its own world, where it does no harm. The travellers can afford to smile. They admire its survival instincts.

The lions had roared in the darkness round the camp.

Tourists are occasionally killed on safari in Africa. Jess always registers reports of these incidents with a slightly sardonic interest. Not many lions and leopards kill tourists, but elephant, buffalo, hippopotamus and crocodile often feature as agents of death.

Her supervisor Guy Brighouse had died in the field, some time ago, while still in his sixties. Well, not quite in the field, but near enough. He had not been killed by wild animals, nor had he succumbed to malaria, as so many missionaries and anthropologists have done. His death had been human, mysterious and violent. He had been killed in a street incident in Harare. It was said that he had been involved in some political protest and had been gunned down by the police, but the facts were never established. There were witnesses, but they told different stories. It was known that in the old Chatham House pre-independence days in London he had been well acquainted with both Robert Mugabe and Joshua Nkomo.

His body was found dumped in a hotel car park.

Guy was the kind of man about whom people told that kind of story. The stories became true because he invoked them. They clustered round him like bees or birds. He drew the gunfire, the flame-thrower. He became his own legend, he made up his own myth, and it ended in a bin bag behind the Brontë Hotel in Harare. Jess believes he experienced a final rush of triumph as he met his death more than halfway. It had all gone according to plan. Wiry, small, tough, provocative, he had provoked his ending.

His memorial service had been very different from Jimmy's Highbury funeral. Camp, baroque, outré. She strings together these words and tests them as she sits on the rattling tube on its way to Finsbury Park.

SOAS had done Guy proud and turned out in force, the peoples of many lands. Americans, Canadians, Africans, Brazilians, Samoans. A bizarre late-twentieth-century international ceremonial had seen Brighouse on his way. Unlike Jimmy Parker, who had known a few square miles of the foundations of North London as though they were the grounds of his own garden and his own estate, and had not strayed far beyond them, Guy had attempted to traverse and interpret the globe. Restless, footloose, he had never stayed anywhere very long – a year or two here, a year or two there. Superficial, his colleagues enviously judged him. He was a natural linguist, famed, like Richard Burton, for being able to pick up a working relationship with any language he encountered, in any part of the world. He hadn't published very much: as one of his eulogists commented, he preferred talking and walking to writing. His flamboyant reputation would not long outlive him. A grasshopper, not an ant.

Jess had seen Guy from time to time, over the years. He cherished a soft spot for her, from those early Bangweulu days. She had been his poppet, his protegée. He had hardened and shrivelled like a nut, a brown dry nut. A dry little hopper, with a sharp jaw.

The memorial had included a reading from the ancestor poetry of the perished tribe of the clay mansions, in its original language, with some presumably freely inventive phrases of translation from Guy. The ancestors are dying, their houses are in ruins, the living have abandoned them, the living have gone to the cities and sold their souls.

There had also been songs, some of them outrageous.

Guy and the Professor had known each other quite well. Guy had warned her off the Professor and his habits, but she had taken no heed.

The Professor had been, in his way, generous about Anna. He had settled money on her. Jess does not like to remember this fact, and has almost managed to forget it.

Jess now knows that she ought to google the Professor, to see if he is alive or dead. The depth of her terror at the thought of initiating this act, this investigation, scares her, and interests her. It reveals to her that she is more fragile than she likes to think she is. She has procrastinated for so many years, and during these years technology has altered beyond any possible expectations. All she needs to do is to type in his name. It will be there, somewhere. An obituary, a final publication, a footnote, a cross-reference on Google Scholar. She is waiting, she thinks, for something to propel her into action. It will come.

Yes, it will come.

When she gets home after her third lunch with Raoul, Anna is not yet back from the day centre, so Jess rings her and Anna says she will be on her way home with one of the minders who is passing the end of their street. Anna sounds subdued, and remains subdued on her return. Jess probes a little but cannot discover any cause for the shadow that lies over her. Anna's emotional landscape is rarely tempestuous, though sometimes dull, and this cloud will surely pass, but it saddens Jess. Is Anna annoyed that her mother broke off her studies on sanitary protection to take lunch with Raoul? Is she jealous of this word called 'Raoul'? Maybe, if Jess is to continue to see Raoul, she should invite him to her home and introduce him to Anna, but this is a step she does not feel ready to take. Her life with Anna is so composed, so settled. To cheer Anna, Jess irresponsibly suggests that next year they might take a trip to Africa, to see the animals.

Anna does not respond to this idea very warmly, and why should she? She has no sense of the old depths, the hinterland from which it proceeds.

She doesn't seem interested in Jess's radical proposal.

Jess is shocked by her own suggestion. It is not like her to be so random. But she is beginning to think that she could perhaps take Anna to Africa. Why not? It wouldn't kill them, would it? It would be an adventure. And they could afford it. According to that poster, it wasn't very expensive.

Anna, the next morning, seemed still to be subdued. Jess decided they should both stay at home for the day, and whiled away some time by emailing her friend Lauren in Colchester. Did Lauren know anything about alleged squatters at Troutwell? Whom should Jess contact in the CMHT? She googled Troutwell, and saw that since she had last looked at the site there were some new photographs which did indeed suggest recent habitation, as well as a greater degree of vandalism than she and Anna had encountered. Breaking into and photographing large derelict listed buildings seemed a not uncommon hobby, according to this website. Jess had not known that and was slightly worried to think of herself as belonging to such a strange and deviant fraternity. She had thought her interests special, but clearly they weren't.

Was Ursula in there somewhere? It seemed neither probable nor improbable. It was a worry to her, but not a very serious worry. It was Raoul's adopted problem, not hers.

Serious worry hit her at lunchtime. Anna, toying half-heartedly with her baked potato and mushrooms, looked up at her mother and said in a solemn, anxious, embarrassed voice, 'Mum, it keeps on coming out.'

Jess put down her fork and looked at her grown-up daughter's worried face. She couldn't think what Anna was talking about.

'What comes out?' she was obliged to ask, as Anna could go no further.

'I can't stop it. And it's red,' said Anna. 'It's the wrong colour. It's like blood.'

At the heavy word 'blood' her face crumpled and tears filled her eyes, tears of sadness for her mother, of worry for herself.

'Where from?' asked Jess, putting her hand comfortingly on her daughter's hand.

'You know,' said Anna apologetically, her face pink with shame. 'When I go to the toilet.'

Slowly, painfully, Anna disclosed that for some time now she had been mildly incontinent, needing to pee all the time, sometimes wetting her pants. And there had been blood in her urine. Pink urine had been trickling into the white lavatory bowl which Jimmy Parker had installed just after Christmas all those years ago. Yes, nearly every time she went to the toilet. And she had to go so often. No, it wasn't anything to do with her monthlies, it wasn't a Tampax thing. (Jess had taught Anna to use tampons; it had been hard to explain the procedure and hard for Anna to learn to do it, but she had learnt and coped with it well. A useful womanly skill.)

How long had this been going on for? Anna couldn't tell. She didn't have a good grasp of the passing of weeks and months and years, although she could latch on to dates, birthdays, promised events. She knew they were going to meet Bob next Tuesday in Kilburn in an African restaurant. She knew it was her mother's birthday in October and hers a month later. But she couldn't tell when the bleeding had started.

It had been going on quite a while, her mother guessed; she'd been hiding this for quite a while, hoping it would stop and go away.

'Don't worry,' said Jess confidently. 'It's nothing. This kind of things often happens. It happened to me once. We'll get it checked out, but we'll find it's nothing. You may have to have some antibiotics, we'll find out.'

'Did it really happen to you?' asked Anna.

'Yes,' lied Jess.

Well, in fact, she now remembered, she had once had some blood apparently coming from the wrong place, but she'd connected that with the irritation caused by an obsolete bit of invasive fish-hook contraception she'd used while sleeping with Zain. That could hardly be the cause of Anna's bleeding.

Jess thought the fish-hook had also given her cystitis.

'Really?' insisted Anna. 'You had it too?'

'Yes,' repeated Jess. 'It was nothing.'

Anna brightened and reached for some more butter to liven up her cooling baked potato.

'Hey, steady on,' said Jess admiringly, as Anna helped herself to a thick slab of New Zealand Anchor. And they both laughed.

Jess knew she shouldn't look at the internet, and she didn't. Self-diagnosing illnesses on the internet is not wise. She rang their GP and made an appointment for later in the week, she made Anna promise next time it happened not to flush the lavatory but to leave what was there for Jess to see. Anna promised.

Anna was relieved, and that was the main thing.

It hadn't been possible to ascertain whether or not Anna was suffering any kind of pain. Looking back, Jess could see she had been unusually quiet for the past few days, but she couldn't cast her mind back further than that. She didn't want to suggest pain. Anna would always deny pain.

The thought of her expert friend Sylvie occurred to Jess during the afternoon. We all hesitated to exploit Sylvie, now she was so busy and so important, but Jess didn't think it would be wrong, in the circumstances, to consult her. She emailed her, giving a brief description of the problem (urine straw-coloured, bleeding pinkish and thin) and asked Sylvie, when she had time, to email or ring her back. She hoped for reassurance.

Jess was more worried than she liked to let herself know.

Anna had enjoyed good health, on the whole. She had been lucky that way. And so had Jess.

Anna had not been told about Jess's fainting fit at Wibletts. It would have worried her needlessly. Jess had blanked it out, ignored it, forgotten it. Raoul had never referred to it. I don't know if Sylvie had ever mentioned it either. I had asked Jess if she had had a check-up, how was her blood pressure, that kind of general query. She'd said she was okay, she was fine, nothing wrong, it had just been the heat. And the stress of mad Victoria, who was enough to make anyone pass out.

No connection with Anna's illness. No proleptic connection. How could there be?

Anna was unwell.

An infection? Kidney stones? Cancer of the bladder? Cancer of the kidneys?

Jess didn't know what to think.

~

Jess didn't call me until after she'd spoken to Sylvie, and until after Anna had seen the doctor and had some tests. It wasn't very good news, and the diagnosis was not facilitated by Jess's inability to answer any questions about her daughter's paternal genetic inheritance. A lot of kidney and some bladder ailments are hereditary. More ailments than we ever thought possible are hereditary. Not, as Jess said to herself, that it would make much difference, would it, at this stage? But it wasn't good to be so unhelpful, to sound so uncertain.

Jess's first guess had been that kidneys were the problem, but it seemed that the bladder was also suspect. Haematuria (a new and unwelcome word in Jess's vocabulary) could suggest either. There would have to be a cystoscopy and a biopsy. Poor Anna was a modest girl. She would not like these procedures.

Jess had never spoken to me so openly about the Professor. We sat there, in that front room I'd known for so many years, on the soft old cushions on the old settee, with our mugs of coffee, as Jess went back over some of the old ground. She told me that she'd no idea what had happened to him, had not wanted to know. I could understand this, up to a point: in the distant past I'd had a few affairs that I would never have wished to own up to, I'd slept with one or two men whom I wouldn't recognise if I sat next to them tomorrow on the bus. But these affairs had had no consequences. They had been light-weight, passing. Anna was a consequence, and the Professor had not been light-weight.

'He took advantage of me,' said Jess, smiling wryly as she clasped her 'Present from Southend' mug. 'I didn't think that at the time, but I suppose I do now. I thought I knew what I was doing, but I didn't. And then there was Anna, and everything changed.'

He'd wanted her to have an abortion, he'd set it all up, with a recuperative week in an expensive, discreet clinic in Hampshire thrown in, but she had refused. And their sexual relationship had lingered on, had been picked up after Anna's birth, had renewed itself, and then had worn itself out slowly. It had come to an end before Jess had learnt of Anna's condition, in the early days when all with Anna was still golden. The ending of the affair had been sealed by his trip to Manchuria, which he and his wife had been planning for a long time. Jess had known he was leaving SOAS, but not that he would be travelling so far afield, for so long, and with his wife. It was a great undertaking, a serious career move that was meant to propel him and his wife into another higher realm of research and fieldwork.

She was relieved, she told me, by the dramatic finality of his departure, by the sense of complete rupture, by his unfeeling demeanour. She had begun to feel shamed by the shabbiness of their hole-in-the corner relationship, their cheap Thursday-afternoon hotel, their inability to greet one another openly in corridors and lecture theatres and on street corners. What had seemed glamorously adult and pleasantly secretive had come to feel inadequate, embarrassing, unnatural.

'I was glad when he disappeared,' said Jess. 'I was all right with Anna, my life was fine. You remember, we were all fine, we were all fine in those days, I knew someone else would turn up, someone less unreal. Because the Prof was unreal, he was really out of touch. I could see that the thought of having a child horrified him. He didn't think much of human beings. He inspected them as though they were insects. I don't think he ran away from me because of Anna – he'd been plotting the move for a long time – but his reaction to the birth of Anna was – well, it was unacceptable.'

I wanted to ask if he had ever seen his daughter, but I didn't dare. We were in dangerous territory, walking on eggshells, I didn't want to interrupt.

'So,' said Jess, bold, brave, independent, proud, self-sufficient Jess, 'I've never dared to try to find out what happened to him. I haven't dared to ask anyone who might know. At Guy's funeral, I nearly spoke to somebody there who would have almost certainly known, but I didn't dare. And since then I've done nothing. I was such a coward. I've been such a coward.'

We both sat silently for a while, contemplating the nature of cowardice.

I had brought Jess some flowers, a little bunch of anemones, and she'd put them in the little green-and-white-striped jug on the mantelpiece, which stood amongst the African rain-maker's stones and the figurines and birds' eggs and tarnished silver candlesticks from Broughborough. They'd been crumpled and drooping when I arrived, the little pink and red and white ones, but now they were beginning to straighten themselves, to stand up and open their bright faces and their mascara-black eyes. You could almost see the water rise through the sap of the pale hairy stems.

I love that little jug on Jess's mantelpiece. I have known it for many years. It's hand-painted, clay, irregularly striped in a soft mossy-yellowy-green and off-white cream with a coarse cracked glaze. It has a deep, high-waisted rim and a soft little lip. A springtime jug, a primavera jug, but lovely with autumn flowers, or with a sprig or two of red winter berries. Jess says you can stick a handful of anything in there and it will fall of its own accord into a perfect shape: weeds or flowers or a bunch of parsley or little twigs will arrange themselves as though nature herself had taken a hand to show them at their best. It had been given to her as a wedding present by Maroussia, and it had been broken once, it had been knocked over by Anna and broken, but Jess had glued it together again with Araldite – not very invisibly but competently, and it was still water-tight. It was the more beautiful for the cracks and the chips and the patching and the marks of age. The brown-pink clay spoke through the gentle pattern. The anemones opened as we watched.

'He gave me some money,' said Jess. 'I made him cancel the abortion and the clinic, but he insisted on giving me some money when he left. He gave me £1,325 precisely, he paid me off with £1,325. That was a lot of money in those days. I was going to invest it for Anna. He called himself a Marxist, you know, but I think he came from quite a grand family. I did invest it at first, but then I thought it was more sensible to use it as a deposit to buy this house, so I did. I had some from my father too, but it was his money that made me think of it, that made it possible.'

She sighed, then shook her head and smiled, in a weary, good-mannered elderly way.

'You know what I paid for this house? I paid £6,000 freehold. I got a good mortgage. And you know what it's valued at now?'

I could guess, but I waited for her to say.

'It's valued at £800,000 . . . £800,000.'

Despite the drug dealers at Finsbury Park and the ricin men of the mosque, Kinderley Road was valued at £800,000. I knew that, because so was my house in Shawcross Street. In fact, mine was worth more. It was worth more than a million pounds. My husband and I had been joint owners, we had paid off the mortgage jointly, and now he was dead and it was mine. Through no fault or virtue of our own, Jess and I had appreciated. By sticking it out in our everyday way, we had become rich.

'I've often thought,' said Jess 'that it would look after Anna when I'm gone. She could be comfortable, even when I had gone.'

This was the unmentionable subject, which Anna's illness had brought to the surface.

The confused tenses of Jess's statement were indicative of her dilemma.

'Comfortable' is good. But it is not best.

We were both silent for a while. Then Jess began to talk about Anna's prognosis, and the suggested surgery or treatments, and how frightened she (Jess, not Anna) was of the surgeon and the oncologist, and how Anna would have to give consent. But Anna would give consent to whatever Jess advised. Her trust in her mother was absolute.

This was part of the dilemma.

Jess did not know what to think of the new would-be enlightened 'consent' legislation. It could make things very difficult for parents and carers. But she knew that not all parents were loving, not all carers caring.

Jess knew that she and Anna would never be able to cope with dialysis, and that Anna would never be high on the waiting list for a transplant. But of course it might not come to that. Her imagination had leapt to the worst, but the worst might not come. It might be a small problem, an infection, a benign growth.

~

Fear of the surgeon overcame Jess's fear of the Professor and the internet. She realised that it did not matter when he had died, what he had died of, whether he had had other children. It did not matter whether or not he had suffered from any form of kidney or bladder disease. It did not matter whether he had ever felt bad about what he had done to Jessica Speight. Maybe he had followed her career guiltily, checking online her articles on the language of the male orgasm and Pearl Buck's daughter and Mungo Park's adventures and Lionel Penrose's chromosomes and the luxury flats of Colney Hatch. Maybe he had forgotten her altogether. Maybe she had been one of many seduced maidens, a forgotten statistic.

Or maybe she and Anna had been a trauma to him, a guilty trauma from which he had fled to the uttermost parts of the earth.

Zain, she knew, had remembered her. And Bob still loved her. And Raoul had sought her out. She comforted herself with these thoughts.

It is surprising, but she is beginning to think that Raoul's interest in her is sexual. It's a bit late in the day for that kind of thing, but nevertheless she thinks it may be so. And she had put on lipstick for him. She doesn't often do that these days.

She must have been responding to something in the quality of his interest in her.

Maybe the Professor had loved her? No, she thought not, she knew not. He had desired her, and had taken some small professional risks to possess her, but he had not loved her.

Grimly, bracing herself, clenching her teeth, she sat down one evening during the days of waiting for Anna's biopsy results and fed the Professor's name into the search engine. She tried Google first, not thinking anything would pop up and that she would resort to Google Scholar, but to her astonishment she achieved an immediate hit. There were dozens of links to somebody called Bernt Gunnar Lindahl. They did not look like good news. Bernt Gunnar Lindahl, it appeared, had murdered his wife in a small town in Scotland. This seemed too good, too bad, to be true, and indeed it was, because as soon as she clicked on the first of the links a photograph of the murderer appeared, and he was of the wrong age group, although the fairly unusual combination of his three Swedish names matched. He was a plump pink smiling man in his fifties with a moustache and spectacles. He was much younger than Jess, not older. She flitted through the murder reports rapidly, discovering that he had stabbed his wife, not in a fit of jealous rage but because of something to do with insurance.

A squalid and uninteresting little murder, but it was recent and it had excited the press, and it was difficult to get beyond it to any other namesakes. The murderer had clogged the net. So she made her way slowly to Google Scholar, where she discovered a Swedish author called Gunnar Lindahl and a cross-country skier of the same name, but they were not very helpful. She trawled and trawled, more and more impatiently, but she couldn't understand the Swedish websites, and eventually was driven back to trying SOAS staff and alumni. But SOAS seemed to have disowned or forgotten the Professor, or tucked him away in a digital corner so obscure she could not find it.

Eventually, after stabbing and jabbing and clicking in an increasingly random manner, she found him. When she typed in the title in English of his doctorate at Uppsala, up it popped, with a link.

The link was an obituary. It was in Swedish, and it appeared to be from some old university listing. The print itself was old, the typeface was old. There was nothing new here.

He had been dead for years, for decades. All the time she'd carefully not been thinking about him, he'd been dead. That was why he had vanished from the academic world and sent no messages from Manchuria. He had published nothing since the doctorate, except for a few papers and a contribution to a book published in Korea on agrarian policy and population control. He'd not left much of a mark.

The Professor, in fact, had not even been a professor. She'd given him that title, in her dialogue with herself and eventually with us, as a joke. He'd been Dr Lindahl, not the Professor. He'd never become Professor Lindahl.

It was late, Dr Speight's eyes ached, the screen quivered and swam, her new varifocals had had enough, and she couldn't be bothered to google the wife.

She went to bed, feeling curiously relieved by this outcome. She was pleased to have extracted a reply from the web, she was pleased not to have to worry about him any more, she was pleased still to be alive. She and Anna were both still alive. They would both move on, as modern jargon has it, they would both go forward together. Anna would be okay. Irrationally, she suddenly felt sure that Anna would be okay. The ogre was dead, poor old ghost, but she and Anna were alive.

She felt sorry for the poor old ghost of the waste lands of Manchuria and Uppsala. He had been driven out of Bloomsbury and his lovenest in the Marchmont Hotel by the unexpected birth of the pure gold baby. A sense of generous sorrow for his disappointing life and long-ago death flowed through her, as she stretched her legs, and then curled herself up in her warm and comfortable bed, and turned the pillow over so that the cool fresh side of it met her cheek. How good it was to sleep alone, in her own house, which was worth £800,000. The Professor, unwittingly, had invested his £1,325 well.

The curious sum that made up the dowry represents, Jess has always suspected, the sale of some asset. A small house on an island in the archipelago, a Sèvres dining set, a ruby necklace. She may never be able to verify this, but it is what she suspects. He had, after all, been a Marxist, of a sort, with a morality, of a sort.

~

It was quite easy to reassure Anna about her condition and her health, or at least it seemed to be so to Jess and to us, though who could tell what Anna's underlying fears were? Confiding in her mother seemed to have satisfied Anna that her illness was not grave and that she would be cured.

Her confidence in Jess was enormous. It had rarely had cause to falter, and it did not falter now. Anna approached the complicated sequence of hospital visits and scans patiently, even cheerfully, and opened her legs and submitted to the embarrassing examinations as bravely as she could. She did not like or understand what was happening, but she did not complain.

Jess sits near by, behind the flimsy little curtain on its metal rail, twisting her silver rings round and round her fingers, helpless. She is too close to her daughter, she suffers in her body for her daughter.

Anna, robed in the long pale hospital robe, a much laundered heavily ironed faded blue robe with a pattern of white daisies, looks angelic. With her fair hair and her timeless, ageless face, she looks like a girl in a fairytale, entranced, charmed, expectant, at the beginning of a story that has yet to unfold. She looks touchingly trusting, bewildered but trusting. The simple round neck of the robe make her look like a vulnerable child. Was it possible that anybody had abused her, and that Anna had never been able to tell, had been too ashamed or frightened to tell? Jess is sure this that could not be so. Anna would have spoken to her mother. She would have found the words. But of course Jess has not kept her under her eyes for every moment of her adolescent and adult life. She has been obliged to trust others.

The tapes that tie the hospital robe across Anna's smooth fair slightly freckled back are the apron strings.

Anna is tied to her mother's apron strings.

Jess's confidence in the hospital is not as strong as Anna's confidence in Jess, although the hospital and the manner of its staff has improved since the days when it had pumped Steve Carter's stomach in such an unforgiving manner. Jess has had little reason to visit it, except for routine blood tests and a mammogram (this was before the days when she found herself summoned to the supermarket mobile-van) and an abortive attempt at physiotherapy for a sprained ankle, but she can tell that it was now more efficient and more patient-friendly than it had been. When they see him next, the urologist/surgeon, Mr Savandra, tries hard to be reassuring as he explains the possible diagnoses and procedures ahead. Jess is in too much of a panic to listen very carefully, and Anna nods and smiles nervously and does not understand a word of what he says. How could she? Mr Savandra is small, dark and courteous, but withdrawn. He does not reach out. He seems to have taken on board Anna's limited understanding, but prefers consulting the file of notes on his desk to attempting to engage in eye contact with either mother or daughter. He looks down at the notes through most of the consultation. But he is respectful and polite. He addresses

Jessica as Dr Speight, which she finds comforting. We cling to status when in danger, when trapped at the mercy of an institution. Jess's doctorate on the impact of missionaries on the practice of traditional remedies in Central Africa stands between her and the sucking gulf of non-being and nonentity and humiliation that hospitals represent.

Mr Savandra is polite, but his sidekick the oncologist is not so friendly. Jess finds him inhuman and alarming, though she knows she may be projecting her fear on to him and turning him into another male ogre. His most human trait appears to be a desire to upstage Mr Savandra and to suggest that oncologists are more important than surgeons and urologists. He talks a great deal about the ever increasing importance of oncology, the decreasing value of surgery. He may be right about that, but why should Jess care? She is not here to support his sense of his status, which is not under attack. His manner towards Anna is an aggressive mix of the profoundly condescending and the jolly. Jess knows that some adults find it hard to talk naturally to Anna, being unsure of the level of her response and understanding, and are over-cautious in their efforts. Dr Newman has no such hesitations. He is, by nature, an overbearing bully. His complexion is a high dark red with a bluish tinge, his hair black and thick and neat and carefully combed, his eyes deep set, his eyebrows prominent and handsome, his square and manly chin aggressively smooth from hard close shaving. He is very pleased with himself. He asks Anna questions about her sexual history that Jess knows (or believes she knows) that Anna cannot understand, but the manner of his interrogation arouses in Jess the slightest faintest tremor of fear. The un-safety spreads, the anxiety of uncertainty spreads.

Jess knows that Anna does not smoke, although she herself smoked when young, but she cannot be certain about everything that has happened to her.

Anna disapproves of smoking, as most young people do. She was taught to disapprove at Marsh Court, and Jessica's generation has long abandoned the habit.

(Except for me. I still smoke, when I am alone, in my own home, once or twice a week. A cigarette comforts me. I am sometimes indeed quite often lonely now, and a cigarette keeps me company, offers me a small act of defiance. I smoked as an undergraduate, and I took it up again when Tom was dying.)

Dr Newman tells Jess that the problem is not with the kidney but with the bladder. Anna has a small tumour, located in what Jess thinks of as Sylvie Raven's domain. With Mr Savandra's approval, he will attempt to shrink it with medication and then they will all see what to do next. He will send the results to Mr Savandra, the surgeon with the knife, and Anna will be summoned back.

Anna's blood pressure is slightly high, she must take medication for that too. How long has her blood pressure been up? Jess shakes her head, she has no idea.

She has neglected her daughter and failed to recognise her symptoms.

What else do we need to do, asks Jess. Has he any dietary advice, what about fluid intake, what about exercise? What about going on living?

Dr Newman has no interest in such questions. He brushes them away. They are beyond his remit. Living is not his specialty.

Sylvie had warned Jess that Dr Newman was not a congenial man, that he was brusque and vain and self-important, but, she had insisted, he was good at his job. He was really good at prescribing the correct dose of toxic pills, and that takes nerve as well as judgement, said Sylvie. The staff disliked him, but they trusted him. His patients were frightened of him, but he cured a lot of them. 'You have to remember,' said Sylvie, 'he spends a lot of time dealing with people with ghastly afflictions.'

But she agrees that his manner is not good.

Sylvie is kind and reassuring to Jess. She thinks Anna will be fine. Bladder cancer very rarely spreads, she says. 'From bladder to bone has never been known' was one of the old saws of the profession. (Sylvie doesn't mention the possibility of a brain tumour; 'From bladder to brain and you go insane?') And it has been caught early, it won't have had time to metastasize, says Sylvie.

Jess doesn't like that word 'metastasize'. Haematuria, metastasis. IVP, CT, MRI. She doesn't like this new vocabulary, with which Sylvie has been familiar for so long.

She doesn't know whether Sylvie is offering comforting platitudes, as an old friend should and would, or whether what she says is to be trusted. How does Sylvie know it has been 'caught early'? What does 'early' mean?

Jess has friends, and her nature is such that she can share her worries. Some cannot, but Jess can. It is a gift, this ability to tell. And during this period of uncertainty and waiting for results, she told us. She told Sylvie, she told me, she told Bob, she told Maroussia.

Maroussia is in a play at the Donmar, she is playing Medea, she offers Jess and Anna tickets, the tickets for the short run are like gold dust, star dust, but Jess hadn't the heart to go. Anna would have liked to have gone, she likes seeing Maroussia on screen and on stage, but Jess can't face it.

We listened to Jess, we offered comfort, but we could not share her grief. It was hers alone. We can feel for one another, but we cannot partake. One of the melancholy Wordsworth poems that Steve used to read to Jess and Anna and anyone who would listen comes back to Jess now, and she recites it to herself as she goes through the terrible countdown of the days of waiting for the next medical event, the next hospital appointment, the next result:

Beyond participation lie
My troubles, and beyond relief:
If any chance to heave a sigh
They pity me, and not my grief . . .

It is a fine distinction, a profound distinction.

~

Jess told us, and she even told the mad Victoria.

Victoria, since the summer meeting, had been persistent in pursuit of Jess, drawn to her, or so we supposed, by some need for absolution, by the need for a new listener. She had poured out her anxieties about Marcus and Wibletts for hour after hour on the phone, in email after email, and over lunch in her Chelsea apartment. Jess knows all about Victoria's love affairs with famous folk, about her first and second husbands, about her other children, about her very famous psychoanalyst, about her aborted career as an opera singer, about the class in needle-work that she attends at the V&A. Victoria's need for attention is extreme, her neurosis disabling. She occupies a glittering point on the spectrum of craziness. Her large high-ceilinged apartment off Cadogan Square is far grander than the homes of any of Jess's friends, and it is furnished with the kind of opulent slightly faded luxury that Jess recognises as belonging to the very rich, the long-term rich. The red and bronze curtains are massy and heavily textured and fringed, and they hang from great poles, looped back by stiff encrusted golden tassels. Marble plinths support huge Art Nouveau pots of lilies, the chaises-longues are heaped with tapestry cushions, and books of art history and photography lie on coffee tables. It is sumptuous, decadent, worn, taken for granted.

Victoria is not wholly part of her background, Jess suspects;

she has been transplanted into it by beauty and by marriage, she is restless and profane in it. Her language is extreme.

Victoria is highly tuned to her own disasters, but just as eagerly tunes in to Jess's anxiety about Anna, and recommends various specialists of her acquaintance, urging Jess not to rely on the NHS. The prince's own surgeon, the man who operated on the prime minister, the gynaecologist who looked after half of Notting Hill and Hollywood – she knows them all by name and by repute. They are the leaders in the field. Mr Dalrymple, Mr Brathwayte, Sonia Everett, Sir Michael Rajah. Jess listens fascinated, over the phone from her small North London kitchen in Kinderley Road, to the names and the dropping of names. Princess Alicia, the Marquis of Aran, the Baron of Bute, the Prince of Wales's cousin's sister-in-law, the half-sister of the governor of the Bank of England. Victoria sounds like a character out of Woolf or Proust, both arch-neurasthenics who distrusted and disliked their doctors and their exorbitant fees, and both of whom died before their time. Jess had thought that old world dead and buried, buried beneath a shattering splintering heap of progress and vulgarity, but it lingers on, entrenched, indestructible. It is the bedrock; its sloping slabs of subservience and sycophancy project solidly upwards like tombstones through the splintering rubble of modernity.

Jess has to remind Victoria that Baroness Raven, whom they had both heard speak in the summer at Wibletts, is one of Jess's best friends. She pulls rank with Sylvie. Sylvie, she reminds Victoria, is a bladder expert, and will give Jess all the advice she needs. (She doesn't put it as rudely as that, as she is touched by Victoria's effusive concern.)

Victoria cedes Sylvie to Jess, a point scored, but is reluctant to relinquish the expertise of Sonia Everett.

'Come round for a drink!' cries Victoria, from time to time. She never asks Jess to take Anna round for a drink.

Victoria's youngest son, Marcus, sits frozen at his chess set or raves round the subtly (and in her view inadequately) wired and hedged perimeters of his expensive prison. Her other children (all are from her first husband, a theatrical impresario relocated in New York) lead 'normal' lives, one married to an American hedge fund manager, the other writing speeches for the president. (The president of what? Jess is not sure. The United States? A university? An international court? A supermarket chain? Victoria's narratives take a lot for granted, they are full of ellipses, and it is too late to ask.)

Victoria has made it clear that there is an impressive inheritance of lunacy on both sides of the family, with ancestors flamboyantly deranged and eccentric, jumping from high windows, eloping with heiresses, shooting butlers and racehorses, starving to death in bothies. She seems proud of the legacy. Well, pride is a brave option, and Jess salutes it. She finds Victoria exotic, exhilarating, a change from our bourgeois ways. Jess often thinks of that strange tableau of Marcus and his chess set. It reminds her of a scene from a late Shakespeare play. The Renaissance prince in prison on the island, playing chess. Her own family is humdrum, ordinary, with only Jack Speight, the simple young man with Down's syndrome, the backward boy from Lincolnshire, to mark a known and not very unusual departure from the norm.

Grandpa Speight had left some money in trust for Anna, his only grandchild, his simple grandchild, whom he had simply loved. There had been no barriers between Anna and her grandpa. He had found Anna easy company. They would chat for hours about her favourite television programmes, her swimming badges, his entertainingly exaggerated dislike of most vegetables, his little dog Phoebus, which he usually left at home with Grandma. They even chatted about architecture. Grandpa would ask her what she thought of this building, what of that, and listen to her opinions gravely. Anna liked the redbrick Victorian church and the double-fronted house with the monkey-puzzle tree and the library and Islington Town Hall.

Anna misses her grandpa. Jess can picture them when Anna was little, hand in hand, walking down Stirling New Park through the autumn leaves. She has one very clear sequence of them, emblematic, receding, as they walked confidentially together towards the bus stop on the corner. They were catching a bus to Highbury Barn, to the cake shop, to buy a lemon cake for tea. Jess would put the kettle on, they'd all have tea.

Jess wonders if she should follow Victoria's advice and find a private urologist, a private oncologist, but she suspects that were she to try to do so she would find herself in exactly the same position, miserable and tongue-tied in front of the same Dr Newman, nervously awaiting an appointment with the same Mr Savandra, but in a different hospital with more sprightly foreign receptionists wearing more lipstick. It hardly seems worth it. Sylvie reassures her that the NHS is quite capable of coping with Anna; she promises to alert Jess if she suspects any neglect, if she can see any better option.

Sylvie is a friend in need. Jess would never have known she would need expert advice on diseases of the bladder, and Sylvie did not train in adult life in order to be there at the right moment to advise Jess. That's not how life arranges itself. But so it happened.

~

During the long anxious hours of waiting, during the hospital visits and the intravenous chemotherapy, Jess plays little count-down games to pass the time. She recites poems to herself silently, she does the Short Crossword, she embarks on a blue-and-yellow tapestry in Bargello stitch, she counts backwards from 500 to nought, she recites nursery rhymes. She cannot concentrate on the book on homelessness and dementia that she is meant to be reviewing, although her thoughts do turn to Raoul and Ursula from time to time. It was in their interests she offered to take on the book, but their interests will have to wait a while.

She shuts her eyes and summons up a vision of herself and Anna sitting by an African lake. It is a picture that develops in strength and in detail like a photographic plate. When Anna is cured, they will go to Africa and sit by the lake. They should have gone earlier. Anna had not at first shown much interest in Africa, but Jess has managed to impart to her some eagerness, some mercifully distracting curiosity. *Z is for Zebra* comes to their aid. She tells Anna the story of Mungo Park, the poor Scotsman who was so brave and so lonely and so well meaning. Anna likes this story. She particularly likes the bit about the black woman who takes pity on Mungo and sings the song about the poor white man who has no mother.

Pity the poor white man, no mother has he . . .

The bereavement journey, the consolation cruise, the anniversary celebration, the fatal illness adventure. The lifetime trip to the Galapagos, for which one can ignore one's anxieties about carbon miles and footprints. One will so very soon be dead, and returning in the body to carbon inert, carbon reclaimed, so why worry?

The month in a palazzo in Venice, the trip to the Great Barrier Reef, the island in the Seychelles.

Angkor Wat, the Taj Mahal.

The price of an easy divorce.

Guy Brighouse, one of whose many dubious mates ran adventure safaris in East Africa, had told Jess the story of a woman who, believing herself to be dying of ovarian cancer, had embarked on the riskiest safari of all, exposing herself to rogue elephants, lions and hippopotami, but, despite having to swim from a capsized dugout through crocodile-infested waters and being charged by a rogue buffalo, she seemed unable to die or to get herself killed. She emerged unshaken from a single-propeller aeroplane that had to make a forced landing in the bush, and she allowed mosquitoes and tsetse flies to feast freely on her flesh. She was indestructible. One of the guides of the party died protecting his flock, but Elissa Freegard survived whatever came her way.

~

It's a pity that Anna has lost her appetite. She tries, gamely, to pretend to continue to enjoy her food, but Jess can tell she's not hungry. Enjoying their simple meals together had meant a lot to Jess and Anna.

The form of chemotherapy that Dr Newman has decreed is derived from the periwinkle flower, also known as the sorcerer's violet. Jess finds this information surprising and comforting. Who would have thought that the little blue flowers could have such strong stuff in them?

Bob is good. He latches on to the African myth, and leaves little phone messages of lions roaring and birds screeching. The sound of the lions is frightening, even on a mobile phone. Their roar has a deep, abstracted, yearning, devouring tone, from the deep throat and the whole body. The birds laugh and mourn and screech and peep and sing. *Go away, go away, tin tin, tin tin,* they cry. *Nkoya, Nokoya, Nkoya Kupwa – I go, go, go to get married*, they cry.

Bob sits with Anna in the hospital, as the periwinkle drip feeds into her pink blue-veined arm, and he makes her laugh. He is the best of stepfathers. It is good that Jess and Bob have never bothered to divorce, as that makes his presence in the hospital more orthodox, more acceptable. Jess is able to refer to him as her 'husband', when it seems convenient. There is something childlike about Bob that bonds him to Anna. He cannot, surely, ever have molested Anna? No, surely not. The very thought is unworthy.

Stepfathers are quite high on the kinship-access table, surprisingly high, and Bob had been party to the meetings that set up the original trust fund for Anna, into which Grandpa's money had later been deposited.

Dr Newman has driven Jess into unworthy thoughts.

~

Jess did not tell Raoul much about Anna's diagnosis and the chemotherapy, but she had to tell him something, in order to explain why she didn't want to fix another lunch just yet, why she wasn't up to helping him to seek out Ursula. They talked on the phone. They deferred meeting, but would meet. Jess has contacted the Approved Mental Health Practitioner and the community health trust and the local-authority housing department for the homeless. She had put about a few queries, but she does not tell Raoul that she has done this.

Jess mentioned the story of Ursula to me, and I knew she was thinking of planning another Wibletts-style expedition. I was quite curious. The class of Halliday Hall had its fascination even at second hand. I was game to go, and would wait until she asked. I was a wanderer with not much aim in life. Although to others no doubt I appeared busy, with my part-time consultancy, my committee work, my friends, my scattered family, my grandchildren. I don't know why life seems emptier when one is older, even when it is full. It thins out, like the hair of one's head.

I knew that those were tedious days for Jess and Anna, and I worried about them, but there wasn't much I could do. And of course part of me was just glad it wasn't me going through that process. I'd been through it with my husband, and I knew what it was like.

It was just after the end of Anna's chemotherapy that I had to go to France, and I thought I would call in while I was there on the Rodin Museum at the Hôtel Biron in Paris. I was going to a *colloque* at Toulouse, but I booked myself a couple of nights in Paris on the way, and went to have another look at the helmet-maker's once beautiful wife, who had haunted me since I was seventeen. Mortality was much on my mind.

The museum was even grander than I remembered, and I lingered in the garden, for this time the sun was shining. Maybe one notices gardens more as one ages. There were the burghers of Calais, there were the gates of hell, there above the tall trimmed hedges arose the beautiful gilded dome. And then I braced myself and went indoors to look for the old woman, but I couldn't find her. Had I imagined her? Had I seen her in some other country? Was she avoiding me?

I wandered from room to room, looking for her, but she wasn't there. I asked a young attendant or two, but the attendants knew nothing of her, indeed knew nothing much of anything, they were just there to keep order. Eventually I went to the bookshop to see if there were any postcards of her (though who but me would want to buy her?) or any listings of the museum's contents, and a very courteous middle-aged woman told me that she was away on loan. I should have known it. The object one goes to see is always away on loan. But, said the well-rounded and physically confident bookshop woman, had I taken time to look at the Camille Claudel room? If it were images of old age I was seeking, that was the room for me.

I now think that the woman knew about the sculpture because she herself was not in her first youth. She saw the shape of things to come.

I didn't know who Camille Claudel was and hadn't knowingly noticed that she had a room. The kindly woman persuaded me to buy a monograph about her, encouraging me by showing me that it had a picture of *La Belle Heaulmière* in it, and off I went, back up the wide marble staircase, and there indeed in Claudel's room, in Rodin's one-time student-mistress's room, were age and youth together.

Camille Claudel's story was a terrible story, hers was a terrible life. But her work was good, and her old women are as fine, as terrible, as Rodin's. Clotho, one of the Three Fates, in plaster not bronze, as white as old rope, as white as an old knitted dishcloth, heroic, erect, skinny, struggling, not bowed and subdued like the helmet-maker's wife, but gauntly struggling with the twisted ropes and snakes of age, spinning her hair into the fatal yarn of destiny. The booklet suggested that Claudel had used the same model as Rodin, an 82-year-old Italian woman called Maria Caira. I hoped they had paid Maria Caira well, to sit, to stand, at that age, in the nude. I hope they kept her warm in her all too visible old age.

Camille Claudel, like Rodin, also sculpted images of youth and beauty, but the process of ageing obsessed her when she was herself yet young. Her work was proleptic. She foresaw her fate. Her older lover thrust it on her, and she fought back, fiercely and at times obscenely. The ageing man in the centre of her massive three-figure sculpture of Maturity is Auguste Rodin, naked, grim, doomed and tragic, caught between his two mistresses, Youth and Age, torn from Youth's imploring grasp and impelled ever and forcefully onwards into the swirling, grasping, enfolding bronze arms of Age. I don't often like such crude and overt symbolism, but the power of this piece was overwhelming. It struck me as the *Belle Heaulmière* had struck me when I was seventeen. It had been waiting for me.

It wouldn't have been on show when I was seventeen. Women's sculpture, women's stories, were less valued then.

Camille Claudel went mad, or so her family said. She sank into a life of squalor, amidst broken furniture and peeling wallpaper, growing fatter and fatter. I don't know what Ronald Laing or Dr Nicholls would have made of her condition. She was salvaged from her dirty Paris apartment and her studio and incarcerated by her family from August 1914 to October 1943 in an asylum near Avignon. She was shut up in there for *nearly thirty years*, this gifted woman, from the beginning of one world war to the middle of another. I remember thinking that Jess would have been interested in this. Reading of her desolate fate in my narrow bed in my cheap, TV-free, antique and historic hotel in the rue de Seine, I thought of Jess's descriptions of Ursula, and remembered Jess's descriptions of Colney Hatch and Halliday Hall and the inmates of Wibletts. Ah, how we have moved on.

Les Sources taries. The dried springs. A group with that name by Rodin was in the same Claudel room, the room of senescence. They grouped with wrinkled hands, with hanging breasts.

Now they huddle not in the asylum but in the care home.

Statuary speaks more to me as I age. It is a question of the ultimate fate of the flesh. The plaster, the terra-cotta, the marble, the bronze, the ebony, the bone. The effigy, the funerary monument.

Maroussia defies time. Rodin would have done her proud. And proud Maroussia is, proud she remains. She is too proud to have had her portrait painted, her bust sculpted. She talked about this to me when we had supper at Chez Simone after *Medea*. Some people succumb to being painted through vanity, said Maroussia, they succumb through self-importance, but I am too vain and too proud to sit.

I admire Maroussia, we all admire Maroussia, we are proud

of Maroussia. Her Medea was classic, noble, grand, majestic, perhaps a little old-fashioned, a little Edwige Feuillère. Feuillère was Paul Claudel's Muse, as Camille Claudel was Auguste Rodin's Muse. I saw Edwige Feuillère, in the flesh, an ageing beauty, at the Aldwych Theatre many years ago, in Paul Claudel's *Partage de midi*. Paul Claudel and Camille Claudel, brother and sister.

I went by TGV from Paris to Toulouse, and felt very modern, although the buffet car was disappointing. The conference in Toulouse was lively, and the participants were young. They were not fat or mad or withered. Our theme was sombre, but we made merry with our luncheon vouchers and our views. The young academics were gracious to me, they treated me with respect, and I was grateful to them for that. We laughed a lot and my French was adequate.

Jess texted me in Toulouse. In these later years we texted one another frequently with small bits of news and mutual encouragement. As a senior participant, I had been treated to a pretty room in a pretty, very French hotel, with striped wallpaper and hard round striped pillows and green shutters and charming shepherdess china. I lay in bed, luxuriously, enjoying my Gallic holiday from North London, but of course could not resist switching on my mobile, and there was a message from Jess, and I worried if I would be wise to open it, but of course I did, and I was glad I did, because it was all good news. RESULTS GOOD EVEN NEWMAN PLEASED CELEBRATED WITH THAI PRAWNS ALL SET FOR AFRICA WHY DON'T YOU COME TOO BOB WILL FIX IT.

~

And Bob did fix it. It took a bit of arranging, and the African seasons had to be taken into consideration, but he managed to fix it for the following spring. Anna's health improved, she regained her appetite, and the dim distracting dream conceived in the hospital became a proper plan. I didn't want to go with them, I couldn't quite face it, I didn't fancy Africa, and I didn't think Jess's suggestion had been serious. Victoria, unwisely apprised of the project, said she wished to go too, but Jess successfully and easily dissuaded her. 'You'd hate it,' said Jess forcefully, as she sipped a porcelain cup of Earl Grey in Chelsea. (Jess didn't really like Earl Grey.) Victoria clearly saw Africa as a hotel swimming pool surrounded by palm trees and bougainvillea and flamboyants with an occasional outing in a Land-Rover to look at giraffe and zebra, followed by a stiff gin and tonic. Sundowners in the bush, in safari gear, watching the pink sky.

Jess said it would not be like that, and anyway, there would be Anna.

The problem with Victoria was that she had nothing to do.

Bob did the bookings, fixed the contacts, arranged to do a little business for a TV natural-history channel on the side. Jess found she was happy to travel with Bob, and Anna was delighted. She liked reconciliations, reparations, family life. She wouldn't have minded now if Bob had moved back to North London from Herne Hill. She was happy to share her mother with Bob. He was no longer a threat. Bob was easy.

Jess also arranged a commission for herself, though not so well paid, for the Social History section of a Sunday colour supplement whose editor had always liked her and indulged her work. Bob, she promised Jason Winter, would provide some photos free of charge, and she would write the text of the story of the Saucepan Graves. Jason liked the title, although he'd no idea what the Saucepan Graves were. He said it was a very Jess title, and he was willing to take a small gamble on them. Jess had a good record. Jess didn't know much about the graves either, but she was eager to know more. And, she assured Jason, they would do the Livingstone Memorial and the moody many-wived Prince Chitombo of Chitombo as a more orthodox backup if the Saucepan Graves didn't work out. You could always get some good copy out of Livingstone.

She had spun him a line about the Saucepan Graves, as she really had very little idea about what they might be, and whether or not they might be of any serious anthropological interest. She'd heard about them from Gus Kovacovic, a SOAS contact who had been travelling in Zambia. He'd told her of a mystifying encounter a few years ago with a Bemba tribe living by a lake, who had yarned on to him about battles with crocodiles, infamous white land-grabbing settlers and a vast graveyard marked by saucepans in a woodland, the site of a massacre. 'Are you sure, *saucepans*?' Jess had asked this adventurer, over their canteen coffee, and he had sworn to the saucepans – ordinary, everyday-looking objects, just like his granny used to have. He hadn't actually seen the site, but his hosts had showed him some pans, they were still using the same sort in the village, they said.

When had all this happened, this massacre? Gus hadn't been able to work it out. African time isn't like European time, she must know that.

He'd have pursued the story further, he assured her, but he had had to move on, to get ahead of the rainy season. But he could tell her how to get there, if she was interested. It wasn't too far off the beaten track.

She was interested. She took down the details and handed them over to Bob, who said he'd work them into their itinerary, if he could.

She couldn't find out anything more about the graves. The Nubians had buried their dead in what were called pan graves, but they were called that because they were the same shape as frying pans, not because they actually were frying pans.

Saucepans were something else. She hoped they'd find them, although she knew already that even if she did she'd have no hope of interpreting them. She didn't have the languages, she didn't have the background. But she'd like to see them, with her own eyes. As she had seen the little children of the lake. They would have their own meaning, just for her.

Margaret Murray, the legendary anthropologist and folklorist, had cast spells in a saucepan to thwart her enemies. Jess hoped she'd be able to get that into her article.

Anthropology is full of strange spirit stories, about shamans and witchcraft and night ridings and animal shape-shiftings, stories which hover between myth and fairytale and religion and tribal memories of historical events, between belief and denial. Many of them feature dwelling places and domestic utensils, but none has ever, as far as Jess knows, named anything as banal, as friendly, as everyday, as a saucepan.

~

Before they set off for Africa, there were one or two things to tidy up. One of the things that needed to be tidied up was the question of Ursula, and Jess's relationship with Raoul.

Raoul had been unsettled by Anna's illness and Jess's distraction. Jess now believed that he had been looking forward to a different kind of development, a different dénouement, as why should he not? No harm in looking forward. She had at one point during the dreary days of waiting for hospital appointments descended to the vulgar curiosity of googling Raoul's ex-wife, a much less stressful inquiry than googling the Professor had been, and she had been at once astonished and not at all surprised by the curious results. Raoul's wife, Marie-Hélène Tissot, of French–Algerian descent, looked exactly like Jessica Speight. Even to Jess, she looked like Jessica Speight. There were quite a few images of her available, some Facebook passport-sized snaps attached to her academic CV and to her publications, and some larger ones from French and Canadian magazines and newspapers illustrating news stories about trips into the interior. Most of the stories are in French, but Jess can read these easily. She has read quite a lot of French anthropology.

Marie-Hélène had blue eyes, and reddish-brown hair, which was cut in an identical manner to Jess's in these latter days – to just below the chin length, with a Julie Christie sixties fringe. Sometimes Marie-Hélène wore spectacles, of which the frames were exactly the same as those selected by Jess. Her body weight looked about the same, and in one of the photos she was standing in exactly the posture Jess always adopted for the camera – arms firmly folded, the right hand over the left elbow, shoulders back, slightly confrontational but at the same time friendly. A don't-mess-with-me but here-I-am pose. Her smile, her dimpled chin, her cheekbones, were similar.

She was Jess's alter ego, her nomadic wandering alter ego. She could have been her sister. She looked far more like Jess than Vee ever did.

Some of the news stories mentioned her distinguished neurologist husband, but most did not. Increasingly, in more recent years, they did not.

All in all, Marie-Hélène was doing a lot better than the poor Swedish professor. She wasn't exactly world-famous, but she had had, was continuing to enjoy, a satisfactory career.

She was ten years younger than Jess, and still active.

Jess, naturally, found this discovery fascinating, and she was glad she had not made it in the earlier days of her reacquaintance with Raoul. The chronological implications were manifold and intriguing. Had Raoul secretly fallen in love with her during those tea parties at Halliday Hall, when he was at his most vulnerable, and had he been disappointed when she made off with Zain? Had her image lingered in his memory subconsciously and been revived when he first met and wooed Marie-Hélène? Maybe she and Marie-Hélène were simply 'his type', and, if so, had there been other intervening or subsequent models? Was Raoul aware of this surprising resemblance? He must be. And was he now pursuing Jess because he had lost his wife?

He could not possibly have planned to encounter her at Wibletts, reasoned Jess, although the similarity of their interests had made it a not very unlikely coincidence that they should meet there. What had been surprising had been his persistence on that day: his determination, having found her, not to let go of her, even though she had not been at her best and the occasion in many ways inauspicious. He could have easily engineered a meeting without the Wibletts encounter, but by temperament, she now thought, he would have been too shy and unassuming to do so. It had taken the intervention of providence and Sylvie Raven and Victoria and my impetuous and self-serving offer of a lift back to London in my car to bring them together.

His pursuit of her since then had been a kind of courtship, she recognised. The little lunches, even the confidences about the Ursula dilemma. Jess was not quite sure what she felt about these developments.

As Anna's health and confidence improved, and as Bob continued to be a regular visitor from over the river, Jess decided that it would be safe to invite Raoul to see her in Kinderley Road. He had several times hinted that he would like to see Steve again, and Jess was half pleased by the thought that somebody really wanted to see Steve. She organised a tea party, with small sandwiches and a special lemon cake from the shop at Highbury Barn. She even cut the sandwiches out in little shapes – stars, crescents, circles – an easy and pleasing trick she'd learnt from Victoria. Raoul and Steve and Anna ate the lot, while Raoul and Steve talked about Halliday and Dr Nicholls and, of course, Ursula. Jess presided, pleased with her little salon.

Steve was very interested in the story of Ursula's religious afterlife. He quoted from Gerard Manley Hopkins. *I have desired to go/ Where springs not fail . . .* It is a short poem, and he knew it by heart. Steve had found no such refuge, no heaven haven, and neither had the poor tormented Hopkins of the Terrible Sonnets.

There had been an ancient spring of fresh water at Troutwell Farm, and in the grounds of the asylum there was an old pump with a stone trough, long since disused, but never dismantled. The old spring was dry. *La Source tarie*. The 1910 Grade II-listed water tower surveyed the grounds like a watch tower in a war, in a war of mental strife.

But some, even in its bad years, had found Troutwell a haven.

Ursula hadn't seemed to be at all religiously inclined at Halliday, Raoul and Steve agreed. Steve was distressed by Raoul's account of Ursula's wanderings and of her alleged return to their alma mater. Raoul gave less detail than he had given to Jess, but it was enough to cause distress. Steve leant forward, earnestly, attentively, solemnly, his large face soft and heavy with a weight of transferred sorrow. Poor woman, he repeated gravely, poor Ursula, poor woman. His voice was as full and gentle as ever, as receptive of grief. Jess remembered him reading the Wordsworth ballads aloud, sonorously, monotonously, all those years ago.

He is a kind man, Steve, she thinks. The pain of others compounds his own, extends his own, offers him some companionship.

Steve was also, of course, interested in Raoul's speciality of phantom pain, and a career which he immediately recognised as a natural consequence of his apprenticeship under the care of Dr Nicholls. Steve wasn't very well informed about mirror neurones and tended towards a metaphysical interpretation of the human condition, but he honoured Raoul's sustained devotion to physical explanations and explorations of mental states as well as pseudo-physical sensations. Voices, visions, apparitions.

Jess wondered whether Ursula in her crazy old age was receiving any kind of medical attention, or whether she had dropped off the map of the social services. There were specialist nurses for the homeless, her Essex friend Lauren had told her, and indeed Jess had tried to contact them, but had drawn a blank. Maybe Ursula had carefully put herself beyond their reach.

Dr Nicholls had been anti-medication. He took what we now call recreational drugs, but he was anti-medication, a not wholly consistent position, Jess had thought. Liberty Hall, that's what Susie had called Halliday Hall. But Susie's boy Vincent had improved beyond all recognition when the right medication had been prescribed for him, and he was now leading a 'normal' life.

Susie and Jess exchange Christmas cards, and keep one another updated on their Marsh Court children.

Anna does not suffer acute mental anguish, as Steve and Raoul and Ursula have so unjustly and unreasonably suffered it. As Hopkins suffered it. But Anna feels, perhaps excessively, for the pain of others. For Polly and Sukie and their unsuccessful tea party. For Joshua Raven in jail and the tears wept by his mother, Sylvie. For Harry Grigson in the lion's den. For Maya at the day centre whose dog had been run over by a bus. Anna had not liked the dog, she had been frightened of it, but she was sorry for Maya.

An allocentric, not an egocentric, personality, that was Anna. Jess had come across that distinction in an article recently. It had seemed to fit Anna. The article had something to do with evolution, but Jess can't remember what. Raoul seems to believe something not wholly materialistic about evolution, something about the free flow of empathetic neurones linking all human consciousness, all human development. Yet he denies the existence of the non-material world.

Jess rang me that evening to report on the success of her tea party. She described Steve's reciting of the two stanzas of 'A Nun Takes the Veil'. Too much of sharp and sided hail had Steve endured, and so it would seem had Ursula.

'But,' said Jess as an afterthought, 'I really, really *didn't* want to be out of the swing of the sea. I wanted to be out there, in the waves. That's what I thought I wanted, when I was young. But here I am, becalmed in Kinderley Road.'

'Nothing wrong with Kinderley Road,' I said, from the nearby safety of Shawcross Street. And we both laughed.

~

Our outing to Troutwell was like a down-market reprise of our outing to Wibletts, though we didn't take Sylvie. Sylvie was too busy being a baroness, and there was a new bill going through the House that was eating up a good deal of her time. She was much absorbed by its many clauses and amendments. She invited Jess and me to go to watch some of it from the Visitors' Gallery, as we'd both taken an interest in it and signed a lot of probably pointless online petitions, but I think we were both overcome by a sense of our own impotence and declined. (Also, the Visitors' Gallery, which I had visited once or twice before, gives me vertigo. It makes me feel as though I am about to hurl myself down into the Chamber. It makes my exposed knees tremble.)

Jess was very worried about the threat to Anna's support structure and in particular to the funding of the day centre.

They wouldn't close it, but they would cut its hours, she guessed.

So off we went, Raoul, Jess and I, in my still new car, in search of Ursula, in search of the potent past.

We didn't take Anna.

We had an appointment with Lauren in a new social services building in the business park that had sprung up and engulfed Troutwell. Lauren might or might not have some clues for us. I was aware by now that Ursula was something of a red herring, that this expedition had some other meaning for Raoul, and that Jess was anxious it should go well for him. Jess chatted along as we went round the M25 towards Essex, telling us we would like Lauren, she was a large, lively and amusing young woman with a colourful dress sense and Essex was lucky to have her, but as she chatted I think we both began to be aware that Raoul was very tense. He was sitting in the back, but I could see in the mirror that he was looking anxious and worried, I began to wonder if he was car sick, my car is very comfortable and not known for causing sickness, but he did look uneasy, and I wondered whether I should propose a coffee break, but that's not easy on the M25. He did at one point say that he'd never been driven along this stretch of motorway, and it is peculiarly bleak and remorseless as it makes its way past exits to Enfield and Potters Bar and Waltham Abbey; wide lanes, grey-white-hard stretches of lanes, brutal surfaces, heavy lorries on their way to Felixstowe, bloody fools driving too fast on your bumper, gigantic guillotines with warnings about accidents and roadworks hanging over your head, but I knew the A12 was just as bad, a horrible unevenly surfaced road out towards Chelmsford and Colchester and drearily beyond, one of the least loved roads in England.

It was one of those grey monochrome February days when the roads and the skies flatten and join and spread to a discouraging infinity. A wide, scoured, abraded, gritted roadway, very different from the deep rich English leafy sunken roads of Suffolk. I remembered the torrential summer rain, the exuberant flowerbeds, the tall poppies and the tall delphiniums of Wibletts, the expense.

I thought there was a Little Chef coming up soon, and planned to take a break, but before I suggested it Raoul with some embarrassment leant forward and said, 'Eleanor, do you mind if we stop soon, I need the bathroom.' 'Of course,' I said, 'of course', sorry I hadn't been able to pre-empt this declaration, and I pulled in at the first Little Chef we came across and we ordered coffee while he disappeared to the gents'. While he was gone Jess said, 'It's nerves, he's worried about seeing the old place again' – and she was right, for when he came back he said so. He had recovered his composure but warned us it might happen again. 'When I get anxious . . .' he said. He didn't need to finish the sentence, we understood all too well.

For him, it was like revisiting an old school, an old prison, after many years. Apart from the Ursula problem, which also loomed.

Raoul said he'd never seen anywhere quite like the Little Chef. Jess and I were well used to them (I, as a committed driver, more accustomed to them than Jess), and we were familiar with their strange mixture of uniformity and individual local eccentricity, but Raoul was more accustomed to the North American chains. The Little Chef is deeply English, a weird offshoot of the old roadhouse and the old tea room, with its bacon and eggs, its scampi and chips and peas, its buttered scones. It's Americanised, in its way, but it's still recognisably English. Old ways linger.

Finding Lauren and Satis House in the business park was hell. I don't have a satnav, but I did have maps and two willing and intelligent map readers, and we still couldn't find it. Jess had warned me about the geography of those parts, but I hadn't quite believed her. I might have got irritated with this wild-goose chase had I not been worried about further worrying Raoul, for there was something about the post-urban landscape that was profoundly depressing – it was a self-repeating maze of leisure centres and municipal offices and car showrooms and windowless storerooms and hospitals, in a nightmare of jaunty red and steel and glass, and not a tree or a blade of grass to be seen. Eventually, as we circled, Raoul spotted the name of the road we were looking for, Mayhew Circus, and there at last was a modest yellow brick office block called Satis House.

Plump Lauren was a relief. She was one of those large young women whose fine complexion glows with health, and she was all smiles and laughter and welcome. She wore blue tracksuit bottoms and stylish silver trainers and a gay pink-and-white-striped jumper and pearl earrings. How she kept her spirits up was a wonder, as her job entailed grim matter.

She hadn't drawn a total blank with Elizabeth Ursula Strawson: she'd found a bit of a paper trail, though not Ursula herself, and she thanked Raoul for bringing her back to official attention. The community mental health team had received a report two summers ago of an elderly woman answering to his description who was sleeping rough, and it had kept an eye on her for a while, but she had disappeared in the autumn, presumably having found some kind of accommodation or left the neighbourhood. She had never applied to the local-authority housing department, or registered herself as homeless, though she might well have qualified for accommodation as a vulnerable person in priority need, so the matter had rested there. She might still be living in the area, and nobody of her name had died in the area, for Lauren had checked. She might be drawing benefits locally, but Lauren hadn't tracked down a likely claimant.

'As you know,' said Lauren robustly, 'in this country we have the right to be as mad as we like, provided we aren't a risk to ourselves or others.'

Raoul took this point, and assured Lauren that he wasn't interfering. He was just responding to all those letters. He offered to show them to Lauren and got a packet of them out of his bag, but Lauren shook her head: she'd seen enough crazy letters. She suggested we all go and have an early lunch instead, so we'd have time to look at Troutwell before it got dark.

Over our cheese-and-ham toasties in the newbuild fakewood royal-purple psychedelic pseudo-pub at the end of the Circus, Lauren told us about cuts in the social services and updated herself on Anna's local-authority funding. (Anna's old social worker Karen was long retired, and had been succeeded by an over-anxious anorexic young woman called Carol, who, according to Jess, was too fond of trying to teach grandmothers to suck eggs.) Then Lauren told us all she knew about the status of the buildings at Troutwell. The stories about old Troutwell died hard. Even the old-fashioned pre-Dr Nicholls pre-Halliday Troutwell was well remembered: it had been one of the biggest employers in that part of the county, and she knew lots of people whose parents had worked there, whose grandparents had been inmates there, and some of them had happy memories of it. It wasn't the prison it was painted as being. 'It was like a world of its own, it was a community,' said young 48-year-old Lauren. 'There was something to be said for places like that, and now they don't know what to do with the buildings – the site was bought up by something called Pipex Properties, but they can't afford to develop it, it just stands there. I think the library is still in there,' said Lauren, as she passed us the dessert menu; 'there was said to have been some interesting stuff in there. Some valuable books and records.

'And there have been squatters, of course there have.

'Halliday Hall was still in use a few years ago, as a day clinic, but even that was boarded up now. Halliday had a good reputation,' Lauren said.

It seemed to us that Lauren had a happy temperament, a sweetness and resilience of spirit that overrode the daily grind. She was one of those lucky people, a pure gold person, with her shining clear skin and her bright brown eyes and her ready laugh and her goodwill. Her black hair was cut in a dashingly short prickly style that cheered one to look at it. Her hands and feet and wrists and ankles were small, her body ample. She was a redistributive person, happy to share the good fortune of her nature with those less fortunate.

I liked her. I asked if she would come with us for the last stage of our journey, but she said she had to get back to work.

We hadn't really counted on seeing Ursula. I certainly hadn't. The outing hadn't been a quest for Ursula; it had been a pilgrimage for Raoul, who had apologetically been twice to the gents' in the Purple Boar. It's not romantic, having to visit the gents' so often. Jess and I were too old to mind, but I could tell he was embarrassed. He is a very polite man.

Lauren had told us that if we went to the East Gate, nobody would stop us going in. Most of the perimeter was electrified, but the contractors had given up with the wiring by the time they got to the East Gate, and there was still pedestrian access to the halted works. We'd see a row of conifers, and a reddish-coloured path, and if we followed that we'd reach the main buildings.

We parked discreetly, not too near the gate. The path was strewn with pine cones. I picked one up and put it in my jacket pocket. It smelled of resin. I've still got it. It's in the car, the now not quite so new but still much loved car, sitting by the digital clock, waiting for time, our time, to end.

As we walked along the red path, we saw Ursula walking towards us. Maybe on one level we had known that we would.

Of course I had never set eyes on her in my life before, but there was no mistaking her. Who else could this person be? There was an inevitability about her apparition. She was walking towards us in a slow, stately and, I have to say, nun-like way, head bowed, contemplative, yet as though aware of our approach. She was wearing a long grey skirt and layers of dark coloured knitwear and jackets, and her abundant, long, steel-grey hair was held to her head and away from her face by a pale and childish Alice band. Maybe some bush telegraph had alerted her to our arrival, for she appeared to be expecting our little delegation.

We converged, I hanging back, for I was only the chauffeur.

Jess later said that she would have known her anywhere, as she had not changed at all. This, as she knew, was an extravagant exaggeration, yet Jess had indeed instantly recognised Ursula's proud yet self-abasing bearing, the elevated way she held her neck and head, the theatrical pacing of her steps, the strange and deliberate drama of her presence and self-presentation. She was distinctive. She was a woman who had missed her vocation, whatever it might have been, yet she walked proudly in those grounds where so many inmates over the years had suffered such a loss of self. She appeared now as the custodian of Troutwell, not as a squatter; nor indeed, it emerged, was she squatting there, although she haunted it. She had found herself a home with an easily manipulated and even more deeply vulnerable householder in the neighbouring council estate who had unwisely let her over her threshold, out of Christian charity. Ursula had settled in with Kathleen and Kathleen's large three-legged dog in a flat on the Saint Osyth Estate. From this base she had posted her missives to Raoul, and there she had awaited his advent.

Jess saw that she had been wrong to think that Ursula had retreated to a little, little space. She was in command of these vast deserted grounds. She was their self-appointed warden.

She greeted us demurely, conventionally, shaking hands with me and Jess, and offering herself to a tentative hug from Raoul. There was no sign from her of any particularly forceful attachment to Raoul, but there was a sense of a proprietary claim on him, an assumed familiarity. Then we turned, and wandered back towards the old derelict buildings, accompanied by a commentary from Ursula on what had been happening with planning permission, contractors, demolition. Nothing much was happening now. The credit crunch had frozen everything.

Jess's mind went back to the first tea party, when she had been so relieved to find Steve so much recovered, when she had first met Zain and brushed against Ursula. She remembered coming back here years later with Anna, with their picnic of tuna sandwiches and cherries, and finding the old fruit trees of the neglected orchard, and the unplumbed lavatory bowls standing in the courtyard. And here she is again, with Ursula and Raoul, the old inmates. It had been summer on her earlier visits, but now it is cold and wan and grey, and there is no light in the air. The light has been sucked out of the sky. Winter is ending, but there is no breath of spring. We have all aged.

The unplumbed sanitaryware is still there in the courtyard. Time has stood still. We gaze at it, perplexed.

Jess mentions the library of which Lauren had spoken, and Ursula leads them along a corridor, where shabby brown leafless weed stalks and seed heads push through the cracked tiles, and brambles and ivy prise their way through broken windows. Jess had seen this corridor in vandal images on the internet, though when she came with Anna she had not dared to penetrate so far. The library door hangs loosely open on its hinges, and there are some shelves and the charred ruins of desks. A lot of it's been burnt, said Ursula. For firewood, said Ursula, last winter, in that cold snap.

But there are one or two books left, and a few ancient brown and buff ledgers and concertina files, heaped haphazardly on the splintering floor and on the remaining shelving. They look unapproachably dirty and tattered and dismal.

Jess, who had fancied she might find a cache of scholarly treasure here, shudders. She cannot bear to touch this stuff. There might still be riches, but if so they are beyond her reach. She gives up on them. She is too old to cope with this unsorted lumber. Although in there may linger yet some saving grace, some precious witness to some long-ago kindness, some record of a forebear who had wished to disimprison the souls of the feeble-minded and the tormented. But she cannot rifle through the heaps of rubbish to find it. Let it go.

The little, nameless, unremembered acts of kindness and of love.

Wordsworth had wished to remember the unremembered.

The Map Room at Wibletts had been gracious and elegant, the books and papers well catalogued, and Wordsworth's letter to the unhappy Felix Holden carefully preserved.

Jess is saddened by the state of the ledgers, but Ursula seems indefatigable, as she directs them through the library and into what she says was the superintendent's office. Signs of her derangement, at first concealed by the unexpected social normality of her manner, begin to manifest themselves. Her assumption of command is surely unnatural, and her possessiveness of Raoul out of place. Jess, increasingly, as they plod along another mile of corridor (and can that be an active red blinker watching them from an angle in the ceiling – was that the sound of feet scuffling through dead leaves?), Jess begins to wonder about those benefits that Lauren had mentioned. What is Ursula living on? Where does she collect her pension, has she got a bank account? On whom has she battened? Well, it is hardly Jess's affair, is it?

(Kathleen, Raoul later discovers, is a fifty-year-old ex-drug-addict and ex-alcoholic who had been reclaimed, greatly to Ursula's advantage, by an evangelical sect offering a Save Your Soul church programme, under the direction of a powerful black woman called Bonny Belle – a far cry from Dr Nicholls, but just as effective. Salvation moves in mysterious ways. The very name of Bonny Belle can save you from despair.)

Raoul allows Ursula's appropriation of him, as we walk the corridors (surely that is rustling behind the partition, surely we are being covertly, unofficially observed?), but from time to time he exchanges glances with Jess, trying to establish another conspiracy, a conspiracy of the sane. Jess reminds herself (as do I) that Raoul is a neurologist of international distinction, although now lonely, divorced and semi-retired. Yet here he is, trudging through a long-abandoned asylum, in the thrall of an ex-primary-schoolteacher from Croydon, as though success had never visited him.

Maybe he is impelled in part by a still active professional curiosity. Ursula, after her vision of God above the pelmet, had heard voices. Raoul has always found auditory hallucinations interesting. Like phantom pain, these voices implicate our view of the brain. Does one hemisphere of the brain speak to the other? Whence come these echoes and instructions? From the past? From priests and kings and warlords? From religious texts, from internalised mythologies? From books unwisely read, from movies unwisely viewed? In her screeds of correspondence, much of which he did not read, Ursula had tried to describe the calls to action which she had been unable to answer. She had struggled against her hallucinations, never completely trusting them (she had, after all, been a competent teacher of primary schoolchildren for some years before the psychotic episodes that brought her to Halliday), but she had never been able to dispel them either. The letters lengthily, tediously, horribly, charted her struggle.

Ursula had come to believe that God had tested her faith by requiring her to slaughter her class of seven-year-olds, and that in obedience to his will *she had done so*. A terrible angel had appeared to her and ordered the massacre of the innocents, who would ascend instantly to heaven. She was torn in two by these instructions. The demonic angel, in her letters, appeared as a symbol, a four-stroke beak and wings. She believed she had stabbed them all to death, all those little children, and had hideous repeating hallucinations (hallucinations was too mild a word) of their bleeding bodies in the classroom. Halliday had released her from these visitations, but they had recurred, and it seems still recur.

Schoolroom massacres are not unknown. But Ursula had not perpetrated one.

I found the phenomenon of Ursula interesting, but not so interesting that I wasn't very relieved to get back to my car at the East Gate. It was getting dark, I wanted to set off and get away from these ruins, this parkland, before the whisperers came out from the leafless bushes, before night fell. There is nothing more pleasing than getting in one's own car after a difficult social passage: shutting the doors, turning on the radio and putting one's foot down on the accelerator, what joy. So I was not pleased when I heard Jess offer Ursula a lift back to the Saint Osyth housing estate. I had visions of driving aimlessly and lost round the outskirts of the business park, or of hearing Ursula demand a lift back to London and moving in with one of us for ever. She accepted the lift, but to my surprise gave me perfectly clear instructions of how to drop her off at her borrowed home. Dear God, what an estate. We do not know, we cannot see, the lives of our fellow-citizens. They live behind a curtain of unknowing, a cloud of unknowing.

I drew the line at going in for a cup of tea to meet the kindly Kathleen. 'No,' I said, 'I've got to get back.' I really could not face a three-legged dog. They couldn't argue with me. I had the wheels. They didn't want to get stranded either. They'd done their duty. They were reassured.

The thought of Shawcross Street was comforting.

I put the radio on, on the way home. I was worn out. Raoul and Jess were silent. They decided to sit in the back together, and I could see that Jess squeezed Raoul's hand as they settled. He didn't need to stop for a pee on the way home: he'd got over his anxious bladder syndrome. I tried Radio 4 and listened for a while to a soothing, well-balanced programme about solar energy and wind farms, then moved to Radio 3 and wintry Sibelius. The natural world would survive us whatever we did to it. We could cement and tarmac it over and turn it into a motorway a mile wide, but it would break through in the end. That's what Sibelius was telling us.

It's not a good message, for us. But I've ceased to care about us.

~

The simple round clay-and-straw hut has a little wooden veranda platform overlooking the waters of the dambo. The hut is earth-coloured, a terra-cotta earth-red, with a cream-and-brown design of zigzags and a conical roof. They sit there together, Jess and her daughter, as the evening sun declines. It has been a long journey, and both are tired, but they have been made welcome. Bob is in the next hut, only a few yards away, shacked up arbitrarily with a young Mexican adventurer with long black ringlets and some very fancy cameras. Jess can hear them laughing. Bob will join them soon for a beer, and maybe the Mexican will come too. Jess and Anna are both well anointed with Jungle Formula against mosquitoes, and neither has been bitten so far, although the mosquito nets over their twin beds are hard to arrange and Anna keeps tripping over hers. They have swathed them round their narrow beds for the night, and will creep in later by lamplight.

All four of them, Bob, Jess, Anna and the Mexican, flew in from the airport of the capital on a little single-propeller plane, the taxi of the skies, and were landed by pilot Brewster on a small runway in the bush. Here they are, not far from the swamps and floating islands of Bangweulu, not far as the crow or the Cessna flies, and in similar, though not quite so watery, terrain. There, a lifetime ago, Jess had seen the shoebill and the lobster-claw children. Time has come full circle, and the river flows with time.

The small flat lake shines calm and blue and silver and pink, reflecting the clouds. Mosquitoes hum, and they hear a pod (Anna reminds Jess that this is the right word; it is a word she likes) of hippos humphing and snorting and laughing in the mud at the margins in the reeds, only fifty yards away. A kite circles overhead. Jess's expectations of an ultimate revelation are moderately high, but for the moment she is content that Anna seems so pleased with the expedition, and that she has survived the journey so well. She has made a remarkable recovery.

A jaçana stalks and picks its way over the marshland, elegant, colourful, the chestnut-fronted lily-trotter bird which seems to walk upon the water. Anna is not very good at using the binoculars (and neither is Jess, who has astigmatic vision), but she is content with what she seems to see through them. Light-heeled little fawn antelope graze and scatter on what may or may not be a wooded island just over the water. Jess thinks they are puku, but she isn't sure.

~

Jess is thinking, peaceably, of Raoul. Shortly before the African departure, he had invited her to his apartment, in an act of return hospitality for her tea party with Steve. This had been a bold initiative on his part, and she had hesitated about accepting, but she had been touched by his confidence, and had made her way one spring evening to Regent's Park and to his mansion flat.

He had offered her a drink in No. 24A on the fourth floor, and dinner in a slightly up-market bistro in Baker Street. The lift up to 24A was old-fashioned but well appointed, its brass gleaming, its woodwork polished. She had been unaccountably nervous as he opened the door, smiling, blinking through his rimless glasses, but when she saw the rooms within she calmed down. She had been fearing bachelor squalor or anonymous clinical tidiness, but the flat is habitable, even cosy, with book shelves and paintings and photographs, with comfortable chairs and oriental rugs, and a large vase of lilac blooms (how did he get hold of those?) scenting the air. It looks well settled: not as deeply settled as Kinderley Road and Shawcross Street, but lived in, cared for. The walls are papered with a warm red paisley print, the curtains are buff and gold. Jess sits, with a glass of white wine, and admires. She has never been to the Middle East, but she fancies there is a touch of the Lebanon here, a touch of ancestral taste in the furnishings, although all of them could easily have been purchased in John Lewis on Oxford Street.

She is looking, covertly, for a photograph of Marie-Hélène, but pretends to be inspecting the paintings. There is a small oil of a Mediterranean harbour scene, and a sand-coloured gouache of a pale house in an oasis beneath a turquoise sky, and a drawing of bomb damage that looks like a Graham Sutherland. She can't see Marie-Hélène, but that must be the clever son, the one and only son, in a proud and ornate silver frame on the drinks cabinet.

The drinks cabinet is almost certainly John Lewis, and it is quite well stocked for a man who seems to drink only wine, and not very much of that. She wonders if he entertains frequently. He is retired, but she knows he still sees colleagues from overseas, associates from the hospital and the university where he taught, publishers and postgraduate students.

They talk of Ursula, and Africa, and Anna. Raoul now knows the full story of Anna's recent illness and her life's condition, and, now he has met Anna, he talks about her in a friendly way, entering into Jess's world of concern. They have spoken several times of Wibletts, of Victoria and her son Marcus, of the gross Dr Nicholls. As they prepare to set off for their dinner, Jess gestures towards the photograph and ventures 'That must be your son?' and Raoul is delighted to admit to him. Yes, that is he. That is the young man who understands subatomic particles, neutrinos and the speed of light.

The son looks more like Raoul than like Marie-Hélène.

They enjoy their dinner, and Jess teases Raoul that he has yet again chosen lamb cutlets. They come adorned with a little paper frill. She likes to watch him nibble. She has Coquilles Saint-Jacques, an old-fashioned dish, which is served, as it should be, in its pilgrims' scallop shell. Over coffee, Raoul reaches for her hand and briefly holds it, then pats it as he relinquishes it. 'You must take care in Africa,' he says; 'you must remember to take all your pills.'

She had been pleased to have her hand patted. She has led a celibate life for years now, and has considered her body a burnt-out case, long past the need for any physical intimacy, but Raoul's mild attentions had been acceptable, indeed welcome. She had wondered if he had been about to make any further move or declaration, but he had left it at that, embracing her warmly but politely as she paused on the steps of the Baker Street tube. He is exactly the same height as she is.

~

Bob is taller than Raoul and Jess. She can hear his loud and happy voice in the next hut. He has recently made one or two friendly attempts to suggest reclaiming his marital rights, but hadn't seemed put out when she declined. He had loved her once, and is fond of her now, but he can take her or leave her.

And now here he is, advancing, carrying a couple of bottles of beer by the neck, with two glasses hooked on his fingers. He pulls up a chair, pours a beer for Anna and Jess (he drinks from the bottle, but knows they don't like to) and settles back creakily to gaze over the lake. All three are recovering from the long flight and the short flight and the jolting of the Land-Rover on the dirt track through the straggling spreading utterly African miombo woodland. (Jess has at least temporarily memorised the word 'miombo', but Anna doesn't like it. Anna has strong views on new words.) Jess is thinking that Bob has organised this camp well: it is remote, but not alarmingly, frighteningly remote. It is well within Anna's comfort range. Tomorrow they will pursue Livingstone and, after that, the missionary settlement and the saucepans, and then they will join Bob's TV people. She tries to remember how much she had told Bob about the BaTwa lobster-claw fisher children. Will any of them be alive today?

There are seventy-three different ethnic groups in modern Zambia, and the BaTwa are considered one of the most 'primitive'.

Bob is more interested in animals than in people. He has already spotted a sitatunga browsing over the lake. He tells Anna that it has webbed feet, which isn't quite true, but it is more or less amphibious.

The hippos make their massive bubbling watery noises, a strange mixture of mirth and menace, and Bob, raising his glass to happy and unworried Anna, says, 'You'd better not go for a plunge here, babe. There's crocs in there too.'

'I've brought my swimming suit,' says Anna in response.

'Seriously,' says Bob, 'you save that for the pool on the way back. They'd snap you up here for a snack at any time of day.'

Anna laughs, but Jess is curiously relieved that Bob has given this ridiculous and surely unnecessary warning. She's already explained the obvious dangers to Anna, that you have to be really careful about a lot of things in Africa, but she hadn't wanted to scare her, and Bob's casual reminder comes in well. Bob is as kind-hearted a man as he was when she first knew him. Indeed he has become more kind-hearted and more understanding. He is on good terms with his daughter and his ex-wife, and he has been more than good with stepdaughter Anna. And Jess knows that, however brief their life together had been, in his way he loves her.

She wonders if he and Raoul would like one another. Raoul is ten times cleverer than Bob and Jess and the Professor and anyone Jess has ever known, but that's just a fluke. It's just a matter of neurones and dendrites and synapses. His are better connected than theirs. Is she, Jess, now upgrading herself intellectually by having a flirtation with Raoul? This very quick thought, flitting through her, makes her laugh and snort into her beer. She makes a note to herself to tell me about it, as she knows it will be right up my street.

Bob laughs too, though he doesn't know what the joke is, and then the Mexican adventurer waves from the men's hut, and they make their way with him by the thin blue light of their clockwork torches (for the sun has now sunk) along the dark path to their supper. The chorus of the frogs grows louder and louder, and the snorting of the hippos fades away, and Venus and Jupiter as clear as wild diamonds ride through the black enormous African sky.

~

Over their fritters and fried tomatoes and sweetcorn they are joined by their pilot and the Zambian guide Emmanuel, and, when the meal is served, by the cook, whose name is Isaac. Isaac has a small son, who watches the party intently from the kitchen doorway; he was allowed to bring them a plastic basket of bread, but backed away shyly when Jess thanked him. Jess suspects the Zambians may have other names, which they do not choose to use in mixed company.

The three white men compete, as men do, with tales of adventure. Jess and Anna and the Zambians listen, an appreciative and tolerant audience, and behind their narratives Jess listens to the sounds of the bush – a roaring, a rustling, an occasional baboon screech. She knows all Bob's stories, some of them too well, but Brewster's accounts of hopping round the country in his little taxi plane are new to her, and not too scary. This is a safe country, unlike the Congo, just over the border. They had flown over a bit of the Congo on their way here – Brewster had pointed down to the Congo Pedicle, thrusting its mineral-rich foot rudely down into Zambia.

The Mexican's tales, in contrast to Brewster's and Bob's, are horrifying. He tells them about his brother, who was kidnapped and held hostage in a sealed room for a hundred days in Mexico City. None of the family dares to live in Mexico now. He is here to relax, to escape, in the deep peace of Africa. Nothing can harm him here. Nobody will kidnap him here.

The Zambians shake their heads and make sympathetic noises as he tells this story. They know life is grim and lawless over the border in the Congo, but they hadn't expected to hear such horrors of a great and civilised city.

The Mexican is sweet and quick-witted with Anna. He gives her a little present, in the form of a nest of a paradise flycatcher. It is tiny, intricately made of feathers and moss, and he had found it that afternoon on the forest floor beneath a mpundu tree. The paradise flycatcher, Emmanuel tells them, is a very small bird with a very long tail. He shows them its picture, in his bird book. Anna holds the nest on her knees proudly, tenderly.

A hippo slumps noisily up from the water, very close to them, and they hear it munch and graze. It is grey and dirty-pink and enormous.

They sit round a wood fire, loosely built in the shape of a star. The logs and branches point inwards, and the charcoal core of the star glows a dull red. Occasionally Emmanuel replaces or moves a grey branch, and the sparks fly upwards, and little flames burst forth. This is the kind of fire they have been making here for many thousands of years. It has burnt through the stone age, through the iron age, through the advent of Speke and Livingstone and Stanley, and it burns on, through the Jet Age, through the age of KK and HIV and climate change and safari tourism. The light of the fire plays dully and dimly on the faces of the group: on Bob, still boyish though grey-bearded; on Anglo-Saxon Brewster, tanned and clean shaven in his khaki shorts; on the fabulously wealthy and stylish young Jewish Mexican with his ringlets; on the dark, taut and gleaming ebony skin of Emmanuel the guide and Isaac the cook; and on Anna's pale, fair, attentive brow. Jess watches, and thinks of the People of Many Lands and of that Christmas when all the children were young. It is a comfort to be here, so peacefully, with this strange group, by this ancient fire.

~

Emmanuel is appointed to take them to the Memorial and then onwards to the Livingstone river crossing and the Holden missionary settlement near the lake and the Saucepan Graves. The Mexican takes an interest in their project, and asks if he can come too, but is reminded that Brewster is due to fly him to the Shoebill Camp at the crack of dawn the next morning, where his strict and serious Zimbabwean bird guide will be waiting for him.

As Jess and Bob and Anna and Emmanuel and a driver casually armed with a gun grind along in the Land-Rover, and clamber in and out of a dugout canoe, and admire the egrets and ibises and kingfishers and storks, Jess's mind probes back to that earlier journey, so many decades ago, with Guy and Graham Slater and all those other chaps, some of whose names she has forgotten. Ghosts of memories of the landscape emerge, prompted by the cry of a bird, a footprint, a cemetery of grey tombstone anthills, the grey trunk and gaunt dead branches of an elephant-stripped tree, the red mud of a river crossing, the smiling eager schoolchildren with their bags of schoolbooks waving from the side of the road. But there is some other memory lying behind them all, something that had preceded them all. It will not come to her. She cannot get it back. It may be the cause of all things, or it may be an irrelevance, but she cannot return to it.

The Livingstone Memorial she had misremembered, although she knows they had picnicked by it long ago, and she knows it cannot have changed much in forty-odd years. There it stood, and there it stands, a small plain blunt brick-and-cement obelisk in a woodland glade, erected more than a hundred years after Livingstone's death, with its inscriptions commemorating him and his 'faithful native followers'. The handsome young woman now in charge of it tells them that some people are agitating for a smarter, more modern monument, but she and the local people like it as it is. 'People expect it to be like this,' she says; 'they don't want a new one. This is the one they all remember. This is the one in all the photographs.'

Jess hadn't remembered it very well and had thought it much smaller, although she politely nods her agreement. But, as she climbs up into the back of the vehicle, another image does come back, an image almost as clear as that of the unplumbed lavatory. It is of a cement-block shed with a handwritten notice on it reading CLINIC. It had stood all alone, somewhere near here, and when they had looked inside it they had found nothing but a wooden bench and a small wooden cabinet, its door swinging open, empty save for a tube of antiseptic cream and a roll of doubtful bandage.

Dr Livingstone had been highly valued for his carefully crafted wooden travelling medicine chest with its treasure of neatly stored and magical little glass bottles. His faith had sustained him, but his quinine, calomel, jalap and rhubarb had saved others.

There is an undergrowth round here that looks like bracken, under the taller woodland trees. It has little curled fronds. But it isn't bracken. It can't be. The fronds are knee-high.

In the rainy season, the high grasses of the marshland close over the watery pathways, forming deep-green arched canals. Through them the children punt their small canoes.

The landscape is at once strange and familiar, unknown and always known. A group of hornbills scuttles past. Anna loves the strange turkey-like hornbills and the speckled guinea fowls. They are grounded, they are safe.

~

Over supper in the tree camp that night, Jess asks Emmanuel about the Holden Missionary Settlement, which they will see the next day. At Wibletts, the brochure had said it was well preserved, but Emmanuel says this is no longer so. The brochure needs updating. There is a building, and there were some graves, but the community has gone, and the villages around it have been abandoned. The illnesses of the past have been replaced by new illnesses, requiring new clinics, new drugs. There are rural health centres now instead of leper colonies.

And Felix Holden himself, as Jess knows, had never penetrated as far inland as this: he had died of malaria way to the east, not far from where he had disembarked after his long journey to Zanzibar. His heirs and followers had founded the settlement in his name, with the legacies that had unexpectedly come his way, but he had never seen the swamps and the lake and the shoebill.

Jess thinks of Mungo Park, who had shown such faith in human nature, but was nevertheless speared to death by a stranger. The needle of his compass had steadfastly pointed to his mother, who outlived him.

Bob had once said to her, decades ago, as they talked about Africa and human nature over a nourishing pig-trotter supper in Kinderley Road, that Jess only saw what she wanted to see, she read into stories what she wanted to read into stories. Africa's full of violence, young Bob had said, of stupid barbaric rituals, of endemic brutality, black on black, Arab on black, white on black, black on white, Arab on white, white on white, war lords, mercenaries, slave traders, colonial exploiters . . . it's the heart of darkness, Conrad got it right, but you won't see that, Bob had said. You don't like photos of animals killing one another and eating one another, you don't like people killing one another and eating one another, you don't like skull- and bone-heap stories, you just look the other way and refuse to listen. Any research denying historical evidence for cannibalism, you jump at it. You don't like to think about all those cannibals. You'd domesticate cannibalism, Jess. If you were forced to accept its existence, you'd provide a recipe book.

Jess had laughed, they had both laughed, all those years ago when they were not quite but nearly 'madly in love'.

It's because I'm a woman, Jess had then said. I see the world like that because I'm a woman. She was, then as now, content to be a woman.

And that, she now thinks, is why she is in pursuit of the Saucepan Graves.

She asks Emmanuel about the graves, but he looks shifty and does not want to talk about them, although he doesn't deny them. They are not a subject he wishes to discuss. She has a sense that he is reluctant to go near them.

To lighten the conversation, Bob reminds them that when he'd been checking the possibilities of their itinerary and working out how much he'd have to pay Brewster, he'd hit on a website that said FUN THINGS TO DO IN MALAWI: VISIT THE MISSIONARY GRAVES. Emmanuel doesn't find this funny, although Jess does. Emmanuel may be a Jehovah's Witness. The woman in charge of Livingstone's obelisk is a Jehovah's Witness.

Jess and Bob and Anna miss their worldly Jewish Mexican billionaire, and they can hear a lion roaring, a little too near. They haven't seen a lion yet, and Jess and Anna don't really want to, or not at night, in an encampment made of straw. Mungo Park had many encounters with lions. And he was alone, sometimes on his poor horse, which he greatly pitied, and sometimes, often, on foot.

They feel better in the morning, as they hurtle bumpily along the unmade red road. They have a new driver, called Stephen, who keeps stopping to try to get a signal on his mobile. Emmanuel and he talk in their own languages, one of the languages of the lake. Bob cannot resist trying his own mobile to see if he can get in touch with the Luangwa crew filming the hyenas and vultures eating the dead hippo (he fails), and even Jess is tempted to switch hers on. But what would be the point?

She could have texted me on her progress, but she didn't. She didn't text me until she reached the Jacaranda Hotel. But she was saving up her stories for me, as she'd promised.

Anna is here, and safe, and with her mother, and she is enjoying the ride. Anna learns to duck when branches hang low over the track, and sips her bottle of tepid water and gazes around at this new but ancient world. She likes the sausage trees, and she even likes the circling vultures. As Jess had hoped, she seems to have forgotten about her illness. She does not have a brooding memory. She has regained health, appetite, confidence. She is comfortable that Bob is here, looking after her mother.

It is all a success, so far, this expedition.

~

The Holden Settlement, as Emmanuel had advised them, is no longer functional. There are no more lepers in this region; instead, there is a new clinic in the chief's village with visiting doctors and vaccinations and a maternity unit and condoms as well as quinine. But they pass the scorched circles of dead and abandoned villages, and vestiges of some of the mission buildings remain. They see the walls of a small brick structure which was once the chapel, built on higher ground that does not flood even in the rainy season. A recent undistinguished twentieth-century plaque set on the ground on a raised cement base states that it marks the settlement dedicated to the memory of the Reverend Felix Holden, 1785–1830. It is not a place of pilgrimage – it is too far from the Livingstone tourist route – but it is there, and not utterly forgotten. It is a far cry from Wibletts, or from Livingstone's polished plaque in Westminster Abbey.

It is sad. It is not really very interesting. There is not much to see, and the immediate landscape lacks charm. It is neither one thing nor the other. Anna and Bob are visibly bored and restless and wanting their lunch of tomato and processed cheese and salami sandwiches, and even Jess finds it hard to summon up much interpretative enthusiasm. Subdued, they hoist themselves back into the Land-Rover. Anna and Bob leap up into the vehicle with energy, but Jess finds it an effort. Her left knee has started, uncharacteristically, to protest. She almost accepts the strong helping hand of Emmanuel. She is not as young as she had been on her first visit.

Ursula had wanted to be a martyr and to save the lepers, or so Raoul had reported, but there weren't any lepers in Sussex or Essex or Somerset. It's odd that she had suffered from such archetypal Roman Catholic aspirations and delusions, when she had been brought up, like Felix Holden, in the Church of England, and in a Low Anglican branch of it at that. Jess, who had hardly ever been taken to church as a child, had once happened to hear a sermon when she was about eight years old on the life of Father Damien and his lepers, which had made an uneasy and confusing but lasting impression on her, but she had not been converted by it to a desire for martyrdom.

Jess hopes for something more elevating from the saucepans in the wood or from the lake's immensity.

~

The Land-Rover judders to a halt on the verge of a stretch of watery terrain from which a sluggishly small but clear rivulet rises and meanders away to the west. They will have to walk from here up the slope and past the termite mounds to the woodland and the graves.

Emmanuel says that they are standing at the headwaters of the Congo. From here, the water rises and flows for many many hundreds of miles, for a thousand miles and more, treacherously, destructively, deceptively, tortuously westward to the Atlantic, gathering strength as it goes. Or so Emmanuel says.

This does not look very likely. It is not an impressive site.

Like the Holden Settlement, it lacks significance. The words Emmanuel used are grand, but the place is not. Maybe, thinks Jess, the mighty Congo has many headwaters, and this is just one of them. Yes, of course that must be so. Livingstone had wandered from headwater to headwater and gave up even trying to chart them. And then he got lost and died. He was wrong about the Nile. This was the Congo, not the Nile. He died in a false belief. In good faith, but false belief.

She gazes around her. It is unsatisfactory. Maybe all revelation, all discovery, is unsatisfactory. Many explorers have come to this conclusion. She stands and stares. The water bubbles. A tall yellow-billed marabou stork flaps a little way along the bank, and contemptuously settles again. Has she come all this way for this? This soggy stretch of marsh? It reminds her of a bog on Exmoor. She thinks of taking off a sandal and sock and dipping one of her itching heat-bumped feet into the Congo, but decides Emmanuel would think this form of baptism too eccentric.

They walk onwards and uphill a little way towards the woodland grove, the cursed but sacred grove where the Saucepan Graves are to be found. Emmanuel, pressed for exegesis, has told them some hopelessly confusing and unconvincing rigmarole about the graves. His version is a tale of warring tribes and clans, of migrations of peoples from east and west, of battles with the massed crocodile enemy, of massacre and flight, of a white colonial invader. The clan of the Royal Crocodile had fought the clan of the Mushroom, and the crocodiles from the lake had taken their vengeance. Real crocodiles, or human crocodiles, or spirit crocodiles? Jess cannot follow or decode it, and Bob and Anna do not even try. Of what century does he speak? Of our own, or of centuries long ago? Time here, as her SOAS friend Gus had reminded her, is not as it is in Western Europe. There have been travellers' accounts, even photographs, of the tribes from the west, but nobody knows the true story. It could have been the BaTwa, it could have been the Unga or the Soli or the Lala or the Bisa, migrating from the west, from the lands of the Congo. Jess can make it all up if she wants. One version is as good as another. The colour supplement will believe her story, whatever she says. They will know no better. It is up to her to find it interesting, to make it interesting.

Emmanuel says the local people will not touch the saucepans. They lie where they lie.

The saucepans are interesting. To Jess, all saucepans are interesting, and these are particularly so. They are of chipped white and blue and dark green enamel, and there are enamel mugs and saucepan lids too, lying, it would seem, haphazardly in the tree roots and leaf mould, some on slightly raised mounds of earth. There are dozens, perhaps hundreds of them. Beneath the mounds, she assumes, lie the victims of a tribal massacre, but she is not very clear even about that. The pans do not look very old. They look post-Livingstone. They look like the pans of a 1950s childhood, but they could be a lot older than that. Enamel kitchenware has a long history. Jess has done some research. Holloware, it used to be called, and most of it was made in the Black Country, in Birmingham and Bilston and in Lye – Lye, known as the Bucket Capital of England. From the foundries of the Black Country kettles and pans and stoves and ovens were exported, and there was a steady trade in large cooking pots with legs known as 'Negro pots'. These are the ones that feature in cartoons of stewing missionaries. They are not indigenous; they come from Lye.

These are not historic Negro pots towards which Emmanuel has reluctantly led them. They look just like the kitchenware still on sale in the Blackstock Road.

And they do mark graves, these pans. They signify a burial rite. Many bodies are here returned to earth.

Jess squats to contemplate the pans. Bob takes Anna off to look at a termite mound and a thorn tree and the neat little spiral earth-holes of the ant lion, leaving Jess to think. She does not like to touch the saucepans, but she picks up a dark blue-brown lump of iron, an iron ingot, lying in the leaf mould, and holds it in her hand. It is warm and shapely and smoothly polished, but it is not an artefact. It is natural. It is the size of a netsuke. She looks at it through her little hand lens.

It is emergent form.

Livingstone had noted burial places, large mounds 'with drinking vessels of rude pottery on them, arranged in circular form like a haycock, with no vestige of any inscription'. The people who left these memorials had not striven to perpetuate their names. Livingstone had attempted to convey the Christian notion of personal immortality and bodily resurrection to those he met on his long, hard, missionary's way, to cheer those who gave him hospitality in his wanderings, but he had failed. And he had come to respect, or at least to acknowledge, the rites of the pagans. He recorded, tenderly, a meeting with a bereaved woman who had walked many miles to build a little miniature replica hut in the burnt-out ruins of her dead mother's house, where she had left offerings of milk and grain. No doubt, he said, this 'comforted the poor mourner's heart'.

Polly, put the kettle on.

The starry fire beneath the stars.

Steve in his Wendy House.

The little nameless unremembered acts of kindness and of love.

Jess feels some communal memory, some folk memory, some memory from her earliest childhood about to well up, some memory that enfolds the swamp children and the pure gold baby that is Anna and Steve in the Secret Garden and the dead of the Saucepan Graves. Something was laid down long ago in the pathways, something that links her to her own story, something that brought her here.

She holds the warm ingot in her hand. It will join the rain stone on the mantelpiece at Kinderley Road.

Stumbling blindly with its pots and pans, the human race. She sees it stumble on.

~

Bob takes a photograph of Jess and the saucepans. She does not know he is taking it. He photographs the graves, of course, for the colour supplement, but he also photographs his wife, Jess, crouching with her arms around her knees, wrapt. She is dissolving into time, she is old now, and she is in the process of transfiguration.

~

The hippo feast is disgusting, in every sense of that word. The smell is appalling. The hippo lies on the wide, sandy, shelving bank of the Luangwa, at the mercy of the teeth and beaks and probosces of scavengers and the exploitation of cameramen. The vast and helpless bulk of its flesh decomposes and is consumed before their eyes. This mountain of rotting beast is a vivid demonstration of the processes of decay and recycling, and the camera team is recording them with a macabre relish. At night in the camp they show Bob their choicest footage and listen to his suggestions. He has been commissioned to take stills, and has been enjoying himself. Jess and Anna watch the film footage with a mixture of pleasure and horror. Bob is pleased to be with the boys, showing off to them, receiving at least a show of deference. He has been patient with Jess and Anna.

The camp by the river is more luxurious than the camp by

the dambo and the tree camp. Jess washes her hair and sits on the river bank to let it dry in the sun. Tall birds wade in the water. The tallest is the Goliath crane, or so her bird book tells her, but she is not sure which he is. What does it matter? The river is yellow-grey and wide and full of living beings of ageless and unchanging forms. The carmine bee-eaters have their tenements in its yellow banks, brilliant in their dazzling plumage. Anna had liked the bee-eaters. She still has her bird's nest, safe if squashed in her pocket.

Soon Jess and Bob and Anna will be in the Jacaranda Hotel, in reach of mobile-phone signals and texts and newspapers and news. What will have happened while they have been away? There has been time for births and deaths, scandals and revelations. The banks may have crashed, governments may have fallen. Emails and letters will be waiting for her.

Jess hopes that nothing much has happened in Kinderley Road. It is quite all right as it is. She is looking forward to being home. She is nearing the end of her journey. Soon she and Anna will again take up their unchanging daily life together.

Livingstone, not far from this spot, had written: 'I am never to have a home again. All my hopes of doing good in my home among the outcasts of Africa have been dispelled.'

He had died in a posture of prayer.

Jess has not aspired to do good to others. Her hopes have been more limited.

Yes, she will be pleased to be home. It has been a good trip, but home, at her age, is better.

~

It was by the pool at the Jacaranda, Jess was to tell me, that she made a small new connection. It didn't seem an appropriate place – it would have been more meaningful to have been enlightened at the shallow headwaters of the Congo or by the Saucepan Graves or on the banks of the ancient and mighty Luangwa – but we cannot choose where our memories may return to us or what may prompt them. We are at the mercy. We believe there is a thread, a story, but we are at the mercy.

Jess was sitting in a striped hammock by the pool in the Jacaranda Hotel, watching Anna swimming and sipping at a glass of beer, in the kind of idle safari scenario that Victoria would have imagined for her, and letting her mind wander over her adventures, over Africa and the children of the lake in their dugout canoes and the photograph of the children at Wibletts and Isaac's little boy, gravely handing her the bread basket before slipping back into the shadows of the night.

Halfway home in spirit, she hadn't been able to resist looking at yesterday's copy of an English newspaper that had been lying in the hotel foyer, from which she had learnt that the FTSE was down by twenty points, that a government minister had resigned over a financial embarrassment, that Maroussia was to appear at the National in a new play by a young woman playwright, that disputes over a third runway at Heathrow were as ever ongoing, and that an anonymous burns victim had received a successful hand transplant with successfully moving fingers by a new technique pioneered in France. But she was trying to put these irrelevant updates on the world out of her mind and to let it drift back over Africa.

A wider view, an aerial view, an uplifting view, a view of the river, a view of time, a view of the shores of the infinite.

Jess's mind wandered, and it wandered over the rift valley and the swamps and the miombo woodland to the burns victim and the transplanted hand, and the sun beat down through the striped turquoise Jacaranda parasol and through her raffia sunhat and on to her eyelids, and very slowly, or was it suddenly, for the apparition was mysteriously both slow and sudden, she began to see the little girl who had been her best friend at East Broughborough Kindergarten when she was five years old. The girl had had a hand with no fingers. She had fallen on to an electric fire as a baby and burnt her hand very badly. She had a little paw, with scarred stumps, a friendly little paw.

She'd been a lobster-claw child. Jess had loved her.

So perhaps that was it, perhaps that was why she had responded so warmly to the beautiful children of the lake? They had reminded her of Christine. Fair-haired, smiling, confident, very slightly damaged Christine Godley, who at the age of five had paid no attention to her disability whatsoever, and seemed to have suffered no trauma.

Jess had hardly thought about Christine in sixty-odd years, she was to tell me, but she'd been waiting there all the time, with her little pink hand and its smooth pinky-blue scar tissue, all laid down in Jess's neurones. In her hippocampus, in her amygdala, whatever, wherever, she wasn't very good at the names of brain parts. She would ask Raoul about it when she saw him next week. Raoul would know.

It wasn't much of a revelation, it didn't really explain anything. There would be no revelation.

Thinking all this over, as they queued at the airport and fastened their seat belts and took off towards the Equator through the night, Jess wondered if there was a Jungian archetype called the wounded child. She knew the Wounded Healer, but she didn't think there was a Wounded Child. She would look into it when she got home. She closed her eyes and waited. In her hand, inside her pocket, she held the iron ingot. It might lead her safely onwards, to whatever still lay ahead.

Anna was happy with her headset. She was amazed by the choice of channels, up there in the sky. She had found an adaptation of *David Copperfield*. She had seen it before and knew the story well, and she'd settled down to the childhood sufferings, the Mum is Dead story, the horrible stepfather, and the sure expectation of a happy ending. Dickens and she were old friends. Her mother was asleep, so that was all right.

Bob, the good Step Dad, sat in the aisle seat, flicking through some of his photos. Jess by the graves presented a peculiarly haunting image – he knew he would do well with that. She was sitting on the shores of time, on the shores of the infinite. He had taken her there, and he had brought her safely home again. He could relax. He plugged his iPod into his ears and his brain, and soon began to snore. He was worn out by looking after his wife and his stepdaughter. He was really good at sleeping on aeroplanes. We don't know what he was listening to while he slept.

~

So that is Jess's story, and the story of Anna. I will leave them in mid-air, but you will know that they landed safely, or I wouldn't have been able to tell their story so far.

I haven't invented much. I've speculated, here and there, I've made up bits of dialogue, but you can tell when I've been doing that, because it shows. I've known Jess a long time, and I've known Anna all her life, but there will be things I have got wrong, things I have misinterpreted. Jess and I talk a lot, but we don't tell each other everything. There are things in my life of which she knows nothing, and she has her secrets too.

I've tried to give a sense of what it was like, in our neighbourhood, in our time. Some of it survives. We are old now, and I heard this week from Maroussia that she has to have what she discreetly calls major surgery, and that the prognosis is not good. She has had to pull out from the National. This is very sad news. We are dying off, one by one.

But Sylvie Raven is in fine form, buoyed up by combat.

I don't think Jess will marry Raoul. My guess is that they

will continue to meet, once a month or so, without commitment. But I may be wrong about that. Marrying Raoul would certainly alter the plot. But it wouldn't solve the problem of Anna's future, would it?

Ollie's mother has just remarried, aged seventy-five. She's on her third husband now, and he's ten years younger than she is. She's had her hair dyed orange. It looks quite good, but not very good. She is tiny, even tinier than she was, and he's six foot three. They make a striking couple.

I'm not very taken with Jess's claim that the whole curve of her life was made clear to her when she was prompted to remember a fingerless child she'd known a hundred years ago. That sounds more like a false memory to me. I think Jess is looking for meaning where there isn't any. She's just a bit too inventive about causation. I'm more resigned to the random and the pointless than Jess.

I'm older now than I was when I started writing this record.

I worry about Anna's future. I don't like to bring up the subject with Jess. But I've resolved that I'll be brave and have a go. I'm going to ask her to supper to talk about it, next week. Or maybe the week after next. I have a practical suggestion I could make. I'll do lamb shank with chick peas, Jess likes lamb shank. And I'll find a DVD for Anna – I don't think she's seen that animated Japanese ghost story Jake gave me for my birthday.

Maybe I'll invite Raoul, one day? I'll ask Jess if she'd like that. Or would that be presumptuous? I don't want to presume.

Jess must have her own plans. It's none of my business. I don't like to meddle.

I shouldn't have written any of this. I hadn't the right.

Bob's photo of Jess crouching by the Saucepan Graves is remarkable. She didn't know he was taking it. She doesn't know I've been writing this. I don't think I'll ever be able to tell her.